DANGEROUS FORTUNE

He stopped, but his gaze swept over her face. "Am I reading you right this time, Sela? We can be friends, but leave it at that?"

She stared back at him, conscious of his fingers, warm and smooth, above her thumping heart. "I . . . I believe so," she said.

As Ben leaned into Sela, she still didn't suspect his intent; then his mouth, feather light, touched hers in intimate persuasion. Her eyes closed as she succumbed to the heady sensation. She didn't think, but parted her lips and raised her face to meet him fully.

When Ben pulled back, Sela was slow to open her eyes, only to find his stare pinned to her, his brows narrowed. At the same time, his hand moved recklessly to her neck, his fingers warm as they began a rhythmic stroke there. Before she could focus and clear her head, she fell back against the sofa, and he followed her. But this time his lips parted hers.

As her mouth softened under his seductive assault, she tried to hold on to her drifting sanity. Her hands, caught between their bodies, pressed into his hard chest.

What am I doing? While she asked herself the question, she met the rhythm of his lips on hers, and gave herself freely to the passionate kiss. Just this once.

DANGEROUS FORTUNE

Shirley Harrison

ARABESQUE BOOKS are published by

BET Publications, LLC
c/o BET BOOKS
One BET Plaza
1900 W Place NE
Washington, DC 20018-1211

First Printing: October 2001
10 9 8 7 6 5 4 3 2 1

Printed in the United States of America

This book is dedicated to my mother,
Minnie Reeves.

ACKNOWLEDGMENTS

Thank you, Jan, Carolyn, and Bridget, for your invaluable opinions and tireless carping that I should just finish the story.

I extend a special thank-you to Mr. Jim Campbell and Dr. Ivan Cazort for coming to my rescue so quickly and so often.

Prologue

"Raise that pretty brown face, Sela, and accept your destiny."

At her aunt's stern command, Sela Bennett, barely five years old, dutifully straightened her back and looked up from the center of the room. Kneeling on the hard plank floor, she gazed through the faint light given off by the flickering candles in the wall sconces, her eyes wide with curiosity and confusion at being summoned to the secret room.

Claire Bennett, a young woman herself, circled her niece. In a swirl of colors, her long skirt floated out to snap at Sela, as though to remind the child of where they were and to pay close attention. She spoke quickly, and in a low, soft voice.

Her words didn't alarm Sela. Her mama and aunt often said and did strange things. She supposed it was because they had "the sight"—they could see things—and it was just their way. What puzzled Sela was why they let her visit this private place. The basement door was always locked, and she wasn't allowed to enter. In fact, she didn't think anyone ever came in here.

Her stomach fluttered with puzzling uncertainty even as her thoughts drifted to her pinched knees. She shifted on the unforgiving floor, careful not to fidget too much. Earlier, when Aunt Claire brought her in from the bright sun outside, she'd been told to remain as still as the water in her favorite pond. She could do that. Her curious gaze swept over a shadowy corner in the nearly empty room and a shiver renewed her reticence at embracing this place. She hadn't decided if she liked being in here after all.

Claire stopped in front of Sela before whisking a long silk scarf through the air. "To your health and continued welfare."

The smell of her aunt's fragrances in the scarf's wake assailed Sela's nose.

"Your own barrier, child," Claire continued, "against the card of dangerous fortune." The scarf swooped through the thin light again. "If Helena won't protect you, then I will." Her fingers released the colorful cloth high in the air, and it slithered like a snake down to the floor.

Sela's confusion grew as she nodded in obedience. Why did Auntie say her mama wouldn't protect her? When her aunt knelt beside her and began a prayer, Sela sneaked a peek at her face before mimicking the older woman's bowed head. Aunt Claire's face was wet with tears. Sela continued to hold her posture for what seemed like forever before a touch came to her shoulder. She opened her eyes in time to see her aunt rise as she pulled her hand from her pocket.

Claire's arm motioned upward in a toss before Sela saw something float for only a moment, then burst into a hundred fireflies. The instruction to remain still was forgotten as Sela's eyes and mouth formed perfect circles at the sparkling spectacle.

"Ohh . . ." With a child's awe, she lifted her hands to catch the darting lights.

"Your destiny is set, my beauty, and it wills your future as a bright one, with much promise. But, we must be careful of the path that leads you there." Satisfied that she'd done right by both her sister and her niece, Claire knelt in front of the child. Gently, she tilted Sela's small face to hers.

"Now you control that path." She studied the face so much like Helena's and searched for understanding in the child's large brown eyes. She saw only confusion . . . and trust. That would do for now.

"You don't have to be afraid. Your mother and I will always watch over you." She kissed Sela's forehead. "We will protect you from the pain that people inflict."

Neither saw the dark eyes in the garden's twilight that peered down through the basement window.

Sela had forgotten her earlier uncertainty until Claire's eyes jerked to the window above them. She followed her aunt's gaze and saw nothing. When she turned to look into the older woman's face, something there made the shiver return.

"Auntie?" Her voice, small and tinny, echoed through the room. "What's wrong?"

"Hush." Claire brushed her hands down Sela's two plaits. "Give fortune a moment to embrace and comfort you." Her gaze was warm before she drew her niece to her chest and uttered a last word against her hair.

"Amen."

One

Twenty years later

The summer sun's warmth was only slightly muted as it poured through the stained glass in the church vestibule. There, alone in the quiet and comforted by the presence of the colorful glass saints, Sela paced impatiently while she waited for her aunt Claire to return and explain her absence.

"Damn, Auntie, where are you?" The moment she spoke the blasphemy out loud, she remembered where she was.

"Oh, hell." She heaved a sigh as she chastised herself. "Gotta watch my mouth." Giving up on decorum in the oval-shaped room of saints, she dug her hand deep into her jeans pocket. Sela had definitely become less than proper these days. Years of being an introverted child had finally given way to a woman who had begun to share her aunt's joy in unconventionality. Of course, *that* mold had been broken with her aunt. The thought brought on a smile.

She crossed the carpeted floor to sit on a padded window seat beneath one of the peaceful colored images. Though the sun felt good against her skin in the air-conditioned room, a cloud of unease she couldn't shake continued to settle over her as she waited for her aunt. That very same ennui had been the reason she'd sought out this antechamber, a reflection room she'd loved since childhood. She ran a hand through thick, curly hair as she stole another impatient peek at her watch. Charles was late, too—highly unusual for her punctual, soon-to-be fiancé.

"Where are you, Auntie?" Again, she whispered her concern at the saints who circled the walls. "And, where in the world is Charles?"

Outside, in the late afternoon haze, Claire Bennett had arrived in the church's side parking lot. She quickly exited her car, refusing the escort offered by a hovering Deacon Freeman, and started for the front steps.

Claire's normally imperious, almost haughty expression was drawn, and her mouth had turned downward in a solid frown. She had unexpected bad news to share with Sela, and it was important that her niece hear it from her—no one else.

"Oh, Claire . . ."

She turned her head toward the singsong greeting and knew it could only have come from Mabel Thornton, well known as both a church matron and a gossip. Mabel stood with Alice Freeman, the deacon's wife. Claire continued at a brisk pace as she imagined the gossip the women discussed like clucking chickens, and immediately dismissed them. She must get to Sela before anyone else.

"Claire—" Mabel now hurried across the parking lot after her. "Just a moment."

By the time Claire reached the church walk, Mabel had managed to catch up. Breathing sharply from her rapid strides, the heavy woman reached out with her arm to stop Claire from ascending the steps.

Claire's frown deepened at the woman's bold intrusion.

"I just heard what happened from Sister Freeman. Is there anything—"

"Where's Sela?" Claire's voice was sharp with forced civility. "Does she know?"

"She was in the sanctuary earlier, waiting for you, I imagine." Mabel shook her head in sympathy. "She's so young for so much tragedy."

Claire mentally sheathed her claws as she turned to continue up the church steps.

"Two beaus inside of four years." Mabel rushed the words at Claire's back. "And both of them end up like this." She clicked her tongue as though to oil her next words. "It's turning out to be true. She's her mother's daughter."

That was the last straw. Claire whirled to face Mabel on the wide step. But, one look at the round little woman's expectant face below her, and she lost the fire in her temper. Her heart was too heavy with other, more important matters.

"Listen to yourself, you silly woman. You ought to be ashamed. Rather than offer a prayer of comfort, you prefer to wallow in another's misery."

Mabel's indignant gasp was already forgotten by the time Claire opened the heavy church door under the columnar portico.

She entered the quiet, empty interior hall of the town's historic church, expecting that her footsteps across the slate floor would quickly announce her arrival. Ahead were the doors to the sanctuary. When Sela didn't appear straightaway, Claire knew where her niece would wait and she veered to another set of doors to the left. It seemed only right that Sela would hear the news in a room she'd considered a source of comfort most of her life. Claire grasped the brass door handle and pushed through the vestibule doors.

Sela looked up from across the room and, at the sight of her aunt, was flooded with relief. She jumped to her feet and blurted an impatient greeting.

"Finally, you're back. I was beginning to think you and Charles had forgotten me," she said, as she grabbed up her sweater and moved to join her aunt. "I'll make sure I drive my own car next time. So, where've you been for almost two hours?"

When Claire remained silent at the door, Sela stopped in the middle of the room, her curiosity roused. "What's wrong?" Her words were hesitant. "You look like you've seen a ghost."

"Sela—" Claire now moved to her side, her eyes never leaving her niece. "Charles has had an accident."

"What kind of accident?" At her aunt's silence, Sela's hand flew to her mouth in a motion of panic. "Oh, no. He's all right, though?" When no ready response came, her eyes narrowed in fear. "Tell me, Auntie . . . he is all right?"

"No." Claire's swallow of sorrow was audible, and she pulled Sela into he embrace. "He didn't make it. When he arrived at the hospital, it was already too late. I just left him. I took the call earlier at the house."

"Oh, my God." Sela's hands dropped to her side as she swayed on her feet, her stable world in a tumble. "This . . . this can't be."

Claire's own face mirrored the stricken and helpless expression that marred Sela's face. Again. She held her niece tight as she explained the terrible accident.

"No . . . no . . ." Sela's eyes closed against the

vision her aunt's words produced, but not fast enough to check the tears that streamed down as the news consumed her. Her denials continued as she sank to the floor, taking Claire with her. "It's happening again . . . just like before."

"Shh . . . It was an accident, my beauty. Don't give it power and make it more than that." With her arms still around Sela, they rocked as one, in anguish over what had happened and the ominous portent it carried.

"Charles is sweet and . . . and kind." Sela's choked words found their way around her sobs. "He never had a chance, though, did he? Andrew didn't either. Not with me." She drew back her head to face her aunt. "Did you see any of this happening, Auntie? Did you?"

Claire took hold of Sela's shoulders and spoke sternly. "This is not your fault—you must believe that this has nothing to do with you."

Sela didn't respond through the fog created by her misery and tears and returned to her aunt's embrace. But, what of Charles's accident? What if another innocent person had suffered because of her? *It won't happen again,* she vowed. *Never.*

As Claire attempted solace with soothing words, the sobs continued to creep from Sela's throat, and played a counterpoint to the women's mournful rock beneath the protective stares of the glass saints.

Two

Three years later, present day

Dark clouds rolled in fast over the small community of Fairlight. Its rural sprawl began at the end of the state highway, punctuated by the beginnings of a dirt road of dubious integrity. Like a sleeping baby, the town lay nestled between low green hills a hundred miles southwest of the cityscapes and bustle of Atlanta.

Sela Bennett jabbed her hand spade at the soil as she kept a wary eye on the summer morning's gray sky. She stuck the last yellow marigold in place near the iron fence that surrounded the manicured lawn and garden.

She wiped the back of her grimy hand across her sweat-laced brow and sat back on her heels. With only a trace of guilt, she drew in a deep breath of summer freedom—long, lazy days without Aunt Claire's well-intentioned interference.

Though it was her aunt's custom to travel in the spring and summer, she still managed to stay in touch with Sela's life, one way or the other. Her aunt's letters, posted from whatever exotic location she happened to find herself in, were usually filled with advice gleaned from unusual sources.

Sela was no longer the naive teenager, or the cautious young adult. She was much older now, a wiser grown woman . . . heading straight for a spinster's life, like her aunt. The thought turned her smile to a frown.

That had been the source of her frustration in their last phone conversation two weeks ago. She didn't want to hear the endless suggestions or puzzling bits of advice—it was all fortune-telling, anyway. And, of course, when she'd hung up, Sela realized her words would hurt the woman who'd replaced the mother she'd lost so long ago.

She shook off the new guilt and promised to make it up to Auntie when she returned from her travels. Everything would be right again. Like always. But, she wouldn't read those damn letters that somehow always hit close to home.

A devilish smile curved Sela's mouth. It must drive Auntie nuts to know her recent letters had remained unopened since that prickly phone call. And, make no mistake; her aunt would know that her letters, which arrived every few days, were being ignored.

Claire Bennett, whom Sela affectionately called "Auntie," the last syllable stressed as only a real southerner could, was clairvoyant. Sela had ultimately accepted this with a mixture of embarrassment and pride. Though Claire intended her advice and prognostics to act as guides, Sela knew their history and purpose. The direction of her thoughts had somehow veered from summer freedom into a trap of dark mist; but, Sela refused the invitation to enter that gloomy place.

Sela dropped the spade and stood to stretch her legs. The simple action allowed her spirit to break free and rise above the overcast, muggy morning.

The freshly planted annuals would provide brilliant color for the emerging perennials to the side of them. If the rain held off a while longer, maybe she'd put a few around the gazebo out back.

"Good Morning, Sela."

She looked up and saw the postman, Jim Lewis, push several pieces of mail into the box attached to the outside of the iron gate. She waited until he finished his languid observations before she spoke.

"Looks like we'll be getting a good soaking soon. I see you got another letter from Claire today." He pushed back his blue cap and lazily scratched his graying head. "What's she trying to do? Run this place herself while she's on vacation?"

"Good morning, Mr. Lewis." She smiled at his reference to the two-story rambling home behind her. Over the years, it had matured into a thriving, seasonal bed-and-breakfast inn, which Claire successfully operated.

"She acts like she don't trust you to house-sit," he continued. "How many letters does that make now?"

"You probably have a better count than I do," she said good-naturedly.

"Leave her alone with all your talkin', Jim, and deliver the rest of the mail before it rains."

They both turned to the voice and saw Mildred Vasser head their way from the other end of the sidewalk, her white toy poodle in tow. She paraded with her signature pink-and-green sunbonnet tied around her head and a Hawaiian muumuu draped over her ample figure. It had been a gift to her from one of Claire's past trips.

"Hey, Sela, dear," she continued. "The flowers you put out are nice. Claire will like that when she gets back."

Sela joined them near her mailbox. "Good morning." The dog on the end of the leash that Mildred held had stuck its miniature head between two bars in the gate. Sela stifled a laugh. The owner and pet reminded Sela of a middle-aged Bo Peep and her miniature sheep. Sela's face turned stern as the dog, ignored by its owner, nosed about in a valiant effort to uproot some of the delicate shoots she'd just planted.

"Hello, Petey." Sela's tone was friendly in its discouragement, but she knew the dog wouldn't buy it. No one liked the surly, cantankerous pooch. The dog gave her a cursory head toss before he let out an unfriendly growl, and then continued his damage.

Jim slapped his cap in the dog's direction. "Mildred, you're gonna let that yappin' little midget dig up her yard? Look at him."

Mildred yanked the leash, and drew the dog back a few steps. "Sela knows Petey isn't capable of doing any harm."

"She's right. He . . . he does this all the time." Sela stooped to pat the soil back in place around the exposed roots. "See? All fixed."

"And don't you start calling him names, Jim. Petey's from a mighty class of—"

"Dwarf mongrels." Jim finished Mildred's sentence with a loud belly laugh.

Sela couldn't stifle her laughter this time. The postman tipped his cap to Sela in an old-time gesture, winked at their shared joke, and moved down the walk with Mildred and Petey trotting close behind. Sela shook her head at the two as they picked up their argument on Petey's lineage, while the subject of their discussion protested at being led away from the redolent soil.

Reaching through the gate, Sela opened the mailbox and retrieved the contents. Hidden among an assortment of bills and junk mail was a powder-blue square envelope that carried her aunt's fluid script. Sela set her mouth in a stubborn line and pushed the mail back into the box. She'd take it all inside later. Right now, before the rain started, she'd put a few more plants out in the backyard. Collecting her bucket of tools, she headed in that direction.

A shrill horn tooted at her from the street. Sela turned in time to see the town's lone police cruiser drive by with Deputy Luther Matthews. He threw his hand up in a greeting. She waved back before she continued across the yard, her good humor restored.

There was no mystery in why she hadn't left Fairlight for good in all these years. She'd been raised here and she loved it with its small-town flavor, nosy neighbors, and even the cranky dogs. She didn't have to live in the big city, as Aunt Claire urged, to get on with her life and meet other people.

The distant rumble of thunder reminded her to move faster. This would be her turnaround summer in Fairlight. While on summer break from her job as media specialist for the county school system, she was giving serious thought to a change in her career. Though she didn't have Auntie's psychic sensibility, the feeling that change was in the air was, somehow, intuitive. She could just tell.

"If you go through those double doors, Mr. Russell, you'll find your rental car waiting in row three."

"Thank you." Ben turned from the direction the attractive agent had pointed out, and returned her smile. "I'll drive around and collect the rest of my luggage."

It was only midmorning, but Ben was bone-tired. A hot shower coupled with a few hours of uninterrupted sleep would be nice. He felt as if he'd been living in airports for days. Actually, that had been pretty much the case. He'd traveled on three different airlines over the last two days to get more than halfway around the world. The last leg, from JFK airport to Atlanta, had been further delayed due to weather conditions.

"Do you need help finding your destination?" The agent seemed motivated by his hesitation. "Will you be staying in town?"

Ben arched a brow as he considered, in no more than the span of a second, whether her questions were innocent inquiries or aggressive flirting. Experience told him it was the latter. He was the dimple-cheeked agent's only customer—faced with her dazzling smile, the least he could do was appear courteous.

"I have business in a small town near here, called Fairlight. Are you familiar with it?"

She deftly pulled out an area map from somewhere behind the counter. Spreading it on the countertop, she tilted her head close to Ben's. "Here it is . . . not too far outside the city." With her pen, she marked the interstate highway he should take, before she turned her gaze to his. Her eyes were bright with interest. "Will you be returning to your hotel here in the city?"

Ben smiled as he gathered up the rental contract, map, and car keys. "Actually, I thought I'd stay in Fairlight."

Disappointment clouded her face. "Are you sure? It looks like it's in the middle of nowhere."

"In that case, I won't have anyone to blame but myself. You've warned me."

She slipped her hand into her pocket and produced a business card, which she handed to him. "If you decide you need help locating a real hotel, or getting around the city, why don't you give me a call?" The dimple in her left cheek deepened. "Day or night."

Ben glanced at the card before he returned a knowing smile to the attentive woman. "Thanks. Maybe I'll do just that."

At that moment, he felt the familiar quiver of his pager in his breast pocket. With an apologetic look to the woman, he stepped away before he checked the call's source. As expected, it was from his younger brother, Montreal, affectionately called Mont. He headed for a row of pay phones near the doors.

Within a couple of minutes, the connection was made, and his brother's anxious voice poured through the telephone.

"Hey, where are you, man?"

"Atlanta," Ben replied, and glanced at his watch. "Getting ready to leave the airport. So, what's up?"

"Plenty. Mom and Dad expected you to show up at the office before you left for Georgia."

"Change of plans. Anyway, Deborah in the office has my schedule." Ben shifted against the phone booth. "I thought Mom was still commuting to that interior design project she's overseeing."

"You really are out of the loop these days, bro. Her project finished ahead of schedule. She's getting ready to start a new one, which means she's got a little time on her hands." A laugh resounded through the phone. "Especially after Marcie called."

At his words, Ben grunted—the reason now crystal clear as to why his little brother and his parents had been so anxious to talk with him. With an impatient spirit, he rubbed his brow as he muttered the obvious. "So, Marcie told them, huh?"

"You didn't think she would?" The humor was thick in his tone. "Hell, yes, she told Mom. The only thing that surprises me is she didn't tell her sooner."

"Thanks for the warning."

"You must be losing your touch, 'cause your stuff needs some serious fixing."

Ben sighed at Mont's take on things. "I'll call Mom and smooth things over when I get to Fairlight."

"Hey, that's the other thing. What about this town you're headed for? I mean, some woman makes you an offer you can't refuse and you bite? If it's too good to be true, you don't accept it unless she has 'supermodel' in the front of her name."

Ben smiled at his young brother's predilection for beautiful women. "I've checked it out, and it's legit. I can't tell you much else until I get there."

"We're all curious, that's all. Hey, good luck, and be safe. Let me know something when you get settled."

After they exchanged good-byes, Ben hung up the receiver and, for a moment, reflected on his brother's words. He should make more time for his family. Maybe they would understand why he broke off an engagement six months ago and they were only now learning about it. He drew his lips inward as he turned and headed for the rental lot.

He disliked mistakes and made a conscious effort not to make them. The engagement to Marcie Hunter had been a huge one. Their long-distance relationship had risen from corporate convenience and, ever since he had started a path in pursuit of his individual goals, the relationship had long outlived its usefulness to either of them. All that had been rectified amicably, and the subject was closed. His mother, though, was big on family and stability, and she'd made it clear that she was anxious for him to settle down, like his eldest brother. She could also be a hound dog when it came to hunting down answers. He began to smile again. He actually missed her caustic take on his lifestyle.

It felt good to be back in the states. First, though, he would enjoy the summer and make this historic church project an unflagging success, come hell or high water, fire or rain. He spied his rental car, and headed for it. Shortly thereafter, he was off to Fairlight, Georgia.

Sela mounted the back steps and walked across the wraparound porch of the Victorian turn-of-the-century home that Aunt Claire had cared for all of Sela's life. She kicked off her red-clay-caked shoes and left them at the door. Working in the yard had been exhilarating, but the promised rain had become reality. Now all she craved was a hot bath before she left for her stint of library duty.

She pulled the door closed behind her and turned to the security alarm pad affixed to the kitchen wall. As she entered the code, she didn't miss the irony. Her aunt thought it wise to have a system installed since the bed-and-breakfast guests usually had big-city sensitivities about unlocked and unguarded doors. Thus, they seldom used the alarm except when tourists were in residence. And while Sela would be the first to tout the safety of Fairlight, she had to admit the alarm gave her a sense of security in the big house where she lived alone during Auntie's absence.

In her damp socks, Sela traversed the hardwood floors, across the living room and past the staircase, which led to the upper floor and the five guest rooms. She moved down a narrow hallway that hid the large, sunny bedroom she'd taken as her own. It looked out across the veranda and over the wide front gardens she so carefully tended. She grabbed her robe from a hook behind her door and headed for the bathroom opposite her room on the other side of the hallway.

Sela leaned across the claw-footed tub and turned on the water jets. As the hot water spewed and the steam rose, she stood to peer at her reflection in the mirror above the sink. The two coiled plaits and dirt-smudged face that lacked makeup all bespoke her recent mood. She was happy with her simple life, wasn't she? She frowned inside, though her reflection didn't. It remained, to her, a rather ordinary face of thick eyebrows and lashes above large eyes—her best feature, she was told.

True, the old restlessness for change had begun to set in again, but hadn't she come to terms with her lot in life? She shook off the contradictory thoughts and proceeded to peel the dirty clothes from her body.

Ben drove along Coty Lane in search of house number 2025. The steady downpour of rain, which had followed him from Atlanta, had mercifully ceased minutes ago. As he strained to read addresses through the rising mist and leafy trees that lined the narrow street, he was struck by the bucolic, storybook look to the wood-framed houses that dotted the road.

There it was—the house he sought sat on his right.

He parked along the street before he got out of the car. Carrying only his jacket, he left the bags to bring in later. He fished in his pocket for the set of house keys he'd been provided.

"Hey, mister, what you doin'?"

Ben jerked around at the dual voices and saw two little boys with heads strained skyward in perfect unison as they watched him from the sidewalk. They were twins, and no more than, maybe, four years old. Dressed alike, they held hands.

His mouth twitched into an unconscious smile. "I, um—"

"Leave the man alone. Didn't I tell you not to get too far ahead?"

Ben turned with the boys and saw a woman, a very pregnant woman, about a block away with her hand pressed to her back, slowly walking toward them.

He glanced back to the boys, then to the woman he presumed was their mother, before he smiled again.

"They're not bothering me," he assured her. He faced the twins as he dropped to their level on one knee. "Don't you think you ought to wait on your mom?"

"She's kinda slow," one twin said.

"Yeah," the other chimed in. "Who are you?"

"Well, I'm going to be your neighbor for a while. Do you two live around here?"

"Uh-huh." They nodded and spoke in a united chant. "Sixteen fifty-two Coty Lane."

The mother arrived and, insinuating herself between the boys, grabbed their hands. "These two," she complained to Ben in a friendly laugh. "No matter how often you tell them not to talk to strangers—"

"They do," he finished.

"You have some of your own, huh?"

"Oh, no." Ben shook his head in firm denial. "All I know came from my parents."

"He's not a stranger, Mama."

"He's a neighbor," the second twin added.

"Oh, is that right?" The pregnant woman gave Ben the once-over. "You must be new in town, then. Welcome to Fairlight. If you have to live in the South, it's a good choice." She stuck out her hand. "I'm Vanessa Stewart and these are my two boys, Brett and Brian."

He shook her proffered hand. "Ben Russell. Thank you."

"Come on boys." She ushered the boys along the sidewalk, but this time she kept their hands safely enclosed within hers. The twins waved to Ben.

He smiled and wondered how she could tell those two apart. He'd turned his attention back to his keys when he heard Vanessa's voice.

"Maybe you can join us at the church for family dinner on Wednesday night."

Ben gave an expected civil nod to the invitation before the little group walked on. Heavily engrossed in thought, he started up the front walk. Small towns had a style and force all their own. The key was to avoid the community-mentality madness. Mind your own business and, hopefully, they'd mind theirs. That was his plan for the summer. It would be nice, though, to end his suitcase existence, even if for only a few months; he had begun to look forward to the plane's breakfast entrée. He took the porch steps two at a time.

He slid the key from the extra ring into the front

door. As it found the slot, he turned the knob and pushed through.

The low-decibel, unbroken ominous beep from a tripped alarm sounded immediately throughout the room.

Ben muttered a loud curse and pulled the key from the lock. As he quickly pushed the door closed behind him, he caught a glimpse of the pregnant mother and her twins on the sidewalk. All three watched him as they stood with arms spread akimbo.

A series of expletives whisked past Ben's lips as he moved around the large, dimly lit living room in search of a control panel for the alarm. Where was it? He suspected he had less than a minute to enter a code he didn't know, so what good would it do to find the damn thing?

"This is just great—"

The loud roar from the alarm's klaxon horn now sounded, announcing that time was up for entering the security code.

The phone. It would ring any moment now and the security company would demand a password, which he didn't know, either. Another expletive. Where in the hell was that control panel? The horn's raucous blast had not abated when Ben turned into a narrow hallway.

A woman in a bulky robe stopped in her tracks in the middle of the hall. She brandished a toilet plunger in one hand while shocked surprise covered her face.

Ben mirrored her surprise and froze in confusion. "What the hell? I didn't know anyone was here."

He took a step toward her just as the phone rang, adding to the noisy racket. The woman screamed and backed away before she turned to run.

"Hey—who are you?" Ben shouted, and then bounded after her.

Screaming at the top of her lungs, she ran toward an open door farther down the hall.

"Wait a sec . . . This isn't what you think." When she was within a hand's grasp, he reached out for her arm, but she turned slightly and her plunger careened down across Ben's head.

"Hold on a minute." Blindly, he grabbed at her and pulled.

She let out another piercing shriek as her robe slipped from her shoulders and was left clutched in Ben's tight fingers. He stared in disbelief as her naked body darted into the open doorway a few steps away. The door slammed shut against him.

"Miss, miss . . . would you stop screaming?" Ben yelled through the locked door. "I'm not going to hurt you. If you give me a moment, I can explain—"

"I'll just bet you can, buddy."

He heard the deeply drawled words clearly above the horn's blare, the phone's ring, and the woman's screams. They came from behind him, and had been issued by the same man who now pressed a gun near Ben's ear.

Three

"What do you make of this?" Vanessa's comment was directed to her friend, Sela, as both stood on the front porch. "We can only hope Luther knows what he's doing."

Neither removed her solemn gaze from the street where the tall intruder now stood with the baby-faced deputy, Luther Matthews. A host of curious neighbors flocked along the sidewalk where the lawman continued his questioning near the man's sleek, late-model car.

Sela crossed her arms tightly over the robe that swallowed her figure, and squinted in disdain at the well-dressed, handcuffed man. She imagined he still argued his innocence to Luther.

"Oh, he'll get to the bottom of this and then cart the guy off to jail."

"We are talking about the same deputy, right?" Vanessa hooked her arm through Sela's. "I'm surprised the sheriff returned his gun after that last incident."

She ignored the truth in Vanessa's comment. "I wonder if this guy's a part of a burglary ring going around. And that story of his about being one of our guests. Since when did we start mailing the guests keys to the house?"

"If he is part of a ring, they've got a unique cover." Vanessa let out a soft laugh as she darted a humorous glance at Sela. "Upwardly mobile criminals with nice manners." She nodded her head toward the street. "Look at him, girl. Take a good look."

She had already done that, or at least for the frightening twenty seconds they'd faced each other in the house before she turned and ran from his formidable figure. He was tall and yes, she could admit it now, handsome in a rugged sort of way. Surprised by the treacherous thought, she quickly pushed it aside.

"What are you talking about?" she asked Vanessa.

"Your ordinary burglar doesn't show up for loot looking all polished and polite in a casual suit."

Sela frowned as her eyes narrowed on the intruder. He seemed to sense her stare, and turned his own onto her. Even from the distance, his blunt gaze disturbed her. Her head shook absently. "It doesn't matter. I want to know why he's in my house and what Luther's going to do about it."

"He seemed pretty harmless when I spoke to him earlier." Vanessa sighed at the puzzle the stranger presented. "Unusual, seeing as he stopped to talk and even offered his name. Said it was Ben Russell. The boys even took to him."

As she watched the intruder turn away when Luther held a cell phone to his ear, Sela realized Vanessa was right. He didn't fit the burglar mold. On top of that, even in the presence of the law who would surely check him out, he acted too cocksure.

"I don't care, Vanessa. Before this morning, I felt safe at home. Now I don't know." She turned to her friend. "And, whose side are you on, anyway? He attacked me in my own residence."

"I know, I know. I'm sure you were scared to death." Vanessa squeezed Sela's hand. "When I saw him leave the street and head up your walk, it surprised me. So, the boys and I stopped to watch him. It didn't look like he was getting ready to break and enter."

"What he did is not your fault. I didn't mean to snap at you, either. In fact, I'm grateful you were around to wave down Luther when he passed."

"One thing is for sure, though. Your visitor was definitely unexpected." She gave Sela another good-humored squeeze. "I can't imagine you planning to meet an inn guest barefoot, in your robe, and your hair sticking out like that."

"Like what?" Sela reached up and fingered one of the unruly plaits that had become uncoiled near her ear before she quickly recrossed her arms against her chest. She also remembered the air against her naked back when her robe fell away. Engulfed by embarrassment, she hardened her resolve against the man. "There's no telling what might have happened if you and Luther hadn't come when you did."

"I guess we're about to find out the verdict on your guest. He and Luther are headed back over here and look—he's not handcuffed anymore, either."

Sela jerked her attention back to the street, and watched the two men eschew the walkway to take a shortcut across the lush grass to the front porch steps. His casual walk afforded her an opportunity to satisfy her curiosity and take a second, longer look at the man who'd frightened her half to death. As they neared the porch, his long strides almost doubling Luther's shorter ones, she saw that his gaze remained steady on her, and that he appeared angry, glaring even.

Vanessa summed it up. "You know, he looks like he's royally pissed about something."

He had some nerve, Sela concluded. It was she who'd stayed huddled in that locked bathroom with only a towel for cover until Vanessa came to the door. And how humiliating was it when the neighborhood showed up to gather gossip from all the ruckus that the alarm and police lights made? This was some public debacle for Auntie to hear about.

The deputy climbed the porch steps first while the intruder brought up the rear.

"Sela," Luther drawled, "I think there's been a little case of mistaken identity."

"What do you mean?" She and Vanessa stepped forward as one.

"Let me finish, let me finish." He punctuated each syllable.

It was obvious the languid drawl was too much for the stranger, who stepped around Luther to confront the women.

"I was invited here." He pushed a sheet of pale blue notepaper, along with a matching envelope, toward Sela.

She immediately recognized the stationery, and stared at it stupidly. It couldn't be. It looked like Aunt Claire's writing stock.

"Well, take it and read it for yourself," he challenged.

She darted a glance to Vanessa before she took the papers thrust at her, then opened them to reveal her aunt's familiar, fluid writing style.

"By the way, my name is Ben Russell—the same name I gave to this lady earlier." He motioned toward Vanessa with a nod. "And what I tried to say to you inside before I had a gun pushed in my ear." When he turned to acknowledge Luther's part in the mistaken identity, the younger man shifted from one foot to the other.

"Oh, my God," Vanessa exclaimed, and rested her hand on her great belly. "I knew there'd be an explanation. I just knew it. Sela, what does the letter say?"

Sela looked up from the condemnable words in Auntie's letter and saw that the hard frown on Ben's face had begun to soften. Probably because he knew he had the upper hand.

"You set off the house alarm, and then you come after me, pulling off my robe in the process." An indignant Sela met his keen stare. "What was I suppose to do? Stand there stark naked while you properly introduced yourself?"

A hint of a smile finally reached his lips. "I wouldn't have minded."

"Not in your lifetime," she replied, with as much sarcasm as could be mustered on the spot.

"All right, now," Luther intervened, resting his hands atop his gun belt. "No harm was done."

"Your robe . . . that was purely accidental," Ben offered. "I honestly didn't mean to frighten you, but you sure as hell didn't give me a chance to explain things." He looked at Luther. "Neither of you did."

"He's right." Luther stood back and rocked on his legs. "That's a letter of introduction. It seems he studies buildings and then draws them. He's going to study some of the old ones around town."

"Your A.M.E. church," Ben clarified.

"I'm still confused. So, what's your connection here?" Vanessa inquired.

It was now Sela's turn to thrust the letter at Vanessa and offer a terse explanation. "Aunt Claire was the one who invited him here."

"Without telling you?" Vanessa quickly began to scan the letter.

Luther continued. "I called Reverend Osborne from the patrol car, and he vouched for Mr. Russell, too. Seems you're the only one who didn't get wind of all this, Sela." He chuckled at the idea.

Sela colored at his words, and was reminded of what had transpired that morning at the mailbox. Another letter had arrived today from Auntie, which she had planned to stack with the others in the house she had yet to open—had any of them mentioned the arrival of this man? At this moment, she'd bet her summer's happiness they did. Absent, Auntie had still managed to beat Sela at her own game of chicken.

Vanessa looked up from the letter. "Miss Claire doesn't mention you in here, Sela, but she did tell Mr. Russell to use the key as necessary and make himself at home."

"Please, call me Ben." He captured Sela's eyes with his, seeming to enjoy her struggle to capture her composure. "I believe you're Miss Bennett's niece. Any more questions I can answer?"

"The name's Sela Bennett," she retorted tartly. "Seeing as my aunt failed to inform you of that little fact."

He extended his hand to her. "All right, Sela. I'm sorry your aunt never mentioned you or the fact that you'd be staying here."

"That makes us even. And, I live here." When she grudgingly stuck her hand out in a truce, it was immediately smothered in his larger one.

"Maybe we could start over, then," he suggested.

The beginnings of a smile played across his lips. "On a better footing."

Vanessa cleared her throat. "And maybe we should take this inside. I think we've attracted a large enough audience." She referred to the curious that continued to mill outside the gates.

Discomfited, Sela pulled her hand from Ben's and buried it in the pocket of her robe. At that moment, she remembered the twins and whirled to Vanessa. "Where are the boys?"

"In the back on the gazebo swing—I can hear them," she answered. "We'll be going as soon as things are okay with you."

Luther doffed his cap to the women. "If you don't need anything else Sela, Vanessa, I'll get on about my rounds." He turned to Ben to shake his hand. "No bad feelings, I hope."

"Just glad you don't have an itchy trigger finger," Ben replied.

"Oh, it's much better now," Vanessa said, laughing. "He's been working on it."

Luther's smile danced clear to his eyes as he explained things to Ben. "Aw, Vanessa's always teasing me about that accident. You see, Chief won't let me put bullets in my weapon anymore, that's all."

"I don't believe this," he said, and arched a disbelieving brow at Luther before he turned to Sela. "I've had one hell of a morning. I'd like to get settled inside if we're finished out here."

"It's what my aunt wants," was Sela's noncommittal answer.

He grunted matter-of-factly at her lingering animosity. "I need to bring some things in from my car." With a backward glance, he walked off.

"I can help you with that," Luther said, and left to follow behind Ben. "Since you're gonna be around town for a while," he called out, "why don't you join us this week at the church for family dinner night?"

As the men moved beyond the porch, Sela turned to enter the house. "Did you hear that? Luther is already inviting the man to the church to eat. We don't even know him."

Vanessa gave Sela a sheepish smile. "I invited him, too."

Sela frowned her disapproval.

Vanessa propped her hands against her hips. "Well, he seemed nice at the time and I figured Ron could introduce a new neighbor to some other folks. Anyway, he said the robe thing was an accident, and he did apologize, which shows character."

"Maybe Ron will think his seven-months pregnant wife is picking up men."

"If you ask my opinion, he'd be a pretty good pick, don't you think?"

"Thank goodness no one's asking you." Sela found herself seeking him out again. There he was, lifting the car trunk's lid.

"Why do you think Miss Claire didn't tell you about her invitation to Ben? You don't think she's up to something, do you? I mean, she'd never put you in this kind of position, not with some stranger."

"Oh, she told me all right." Sela's tone was soft, but her thoughts were sharp as they flitted over the recent events. "Only, she knew I wouldn't listen."

"You're not making sense, girl. Not much of this does."

Vanessa was right about Aunt Claire. She was up to something. What, Sela hadn't quite figured out yet; but she'd find out soon enough.

And, exactly how did Mr. Ben Russell fit into all of this?

The tarot cards seemed at one with the knowledgeable fingers that dispensed them facedown onto the small, scarf-covered table in the ship's upper-deck suite. The cards relaxed Claire, and had become more a simple tool she used to free her mind than a medium for predictions. In less than a minute, the cards were lined up in a Celtic Cross spread.

Claire Bennett expertly revealed the cards, one at a time, nodding sagely as she performed this ritual morning read. When the fourth card, the moon, was revealed, a frown creased her brow. Resistance.

"Resistance?" She muttered the word out loud, questioning her own interpretation of her niece's card. Of course, resistance can occur before one finally relents, she decided, then smiled broadly. Maybe that particular insight wouldn't be shared in her next letter to Sela.

A sharp rap at the stateroom door averted her attention. Claire turned to the sound, not expecting a visitor.

"Yes?"

A deep voice came from the other side of the narrow door. "The captain wanted to make sure you remembered your promise to join him at his table this morning."

Claire recognized the southeastern drawl of the ship's junior officer. She glanced at her gold watch before she caught the tarot cards into the folds of the silk scarf with her other hand. Time had flown by, and a promise made to the wonderful Captain Powell was a promise. Swiftly, she moved across the room and dropped the silk-cloaked cards into an ornate wooden box on the nightstand. Heading for the door, she scooped up the light wrap from across the bed.

"Forgive me." Claire started the apology before the door was fully opened. "It seems I've lost track of time." When the officer looked up—he stood no taller than her own average height—she remembered his name and matched his smile.

"Mr. Little, it's good to see you again."

"The pleasure is mine, ma'am. The captain didn't want to start breakfast without you. If you're ready, I can escort you to the dining room."

"I am, and thank you." While Claire closed her door, the young officer waited patiently nearby. She liked his drawl. It was her own private reminder of how much she missed home and her dear Sela as the cruise ship drifted through the icy beauty and solitude of the Alaskan coast.

"Do you have any more of those letters to your niece that need posting?"

"For the time being, no." Claire let him help her with her wrap before following his lead down the narrow corridor toward the dining deck. "Right about now, I think my beauty has more than enough to keep her busy."

Four

In fifteen minutes, Vanessa had gathered the boys from the backyard gazebo and followed Luther to the street, passing among a few bystanders who still milled outside the gate.

Meanwhile, inside the house, Sela settled into the comforting folds of her robe as she stood in the middle of the living room and cast a suspicious eye toward Ben. Still grasping his luggage, he turned to survey the room's eclectic decor. He broke their heavy silence first.

"I didn't notice these pieces before." He stopped in front of a large carved African tribal mask and shield, suspended from the wall, before moving on to the fireplace and a complicated teardrop-shaped Indian dream catcher, which jutted out from the mantel where it hung. He paused to peer at it closely.

"A dream catcher. Now, this is nice. You can see a lot of the intricate webbing details. I'll bet it was specially made." He turned to Sela. "For you?"

"No. I sleep just fine. It was made for Aunt Claire by a Native American friend of hers in the northwest." She moved restlessly about the room. "You'll find mementos from Aunt Claire's globetrotting all over the house." With a slight toss of her head, she added, "You must have missed that in her letters."

"Are you having second thoughts about my staying here?"

"I—" She was caught off guard as he turned and attracted her stare with dark, deep-set eyes set under heavy brows. "I just need a little time to get used to this."

In a few easy strides, he planted himself in front of her. "Listen, your deputy checked me out, and your aunt and minister vouched for me. I don't know what else I'm supposed to do to get your approval. It's been a long twenty-four hours, and I do know I'd like to get settled in somewhere. So, make up your mind and either show me a room where I can put my things"—he lowered his luggage to the floor—"or, if you want me to leave, say it and stop shooting daggers at my back. Just tell me what you want."

Sela inhaled a deep breath and looked away. She disliked being put on the defensive. Again. Frowning, she knew she couldn't ask Aunt Claire's guest to find other lodging just because she was caught off guard by . . . what?

She had to face it; there was no tactful way to tell this man to get lost—at least not one she could think of right off. She turned back to him and faced what she considered his overconfident smirk.

"I wouldn't think of putting you out. You're my aunt's guest." She walked across the hardwood floor to the similarly polished wood staircase that led to the second floor, assuming he'd follow. At the base of the staircase, another of Aunt Claire's treasures, a surprisingly tall suit of authentic English armor, stood as sentry.

"I have things to keep me occupied—I suppose

you will, too. At least we don't have to worry about getting in each other's way." She tossed him a withering glance from over her shoulder as she sailed past the armor.

He gathered his bags to follow her up the staircase. "I can live with that."

"Guests stay on the second floor."

"Your house is a gem. It's interesting and quite large—more than it appears to be from the outside."

"You were expecting what—a plain little farmhouse because we live in a rural area?" Sela's bare feet rapidly thumped over the wood steps ahead of him.

"No, but I sure need to figure out how to pay you a compliment without getting my head chewed off."

His deep voice rumbled over Sela, keeping her senses alive to the fact that he was close behind. His compliments had emulated those made by inn guests in the past, any of whom he could easily have been, until she remembered the embarrassment she suffered when he arrived. Did she have a problem with him? Of course—his presence now threatened the direction of her entire summer. Surely, that was the reason for her discomfort around him.

When she reached the first bedroom off the landing, instead of berating his comment, she gave him her practiced tourist spiel.

"The rooms on this level are numbered one through five, but only one and five, the end rooms, include a private bath; the middle three share a fairly large bathroom that's just around the corner of this L-shaped hall." She arrived at the third bedroom door and pushed it wide. "You can use this one, and I'll get some fresh linens for you."

Ben joined her in the bedroom where she walked to the window and pushed back the chintz curtains.

"Technically, the B and B is closed down until Labor Day weekend, you know. That's when our season starts up again." When he didn't respond, she looked at him over her shoulder and added, "Didn't Auntie tell you?"

He had already turned to leave the room. "She mentioned it. That's why I didn't expect anyone when I showed up."

"That's great," Sela pronounced with disgust as she turned and crossed her arms. "She tells you about everything *but* me."

"You I would've remembered." He walked through the door and out of her view.

"Hey—" Sela crossed the room and stuck her head out of the door. "Where are you going?"

"I don't rate a room with a private bath?" He set his bags down in front of room five, which faced the end of the hall.

"No." Aware that she'd sounded harsh, Sela explained her answer as she rushed out of the room to join him. "Well, room one isn't available because the mattress has to be replaced, and—"

"What about this?" He tried room five's doorknob, and when it turned under his persuasion, he entered.

Ben studied the cool, quiet interior with a skilled eye. It was an airy corner room with interesting architecture offered by the sloping planes of the open-beamed ceiling that followed the roof's eaves. A large bay window provided lots of sunlight. That would be a good spot for his drafting board and books. A double bed, turned down with a colorful quilt at the foot, also looked inviting. Nearby stood a dresser. On its top sat an ornate, sectioned box with a framed picture turned down next to it. The door tucked in the corner most likely led to the bathroom. Yes, he'd just as well get settled in this room as another. He turned, expecting to see Sela.

"I'll settle with this one, if it's all right with you."

"No, it's not." She spoke from the hallway, her face a stony mask as she tugged her robe close around her body.

"Oh, and why not?" he asked. "It's got a bed, and everything else looks fine to me."

Faced with his insistence, she raised her voice an octave. "That doesn't matter. It's not used during the summer. Now, if you'll come out and close the door . . ."

Puzzled, Ben cocked a brow at the serious frown on Sela's face.

As though she sensed his heightened interest, she lowered her voice. "Mr. Russell, please."

Intrigued by her plea, Ben did as she asked. Once the door was closed, he watched as she visibly relaxed, her shoulders sloping once more to a more casual slant.

"Call me Ben. You don't mind if I call you Sela?"

She looked up and managed to reply through stiff lips. "Sure . . . Ben."

She had striking eyes. They were large and intense, and he could see within them her attempt at composure. "Sela, are you all right?"

"Of course, why wouldn't I be?" She offered a small smile as proof. "I'm sorry you won't be able to get a private bath this visit. So, what's your choice for a room? Two, three, or four?"

He retrieved his bags from the hallway and started for room three, her first suggestion. "Why don't I take the one you willingly offered, since you refused me my choice?"

She shook her head, and sloughed off the entire incident. "It's not like that at all. We just don't use certain rooms during the off-season, that's all."

Ben didn't question her reasoning, and decided, instead, to keep his thoughts to himself. He strode into the room and set his luggage on the low rack next to the wall before he turned to Sela. In the seconds it took to take in her figure leaning against the door frame, he saw, instead, the smooth length of golden brown hips and legs that had been exposed to his gaze not an hour before. He blinked at the erotic image spread across his mind's eye.

At the same time, she straightened up and tightened her arms across her chest again. Was she ever going to get rid of that damn robe so he could satisfy this craving of his to see what she really looked like? It didn't take a lot of mental effort to remember her curves from the back and how they flowed down to become a nicely rounded bottom above legs that moved like the wind. He imagined her front side was just as interesting. He blinked again.

Sela looked at Ben's expression. *Why is he blinking like an idiot?* Uncomfortable in what was now *his* domain, she fumbled with the robe.

"I—I'd better get back downstairs. I was supposed to help out at the library quite a while ago."

"Yeah, I've taken up too much of your time, as it is." He shrugged out of his jacket. "I think I'll change before I meet your Reverend Osborne over at the church."

Fascinated by the way his chest muscles strained against the shirt's thin fabric, Sela stared at his movements. She quickly raised her eyes to his as she felt the glow of a warm flush. "Well, um, do . . . do you know how to get there?" She cleared her throat.

Ben chuckled. "I think I can find my way."

Embarrassed that he'd caught her staring, she looked away as she hastened to leave the room. "Good. I'll . . . I'll see you back here tonight, then."

At that moment, the downstairs door chime sang out. They both turned to the sound as a series of knocks followed.

"I wonder who that is?" Sela walked over to the balcony rail where she could see the bottom of the downstairs front door as it was being pushed open.

"Sela . . . Sela." The authoritative male voice floated up from the ever-widening door.

She recognized the voice immediately and headed for the stairs, turning to Ben, who had joined her. "It's the reverend. He's come here to see you, I guess."

Ben smiled as he swung his coat over his shoulders and slipped it back on. "I see you have an open door policy for everyone, huh?"

"I'm not used to locking everything up tightly," she replied smartly without looking back. "Now that you're here, I'll probably have to change that." She sped ahead of him, and danced down the stairs to meet the minister.

Reverend Osborne was waiting near the front door when she reached him. Barely Sela's height, showing the beginnings of pattern baldness, and with bifocals balanced on his nose, he more closely resembled a character actor in his full black suit and cleric collar than a middle-aged man of God. She greeted him with a meaningful smile—he had dressed to impress the out-of-town visitor.

"Sela, I didn't know what was going on after that odd call from Luther and Mr. Russell." His gaze darted beyond her and upward to Ben. "And you must be our guest."

"Yes, sir. I'm Ben Russell, and I'm pleased to meet you in the flesh, Reverend Osborne." He moved from around Sela and stretched out his hand. "You don't know how glad I was that you were in your office to take the call from your deputy."

They shook hands heartily. "I was glad to vouch for you with Luther. Course, I don't know why all that was necessary. Luther doesn't usually treat Claire's guests so suspiciously."

"That's good to know," Ben said with a good-natured smile.

Sela sighed. It was obvious the reverend didn't know the full story of what had happened. The gossips were going to have a field day when they told their version of her run-in with a stranger she was now letting stay with her at the inn.

"Why didn't you tell me you knew he was coming here?" she asked Reverend Osborne, smarting from the fact that no one took into account how put upon she'd been all day.

He scratched his shiny brown forehead and tried to explain. "Claire wrote and said she didn't want me telling everybody about the young man just yet. She wanted things settled with him first. She said she wrote you the same thing." He squinted across his glasses. "Why couldn't you explain things to Luther?"

She crossed her arms. "Never mind."

He turned back to Ben. "Listen, Mr. Russell—"

"Please, call me Ben."

"All right then, Ben. If you want, we can go on over to the church now so you can get a chance to see how it's laid out, meet our secretary, learn where everything is, and get a general feel for our little church." He chuckled. "After all, you'll be spending a lot of time in it over the next few months."

"That suits me fine," Ben replied. "I can follow you in my car."

"Good, good," the minister said. "That way, you can stay as long as you like today."

Ben turned to Sela. "Can I talk to you for a moment?" He motioned toward the next room, away from the reverend.

She frowned, but only obliged him with a few steps before she spoke. "What?"

Ben tried to lower his deep voice. "Do you want to share the security code with me, or do you want to just wait up for me later? Either way, we won't have to go through a repeat of what happened earlier."

Sela flushed again at Ben's subtle reminder, the warmth creeping up her neck to her face.

"Anything wrong?" Reverend Osborne looked from Sela to Ben.

"No," Sela declared. "We're just working out our schedules, that's all." She gave Ben her best glare. "That way, we can be sure not to get in each other's way. Again."

"I'm only trying to accommodate you," Ben offered.

"Don't worry about me." Sela lowered her voice for his ears only. "I won't set the alarm."

"If you want me to, I can ring the doorbell so you won't—"

"Just use your key to get in," she cut in with a whisper. Her patience had worn thin and she didn't care that he was being nice and accommodating. "We'll work out the details later."

Ben seemed all the more amused by her consternation. "As you wish." To the minister, he said, "If you're ready, I'll get some notes I have upstairs and be right back."

"Sure, sure, go on and get them," Reverend Osborne said, shooing him off.

Ben turned on his heels and headed for the stairs and his bedroom.

Sela sighed as she watched him leave, surprised that she was still reacting to the man. She needed some air, which reminded her that she'd better get changed if she was going to put in any hours at the library.

"Reverend, I'm already late for my volunteer shift at the library. Can you see yourself out when Ben comes back down?"

He nodded, but it was obvious he was anxious to say something else. "Before you go, Sela, tell me what you think about Mr. Russell. That Claire sure knows a good idea when she comes across one. I mean, she got this smart young architect to come here and write about us and our rebuilding efforts at the church. And mind you, he's not just any kind of architect. No, no. Claire says he's an architectural engineer." He took pride in enunciating each syllable. "You know, we could even find ourselves in that magazine Doc Harris keeps in his office, the *Architectural Digest.*"

Sela smiled at his enthusiasm, and realized he didn't care a whit about what she thought of Ben. "I think it's the church building he's interested in, not us."

"But there's no church without the community and congregation. They're all twined together with history. Which reminds me, Sela. Didn't you promise to go through those boxes of water-damaged files in the basement at the church?"

She groaned at both his non sequitur and the reminder of the loathsome chore. "Yes, a promise you pulled from me last summer in the middle of a softball game. You've still got the memory of an elephant." Her smile grew a notch. "I haven't forgotten. I've just been waiting for the opportunity to blackmail you into taking it back during this year's game."

With his hands clasped piously behind his back, Reverend Osborne winked at Sela. "I've still got my work cut out saving your soul, young lady. Claire won't be happy to learn you've slipped again."

"We just won't tell her then, will we?" Sela offered in good humor as Ben returned to join them.

"I'm ready," Ben said, his glance once again curious and assessing as he hefted a slim valise under one arm, and hoisted his camera's shoulder strap on the other.

"Great. Let's go." Reverend Osborne held the front door open for him. "You know, Ben, I'm sure you'll like our little town. In fact, I think the perfect opportunity for you to meet the congregation is this Wednesday night."

Sela's eyes rolled heavenward, her amusement swiftly dying. What was it about Ben and unsolicited invitations? She followed them and prepared to close the door on this particularly bad morning, but the minister's final comments managed to slip through the closing portal.

"Why don't you plan on joining us for our family supper?" he suggested to Ben. "I've got a good feeling about you and this project of yours. You'll be getting a lot done this summer, and I think it'll make a difference for Fairlight."

Five

Sela wasn't normally a clock-watcher. This evening, however, from her chair behind the library's main desk, she kept a wary eye on the large clock fixed to the wall above the copy machine. The fact that she'd soon be going home—and the inescapable certainty that Ben would be there, too—had left a deep tread in her thoughts. Try as she might, she couldn't lose sight of him as he boldly paraded, front and center, across her mind.

She sighed at the irritation to her summer solitude. Under normal circumstances, she was quite comfortable with the inn's guests. But, this was hardly normal; it was a different matter altogether when the arrangement was so inconveniently forced. Her hope was that the unopened letters would reveal what had possessed Aunt Claire to invite *him* to the house. She would read them tonight. If her aunt had a reason behind the invitation, Sela would unearth it.

As the media specialist for both the elementary and high schools in Fairlight for the last three years, Sela's natural progression when school was closed was to spend her summer working with Ophelia Glover in the town's library. With only a handful of people present this evening, she fidgeted in the chair, restless with what she'd never admit might be anticipation. She sighed again when her furtive glance told her the clock's hands had still failed to move fast enough.

"Okay, I'm back." The cheerful greeting signaled Ophelia's return through the library's wood-framed glass doors. "The way you're glaring at that clock, it's not a moment too soon, either. You look like you can't wait to get out of here tonight."

Embarrassed by the accurate observation, Sela laughed it off. "No, I'm fine. I promised you I'd make up for being late, and I will." Ophelia had been the town's librarian for as long as Sela could remember—at least since Sela had been in grade school—and had always shown appreciation for her help. So, the last thing she wanted to do was offend the older woman. "Hey, your new hairdo looks great. Juanita outdid herself this time."

Ophelia smoothed her fingers across her upswept French twist as she joined Sela behind the desk. "Thanks. I could never get away with wearing my hair in a plait like you. When you're young, you can do so much with what God gave you."

"Oh, please." She drawled the words with a smile and brushed back the tight braid that was twisted and then pinned to the back of her head. "Let me guess—Juanita was mouthing off about my hair again. I know she thinks it's the lost cause of the century."

"Not only Juanita. Everybody was running their mouths about you today, girl."

"Oh?" Not expecting that response, she became both curious and defensive. "Well, they all know that summer is my own personal break. I want to relax, not worry about perms and hairstyles every day."

Ophelia's eyes carried a distinct twinkle. "Sela, they were talking about you and that good-looking man who's staying with you."

"Ben?" The name easily slipped past her lips.

"You know who I'm talking about, huh?" She lowered her voice conspiratorially. "So, it's true he's staying with you at the B and B?" Then, she laughed as the answers reflected in Sela's face. "Course, I wouldn't be blaming you for wanting to get back over there, to take care of your guest and all. Maybe that's why you were watching the clock, hmm?"

"His name is Ben Russell in case you want to tell Juanita and the rest of the town." Sela threw a playful scowl at the older woman before she moved to a stack of returned books on the counter and busily set about checking them in with a library stamp. Vanessa had warned her that news of Ben would circulate in a hurry, but she was surprised at how fast.

"What else did you hear?" she asked as nonchalantly as possible, wondering if Luther's loose lips had sped up her public embarrassment. "And, he's not my guest."

Ophelia followed her to the counter and whispered, "That's not what the girls at the shop are saying. Why, you didn't even tell me he was the reason you were late getting over here . . . something about you having Luther check him out first because he'll be staying with you in that big house—alone."

Sela looked up from the books and feigned shock. "Ophelia, that's pure gossip you're spreading."

"Not if it's the truth." When Sela didn't offer a comment, Ophelia added, "Well, is it?"

"What?"

"The truth." A devilish smile played across

Ophelia's lips. "I also hear he's not bad on the eyes; tall, handsome—and my personal favorite, broad shoulders—and—"

She was interrupted by the loud *clunk* Sela made with the stamp. "He's with Reverend Osborne now. You can tell Juanita and the others he'll be spending his time over at the church if they want to hunt him down to drool. I don't want them ringing the bell over at the B and B to chase him."

Ophelia pressed her hand against her heart in mock shock. "Oh, my Lord, don't tell me. He's a minister? Seems like the good-looking ones always turn to religion. Still, though, he sounds like a fine catch for you."

"That's not funny." She turned so she could face Ophelia. "He's an architect and he studies buildings, especially old churches."

"Oh, I see."

When Sela saw the grin clinging to the librarian's face, she slanted her eyes in frustration. "No, you don't. Anyway, that's all I know, so don't ask me anything else." She turned away to move the canceled books to a nearby cart.

"All right, Sela. Don't be flashing those big old eyes at me, looking all hurt. You know I'm just kidding about you and him, don't you?" Her tone turned serious. "You still get as skittish as a colt when subjects turn personal. Honey, everybody in town knows what you've gone through, and respects your feelings about it. We were just having a little fun at your expense."

Sela looked up and took a deep breath. "I know. You'd think with my track record, I should be able to take a joke better."

"So, why do you have a boarder when the B and B is closed until the fall?"

"He's not a real guest. He's Auntie's friend. She invited him to stay while he's in town studying the church renovations with Reverend Osborne."

"Okay, it's beginning to make sense, now, since our church is over a hundred years old. But, isn't Claire still traveling outside of the country somewhere?"

Sela nodded. "And she won't return for a while. This was all arranged a while back."

"And, it's just the two of you at the house?"

"Ophelia." This time, she smiled good-naturedly at the ribald suggestion. "Stop it. We're all adults here."

"That's what I'm talking about, girl." They both laughed before quickly quieting when they remembered their surroundings. "Anyway," Ophelia continued, "if Claire invited him here, he must be all right. Otherwise, she'd never have let him stay at the inn. He's probably married with four kids."

"Like you." Sela grinned. She was sure she had not seen a wedding ring on his finger. That's something she'd have remembered. She stole another look at the clock.

"Hey, it's already seven," she announced, happily changing the subject. "Do you want me to help file this last cart of books before I leave?"

"No, I can handle things. You're still coming tomorrow, right?"

Sela returned to the main desk while Ophelia followed. "Of course."

"I wasn't sure if your schedule had changed and all, what with *Ben* in town."

"He won't be a problem." She reached into the desk drawer and retrieved her shoulder bag. "He knows he's simply a houseguest, not an inn guest. He'll have to get his own meals at the diner and make up and change his own bed."

Both women now strolled toward the front doors. "In fact," Sela said, "we've already agreed to stay out of each other's way. I mean, I doubt we'll even notice each other around."

Ophelia's glance was suspect. "I wouldn't put money on that happening."

"Just watch." Sela smiled, then slipped through the door as Ophelia threw out her final rejoinder. "Somehow, I can't believe Claire expects that to happen, either."

It had been at least six months since Ben had tasted southern fried chicken, and this had actually been cooked in a bona fide southern kitchen. Mrs. Osborne's special preparation of the bird had been well worth the wait, not to mention the accompanying carrot soufflé, string bean casserole, and a layered salad concoction that tasted heavenly, though it defied description.

From the moment he'd entered their modest brick home, located in a clearing to the rear of the church's sprawling property, Mrs. Osborne began to practice her own brand of hospitality with a vengeance. It had been unexpected and certainly disconcerting, especially when Ben's own set of rules for visiting this small town included keeping a low profile and staying clear of local entanglements. Thus, he had initially begged off the dinner invitation; but Reverend Osborne wouldn't hear of it. And so, Ben had broken his own rule. Now, in retrospect, he didn't think the damage was too great—the evening so far had turned out pretty well.

"Do you want more dessert?" Mrs. Osborne's plea, accompanied by an expectant look from across the pristine white linen tablecloth, washed over him.

Reverend Osborne had already pushed his plate away and simply smiled at his wife's efforts to press more food into their guest.

Ben waved his free hand, refusing more red velvet cake while he downed the last forkful from his plate.

"And the banana pudding . . . I can pack it for you to take back to the inn." Mrs. Osborne, a heavy-set woman with a round, pretty face, made it hard to refuse. She was short like her husband; they appeared as a perfectly matched set.

Ben reached for the water glass and downed a swallow before glancing at the minister, who offered an imperceptible nod. "Okay," Ben said. "That would be nice. And thank you, Mrs. Osborne, for everything. It's been a long time since I had a home-cooked meal of this caliber—a very long time."

Mrs. Osborne beamed a smile and left the table.

"I'm glad you took my advice; otherwise she wouldn't have given up, you know. She's taken a liking to you," the reverend stated matter-of-factly. "So, she'll feed you. Now, if she didn't like you, you wouldn't be taking her food out of the house." They both grinned at the observation. "The sooner you know this, the sooner you'll learn not to argue with her. Just take the food."

"I like her, too." Ben enjoyed the relaxed atmosphere and leaned back in his chair. "Of course, our mutual admiration means I may have to start running a few extra miles each morning."

"She also likes Sela. She'll probably come back in here with dessert packed for the both of you." He tented his hands in thought for a short moment. "Tell me, what do you think of our Sela?"

Ben's brows had risen at the mention of her name. Ahh . . . Sela. If nothing else, she had all the makings for an interesting landlord. He sat forward in his chair, warming to the subject. "Well, let's just say getting her to like me is probably too big an order."

"I take it there was some friction earlier between the two of you?"

"You could say that. She's taken an instant dislike to me." Ben smiled, knowing at least one of her reasons why. "Actually, I believe we can work out a plan to stay civil to each other."

Reverend Osborne leaned forward and rested his arms on the table. "You know, Sela is pretty special to us. Everyone in town knows her—she's lived here all her life."

Ben nodded, though he didn't quite understand what the minister was getting at. So, he waited patiently for the older man to make his point.

"Of course, you've met her aunt, Claire Bennett."

"Yes. We became acquainted when I hosted a design seminar for university students in, of all places, Italy, and she happened to be staying at the same working farmhouse set out in the valley."

"A charming woman, don't you think?"

"Quite. Persuasive, too." They both laughed at what was obviously an accurate description.

"You never regret meeting someone like her," the minister said.

Ben's eyes grew openly amused. "Within a day of our meeting, she had become like an old friend. I ended up telling her my plans for a book on church architecture, and how I collected research on old structures. That's when she told me about Fairlight and the church here, and that we had been brought together for this very purpose. Now that I think about it, maybe *intrepid* fits her better. I understand she travels all over every summer—no fear."

"Yes, she does, but she seems to have a lot of trust

in you. I could tell in her letter. From there, it was an easy enough matter for her to invite you here."

"Sometimes she could be uncanny." Ben tilted his head at the memory. "One time, she told my fortune. She pointed out little things here and there to make it interesting. Of course, I'm not a big believer, but I didn't tell her."

Reverend Osborne frowned. "Yes, that's our Claire, all right. And, she didn't expect you to believe her. No matter her faults, though. She's a friend with a good heart."

He paused a moment. "I mention her so you can see the woman that Sela really is once she gets to know you. I wouldn't judge Sela too harshly after one meeting. She's very much like her aunt, and persuasive, too."

Ben was still not sure what all this meant. "We probably won't have many run-ins anyway. I expect I'll be out most of each day, so it should all work out."

"Good." At that moment, Mrs. Osborne returned, and true to her husband's word, she had two containers of food prepared for travel.

"I thought I'd pack something for both you and Sela." She set the package next to Ben.

He stood up from the table. "Thank you, Mrs. Osborne. Both of you have been more than gracious. I should be going, though. It's getting late and it's been a long day."

Reverend Osborne also stood. "One last cup of coffee in the den before you leave?"

An unbidden vision of Sela, shapely backside and all, swept through Ben's mind, and it occurred to him that he was looking forward to seeing her again. It wasn't too late, he surmised; she'd still be awake when he returned.

"I believe I can make room for one cup," he said and followed them into the den.

Sela rapped on Vanessa's back door. Through the pane glass, she could see the twins at the small kitchen table eating dinner. They hadn't noticed her yet.

"Coming." Vanessa's faint response came from somewhere inside the house.

Brett looked up at the door. "It's Aunt Sela," he blurted, and slid from his chair. The race was on with his brother, Brian, to see who'd get to the door first.

Both boys arrived together, two pairs of sticky hands grabbing at the doorknob before Vanessa walked into the kitchen behind them.

"Get back to that table," she ordered the boys, and pointed them in the opposite direction before she opened the door.

"Hey, fellas," Sela greeted them as they climbed back into their chairs. She then turned to Vanessa, who was now leaning against the counter, her hand curved around her belly. "Are you all right? Where's Ron?"

"I was just with him on the phone." She sighed. "Late at the office again."

With another baby on the way, Vanessa was no longer working as a registered nurse at Talbot County Hospital, so Ron was determined to make his independent real estate business more lucrative by drumming up new clients, and that often required him to travel to neighboring counties for listings.

"Well, since I'm over here, I'll help the boys get

ready for bed and you can put your feet up for a while. How's that?"

Vanessa smiled. "I am a little tired. Thanks, Sela. What do you say, guys?"

"Okay," Brian agreed between chews.

"Can you read us a story, too?" Brett added.

"Only if you finish all of your dinner." She turned to Vanessa. "We have a few minutes. I need to talk." She pointed toward the living room. "In there." At Vanessa's nod, she returned her attention to the boys. "No funny stuff 'cause Mommy and I'll be right back."

She led Vanessa into the next room. The carpet was thick underfoot in the tastefully furnished room of dark wood pieces and stuffed, footed chairs. And plants. The room flourished with them. They hung from corners and flowed down the sides of shelves. They graced the fireplace opening as well as the coffee table. The soft, indirect lighting made the room calm and soothing, something Sela needed right now.

Vanessa lowered herself into the wing chair next to the fireplace and watched Sela pace across the room. "Okay, what's going on? I can see it in those eyes."

"When I left the library a while ago, I went home and opened Aunt Claire's letters." She stopped momentarily in front of Vanessa. "You know, those last ones I decided to ignore because of all that daily advice about—"

"I know . . . what did they say?"

She stuck her hands in the back pockets of her jeans and resumed her pace. "The first two said about the same: advice, things to be careful of, places she had been—and by the way, she sends her love to you and the boys."

"Of course, but, go on."

"Well, finally in the third letter, she mentioned that she had made arrangements with a nice gentleman—that would be Ben, of course—to meet Reverend Osborne about studying the church, and that she would write and tell me how things were progressing with the arrangement."

"So, she did tell you about Ben."

"In painful detail, I might add. She was obviously impressed by his handsome list of credentials."

"Not to mention the handsome face," Vanessa said with a grin.

"But, she doesn't mention a thing about him staying at the house until the letter I received in this morning's mail. Then, she warned me that when Ben arrived, he would probably stay through the summer, that she didn't want me to be overly surprised or anxious about that, and that I should make sure when I meet him to be as hospitable to *our* summer guest as I could. She ends it by asking that I please do it for her. How's that for a request?"

"Well, for one thing, it's obvious she knows you." Vanessa arched a kink out of her back. "Sela, blame yourself for not reading the letters when they arrived. Face it, Miss Claire did try to warn you he was coming."

"You know Auntie, and Auntie knows me. She knew I wouldn't read those letters after I asserted myself all over the place on the phone with her. Of course I blame myself entirely. I'm so mad at me I could spit nails."

"That's not gonna help. He was coming whether you knew it or not, right?"

"But see, with me not being prepared, his showing up has created gossip." Sela curled onto the settee opposite Vanessa. "Ophelia says everybody in the beauty shop was talking about me and . . . and Ben staying at the inn. And when I was walking home from the library a while ago, two more people greeted me with this kind of sly smile on their faces, like they knew something was going on."

"So what? It's not like there's some kind of hanky-panky going on with the man."

"That's what I'm talking about," Sela declared. "You think Luther told what happened, how I was trapped in the bathroom and didn't know Ben from a burglar? I can imagine how everybody'll fill in the blank spaces. I swear, Vanessa, somebody's going to pay if he gave out details." She grabbed the sofa cushion to her chest.

"Every neighbor on our street was lined up outside the gate when Luther's patrol car light was flashing this afternoon. They were bound to know something was up."

She dropped her head back on the sofa, and grimly gagged. "Aargh . . . I don't like being the butt of this gossip."

"You've survived worse, and you'll survive this raindrop in Hunter's Pond. Don't let it get to you."

Sela drew in a strong breath of air. Vanessa was right, she had survived the last gossip fest from three years ago. In fact, it had taken a year before rumors died down enough that she felt she could walk comfortably among her neighbors.

"Miss Claire wouldn't put you in the middle of anything she didn't think you could handle. That, I know."

"I just don't like the jokes insinuating that he's more than a guest. I mean, not only is it unfair to him, but I don't want ideas put in anybody's head about how I feel."

"You're letting your pride take control, girl. Let

them talk, laugh, make jokes, whatever—it'll die down soon enough. And Ben Russell is a big boy. He can take care of himself. But, if you start looking guilty and get all upset, they're gonna figure where there's smoke, there must be a fire ready to spark."

"Not here and not any time soon," she answered smartly. When Vanessa didn't respond, she sat up on the sofa and saw the serious slant on her friend's face. "Why are you looking at me like that?"

" 'Cause I can't remember the last time you were so concerned about what people think. Good or bad, and whether you like it or not, he's pulled some strong reactions from you. It won't be so easy keeping that vow to ignore the opposite sex, will it?"

In truth, Sela hadn't really analyzed what her feelings were on the matter or on the promise she made almost three years ago. And, she didn't want to think about it. The consequences were too great to contemplate, and Vanessa knew it. That's why Sela wouldn't lie to her best friend.

"I'll admit," Sela began, "when we learned who he really was, I was ticked off, and probably with Aunt Claire more than him. Then, everybody he met, even people who hadn't met him, thought he was great, including you and the boys." She paused to catch her breath as she curled around the cushion again. "Common sense tells me I can't blame him for that."

"He's as much a victim of Miss Claire's planning as you are."

"Maybe," she agreed stubbornly.

"You didn't answer my question, though," Vanessa said. "You told me what everybody else thinks about him. I asked if you were keeping that ridiculous promise you made."

"And I wasn't finished." Sela swallowed hard, and looked Vanessa straight in the eye. "I'm more determined than ever."

Ben parked the car in front of the house and got out, only to be blanketed by the humidity drawn from the hot, damp day and now warm evening. The empty street was quiet, the only sound coming from the staccato chirps of what must have been hundreds of crickets. The gate to the drive had been closed, so rather than upset Sela by parking in her driveway without specific permission, he thought it best to leave the car outside until tomorrow morning.

The porch lights were on, as were the twin floodlights that lit the upper gables of the two-story home, showing off the interesting roofline and handiwork from early-century craftsmen. You couldn't find that kind of work anymore on a regular house. Everything had become prefab, Ben lamented. He made a mental note to spend some time riding around the town taking snapshots of homes he suspected were easily seventy to a hundred years old. Most of the ones he had driven past were in very good condition, some with extensive and obvious renovations.

As he made his way toward the gate, he heard a rustle of leaves break the silence. It came from near the shrubs that surrounded the mailbox. Ben slowed his steps, but with ears keened, he heard nothing else. By the time he passed through the gate, he felt more than heard something else; this time, it came from the other side, his left. Turning, he saw a shadow approach him from the gate he'd just entered.

With a quickness learned from traveling alone and in foreign places, he pivoted to confront the dark figure.

Six

"Ben."

It was Sela's voice. As she came out of the shadows cast by the trees and into view, Ben saw that she walked alongside a man, her arm possessively folded into the crook of his. He was taller than she as their matched strides brought them across the yard. Dressed in a business shirt and pants, his tie was pulled loose from his neck.

The uncomfortable humidity was forgotten as disappointment enveloped Ben. She was returning home with her date—a boyfriend, no doubt. He hadn't noticed a wedding band on her finger earlier; he was sure of it. He would have remembered. And she—well, she was definitely not a disappointment under the robe.

"We weren't sure it was you," he heard her say as she drew closer.

Ben caught a full view of her in the moonlight and drew a deep breath as his appreciative eye traveled from her sandaled feet upward across her shirt. She looked delicate, more vulnerable with the light casting an ethereal glow about her. She had exchanged the robe for hip-hugging jeans that draped her figure well, and a white shirt of soft material that did the same. The inch of skin the shirt left exposed at her waist charmed him into a stare.

His heart lurched in his chest. Not only was the sight of her an unexpected pleasure, she smelled good, too. That's when he realized she'd stopped in front of him. His gaze quickly roamed higher, over her breasts, along her slender throat, only to meet her eyes—large, dancing pools of black—that seemed to frown a warning. The man with her was saying something.

Ben exhaled and dragged his eyes from hers to her friend. "I'm sorry. You were saying?"

"Sela was just telling me about you," the man said.

"Ron," she interrupted, "this is Ben Russell." She disengaged her arm from Ron's before she continued the introduction. "And, Ben, meet Ron Stewart."

The men shook hands as they exchanged greetings.

There was something familiar about his name. While Ben culled his brain to remember, he joined in small talk. "So, what did Sela have to say about me? I hope it wasn't too bad."

Ron exchanged a glance with Sela before answering. "She did say you'd be around the neighborhood for a while."

"It looks that way. You live near here?"

"Right down the street on the corner, in the two-story number painted with pastel colors." He looked apologetic as he explained. "You met Vanessa earlier today—the pregnant lady? Well, she's my wife." Now he smiled. "She dreamed up those colors during her first trimester."

Now Ben remembered the name. His humor returned and he chuckled. "I met your twin boys, too. You have a good-looking family."

"With another one on the way." Ron beamed with pride as he crossed his arms against his chest.

"And don't you forget it, either." Sela playfully socked Ron's shoulder. "You'd better get home earlier tomorrow night."

Ben watched their exchange and the wide smile on Sela's face, amused by their obvious camaraderie.

"What's that?" Sela asked, referring to the bag dangling from Ben's hand. "Did you bring back leftovers from the diner?"

"Oh, this." Ben raised the bundle. "I had dinner with the Osbornes."

"Ahh . . . I'll bet that's Mrs. Osborne's dessert," she announced. "Ron, do you want to come inside?"

"No, I'm not staying. Like you said, I should be getting back home."

"In that case, you two can get acquainted while I go in." She gave Ron a peck on the cheek. "Thanks for walking me home. Tell Vanessa I'll see her tomorrow." She then pivoted to Ben. "If you'd like, I can take that bag inside with me."

He exchanged a smile with her and handed it over, then shook his head as he watched her cross the driveway under the floodlights.

"Vanessa figured it was a good idea for me to come over here and introduce myself," Ron said. "You know how small towns can be when you don't know anybody and there's not much to do."

Ben turned to Ron. "I've been through a few, but I expect this new project will keep me pretty busy."

"I never met an architect before. I bet it's pretty interesting."

Ben laughed. "Most days it is. But like everything,

there's always the inevitable downside. What do you do for a living?"

"I sell real estate, both residential and commercial. I've got my own business out on the main highway. So, if anything catches your eye in these parts, I can get it for you."

Ben's left brow arched a fraction as he read a wealth of unintended meaning into Ron's words. "I'll keep that in mind." He unhooked a couple more buttons at the top of his shirt. "One thing is for sure. I've got to get used to your heat and humidity."

"Yeah, it's barely June and we're already getting into the nineties."

The windows on the main floor of the house began to illuminate, one at a time. "I think I'll call it a day, too," Ben said, and extended his hand again. "It was nice meeting you."

Ron shook his hand before thrusting his own deep into his pocket, but he didn't move away. "Maybe the four of us can go out to eat or something once you get settled in. Maybe bowling."

Ben's look became one of faint amusement.

"The bowling, that was my idea," Ron added.

"And Sela has agreed to this?"

"I guess you've already learned it takes a little time for her to get warmed up to new folks." Ron chuckled knowingly.

"Actually, I'm wondering, is it me or the fact that we'll share quarters for a while that she dislikes more?" He shrugged matter-of-factly.

"I figure you don't hold the same opinion about her."

Ben sighed at the assessment. "Hey, I was invited here, and didn't know what to expect. But, to be fair, I guess she was as surprised as I was."

"When you get to know Sela, you'll learn she doesn't open up too easily at first. In a week or so, though, she'll be treating you no differently than she does everybody else. Until then, just don't take it personally."

"So, is she seeing anyone?"

Ron took a moment to answer. "You know, she's been through some rough spots in the past, and it's probably best if you give her some space, if you catch my drift."

"I do," Ben said. "And thanks, Ron."

"Later," he replied, before stepping away, leaving through the gate to merge once again with the shadows that fell onto the sidewalk.

Ben heard a dog's discordant bark in the distance. It broke the otherwise eerie tranquility that stroked the warm evening. Hefting his valise under his arm, he headed for the house. So, Sela had been through some rough spots. Usually that meant it had something to do with a man. It also helped to explain her reserved attitude toward him. Funny, but everyone in town made excuses for her poor manners. That was because she had the lot of them twisted around her lovely fingers. He'd have to be careful in this small town not to let that happen to him. The thought brought on a smile.

Sela stooped to peer inside the refrigerator before she pushed the carton of food in place on the lower shelf.

"Mrs. Osborne included a dessert for you."

She jumped at the words that came from somewhere behind her. Quickly, she straightened and turned to see Ben's tall, imposing figure fill the kitchen doorway like a sentinel.

"I thought you'd still be outside with Ron." She closed the refrigerator door and started across the brightly lit country kitchen to the slate-topped island counter that sat in the center.

"He left." Ben joined her at the counter. He looked up at the shiny copper pots above the island that hung from a metal ring suspended from the ceiling. "You've got a great cook's kitchen here." His survey took in the shiny appliances set along the long counter that wrapped the walls, the rectangular table set for eight near the bay windows, the oak hardwood floors, and the multitude of oak cabinets.

"The kitchen is not my specialty, but you're welcome to anything you find in here."

As she watched him set his valise on the counter between them, she knew Vanessa had been right. He had done nothing wrong, had not even been rude, and was only here by invitation. Unexpectedly nervous, she moistened her lips to form an apology, and raised her eyes to his, only to find that he studied her as well with an inscrutable expression.

"If you have time, maybe I can show you around the house tomorrow." At the slight arch of his brow, she added, "I'm trying to apologize for earlier. Vanessa was quick to point out that I was venting my anger on you. Unfairly, I might add."

The beginning of a smile tipped the corners of Ben's mouth. "Everyone keeps warning me not to take your cold shoulder personally and that you'll come around in time," his deep voice rumbled. "I didn't really expect it to happen this quickly . . . not that I'm complaining."

They looked at each other and now smiled in earnest.

"I came home from the library expecting you to

be here," Sela said. "I'd intended to tell you about the diner so you wouldn't have to eat at McDonald's downtown."

"I don't think Reverend Osborne was going to let that happen."

"So all went well at the church?" she inquired.

"I got the full tour. It's an interesting structure with an interesting history."

"I hope the reverend didn't start in on you with all his tales about that place. He likes to say that he knows all of the secrets around here and most, he claims, are buried at the church. All in all, he's an interesting man to know. I think you'll like Ron, too."

"When I first saw you two, I thought he was your date."

"Ron? Whatever in the world made you think that?"

"It was an easy enough mistake on my part. You probably go on lots of dates, or as many as this town can offer."

Her lips parted in surprise at the backhanded compliment. "Where did that come from?"

Ben seemed totally unaware that she was insulted. "You're a very attractive woman who goes out—"

"I am not attractive. I'm a librarian—a county school district librarian, at that."

"Whoa," he charged, enjoying her annoyance. "Hold on a minute. The two don't have to be mutually exclusive, you know."

"I'm more concerned about your insult to Fairlight." She repeated his words with a snort. "As many as this town can offer?"

"It wasn't an insult, just an observation. The population is pretty small—less than two thousand,

I'd guess. I figure it doesn't leave someone like yourself much of a choice."

Sela frowned. "I have plenty to choose from, including dates if I wanted them." She crossed her arms and shifted indignantly. "You don't think much of small towns, do you?"

"If that's what you want."

"Obviously, it's not what you want, and we'd better change the subject before I take back my apology."

"Deal," Ben said good-naturedly, and drew his hand across his forehead. "Anyway, I'm ready to hit the shower. When it's as hot as it was today, I can appreciate what our grandparents went through without air conditioners."

"I figure they did what we did—sweat."

"The difference is I'm pretty much wilted by the humidity. You, on the other hand, clean up quite well."

Sela enjoyed the subtle compliment more than she intended, but she didn't think he looked wilted at all. He was superbly well groomed—his clean-shaven face sported neatly trimmed sideburns, and his black hair was cut low. His lips, firm and well shaped, revealed with each smile a dazzling display of straight white teeth. All in all, he presented a massive, self-confident presence.

As her eyes lowered to the open neck of his shirt, they lingered to appreciate the way his shoulders filled his jacket and to observe his bare throat slightly moist from perspiration . . . mmm . . . she detected the smell of his aftershave.

She jerked her eyes back to his face. "You said something?"

His white smile blazed down on her. "Nothing

important. I'll see you in the morning. Maybe we can do the house tour, even the town, tomorrow?"

"Sure," she said, and watched him pick up his leather bag.

"By the way, are you a light sleeper?"

Caught off guard by the question, she asked her own. "Why?"

He started for the doorway. "Sometimes I work into the middle of the night," he called back to her. "You don't mind if I come down here to eat leftover dessert?"

She crossed her arms and leaned against the counter. "Help yourself. In fact, feel free to raid the kitchen whenever you want."

He threw her a backward glance as he strolled to the door. "I'll remember that."

A few hours later, Sela lay supine in bed and listened as, once again, the house settled into a relentless silence. She had become attuned to the manner of the quiet house, and Ben's heavy footsteps along the old staircase had been easily noticed. She had even imagined the moment he opened the refrigerator door and searched out the dessert on the bottom shelf, making good on his promise to raid the kitchen.

She turned onto her side, suddenly restless. Ben was an interesting man. Clearly, he was smart, articulate, and with all that had occurred since his arrival, a quick thinker. Had Aunt Claire divined those characteristics when she first met him? Sela raised her head at the soft patter coming from outside. It had started to rain. Using her fist, she gave her pillow a healthy punch before she lay back down. She wished Auntie would call. Sure, there were a lot of questions; but mostly, she missed her and just wanted to talk. This time, she curved into a fetal position.

Meanwhile, Ben had made it across the darkened living room without tipping anything completely over. He now climbed the stairs to return to his bedroom, noticing that Sela had long since retired the house and gone to bed. All was quiet and dark, the only sound coming from the downstairs grandfather clock's quarterly chime; the only illumination came from a row of small night-lights plugged along the staircase.

When he reached the top of the stairs and started for his room, he looked farther down the yawning hallway stretched out before him. There, nestled in the corner at the end of the hall, was room five, the one that caused Sela's anxious reaction.

Curious, he continued past his door until he reached the fifth room. He reached out and turned the knob. It wouldn't budge; he tried again. Locked. So, she'd taken the time to lock it after he left? Moving away from the door, he stepped near the balcony railing and looked over it toward the hallway that led to Sela's bedroom. An interesting woman any way you looked at her. She had gone through the trouble to make sure he wouldn't be able to enter guest room five later, but why?

A scrape against glass, and he turned to the sound. It was coming from the keyhole window high in the wall. He could see that it had started to rain and a branch from the large oak tree in the yard scrubbed against the pane. Stifling a yawn, he returned to his room, finally ready to retire.

Outside the window, near the ground, the earlier rustle by the mailbox had long quieted, and had faded in with the other evening sounds. But, the onset of the night rain had once again kicked up the crackle of shadowy branches. One such branch separated from the bushes in the form of a large silhouette that crept stealthily up the moon-grayed sidewalk.

Seven

Sela could smell the blueberry muffins hot from the oven, soon to be on her plate dripping with warm butter. But this morning, she couldn't quite pull herself from the tub of warm bathwater to quench her appetite. Sighing with pleasure, she leaned her head back and let it dip into the water. This was heaven—the water's quiet lull, its relaxing heat as it swayed against her skin, the scented steam.

When the bathroom door abruptly opened, she looked up. It was Ben. He had donned her robe and now beckoned her from the tub. As he moved toward her, closer and closer, he loosed the tie that held the robe close. She took in his tempting male physique as he stood tall, proud of his powerful build. It was obvious he was prepared to quench another, quite different appetite of hers.

Sela groaned loudly as she sat straight up.

"It's about time you were getting out of that bed."

The grating voice pierced Sela's consciousness.

"You must've been having a good dream seeing as how you been sighing and humming for the last five minutes."

Sela knew that voice and, through sleep-fogged eyes, strained to see the face across the bedroom. It was Fontella, all right. What was she doing here?

"And put some clothes on that body of yours. I still can't see how you sleep with nary a stitch on."

"Fontella." Sela rasped out the name before dropping back to the bed and rolling up in the sheet. "What are you doing here?"

"I heard we had a guest, so I got on over here this morning to get breakfast started and get a leg up on the cleaning."

With that said, she thumbed the vacuum cleaner's power switch before pushing it across the carpet, drowning out Sela's protest in the process.

"Please, give me a few minutes to wake up, for heaven's sake." Sela croaked her plea above the noise of the vacuum. "And we don't have any guests—paying ones, that is."

As suddenly as the older woman had started up the noise, she ended it with a click before she propped one of her thin arms on an equally bony hip. Fontella Carter was part cook and housekeeper, as well as a longtime friend to the Bennetts. It had always been a puzzle how a woman who enjoyed cooking as much as she did could manage to keep the evidence off her middle-aged frame.

"You talking 'bout Mr. Russell?" she argued back at Sela. "He's at the kitchen table working his way through my muffins."

Sela sat up on the bed and rubbed her face. "You've already met him?"

"In the flesh. Why?"

"Then he must have told you how he happened to be here, so there's no need to handle house duties like during the normal season."

"It's my job around here to get folks fed and the beds fluffed, and I'm not changing that just 'cause we only got one boarder on the premises."

Sela stifled a yawn. "You want to tell me why

you're set on aggravating me so early this morning?"

"Soon as you tell *me* about that dream you were having a while ago." Fontella arched her dark eyebrows as only she could. "Or, do you want me to give you fifteen minutes to get your rump out of that bed so I can vacuum this floor?"

Sela attempted to ease her embarrassment by moving to the side of the bed. "You win this one. Fifteen minutes, and you can have my room."

When Fontella left, Sela crawled from under the sheets and stood to stretch, touching her toes repeatedly. Sleeping in little or nothing over the years had become such a natural habit that she thought nothing of it, except when it was repeatedly called to her attention by Fontella. She drew in deep breaths as her rapid movements chased the last vestiges of sleep away.

Grabbing her robe from the foot of the bed, she slid her arms into the sleeves and headed for the bathroom across the hall. That's when she was reminded of her odd, yet memorable dream. Ben naked, and in her robe? Her mouth twitched with the need to giggle at that image as she closed the bathroom door.

A quick glance as she passed the hall mirror told Sela she looked fine in the aftermath of her hurried, fifteen-minute toilette. As usual, her hair was neatly slicked back in a pinned braid, and her feet were bare. When she reached the doorway to the kitchen, she paused a moment, unconsciously smoothing her hands down her slacks.

The mixed aromas from breakfast were heady, reminding her that she was hungrier than she'd realized. Ben was dressed—much more casually than the day before—and sitting at the table while he conversed with Fontella, who stood at the sink. When Sela neared the table, Ben looked up, and stood.

"Good morning," he said smoothly. His eyes swept over her as she approached.

Fontella turned from the sink and started across the room to the walk-in pantry.

"Come on in here and get some breakfast in you before it gets cold," she urged. "I put chives in your eggs the way you like them, and I've got some hot buttery grits on the stove."

"Thanks," Sela called out as Fontella disappeared behind the slatted doors. She then returned Ben's greeting and sat in the chair he had pulled out for her. "And what's made you look so fresh and alert this morning?" she asked, slanting her eyes playfully at him. When she reached for the juice, Ben beat her to it and proceeded to fill her glass.

"I was persuaded out of my room with the promise of a hot breakfast," he said.

She raised her juice in a mock toast. "Welcome to Claire's Inn, with breakfast and brunch run by none other than Fontella Carter."

"The view from the breakfast table is pretty remarkable, too."

Sela sipped from her glass as she looked through the wide bay window at the lattice-trimmed gazebo surrounded by a cornucopia of blooming flowers, her personal handiwork. She had to agree, the backyard was magnificent. When she turned her gaze back to Ben, his eyes were centered on her. An unexpected warmth surged through her. She looked away, inexplicably wary.

"You, Sela Bennett, look pretty rested for someone who was dead to the world twenty minutes ago," he said, resting his elbows on the table.

"That piece of news must have come from Fontella, huh? I'm almost afraid to find out what else she's told you." She scraped a helping of eggs onto her plate.

He grinned. "At least she's a cook who knows how to put this great kitchen to use."

"The inn guests think she's memorable, too." She added a muffin near her eggs. "After she kicks them out of bed a few times."

This time he laughed. "You have to admit her blueberry muffins are extraordinary. I've never had anything like them."

"It's her own special recipe. They're well known around town. We even advertise them in our B and B brochure." Sela took another swallow of juice before she looked at his plate.

Her eyes twinkled as she asked, "Did Fontella make you eat the grits?"

Ben laughed. "One taste is all I could muster." He made a face. "It's not my dish. What about you? Aren't you getting any of them?"

"Too heavy this early in the morning. She only makes the guests sample them, anyway."

"I see," Ben said, smiling.

"So, did you sleep okay last night? Does the inn meet with your approval?"

He shrugged with satisfaction. "It was quiet, and surprisingly relaxing. I'm used to sleeping in strange places, though."

"That's right, I forgot. You did say you've been traveling out of the country this last year."

"What about you?" he asked.

She looked up from her muffin. "What about me?"

"What have you been doing this past year? I know you're a librarian and—"

"—Media specialist is the correct title."

"All right, but that's during the school year. How do you spend your summers?"

"Wasting her time around here, for one thing," Fontella shot back as she crossed the room to the sink. "Maybe you can tell her what a young woman like her is missing by hiding herself here in town."

Sela turned to the housekeeper, a devilish gleam in her eyes. "Even for you, isn't it a little early in the day to start in on me?"

Ben watched their exchange with curiosity. "Is that what you're doing, Sela, hiding yourself?" he joked.

Fontella chuckled as she untied her apron from her middle. "Since Claire's away, it's my job to step up to the plate and stay on her case."

"Aunt Claire and Fontella believe they have my best interests at heart when they urge me to leave town," Sela informed Ben.

"That's 'cause we been around a lot longer than you and know what's good for you. Anyway," Fontella added, "I got to go freshen up the linens." As she dropped her apron on the counter, her gaze was drawn to the bay window behind Sela and Ben.

"Sela—" Fontella walked back toward them. "Look who's at the back door. It's Jim. I wonder what he's doing here."

Sela twisted around in her chair to see the mailman, his blue mailbag tossed across his shoulder. He waved as he trampled across the grass, then marched up the porch steps. Fontella threw open the back door.

"Jim," she said, crossing her arms, "what are you doing here?"

"Stopped by, that's all." Jim side-stepped Fontella and moved into the kitchen where Ben and Sela sat. He looked from one to the other. "I just heard down the street you had a boarder in the house, Sela. I was surprised since you didn't mention it yesterday morning."

Jim frowned as his roving glance caught Ben's eye. "Since yours is the only strange face I see in here, you must be that architect everybody's rattlin' on about."

Ben stood and in a genial gesture, extended his hand across the table to the burly postman. "Ben Russell. It's nice to meet you, sir."

"Uh-huh," Jim grunted as he grabbed up the proffered hand and slowly shook it, all the time studying Ben.

Sela spoke up. "This is Jim Lewis, Ben. He's our mailman, but he's also a good family friend."

The men dropped their hands, each stepping back a pace to their respective corners. Ben folded his arms across his chest while Jim pulled off his cap.

"So, what brings you to Fairlight?" Jim asked. "I didn't think the B and B was open to boarders 'til the fall." He gave Sela a quick glance before his interest returned to Ben. "When did Claire start taking on summer boarders when she's traveling and you're the only one at the house?"

Both Sela and Ben began to answer in unison, stopped, and then laughed, realizing the futility in answering all of the man's rapid-fire questions.

"Seeing as you're fixin' to do your twenty questions routine, you might as well stay," Fontella said to Jim. "Sit down and have a muffin and some coffee."

"Don't mind if I do," he said, a grin beginning

to split his grizzled face as he sat down. "Thanks." While he scooped up a muffin from the basket, Fontella poured him a cup of coffee.

"I didn't say anything at the mailbox because Ben didn't arrive until later in the day."

"Uh-huh . . ." He talked around the muffin. "Heard about that, too. By the way, here's your mail." Jim dug into his mailbag and handed her a slim packet of envelopes before his attention switched to Ben, who had returned to his seat.

"Should I be on the lookout for your mail, too? You know, things like letters from your family—" He paused imperceptibly. "—Your missus?"

Ben felt a wave of humor ride through him. The nosy mailman was trying to find out if he was married.

Sela looked up to speak, but Fontella beat her to it.

"Ben's not married. He's footloose just like you, though I'm sure he puts that fact to use better than you do." Fontella laughed at her own joke before she looked over at Sela, who was thumbing through the letters. "Anything from Claire today?"

"No," Sela answered without looking up.

Ben cleared his throat and answered the mailman. "I'll probably get a letter or package from my business office, from time to time."

"Then Mr. Lewis is a good person to keep watch for you," Sela said, setting her mail away from her. "Just let him know the names or when you're expecting something."

"I can do that for you, all right," Jim replied. He sipped from his coffee before he once again trained his eyes on Ben. "Well, you want to answer my first question? What brings you here?" Before he received an answer, he settled back in the chair and turned to Sela. "You two know each other from one of your trips out of town or something?"

Ben smiled as he shook his head in disbelief at the man's stream of assumptions.

"There you go bringing up her trips out of town," Fontella argued. "Just 'cause you think she should stay in Fairlight for the rest of her life is no reason to think—"

"Nothing good comes of those trips you and Claire are always pushing her into taking," Jim interjected. "I told Claire—"

"Mr. Lewis, Aunt Claire invited him as her guest," Sela answered evenly. "He'll be around for the rest of the summer, so be nice. Aunt Claire would want you to."

"You tell him, Sela. Claire knows best," Fontella chimed in gleefully.

Jim grunted in disdain as he looked at Ben. "And what are you going to be doing around here for that long?"

Ben had listened to their interplay with growing amusement, wondering when he had taken over the role of the high school kid meeting his date's family. "I'll be studying the original historic structure of your New Hope A.M.E. church," he said, then added, "with Reverend Osborne's blessings, of course. Hopefully, I'll be able to make suggestions for your planned renovations."

Fontella turned to leave the room. "I've got to get some work done. I'll see you later, Jim. And you better be nice or you won't be getting any more of my muffins."

Jim grunted at her departing figure. "Whatever got in Claire's head to do something like this when she's traipsing the globe the whole summer?" He turned to Sela. "I guess it's up to me to look out for you while she's gone."

Sela smiled sweetly at the mailman. "Last time I checked I was neither under eighteen nor feeble-minded."

Both men grinned as the front door chime rang.

Sela scraped back her chair and rose from the table. "Stay put, everybody; I'll get it. Suddenly, this house has become Grand Central Station." She left them in the kitchen.

Jim turned to speak conspiratorially with Ben. "You know, I tease with Sela all the time—it keeps her on her toes. She means a lot to us."

"So I've heard," he replied.

"Ever since her mother died, we all did our part to raise her to an adult. Of course, Claire did the lion's share back then, but we were always here for her. Now it's sort of hard to back down. She don't always like it, but we're gonna be here for her. Just thought you oughta know that."

Ben nodded as his brows furrowed in thought. It explained a lot, especially why Sela's welfare seemed to be the town's priority.

"You see, when Claire's out of town like this, we have an unspoken agreement that I'll check on things from time to time, seeing as I'm around, what with the mail and all." He finished up his coffee in one long, full swallow, then set the cup down before he stood.

Ben nodded again with respectful agreement. Claire Bennett had never mentioned the mailman, a fact that gave credence to Ben's observation that the sly codger was nosy and simply wanted to know Sela's business.

Voices from the other room caused Ben to look toward the doorway. He saw Sela return to the kitchen with Fontella and yet another visitor, a middle-aged man dressed in a business suit with serious eyes focused behind black-rimmed glasses. In his arms he juggled three slender cardboard tubes, the longest at least four feet in length, and the use of which Ben immediately recognized.

"Deacon Freeman stopped by," Sela announced. "He's brought some things for you, Ben."

The neatly dressed man separated himself from the women. He greeted Jim as he passed and managed to reach across the table to shake Ben's hand.

"Reverend Osborne called me last night after you left his house." The deacon set the unwieldy tubes on the table. "First, he told me about you being here." He darted a glance to Ben before he continued. "Then, he told me to get you copies of the building plans from some of the earlier renovations so you could study them before you began poking around."

"Thank you, sir. You saved me considerable time." Ben had come around the table to collect the tubes. "I can begin going over them today."

"Good." Deacon Freeman took off his glasses and, producing a snowy handkerchief, quickly wiped them. "I keep the keys to the church offices, so if you need any other documents, no matter if it's a bad time, or any day of the week, just let me know." He squinted at the glasses before putting them on. "Reverend Osborne's orders."

Ben detected the pride in his voice and choice of words. "Again, thank you. I'll remember that."

Fontella rested her hands against her hips. "And where, pray tell, do you plan on putting this stuff, not to mention there might be more? I saw your computer and those books in your bedroom," she said. "You'll be needing another room to fit all that."

"Is that true?" Sela turned to Ben. "You need more space?"

"I didn't think about it until I started unpacking last night. I haven't even tried setting up my drafting desk."

"We have space you can spread out in down at the church," Deacon Freeman suggested.

"That's all well and good to use when he's over there," Fontella said, as she turned to Sela. "But, I have an idea. How about we set him up in the basement?"

Jim and the deacon exchanged a hesitant glance before they both spoke at once.

"The basement?" Jim grunted.

"Why you puttin' him down there?" Deacon Freeman asked.

"It's okay for Ben's work," Sela said. "I just hadn't thought about it."

Ben saw the range of expressions that covered their faces. "And I wouldn't mind using the space if it's available. Is there something wrong with it?"

"I'd say so," Deacon Freeman blurted. "That's where Claire practices that black magic of hers, and with you working at the church, I don't think you ought to be down there."

"Deacon—" Sela started.

"Don't you be talking about Claire like that," Fontella argued. "You wouldn't be saying that if she was here to hear you."

Sela's eyes had turned stony. "That's not fair, Deacon Freeman, and you know it."

"What's he talking about?" Ben asked. "Black magic?"

"I guess Claire didn't tell you everything, huh?"

Jim brushed his graying hair back as he slid his cap back over his head. "The plain truth is Claire's psychic, and pretty good at it when she wants to be."

Ben stared at the little group in disbelief. "She's what?"

Eight

Sela shifted uneasily at the surprise revelation—common knowledge to the community, but not generally known to outsiders—and directed her annoyance at the deacon.

"The even plainer truth is that she's never practiced what you call 'black magic,' and you know it." She stole a quick glance at Ben, mortified by the interest that lit his eyes. In an attempt to ease her mounting anger, she summoned a smile. "Think about the impression of us you're giving when you say those kinds of things."

"All I know is I hear the same thing everybody else hears and, well . . ." He drew his eyes up apologetically. "Maybe she did stop, and maybe it was a long time ago, but I suspect there's some lingering dregs down there from working the devil's art."

Sela clenched her teeth over a retort. There was no longer a point to be made—she had heard so much of it before.

"You've delivered the package for Mr. Russell," Fontella pointed out, her voice firm. "Maybe you ought to leave before that nice apology of yours starts to wear off."

He cleared his throat before he pivoted on his

heel to face Ben. "I'll see you at the church, I imagine."

Ben acknowledged his good-bye.

In the thirty seconds it took the deacon to clear the front door, no one in the kitchen said anything.

Though, the minute the front door clicked shut, Fontella was first to break the silence. "You know, I believe he's been ticked off ever since Claire talked Helena out of going on a date with him back in high school."

At Ben's confused frown, Sela explained. "Helena—that's my mother."

"Now, that had to be over twenty-five years ago," Fontella continued. "How long you figure he's gonna carry that grudge?"

Ben moved to stand next to Sela. "Why didn't someone tell me about Miss Bennett's gift?"

"Gift?" Sela spat sarcastically. "Since when has being unfairly ridiculed at every turn been a gift?" She turned from the group and quickly swept across the room. "I have to get some air," she called back over her shoulder.

Caught off guard by her displeasure, Ben started after her, only to be stopped by Fontella.

"Leave her alone for a bit. She always tightens up when she hears that kind of talk about Claire."

"I hope nothing I said made things worse."

Jim hefted his mailbag onto his shoulder. "No, this was all the deacon's doing. Normally, he'd never hurt Sela with his words, but he just refuses to leave some things alone. Claire's sight, or whatever you want to call it, is one. Sometimes I think it's folks like him at the church who hurt Claire and Helena most."

"I take it her aunt still draws grief from the others in town?" Ben inquired.

Jim nodded. "There're still a few folks who think like him."

Fontella had moved away to clear the breakfast table. "Like that nosy Mabel Thornton, who likes to think that Claire is no better than those phony TV psychics. Mind you, now, Claire was the one who knew where her little nephew was when he got lost on that visit a while back."

"No point in going over all that, Fontella," Jim said. "Anyway, it's late for me, and I better be getting on." He walked to the back door. And, as he turned the knob, he looked at Ben. "Tell Sela I'll be stopping by from time to time."

"She's probably figured that out already; but, I'm sure she'll be all right." Ben's reply was cordial, yet firm. He didn't like the idea of being considered some sort of vague threat to Miss Bennett's niece.

"Yeah," Jim said as he lingered at the door a moment. "If that's the case, then why was Luther over here yesterday with the patrol car?"

"You know, I heard that, too," Fontella chimed in.

Ben shrugged at the sticky question. "That's easy enough to explain," he began. "It was a case of temporary mistaken identity, that's all. Everything was cleared up very quickly with no problem."

"If you say so." Jim stepped out onto the back porch. "Fontella, you let me know if you have any problems."

Ben sank his hands deep into his pockets as he watched her close the door. "Whew, that guy's a hard sell."

"Don't worry about Jim none; he's harmless. That bark of his is worse than his bite. He's just got too much time on his hands, what with no family of his own, and he thinks of Claire and Sela as his extended family, that's all."

A movement from the opposite doorway revealed Sela's return into the kitchen. She now wore sandals. Ben smiled—he was just getting used to seeing her bare feet. He also noticed that her eyes, so striking in an already attractive face, seemed guarded and not as cheerful as when she first joined him that morning.

"Fontella's right about Mr. Lewis," she said. "He jokes with everyone and prides himself with checking up on the folks along his route. So, don't feel like he's picking on you."

"All right, I won't." Ben smiled as he walked forward and stopped in front of her. "I thought I might not see you for the rest of the day."

"I was about to go over to Vanessa's; then I remembered you."

He arched a brow that was coupled with a devilish grin. "I think I'm honored."

Her eyes showed a glint of humor. "Don't be. I just want to show you the basement so you can decide if it'll work out for you." She nodded toward the doorway she had just come through. "Come on."

"All right," he agreed, and swung his head around to Fontella. "Breakfast was fantastic. Thank you."

"As good as that fancy foreign food you've been eating?"

He grinned at the cook, and then winked. "Better."

"In that case, it was my pleasure," she crowed. "We'll do it again tomorrow." She returned her attention to the sink.

Sela sighed loudly before she spoke for Ben's ears

only. "You're really good, and you made her day." She started down the hallway.

Ben was buoyed by her interest. "She knows a compliment when she hears one, that's all," he said as he followed her. "So, Miss Bennett's ah . . . talent. It's the real thing, huh? She's a bona fide clairvoyant?"

Sela made an abrupt stop in her tracks and, in one swift motion, turned to Ben and grabbed on to his arm. "Yes," she uttered in her best spooky voice. "Sometimes just clutching your arm is all she needs to see into your head and accurately predict your destiny."

Ben grinned at her silly attempt to ridicule his question. "Now, I'm really scared," he said. "That voice sounds awful on you."

Sela dropped her hands from his arm and smiled, too. "Yeah, that's what I grew up with, people thinking we had some sort of sacrificial altar in the house where we mixed powder and potions and drained blood from poor, defenseless animals."

"That must have been hard on you while growing up."

She continued down the hall. "It really ticked me off back then, but you get used to it. After a while, though, people learn to separate the facts from fiction. Then, someone comes up with a really stupid remark, like the one from Deacon Freeman." She groaned. "And, even though I haven't particularly jumped at the idea of sharing my summer with you, I don't want you saddled with old tales about us and get the wrong idea."

She stopped as she came upon a door set in the middle of the back hall. "To set the record straight, Aunt Claire does not cast spells, and for heaven's sake, she doesn't go around reading minds on a whim."

Ben realized the source of her discomfort about the revelation. "After all these years, it still manages to embarrass you, doesn't it?"

She turned in the dim and narrow hallway to face him. "Does it show?"

"You're just a little bit defensive."

"Okay, it bothers me some," she replied. When she reached past Ben to flick the hall light switch on, her arm brushed against his side.

Ben blinked, as much at the abruptness of the bright light as his proximity in the small space to his intriguing housemate. Bathed in the light, she was luminous. If he wanted to, he could easily reach out, touch her face, her neck . . . He looked away and swallowed hard. "So, what, if anything, did happen in the basement?"

Sela opened the basement door, reached in, and flicked another wall switch, which illuminated the wide expanse of white walls and lightly colored carpeted steps that lead down. She took the steps ahead of him.

"First, let's find out if you even want to work down here." She darted a glance at him over her shoulder that seemed both secretive and shrewd. "Then, we can talk about the other stuff."

Puzzled once again over her seesaw behavior, Ben shook his head as he followed her lead.

The basement turned out to be instantly compatible with Ben. He was prepared to find a dark and dusty, unused space under the house. Instead, he was drawn into a high-ceilinged room where most of the walls were hidden by shelves lined with books—old ones, new ones, arcane and contemporary subjects—and bric-a-brac, most of it the obvious product of her aunt's travels.

The sofas and chairs were covered in light colors, which provided a comfortable haven for escape while helping to combat the shadows from the dark wood paneling. Though the room spanned the length of the house, the basement was only partially underground. Its three windows were set at the ground level outside and allowed natural light to enter. From inside, those same windows appeared high, near the ceiling, and worked to ease any claustrophobic effect.

"So, does it meet with your approval?" Sela watched with interest as Ben inspected the room, satisfying his curiosity from time to time by lifting a book or some other object for closer study.

"I suspect you knew all along that it would." He replaced a wooden fertility statue on a bookcase before he turned to her.

"It's become a favorite room for the inn guests during our season. I figured you'd probably like it as much as they do. Otherwise, it doesn't get much use."

He looked around the room. "This house has lots of character, and you've done a good job of preserving much of it. Has it been in your family long?"

"My mother and Auntie were raised here. When my grandfather died, my grandmother moved to Mobile with other older family members, and Aunt Claire managed to take over the house to keep it in the family. I've lived here all of my life, as well." Sela had walked to the far end of the room, her back to Ben. When he didn't respond, she turned and saw that his attention had been drawn to another discovery at the opposite end.

The corner where he stood was set apart from the rest of the room by a six-foot tall wood and metal triptych divider embedded with African ornamentation. When Ben walked around the panels, Sela knew what he'd see and quickly moved to join him. Behind the divider was a table, upon which rested a late-model computer with all of the prescribed trappings—printer, scanner, and fax machine. Neat stacks of printed information on bond paper sat on the tabletop while a small, three-drawer metal cabinet was stored underneath, next to the computer chair. Ben turned to Sela and smiled at this revelation.

"Despite your willingness to continue to play the barefoot country girl, I see you're well in step with the electronic world," he teased, and fingered one of the inch-high stacks of paper. "Looks like you've been working hard on a scholarly paper or something."

"Oh, it's just a pet project I've been doing in my spare time," she explained lightly as she restacked the piles, one atop the other, before sliding them into the table drawer. After the papers were safely stored away, she returned her attention to him, crossing her arms in front of her chest.

He glanced at her. "You know, I don't think I've ever met an educator who wasn't involved in some type of continuing education class."

"I'm sure you'll need to hook up the computer you brought with you, right?"

When he nodded, she said, "There's an extra phone outlet down here you can use for e-mail."

"Thanks. I'll need that."

"Then, you're all set. I'll leave you to unpack." She started to move toward the stairs. "I'm supposed to meet Vanessa in a bit. She and Ron want—"

"Hold on a minute before you leave," Ben interrupted. "You promised to clue me in on what that deacon was talking about."

Sela stopped and turned to him, deciding she would only tell him enough to satisfy his curiosity. "What do you want to know?"

"Well," he said as he approached her, "you can start by telling me about your aunt's psychic powers. You know, she read my fortune when I first met her. I wish I could remember what she predicted, but at the time I thought it was a joke."

She leaned against the doorway and sighed. "It probably was. She hasn't done a stunt like that for outsiders in years. It always made her feel like a performer. And, she prefers the term clairvoyant."

"Do you and everybody else really believe she's a clairvoyant?"

Sela inhaled a deep breath of patience. "Everyone's heard about it, Ben. Beliefs, though, are quite personal and are another matter altogether."

"What about you, then?" He moved to lean on the other side of the doorway. "You're closest to her, I imagine. What do you believe?"

She looked away for a moment. "Sometimes, absent explanations, you have no choice but to believe. That's what happened in my family." She leaned her head back and gazed matter-of-factly into his eyes. "There have been tales of clairvoyants routing about my family tree as far back as the family can remember. What's strange is that this ability only shows up every other generation, and only in the females."

Ben let out a soft whistle. "Damn. That's a hell of a legacy."

"I know, and imagine how it must be if you're the subject under inspection while the family waits for the telltale signs. My mother and aunt were damned by it. So, what others think of their ability is of no consequence. What matters is my mother and my aunt believe."

"Okay, you were lucky getting skipped over. But, what if you have a daughter? Won't she be faced with the same dilemmas you're straddling the fence over?"

A disturbing wave rolled through Sela's serenity. "I don't consider what-ifs," she offered quickly. "I've decided that, given enough facts and information, fate can be malleable. You make your destiny."

"I always thought it was the opposite, that fate—or destiny if you want to call it that—is set. You can avoid it for a time, but it'll ultimately find you."

She snorted. "You look at it that way because you're a romantic—it's obvious, what with your love of architecture, design, old things." She smiled. "Me, I just want the facts."

He snorted back at her. "Let's see, you're telling me you'd choose opinionated rather than thoughtful dialogue. Yep, you're the pragmatist here." He crossed his arms and stared down at her. "That must be some war of wills going on inside you, Sela, what with your family background deeply embedded in the paranormal, and you trying to stay above it. Your mother, Helena. I guess she ran into the same prejudices?"

She nodded. "Actually, Aunt Claire was the younger of the two sisters and she showed signs first, like knowing who was calling on the phone, predicting visitors, that sort of thing. My mother's ability surfaced later on."

"Your father . . . you don't mention him."

"I don't know my father. I never have." At the sight of Ben's clenched jaw, she suspected his manners made him regret his words. Smiling, she said, "Surely that's not too much of a surprise. You've noticed by now that my last name is the same as that of my aunt and mother."

"Reverend Osborne mentioned that you were orphaned at a young age," he offered contritely. "But that's all he said. I didn't intend to pry. I'm sorry."

Sela shifted indignantly, keenly aware of his scrutiny. "You don't have to say nice things to me because of it, Ben. I don't want your sympathy. Others have suffered through worse. Anyway, Aunt Claire was wonderful to me—and though I've been tagged an orphan, I've never in my life felt like one, and I've done just fine."

He smiled. "I can see that."

They stood across from each other as seconds passed. Neither moved as each took in a vital essence of the other through their short conversation. Finally, as if they realized how queer they'd begun to act, Sela cleared her throat while Ben straightened from the wall.

"So," he began. "You were on your way to Vanessa's. I was thinking, maybe you could show me the town diner you've mentioned before and we could have dinner there tonight."

"Oh, I meant to tell you that Vanessa and Ron wanted you to eat with them tonight." Her large eyes flashed up at him.

"Will you be there, too?"

She nodded and smiled.

"Then, make sure you tell them I accept."

"Good," she said. "I'll be home before it gets dark, and we can walk over there together, say around six?"

"Sounds fine to me."

Sela backed away a couple of steps before she

turned from his relentless gaze, and then bounded up the stairs. Only when she reached the door, and stepped through did her breaths become even again. There was something about him—she couldn't put her finger on it, but it was hard to remain focused when she was close to him. She'd have to be careful, that's all. She didn't think being put off-balance was a safe option around this particular man.

Ben watched Sela slowly disappear up the stairway before he rubbed his chin in thought. Damn, but she was distracting. Annoyed by the thought, he acknowledged that it was also oddly exhilarating. She was a complication he had not expected this summer. He'd only sought some downtime from making a decision, time away from the pressures forced on him by the family and the business.

At the time of her offer, Claire Bennett had seemed too good to be true, but earnest in her proposal. She had seemingly appeared from nowhere and, literally, changed the direction he had been headed. Now, he wondered on that. He also wondered about the talk of her being clairvoyant—something he'd never had to take seriously.

One thing was certain: he didn't expect that his summer would be spent sleeping in the same house with the woman's niece. And, to avoid complications in a small town, he intended to make sure he and Sela continued to sleep on separate floors. Unless, of course, she made the move to change the rules. He smiled at this curiously unusual lapse of focus on his part.

***

Claire leaned against the railing of the cruise ship near another group of tourists who had hastily abandoned their breakfast to watch as a whale resurfaced, breaking through the icy, cerulean water as if on cue and, seemingly, for the building crowd's enjoyment. The lumbering giant then disappeared again into a great white crest of water.

Magnificent though the nature scene was, Claire's thoughts were elsewhere. She missed Sela. She wanted to learn how things were progressing. But, she steadfastly fought the urge. She hugged her wrap tighter about her shoulders. She would wait. Yes, the weekend would do before she made a call. There was no need to remind her obstinate, though astute niece that she was being manipulated—but only somewhat.

"There you are, Claire."

She turned her head to the familiar, clipped English accent and saw Captain Powell's purposeful stride head her way. As was the usual case, she enjoyed a sweet rush of pleasure when he appeared, and cocked her head to the side. After so many years of planning their time together on these annual trips, she wondered if it still carried the same thrill for him, as well.

Nine

"That sly old Jim asked you what?" Ron laughed as he asked the question of Ben.

They sat across from each other at the Stewarts' dinner table where they topped off their meal with Vanessa's apple pie. The others present—Vanessa, Sela, and Rosalie Carter, Fontella's daughter—were also amused.

"He was harmless, and just trying to get information out of me, that's all," Ben replied with a grin. "I knew where he was coming from, so I was cool with it."

"Barely," Sela added dryly, before forking up another piece of her pie. "Anyway, I doubt he'll bother you anymore now that he knows who you are."

Rosalie's seat was next to Ben, and she tilted her head near his. "Mr. Lewis just acts like that. If you show up at the B and B, he'll make it his business to get the details." She nodded sagely as she swept back the long curls Juanita had artfully arranged to drape her head.

"Who cares about that?" Ron asked. "Ben shouldn't have to go through the third degree for anyone." He winked at Vanessa. "Except maybe from your future in-laws."

Ben had watched the silent exchanges—a nod, a

smile, a glance—between husband and wife all evening, and now marveled at their invisible bond. Surprised by what he recognized as a measure of envy, he tried to imagine himself within the thralls of such a bond.

"I mean, when your only offense is being a stranger in town," Ron continued, "it gives us all a bad name."

"I promise you," Ben said, "I was never insulted." He raised his eyes to Sela across the table. "In fact, I enjoyed having Sela defend my honor and intentions."

Everyone laughed while Sela raised her voice above their din. "I did it for Aunt Claire. You are, after all, her guest."At Ben's quirked brow, she amended her words. "Okay, our guest. It's the least I could do."

"You have to admit, though," Vanessa added in Ben's defense, "Mr. Lewis can be a hard pill to swallow, especially if you're new in town to start with." Flanked by the twins at the table, she turned to wipe little Brett's mouth. "The only person who keeps him in line is Miss Claire," she remarked absently.

"You're right about that. If anybody can, she can," Ron said.

Rosalie turned to Ben. "It's only because he's scared Miss Claire'll put a curse on him."

"Really?" Ben asked, and dropped his napkin to the table. "You believe that?"

"I'm not scared of Miss Claire," Brett said to no one in particular as he played with his food.

"Me neither," Brian chimed in from the other side of the table.

"Of course not, guys," Ron said to the boys, all the while sending a careful glance to his wife. "We love Miss Claire."

"Big ears," Vanessa whispered as she picked up Brian's napkin and wiped his mouth.

"Rosalie, don't start that business," Sela warned.

"Well, it happens to be true," she continued on blithely. "He thinks she can do it."

Ben watched with interest as both Ron and Vanessa tried to signal Rosalie into silence, but the young woman simply raised her eyes innocently. Sela, on the other hand, had found a fascination with the remnants on her pie plate.

"You can ask Mama," Rosalie said. "And Mabel Thornton always mutters a counter-spell when she gets around Miss Claire. Watch her lips when they're in the same room." She started laughing. "It's a hoot."

Ben stifled his laugh into a grin as he shook his head at her chattering. It was hard to believe Rosalie—she couldn't be too much older than twenty—so easily talked of the possibility of spells and counterspells. He looked across the table to draw Sela's gaze. When she met his eyes, she, too, seemed amused over Rosalie's comments—not at all upset. Good. She'd received enough grief from that deacon.

Ron crossed his arms on the table and stared down Rosalie. "Girl, don't they teach you anything over at that college? Aren't you getting ready to complete your last year?"

Vanessa cleaned Brian's hands as she spoke. "I'd think by now you wouldn't believe everything you hear in these parts like some backwoods jackal scared of their own shadow."

"I didn't say I believed it all," Rosalie protested, though none too fiercely. "Just that everybody knows it. Fairlight has had 'haints' and ghosts around for years. Y'all know that."

After a few moments of uncomfortable silence, Sela cleared her throat. "So, what are you planning on doing after you graduate next year, Rosalie?"

"Besides hide out from the town ghosts," Ron added with a grin.

"Oh, stop teasing," Rosalie chided him. "I don't know, Sela. Teach, probably, but maybe I'll go up to Atlanta and find a job instead of staying here."

"You don't want to stay in Fairlight?" Ben asked.

"She's right," Ron said. "The sad fact is, these days there are more opportunities outside of the county. When kids leave town for college now, they don't return."

"We did," Sela said.

"Yeah, but our situations were unique. I bought out Miss Claire's real estate business after a few years and you were able to snare a good job working with the county."

"It's not that I don't like Fairlight," Rosalie said. "I love it here, what with Mama and Daddy still here," Rosalie said. "It's just that you're limited to what you can do if you stay in town." She looked at Sela. "Now, Sela, she hit the jackpot when she went off to school and managed to come back with a fine catch after her first year."

"Um, Rosalie, that story's best left for another time," Vanessa began, but it wasn't a strong enough warning to stop Rosalie.

"I figure I can still do the same. You know, luck up and find myself somebody like that. Course, I'm hoping it'll last longer than Sela's did. Or, heaven forbid, at least not end the same way."

"Rosalie." The admonishment came in unison from Ron and Vanessa. Ben frowned as his gaze shifted, once again, to Sela. Surprisingly, she didn't seem in the least disturbed by the unexpected revelation.

"Oh," Rosalie said as she looked around belatedly. "I didn't mean that in a bad way, Sela."

"Hey, good luck to you," Sela replied.

Ron quickly spoke. "Ah, Rosalie, you want to grab some ice cream from the freezer and bring the pie out here so we can all have seconds?"

"Sure," she said and, with Ben's help, left her chair and the table.

Vanessa rolled her eyes at Rosalie's exit before she pushed back her own chair. "The boys are through messing over their food, so I'm going to get them cleaned up and ready for bed." She glanced at Ben before she hustled the twin closest to her from his chair. "By the time you have a little more dessert, I'll be right back."

Both men rose at the same time. "Honey, you want me to help?" Ron asked.

"Why don't you stay with Ben?" Sela interjected, and swiftly left her chair to help the remaining twin down. "I can help out. We can handle things faster and get on back."

Ron's humor was evident as he spoke in a low voice. "I'll try to keep you-know-who in the kitchen muzzled until then."

With a final backward glance toward the women, Ben caught Sela's unexpected gaze as she led the boys from the dining room. Another shared smile stretched below her bright eyes, and she was gone. Ben sighed as he already anticipated her return.

Safely upstairs with the boys, Sela tackled the dresser drawer in her search for their pajamas.

"Why didn't you tell me you'd invited Rosalie to dinner, too?"

"I didn't know I would," Vanessa said from somewhere behind her. "She dropped by to do an interview with Ron this afternoon. Mind you, I get him to come home early one day for dinner, and there she is, on the doorstep, looking all helpless, and telling Ron only he can help her."

Sela handed a pair of pajamas to Vanessa, and they each took charge of a twin for changing.

"She's doing some kind of paper for school," Vanessa explained. "Anyway, it was close to dinner, and she was still here, so I asked her to stay."

"I love Fontella," Sela said as she sat next to Vanessa on the edge of the twin bed and dressed Brian. "But, I swear, that daughter of hers is twenty-one going on ten. Sometimes, she doesn't act like she has the common sense she was born with."

Vanessa stopped and squeezed Sela's hand for a moment. "I wanted to scream when she shot her mouth off about you and Andrew meeting at school. I'm sorry."

"Oh, that was nothing. Water under the bridge. Though I would have preferred she not discuss it in front of Ben. He's pretty thorough, you know, always wanting details, and curious on how things fit together. I guess it goes hand in hand with him being an architect."

"Is that why you didn't want to be left at the table with him? Afraid he might ask the wrong questions?"

"He's already asked enough about Auntie and the basement, courtesy of Deacon Freeman." She slipped the pajama top over Brian's head, then reached into her pants pocket and took out a folded business envelope. "Actually, I wanted to tell you about this." She handed the envelope to Vanessa. "It came in today's mail."

Vanessa stopped what she was doing and looked at the envelope. When she read the return address, she turned to Sela, her eyes wide and a smile on her face. "Sela, you got a response. So, tell me. What did they say?"

"They liked the articles and want me to send in a few more."

"Congratulations. I knew this would happen. So, when are you going to send the others?"

"I'm not." When she saw Vanessa's stricken expression, she said, "I don't want to relocate and leave Fairlight, that's all there is to it." She brushed a loving hand across Brian's head. "It's all a pipe dream, anyway, and I responded to the article before I really thought it all out."

"But, Sela, you love writing and editing, and all that stuff. You know you won't find that opportunity around here. This job is a chance of a lifetime, and was made to order for you."

"Not if it means leaving town."

Vanessa let out a loud exhale of exasperation. "Then do this. Promise me you'll tell Miss Claire about it before you refuse any offer they make."

Sela responded to the coaxing from her friend. "All right, but no pressure, just like you promised before."

"Deal," Vanessa said and handed the envelope back to Sela. "We need to finish up with the boys. The guys will wonder what happened to us."

"I imagine Rosalie's okay with their undivided attention."

"Yeah. Did you see how she took to Ben?" Vanessa glanced at Sela. "I think she likes him."

"I like Ben," Brian said as he protested at being buttoned and snapped.

"Me, too," Brett intoned.

"That's Mr. Russell to you two," Vanessa corrected.

Sela laughed as Vanessa sighed and said, "See what I mean? Really big ears."

A rap at the door drew their attention. Standing in the open doorway was Rosalie. She had a big smile on her face.

"That's one nice hunk of a guest you got downstairs at your table, Vanessa." She crossed her arms and rested her hip against the door, her eyes sparked with interest. "Where has he been hiding?"

Sela was careful to keep the sarcasm from her voice as she smiled. "You're talking about Ben?"

"None other, honey. Maybe one of you can put in a good word with him about me, huh?" She looked from Sela to Vanessa before her attention was once again focused on Sela. "That is, I mean, if you don't have your own cap set for him."

"No, not at all," she said and busied herself with Brian's buttons before she dared look up again, only to catch a view of Vanessa's strained face in the process. "Not at all."

Ten

Thirty minutes later, Rosalie left to go home. Soon after, Ben and Sela took their leave into the humid, dusky evening. As they moved down the garden walk, side by side, then through the whitewashed gate to the street, they said nothing as they breathed in the rampant fragrances of mint and sweet woodruff planted all around.

Sela's thoughts were otherwise occupied due to the inevitable brushes she endured against Ben along the narrow street sidewalk. Each touch upped the ante of her already heightened awareness. After the third brush, she swiftly folded her arms across her chest.

"A chill?" he asked.

Sela watched his stare drill into her. Had he guessed she had been unnerved? "No," she said with a gulp. "I was thinking back over our evening, that's all."

"Ron and Vanessa are all right. I like them," Ben said. "They seem to have a pretty good relationship."

"They're my dearest friends," Sela gushed, pleased at his words. "Ron and I grew up together. When he married Vanessa, it was perfect because she and I got along well, too. And their two little boys are darlings."

She could see Ben's white smile growing through the pale light. "What's so funny?"

"Well, if you overlook the mess their two little hellions made at the table, they're okay, too."

Sela tilted her head to look up at him. "They're children—what do you expect?"

"My philosophy is that the best kids are those who belong to someone else." When she let out a loud snort, he gave her a sidelong glance. "Don't get me wrong. I respect their choice. They seem like a happy family unit, and that's what's important."

"You've probably had limited personal experience around children, right?"

He glanced at her. "My older brother, Will, has two—both under three years old."

She snorted at him again. "Then you'd know better if you spent time with them."

"Speaking of spending, they're costly little devils, too." He dug his hands into his pockets as they continued to stroll. "I understand raising one today can easily cost you two hundred grand, and your friends own two, with a third on the way." He shook his head.

Sela couldn't help herself as she burst out laughing, dropping her hands. "You're quite the cynic, aren't you?" As they brushed against each other, she quickly drew her arms into a fold again.

They continued their leisurely stroll down the block where Sela was scrupulously aware of his presence.

"You don't have much need of a car around here," he said.

"I have a car, but it's an easy walk to friends' houses, the library, or even the park over on Jefferson Street. Why? You don't like walking?" She glanced over at him and surveyed his length in the dim streetlight. "A big guy like yourself, I would think two blocks wouldn't be too much exercise for you."

He chuckled at her put-down. "No, I'm fine with it. I exercise on a regular basis. I just think this is a . . . quaint practice."

Sela laughed at his description. "Now you make us sound like some throwback to the nineteenth-century. You think this is all old-fashioned and pretty country, don't you?"

"Not at all. I've had to live in a few dated villages, and this is definitely not one of them."

"I shouldn't forget you are well traveled. Don't you ever want to settle into one place, put down some roots, and have a bunch of horrible, expensive kids?"

"I'll probably have to one day, but only when I find someone worth the sacrifice. Until then, what's the rush?" Ben turned to her. "I believe Rosalie said you had that same opportunity at one point, and you turned it down."

Caught by the subject change, she answered the personal query hastily. "I didn't have much choice in the matter. The decision and opportunity were taken away from me."

Sela watched as he turned ever so slightly to her, without ever breaking his stride, and momentarily studied her face. She knew he tried to glean meaning from a statement she'd purposely left obtuse.

"Somehow, we manage to find our way through broken relationships, don't we?" he said carefully.

She tossed her head at him, taking careful note of his use of "we."

"Yes, we do. You met Rosalie tonight; so, what did you think of her?"

Ben let out a deep breath as he stuffed his hands

into his pockets. "I have a great deal of respect for her mother." He took another breath. "And the daughter is . . . lively company at the dinner table."

"Apparently she thinks highly of you."

"Oh," he replied.

They had reached the house and the iron gate. Ben unlatched the bar, and as he pushed it open, he stepped aside so Sela could enter before him. "And, what do you think?"

Sela felt a warm glow—like heated molasses flowing upward from her chest—seep into her neck and face. Under cover of darkness, she endured the sensation, glad that Ben was not privy to her discomfort. She moved past him, through the gate.

"What I think isn't important. Rosalie can be interesting when she chooses, and she's a nice person."

"In a flighty sort of way?" he added.

She let out a laugh at the right-on description as Ben came up alongside her. "Well, you could do worse for a date, you know."

With the front porch only a short distance away, Ben moved ahead and turned to face her, barring her way up the steps.

"I think you're interesting, Sela. How about I ask you for a date?"

Thrown by the gruff pronouncement, she squinted stupidly at him, acutely aware of his proximity, his face above hers, his lips . . . A whispering breeze from the line of shrubs around the house interrupted her reverie. She hugged her arms tighter around her chest and looked away.

"Well, what do you say?" Ben's voice was as smooth and confident as the unexpected breeze.

Swallowing hard, Sela stepped back from him. "We were talking about Rosalie."

"You were doing that. Anyway, she still has time to find the man of her dreams at school . . ." He cocked his brow in a wry expression and finished his sentence. "The way you did."

His mention of Andrew in that vein was like a cold splash of water to her hot face. "We live in the same house—we don't need to date in order to go out together."

He seemed to think on the idea before he nodded his head. "All right, then have dinner with me tomorrow night."

"You mean, like, just the two of us over at the diner?"

"That'll do."

Deep within, Sela heard the rumblings of a refusal coming from her protective self, with which she had always complied. Until now. This time, anticipation surrounding Ben won out. They could talk like old friends one moment, and his look or touch could render her uncomfortable in the next. It was this curiosity of reactions that she wanted to explore.

"Okay, but it won't be a date." Her eyes narrowed for emphasis. "And, I can't go tomorrow because of the church supper. You were invited, too," she reminded him.

"I'll remember not to call it a date, and we can't go tomorrow," he said with a grin. When he turned and they started up the steps, he placed his hand on the small of her back.

The subtle, unexpected touch was heady and seized her senses. She jerked from his hand as though burned, thereby missing the next step. In the process, she stumbled backward, right into the crook of Ben's arm and chest.

Easily balancing her weight, he looked down at

her, his smile hidden behind a look of concern. "Are you okay?"

"I think so." She regained her footing and quickly straightened as she almost leaped from his helpful hands. She then flew up the steps before she slid the key into the lock. Pushing it open, she entered the low-lit foyer.

"I don't think you've had your alarm on since the day I arrived," Ben said from behind her.

"I . . . It's not used all the time," she explained, her hand still on the doorknob. "Just on occasion, when I'm alone. You see, I was about to shower that morning, and it was the middle of the day."

"I remember," he said as he came around her. "I remember it quite well. Good night." He sauntered past Sela and across the living room. "I'm going to work downstairs for a while," he called back to her. "So I'll see you in the morning."

Sela still stood at the open door. "Good night," she muttered, though he was already out of sight.

As she began to close the door, the crack of a branch, and a distant dog's bark drew her attention. She looked out the door and into the uneventful dark night. What greeted her was a restful scene not unlike the ones from any other night. She closed, then locked the door before starting for her bedroom.

A breath of melancholy began its transformation of her as she turned into the hallway that led to her room. Her need to talk with Aunt Claire had grown.

Ben's presence at the house, initially, was of no consequence, and Sela believed that. Even when she began to accept him in a new light—as a family friend—that was okay, too. Now Ben had shown an interest in her. Slight though it may be, it was surely more than just a friendly one. And, Lord help her, she was beginning to react to that interest with her own bit of fluster.

When she reached her bedroom, she closed the door behind her and leaned against it, as though that simple act would lock away her doubts and return her to the easy thoughts she had enjoyed only a few days before.

Sela squeezed her eyes tight, then opened them, whereon they immediately lit upon the dresser across the room, and settled on the jewelry box. Pushing away from the door, she went to the box. It was a footed mahogany jewelry case with brass fittings and hinges that supported three separate drawers, resembling a Chinese treasure chest. With both hands, as though the burden she undertook were an immense one, she lifted the lid at either corner.

In the velvet-lined center section, flanked by a string of pearls and an assortment of bracelets, lay a gold locket with intricate filigree detail along its outer edge. It was attached to a delicate gold chain. She lifted it from the case, then moved to sit on the edge of her bed with the jewelry carefully cradled in her hand.

She turned over her mother's locket several times. Aunt Claire had presented it to Sela on the occasion of her twelfth birthday. She had put off giving it to Sela for almost seven years because she had wanted Sela to be old enough to understand the details of her mother's death.

It had been the last time Aunt Claire had openly discussed that tragic day with Sela. For her part, Sela no longer dwelled on the loss of her mother; but she kept the locket close by, her link to childhood emotions that she still wrestled with. True, the sudden death of her mother had been an extraordinary ordeal for a five-year-old. Even now, she easily recalled the painful details. But, Aunt Claire's unselfish gift of consistent, unconditional love eventually blunted the pain and ultimately saved her. Sela was sure of it.

Though she believed she owed much to her aunt, Aunt Claire would be the first to insist that Sela had done the same for her own healing as an adult. She had, after all, lost a sister with whom she had been extremely close and shared a psychic history. Over the years, Aunt Claire's support was constantly evidenced, especially during the tragic deaths of Andrew and Charles, Sela's last two loves.

She raised the locket to her chest and pressed it there. "Why did you leave me, Mama?" It was a refrain she had repeated often in the privacy of her quiet room. "Why do I have to lose the ones I love?"

As stabs of regret pummeled her chest, she closed her eyes and the locket slipped through her fingers. It fell from her lap, struck the metal leg of the bed, and then dropped to the carpeted floor.

When Sela knelt to retrieve it, she found it had popped open and was empty. Her eyes expertly sought out the contents she knew had spilled nearby. There it was. A pale strip of paper, in an accordion fold, lay just beneath the bed. She picked up the paper first, then the locket, and returned to where she sat on the edge of the bed.

Carefully stretching out the paper, she read the memorized words penned across two lines:

> Good-bye. I love you, Sela, more than anything else in the world.

She refolded the paper with care and placed it inside the locket cavity before she snapped it shut.

After a lengthy moment, during which she imposed an iron control on her emotions, she pushed off the bed and returned the locket to her jewelry case.

"So, you're still alive and well in Fairlight, huh?" Montreal's humor spilled out at his brother from the phone.

Ben smiled as he leaned back against the chair in the basement. "A little rocky at first, but most everything is smoothed out now. Did you get my E-mail the other day?"

"Yeah. I put together the work papers you prepared for that historical building renovation last year. What do you want me to do with them?"

Ben stretched his hand across the desk and reached for one of the inn's brochures. "How about expressing the box to me down here? I'll give you the address."

"In that case, I have a better suggestion," Mont said. "I'm sitting in for Dad at a meeting down in Miami this weekend, and I have a two-hour layover in Atlanta. We can meet up then."

"Since when did you move up from gopher to Dad's stand-in?"

"Since you don't show up in the office anymore and he and Mom have to attend one of those booze and schmooze affairs."

Ben remembered the scathing name he and his brothers had given the seemingly endless succession of business parties their parents attended. The boys had only been teenagers at the time, unaware that they were destined for a similar fate.

"In that case, you got the better deal," Ben said. "We had to restructure a job bid for this new project's bean counters. I guess Dad and Will figure I can't mess up a prepared delivery too much."

Ben understood his little brother's deprecating comments. It wasn't an easy job living up to their father's expectations. The stoic, successful head of Russell Architects & Engineers expected few faults from his three sons and an almost debilitating work ethic was mandatory. If not for their mother's intervention—she was also a business partner—on more than a few occasions, the situation could have been drastic. She never let things get too far out of hand.

So far, their father had managed to wrest the appropriate success from the eldest son, and the youngest would continue to try. But, it was Ben, the middle son, who had kept his life, ambitions, and goals out of reach of his father's far-flung vision.

"Anyway," Mont was saying, "Miami can be hard to turn down. I mean, think of all the possibilities on the beach."

"Get your mind straight and your tail in gear," Ben warned. "You know what Dad expects, and it's not mixing business and pleasure. There will be no excuse if things go wrong."

"I'm on it, I swear. Why don't you drive up and meet me at the airport? I mean, nothing's keeping you in that farm town over the weekend, right?"

Ben smiled as he pictured the scene Sela would cause if she'd heard Mont's innocent remark about Fairlight. He rubbed his chin as he savored the possibility of her riding up with him. Without realizing it, he voiced his thought out loud. "Sela might want to come."

"Who?" Mont asked. "You've been down there a few days and you've already hooked up with somebody?"

Ben straightened in his chair. "It's more like we ran into each other." When Mont remained silent, waiting for an explanation, Ben tried to give him one. "She's, ah, Miss Bennett's niece and . . ." He looked toward the stairs to insure he was still alone in the basement. "She lives at the inn."

"I thought nobody was there this time of the year."

"It's just the two of us."

"Oh, I see." Mont chortled his understanding with racy glee. "You get all the breaks, bro. I swear, you must be living right. So, what's the scoop on her?"

"In other words, is she available and what does she look like?"

"You know me," Mont crowed. "Personally, I think it's about time you get the R and R you deserve."

Ben laughed at his brother's logic as he rubbed his chin. "She's too standoffish to be the partying type, but she definitely has the looks." Both brothers laughed. Ben went on to share a little about the people he'd met, including the over-the-top postman.

"You sure you want to hang around there all summer?" Mont exclaimed.

"You want to hear the kicker?" Ben asked. "Miss Bennett is apparently a well-known clairvoyant around here, something she forgot to tell me."

Mont released an expletive behind his long whistle. "Man, I don't know if this thing can get any weirder. You know, Dad wasn't too keen about you taking this project so soon after you got back in the country. Maybe you ought to keep this spooky stuff under your hat a while longer."

Ben smiled at his young brother's advice. "Why

don't I just plan to drive up and meet you at the airport? I can treat your usually broke butt to lunch."

"Hey, I'll be on the expense account, so I can give it up for you for a change. And, bring Sela. I'd like to see and hear the real deal about your landlord."

Ben grinned, clearly enjoying his brother's humor. He jotted down the flight information Mont provided, then exchanged good-byes.

"Be safe."

"You, too. Later."

Ben clicked off the cell phone, then stood to stretch. He felt good. In fact, he felt damn good. He wondered if it had anything to do with a certain standoffish, yet interesting female who was probably asleep just up the stairs.

Frisco wasn't sleeping. And, it wasn't for lack of trying in the pitch-black room. He remained troubled by what he had witnessed and heard, and now found himself being tossed and turned through this waking nightmare. He sat up in the bed and took a swing at the headboard.

"Why is she doing this?" The words ran together in an indecipherable mewl of pain as his fist crashed into the headboard a second time, then again, before he slumped back on the bed.

Through the throbbing pain, her beauty circled his head like a panoramic slide show. Why would she flaunt it to his face on one hand, then cuckold him on the other? It wasn't fair.

She knew the consequences of his anger—but, so did he. So, he had to be sure. She was, after all, only a woman, and capable of emotional mistakes.

If he caught it early, and made her aware of it, it didn't have to be too late this time.

When he felt calmer, Frisco smoothed down the lumpy pillow. He would be cautious and careful, making sure this was no mistake. He didn't want to make her cry again. It wasn't a pleasant thing to witness. But, if punishment was necessary, he would do it, if only for her own good.

Frisco's decision settled him down, and he eased his head back on the pillow. Turning his face into the soft mass, he smiled, the nervous tic near his eye finally slowing down.

Eleven

The next morning, Sela didn't leave her bedroom for breakfast. So, when Fontella poked her head into Sela's bedroom later on, her visit wasn't totally unexpected.

"You can show your face again now that he's gone."

Sela sat cross-legged in the center of her bed as she thumbed through a few education articles she had written, and responded without looking up. "What are you talking about?"

"I'm talking about you avoiding that nice young man at breakfast this morning, that's what." She rested her hand on her hip. "He asked about you."

"It's not like I can avoid him when we're living in the same house," she replied, before she turned to Fontella. "What did he say?"

"He wanted you to know he'd meet up with you tonight at the church supper."

"Fine." She spoke nonchalantly and returned to the articles. When she saw Fontella leave, she gave up the charade of sorting articles and leaned back against the headboard. She sighed and supposed that maybe she had avoided Ben. After last night, who could blame her? She preferred a little distance between them for a while, just to get her thoughts straight. And, she only had about eight hours to accomplish it. She swung her legs over the side of the bed, deciding to get in a jog this morning before the rain came. It would help to clear her head.

About eight hours later, Sela stood at the window of the Methodist church's Life Center, which offered an unrestricted second-floor view of the parking lot and sanctuary. She recognized Ben's car and wondered if Reverend Osborne had already commandeered him for the expected round of introductions in the cafeteria.

She returned her attention to the adult computer class she taught once a week. Their session would be over shortly, and the six female students were busy conferring with one another from behind their computers. This particular class was one she both enjoyed and taught with pride. They were at-risk women who needed computer skills to better their job worthiness, which, in turn, helped their economic situation.

She enjoyed the interactive experience on this busy night. There were a host of other activities going on around the church, including Bible study in the sanctuary, all meant to encourage members to involve their families. Thus, it was the only weeknight a full dinner was served in the church cafeteria. She glanced at her watch.

"That's about it for the evening, ladies," Sela announced. "I don't know about you, but I can smell the aroma from the buttered rolls downstairs." While the women laughed in agreement, she said, "Well then, maybe I'll see you in the cafeteria."

Amid friendly chatter, the women began the learned, orderly process of closing files and cutting off their computers before they packed their bags and prepared to retrieve their children from other programs in session around the church.

As Sela leaned on the edge of her desk, her mind engaged in other thoughts, she noticed the women's conversations had died out. She looked up, and realized they were engrossed by something at the door. She turned and saw Ben standing just outside the open doorway, as though he didn't want to disturb them. Her heart did its now familiar leap before she jumped from the desk.

"Oh," she exclaimed to no one in particular before she dropped the papers she held to the desk. Then, smoothing her hands down her skirt, she made her way to the door.

"Hi." His smile warmed his eyes as he greeted her first. "I ran into Vanessa downstairs, and she told me how to find you here." Almost as an afterthought, he lowered his voice. "Did I interrupt your class?"

Sela brushed her hand across her brow. "No, no, your timing is great. I was dismissing the class right now."

"Who's your friend, Ms. Bennett?" The question came from Willene Jackson, her youngest student at twenty, and the only one who didn't call Sela by her given name.

She stared up blankly into Ben's smiling face, then turned and rejoined the class. He followed her into the room.

"This is Ben Russell," she began. "He's an architect visiting Fairlight and studying our church, sort of offering us advice on restoration work, as well as collecting material for his own use."

While the women crowded around to make their acquaintance with Ben, Sela returned to her desk and packed her things into a small briefcase. She followed the group out of the classroom door and closed it behind her. After the women offered their good-byes and dispersed in different directions, Sela turned to Ben with an arched brow.

"That was just a taste of what's going to happen in the cafeteria. So, are you hungry enough to brave those kind of interruptions from most of the congregation?"

"That's why I wanted to find you," he said, laughing. "I think I like having you as my protector—I wouldn't have it any other way."

She joined him with a smile. "Don't say I didn't warn you. Come on," she said, and led him to the dining room.

Sela sipped her lemonade, her eyes browsing over the cup's edge as she followed the odyssey Reverend Osborne and Ben made around the tables set up on the gym floor. They were still shaking hands. It seemed everyone at the church had heard about Ben and most had made their way to the table to meet him. Through the interruptions, dinner had still gone well. A few surprise faces appeared, including a subdued Deacon Freeman, and a jocular Mr. Lewis.

"Why don't you stop staring holes in their backs," Vanessa said from the other side of the table.

Embarrassed, Sela slanted a look to her friend. "Was I doing that?"

Vanessa nodded. "Something's on your mind. What's up?"

She set the cup down. "Last night, after dinner at your house, I was talking up Rosalie to Ben. Then, straight out of the blue, he asked me out instead. A date. How crazy is that?"

"I figured something had happened." She rested her hand across her belly before she continued. "And, it's not crazy at all. He seems pretty red-blooded to me, so why wouldn't he ask you out?"

"Oh, I don't know," Sela replied flippantly. "Maybe it has something to do with the fact that I don't do dates, I'm bad news, I have issues, and so on, and so on."

Vanessa leaned forward. "That's how you see things, and unless you've filled him in with certain pertinent details, how's he supposed to know your ground rules?"

Sela allowed her eyes to dart around the room again in search of Ben and the reverend. "Well, I did clear up one thing."

"You did?"

"I told him I consider him a family friend; and probably against my better judgment, I agreed to have dinner with him."

When she didn't hear a reaction, Sela turned to Vanessa and witnessed her wide smile below twinkling eyes.

"Sela, I . . . I don't know what to say. I think that's great, and it's a big step for you."

"Hey, don't go getting carried away. I also made it clear that it won't be a date."

"Well, I think Ben is a nice guy, and Ron likes him, too. Of course, there's no way Miss Claire would have let him in her house otherwise. You're going to have a nice time."

Sela blinked with surprise at her friend's enthusiasm. "Will you calm down? It's no big deal. All we're having is a meal together at the diner."

She watched as Vanessa's face dropped, her stare

fixed at some point beyond the two of them. Too late, a firm hand rested against Sela's shoulder just as she caught the distinctive fragrance of vanilla.

"Oh, Sela, there you are." The singsong voice that belonged to Mabel Thornton was inimitable. She came around the chair and into view.

As Sela and Vanessa exchanged glances, Mabel thrust her ample body onto the armless metal chair before she announced, "I just met Ben Russell."

Sela couldn't believe her bad luck at having garnered the attention of one of the busiest bodies in town. On a singular quest to gain or dispense information, Mrs. Thornton was a force Sela had reckoned with before, so she was up to the task. If there were such a thing as good luck, Sela figured Reverend Osborne had kept the woman under control while in Ben's presence.

"I made it clear to Reverend Osborne that the young man should have been formally introduced to the church right after he arrived," Mrs. Thornton said.

"He's barely had time to get his office space arranged," Vanessa said. "After all, he's only been in town a few days."

"Even so, the deacons are just now meeting him, except for Deacon Freeman, of course, and Sister Freeman said she didn't even get to meet him until yesterday."

Sela exhaled an impatient sigh at the mention of Alice Freeman, the deacon's wife. The two women were like peas in a pod. "Well, I think it's understandable that Reverend Osborne didn't want him thrown to the wolves too early. The point is to get him to stay."

"Don't be fresh, Sela," Mrs. Thornton admonished.

"But, he's here to study the church and the repairs it will need, not fellowship and politick with the governing members," she replied.

"Or the local residents, either, I imagine," Mrs. Thornton shot back, her brows knitted in a frown. The older woman's florid complexion, along with the tiny beads of sweat that dotted her graying hairline, confirmed her agitation with Sela.

If the truth were known, both Sela and Vanessa also waged a war with comfort as they anticipated the conversation's end.

Mrs. Thornton turned her attention on Vanessa. "Now that I've met Mr. Russell for myself, I'm impressed. Not only is he well-spoken, he's smart." She looked back at Sela. "Of course, you always were attracted to quality young men, like your Andrew and Charles."

As warning bells sounded, Sela smiled stiffly to cover her annoyance. "What are you trying to say, Mrs. Thornton?"

"Only that the church council wants to put its best foot forward now that we have this opportunity for Fairlight. And, with that said, do you really think it wise to let Mr. Russell stay at the inn?"

Struck by the woman's gall, Sela's patience screeched to a halt. "Mrs. Thornton, how do you come up with these cockamamie conclusions?"

"The only reason Ben is here is because of Miss Claire," Vanessa said. "He's *her* friend."

Mabel nodded, as though she was not the least bit affected by their indignation. "Leave it to our Claire to arrange for someone of his stature to come to town. Lord knows, she meets all types when she's off traveling like a Gypsy." When Sela's audible sigh rose up between them, the older woman's voice became amiable—a girlish lilt that struck a false note.

"Now, I know my frankness is considered a fault by some, and I apologize if the truth isn't always pretty, Sela."

Auntie had once observed that the joy in Mrs. Thornton's voice never quite reached her eyes. Sela looked into those cool orbs now.

"You know Claire's house has a history of, well, to put it frankly, pain and misery," Mabel continued. "And with only you there, what'll Mr. Russell think when he learns the truth about young Andrew and Charles? Fairlight's a small town, and he's bound to hear it all someplace, sooner or later."

"Rumor and gossip are not the truth," Sela warned.

"Mrs. Thornton, I just left Reverend Osborne."

Ben's mellow baritone blanketed an irritated Sela.

"He's on his way to the sanctuary and wanted you to meet him there," Ben continued.

"Thank you very much, young man," the older woman said.

Sela's gaze caromed across Mabel only to collide with Ben's as he stood there, tall as ever, with curiosity in his eyes. Had he heard any part of their exchange? Sela straightened as he came to reclaim his chair alongside her.

"Ben." She swallowed hard as she prepared a feeble response. "We were wondering where you had gone."

"So, it's already Ben, is it?" Mrs. Thornton lifted a carefully plucked brow while she surveyed the two. "And what's this about you two planning to eat over at the diner?" she added.

Frowning, Ben shot her a penetrating look. "Don't tell me you're psychic, too, Mrs. Thornton."

"Heaven's no," she exclaimed, shaking her head.

"I don't abide by that stuff. I overheard Vanessa and Sela talking about it."

Sela's irritation quickly turned to embarrassment. "You what?"

"You eavesdropped on us?" Vanessa exclaimed.

"Nonsense," the matronly woman quickly retorted. "There's a big difference between the two." She dismissed their concerns by smiling at Ben. "Now that you're a part of us, or at least for the summer, you'll have to meet your neighbors, mix with them, which means you don't have to eat at that diner. It's what we call hospitality. In fact, I'm giving you an open invitation for dinner at my house."

Ben smiled as he refused her offer. "My work hours won't be normal, so there's no telling when I'll be able to grab a bite to eat. What I get at the inn and the diner will do fine." When he leaned forward, he rested his arm along the top of Sela's chair.

"As long as he's staying at the inn," Sela added, inching forward on her chair in the process, "he won't starve."

"Just you remember that vow of yours," Mrs. Thornton replied sharply at her. "It's kept us from tragedy's door for the last three years, so you take care with what you do." She turned to Vanessa before she rose from her chair and said sweetly, "Give a kiss to the boys for me."

Thoroughly offended, Sela clamped her lips tightly over her teeth, and swallowed her retort. At the same time, she signaled silence from Vanessa.

Mrs. Thornton had turned to address Ben. "It's been a blessing meeting you, young man, and I expect to see you often, but right now I have to go. I don't want to keep the reverend waiting."

As Mrs. Thornton left the cafeteria, Vanessa said,

"Well, Ben, you had to meet her sooner or later. I'm sorry it wasn't later."

"Hey, I'm fine with it."He glanced at a quiet Sela, and read a combination of things in her stubborn frown and folded arms.

"Everyone who knows Mrs. Thornton understands that she thrives on drama. And, like tonight, if it's not around, she'll create some."

Ben smiled at Vanessa's assessment.

"The best thing to do is put her out of your mind," Vanessa said. "She doesn't make much sense, anyway."

That was exactly what Ben had been thinking. The older woman's comments didn't click with anything he'd learned so far about Sela. A vow? Some sort of tragedy? And, the woman's parting warning had visibly upset Sela. Obviously, he was totally ignorant about something well known by the locals; but to ask about it now would endanger the gentle trust he had built with Sela. He watched as she pushed back from the table, though she avoided looking into his face.

"I hope you enjoyed yourself tonight. I know Reverend Osborne probably did." Sela looked across the table at Vanessa. "Are you ready to leave?"

"Now?" Vanessa asked as she wiped her hands on her napkin.

In a nervous gesture, Sela smoothed her hand across her pulled-back hair. "I'd like to get home, that's all."

"Then, I'll take you," Ben said as he stood up. "Come on."

"No," she said, and looked at Ben, albeit apologetically. "You should be here with Reverend Osborne and the others at the church. This is business for you. Anyway, I rode with Vanessa." She turned to her friend, and spoke with a light plead to her voice. "Can't you leave now?"

Vanessa was clearly torn by Sela's predicament. "I . . . I'm supposed to wait for Ron so we can collect the boys." She looked at her watch. "Maybe if we wait a while longer he'll be finished—"

"Don't worry yourself, Vanessa." Ben's voice broke with huskiness, and his eyes never left Sela. "I'll take her home." A small smile softened his angular mouth. "After all, it's not out of my way, and we're beginning to draw attention standing here arguing over a simple matter."

The long sigh from Sela as she looked around them signaled her concession.

After they bid Vanessa good night, Ben followed a quiet and compliant Sela out to the parking lot.

Twelve

Sela leaned against the headrest and closed her eyes. The steady hum from the car, coupled with Ben's silence, gave her peace to think. Maybe the past was not as buried as she had hoped, seeing as how easily Mrs. Thornton's words had aggravated her scars. And maybe it wasn't just the pain of loss. Maybe it was resentment that she was considered different, a plague lurking in the shadows waiting to inflict harm at the expense of Fairlight's citizens. Maybe.

There was no avoiding the label, and she didn't want Ben to see her as an embarrassing anomaly. That she cared a whit about what he thought surprised even her. Instead of settling down, her life had taken some decidedly eventful turns.

"What do you call this place?" Ben asked.

Sela broke from her reverie, and glanced at Ben first before she turned to look out the window. They were driving along an empty stretch of country road she knew well. It ran adjacent to a wide pool of water, a halfway point between the church and the house. She sat up quickly.

"It's called Hunter's Pond." These days, Sela could ride past the landmark without the lingering pain of having known what had happened here.

Mrs. Thornton's cruel reminder, however, brought it sharply back into focus.

"Looks like it's a popular spot with the teenagers. Every town has one." Even with the night sky as its only illumination, they could see the outlines of a spattering of cars parked on the grassy knoll.

Fighting the melancholy mood she'd sunk into, Sela smiled, the feel of Ben's gaze warm on her skin. She hugged her arms.

"I guess it still is," she admitted. "It has lots of trees, a great view of the sunset, and it offers the best chance of privacy around here when you're a teen with use of a car."

"Is that from personal experience?"

They both laughed.

"That sounds good coming from you," Ben said. "I figure you've sulked long enough after that dinner."

"What are you talking about?" she asked, and jerked her head around at him. "So, you've decided it's time I get over Mrs. Thornton?"

"Something like that. Admit it, she did get to you, didn't she?"

"She only talks gossip, that's all."

"Are you admitting it's a given to gossip and have your life scrutinized by everybody in a small town?"

Sela sloughed off his insult wrapped in concern. "I only put up with her out of respect for Reverend Osborne. He just hates it when fights break out at the church."

As they both laughed at the absurdity, Sela, more comfortable now than she had earlier thought possible, settled into her seat again.

Shortly after, they arrived at the house. As they walked up the drive of the dark house, Sela's arms developed goose bumps from a chill, and she hugged her arms to her middle.

"What's wrong? Are you cold?" Ben asked.

"No, just a sudden chill." She looked at him. "Like somebody walked over my grave."

Ben swung behind her and took up his steps. "I thought you weren't superstitious. Your real problem is you don't have any blood in these arms." And with both hands, he started a vigorous massage of her upper arms. "In fact, my mom would say you're too skinny."

Sela steeled herself to his touch, both attracted and resistant to it at the same time. "She sounds a lot like Fontella and Auntie."

A high-pitched series of sharp barks rang through the air. Both Sela and Ben turned to the gate where the noise came from and saw a toy poodle trot toward them. Ben dropped his arms.

"Is that your dog barking at us?" he asked.

"No, that's just Petey," Sela said and dropped to one knee as she motioned to the still yelping dog.

"Isn't he kind of little to be so aggressive?" Ben asked. "Why is he out after dark?"

"Sometimes he sneaks out. His owner is Mildred Vasser. She lives just down the street, and is probably looking for him." She snapped her fingers at the dog. "Come here, boy."

The dog stopped to give Ben an ineffective growl before he jogged over to Sela and sniffed at her fingers.

While she cooed over the animal, Ben said, "Dogs don't get along with me, and I don't think this little guy is going to be any different."

Sela stood up and challenged Ben with a look. "Petey can be irascible, but he has a good heart.

Go on, give him a scratch behind the ears. I'll bet he takes to you."

Ben appeared skeptical, but seemed willing to try. He stooped to scratch the little dog's ear. "Hi, Fella," he said, but the poodle seemed more interested in sniffing at his leather shoes.

Sela rested her hands on her hips. "See, he's not growling at you anymore. That's a start." She watched Ben as he rose to his feet in one fluid motion, giving up on the pooch.

"Nope. That's enough, if you ask me." The dog had now sidled in closer to Ben, and lifted his wiry little leg.

Sela's hand flew to her mouth as she jumped back. "Ben, look at Petey."

Ben recognized the dog's squat in record time and jerked his shoe away before more than a spray of urine trickled across its toe. Sela laughed hysterically nearby while Ben shook his leg and then rubbed the tip of his shoe across the grass, all the time glaring at the once more growling dog.

"I'm gonna kill that mutt, Sela. I swear I am."

"Don't you dare," she said, dabbing at her teary eyes. She shook her finger at the dog. "Bad dog, Petey, bad dog."

At that moment, they heard someone call for Petey from the street. With his head erect, the dog froze. Then, he took off across the yard, before he disappeared outside the gate.

"That's Mrs. Vasser calling him," Sela said. She gave Ben an open, friendly smile. "Come on, now. You're not still mad at Petey, are you?" Her answer was his smile that sent her pulse racing. She was impressed at how it warmed his eyes and made them crinkle at the corners.

"All I know is if I see that dog again, I'm killing him."

Sela giggled before she tugged at his arm and drew him back to the walk and up to the front door, comfortable with how natural it all felt. "Let's see, you can't stand lovable kids and you plan on murdering my neighbor's defenseless little dog. What ever am I going to do with you, Ben Russell?"

Later on, Sela was curled up around a pillow on one of the sofas in the den. She was listening to the late news when Ben walked in. He had changed into a pair of worn jeans that hugged his lean form and a black T-shirt that left his muscular arms bare. She blinked, her heart suddenly hammering loudly in her chest. His appeal was extreme. But, had she noticed that before? Suddenly conscious of her own dress, a tank top over lounging pants, she curled tighter into the pillow.

"Still up?" he asked.

"For a while. Have you cleaned your shoes yet?" she teased.

He smiled tiredly as he rubbed his neck. "Maybe I'll take them by a shine shop at the airport this weekend."

"In Atlanta?" She lifted her head, confused. "You're leaving?"

"No, no," he said, smiling. He dropped to the sofa across from her and leaned forward, resting his arms on his legs. "My brother, Mont, has a layover in Atlanta, so I'm going to meet him to pick up a package he's brought along for me."

"Oh," she said, satisfied with the explanation. "You've spoken of him before. Your younger brother, right?"

He nodded as he eyed her keenly. "I was wondering if . . . I mean, do you want to ride up to Atlanta with me this weekend?"

The unexpected request, coupled with his stare, caught Sela off guard, and she hesitated with an answer.

"I plan on driving up and returning that same day," he clarified. "I thought we could have lunch with Mont, you'd get a chance to meet each other; then later on you and I could have that dinner you promised me. What about it?"

She looked away as her guard began to rise. "No, this isn't a good weekend for me."

"Why?" he asked. "What can you possibly be doing around here that's so important that you can't spare one afternoon away for the chance to go into the city and do something spontaneous and different?"

Sela didn't appreciate his arrogance and allowed a window of opportunity to slam shut when she exhibited a little self-righteousness of her own. "For your information, there's plenty to do around here."

"Like what?" he persisted.

"Lots of things," she bluffed, before redirecting blame. "You know, you're beginning to sound like a snob when you talk about Fairlight. What makes you think you're the only one around here with a life?"

He stood up. "Fine."

"Fine." Mimicking him was childish, but it was all she could think to do at the moment.

"I just thought I'd ask, that's all." He slid his hands into his pockets. "I didn't mean to imply that anything was wrong with your life around here, and I sure didn't intend to pry."

His attempt at an apology immediately softened her. "So, when will you leave?"

"You don't have to act like you care." It was a matter-of-fact statement that held no malice. He strode across the room and returned down the stairs to his office.

Well, Sela thought haughtily, *so much for his apology, if it had ever been one.* For the life of her, she couldn't figure out what had just happened. Whatever it was, it had quickly undone the wealth of emotions she'd savored earlier simply by being with Ben, a pleasure she hadn't experienced in a long time.

The idea that she had blithely welcomed the sensations in the first place chilled her. And, as she sat up on the sofa, it became clear to her that she shouldn't warm to the man too much. She knew that would be for the better.

Deep in thought, she mutely stared at the flickering television screen as another, more physical chill draped her shoulders, and caused her to shudder. Mabel Thornton may be crude, but she had a point. What right did she, Sela, have to draw tragedy back into Fairlight?

Hunter's Pond glistened from the moonlight. Parked along the bank, and still sitting behind his wheel, Frisco sank his teeth into a thick drumstick he'd brought with him from the church. He knew the area well and often sat out here, unnoticed, among the lusty county teenagers. The water was Frisco's quiet messenger, and often talked to him, showing him the error of his ways as well as the correct paths he had followed. That's what he waited for now. Another sign.

Nothing like mixing it up with folks once in a while to

keep up on what's going on, he mused. *That is, until the outsider came up and shook hands with everybody.*

What did he do that for? Frisco took a vicious bite out of the chicken as his thoughts ran helter-skelter. Couldn't the man see the cat was out of the bag and he was on notice? *Maybe not,* he thought. *Pretty boys never think their vices catch up with them. They're used to taking what they want, then running from the responsibility.* Not on his watch, though. This time, if the stranger wanted to dance to the music, he'd have to pay the piper. Frisco rubbed at the nervous tic near his eye and smiled.

He took another bite off the drumstick and looked out at the dark water as he waited for his sign.

When Sela rose the next morning, she wanted to make amends with Ben and looked forward to breakfast with him. Unfortunately, Fontella quickly informed her that Ben had left almost an hour earlier. Spurred by the early morning disappointment, Sela went through her daily regimen at the house in a record whirl, topping it off with a visit to Vanessa's and a volunteer stint at the library with Ophelia. When she finally returned home for dinner in the closing shadows of the day, she expected that Ben would have returned, too, but it wasn't to be.

Late that night, after she had retired to her own room, she heard his car drive up. When the front door opened, Sela lay back across her bed and decided against greeting him. It was obvious that he had wanted to avoid her, and she'd grant him his wish. After all, hadn't she done the very same thing only the day before? *Be careful what you wish for,* she reminded herself. She turned onto her belly to suffocate the thuds from her heart.

When Ben entered the darkened house, he knew Sela had retired. As he passed the hallway that led to her room, the break in his stride was slight, but it was a pause nonetheless. He had been so sure she enjoyed his company and would agree to ride up to Atlanta with him, that when she gave him the brush-off, it had taken him totally by surprise, and was a blow to his pride.

What was he thinking, anyway, when he even considered making a move on his landlord's niece? Simple. He'd misread her signals. Granted, she was no pushover, and she'd made her feelings known, so he wouldn't trespass again. Seeing as little of her as possible was what he needed. Anyway, that's what he got for breaking his own rules.

He took the stairs two at a time, swinging the bulging briefcase and camera by his side in the process. Once he reached his bedroom, everything was tossed to the bed while he removed his jacket.

Ben had spent most of the day climbing around the interior woodwork at the church to get a better look at its underlying structure, and to take numerous difficult photographs. Tomorrow would be more of the same. As for now, he only craved a shower. That and another long day of crawling through the church building should keep Sela out of his sight and off his mind. He dropped to the bed and began to remove his clothes.

Thirteen

"I sure wanted to meet your Sela this trip," Mont said.

Ben frowned as he placed his fork on his finished plate, and looked across the table at his fashionably attired brother. Though six years separated them, it was easy to recognize that they were related.

"She's not mine," he stressed. "Anyway, she had something else to do."

Mont leaned his arms on the table as he seemed to warm to the subject his brother had shown a reticence to discuss over lunch. "Well, tell me something about her, like, is she hot?"

Ben grimaced in good humor. He knew his brother would eventually reduce everything to the physical. So, reluctantly, he nodded his head and smiled in agreement.

"Actually, she is."

"I knew it, I knew it," Mont crowed at the admission. "You know, if her family can read minds, maybe Sela's been reading yours." He laughed. "For your sake, I hope that's not true."

"Only the aunt is psychic, and don't call it mind-reading around Sela. If you ever meet her, you'll know why."

"All I can say is she must be something for you

to put up with all this drama." Mont shook his head. "I mean, you're already cut off from real civilization; then you got psychics, nosy neighbors—"

"I didn't tell you about the dog who's got a thing for Italian leather," Ben added.

"What?"

"Don't ask," Ben said with a grin. "Even with all that, the place is beginning to grow on me."

"By the look on your face, she's what's growing on you, man, and I don't think you were too happy with her decision not to come. Could be somebody else is in her picture."

"I don't think so, but I'm just a tenant, that's all." Ben's eyes stabbed caution at his brother to drop the subject.

Mont held his hands up defensively. "I'm only following your lead, that's all. Course, I can always find some free time and see you down there. Hey, I could be more her type. If not, maybe I can hook up with another farmer's daughter."

Ben gave up and shook his head at Mont's humor. As he looked around, he noticed how the trendy airport restaurant's Saturday afternoon lunch crowd had increased, so he glanced at his watch. Mont still had an hour before his flight left.

"Shouldn't you be boning up on your notes for this business trip, instead of instigating rumors to circulate back home?" Ben suggested. "I don't need that."

"You know what I think? You need to chill out with some serious R and R and a dose of female companionship." He leaned forward on his elbow toward Ben. "Take a look at the table two rows over."

Ben took the bait and followed his brother's directions. The woman was, indeed, attractive, and to his brother's taste.

"The sister's been eyeing us since we sat down," Mont said.

True enough, she now made leisurely eye contact with Ben and smiled.

"Bingo," Mont gloated smoothly. "Just what the doctor ordered."

Ben waved off the comment with a grin. "I need that even less."

"Well, if you won't go there, why don't you come down to Miami with me? You need a break, my man, not more work."

Ben grunted at his brother's interference. "Has Mom or Dad said anything else to you about me coming into the company as a partner?"

"Mom's okay since you called her the other day and talked. She's filled Dad in and told him to stay out of your decision. But, you know Mom. She expects we can manage our own lives by now without them."

"Good." He took a long swallow of water just as the waiter walked up to present the check.

"Remember, this is my treat," Mont said as he reached for the check. "It's the least Dad can do for us." He glanced at the bill before he looked up, and asked, "You got a pen?"

"Sure." Ben reached into his inside coat pocket and produced one, handing it over to Mont. Something else shared the pocket, too, and he now fished it out. He looked at the small white business card emblazoned with a name and a car rental business. Sherita Taylor. He'd all but forgotten about the card handed to him the week before.

"What's that?" Mont asked.

Ben turned the card over in his hand as he remembered the friendly, dimple-faced rental car agent. Mont's advice may not be so bad after all . . .

female companionship. What an idea—spend time with a woman who wanted to be with him.

"Maybe it's my ticket to that R and R you suggested," Ben replied with a wry twist of his mouth, and replaced the card in his pocket. "I can always find out."

The phone's shrill ring sounded for the third time before Sela fumbled across the dark bed for it.

"Hello."

"Well, my beauty, what are you doing home on a Saturday night?"

Instantly awakened by the crisp, articulate voice, Sela's eyes stretched wide. "Auntie," she exclaimed, and rolled to sit up in the bed. "I've been waiting for you to call," she said in a voice filled with affection.

"How are you, dear? I've missed you."

"I'm fine, and I'm missing you, too. I'm sorry I lost my temper last time we talked. I really didn't mean it."

"I know that. And, in the future I promise not to be so intrusive with my advice."

Sela was amused by her aunt's pledge. "That brings us to your friend you sent here. Auntie, we need to talk."

"And how are you getting along with Ben? Is he around?"

"No, he's the one out on Saturday night. But, how could you do this, send someone here and not tell me about it? I was embarrassed to be the last to know."

"But, Sela, my letters—"

"You knew would go unread after our little tiff."

Sighing, she smiled. "Don't you think we're too old now to play these games, Auntie?"

"Probably," she admitted. "He's a nice young man with a really good heart, don't you think? And, I wanted to help him with his project. It fit right in, and to a T, with the town and church."

"Okay, okay, Auntie, but—"

"Sela," she interrupted. "For us to bump into each other the way we did, and in another country, was quite extraordinary."

"What made you read his fortune?"

"Ah, that. He had sad eyes the first time I met him and I wanted to make him smile. And I did . . . with the tarot cards." She paused. "That's when I decided to hug him."

The hug was a transfer process her aunt employed when she wished to "see" an emotion, or a consciousness, in an individual. The sight could materialize in many ways, which only her aunt, through experience, could interpret. A highly effective gift, it was less useful on someone with whom Aunt Claire shared an emotional bond.

"Sela, are you still there?"

Her heart quickened with the fear of knowledge. So, she had used her gift to see into Ben. "And what did you learn, Auntie?"

"I can only compare it to a splash of water in the face. For a moment, nothing was recognizable; everything had a different face, a tainted meaning. Nothing was as it appeared."

"Did you see any kind of danger for him?"

"It wasn't danger, it was more family honor, still fresh, so he questions his worthiness in the present." She drew in an audible breath. "Overall, I would call it a favorable hug. When I learned his occupation and told him about Fairlight, it all worked out, like the finger of fate."

Mercy, Sela thought. It was hard to interpret Auntie's spoken impressions, especially if she was being deliberately oblique, like now. What had she omitted? Sela wondered.

"Auntie, when was the last time you left anything to chance? Tell me you didn't have ulterior motives with his invitation."

"You know how strongly I believe in fate."

"Only when you give it a hand." She rubbed at her sleepy eyes. "I love you, but don't forget I know you, too. You don't perform hugs with just anyone. On the contrary, you don't even like to do it anymore."

"Sela, he's a well-traveled young man and I sensed in him a bit of a need to settle down. Look at how he jumped at the opportunity to stay in one place for the summer, and from a total stranger."

"Does this have anything to do with me?"

"You, my beauty, are restless. Don't you think I've noticed it? You need the chance to interact with someone who can tell you about the world outside of Fairlight, someone your age. He, on the other hand, needs the peace and stability you and our town can bring. The two of you can only help each other's spirit."

Sela gnashed her teeth. Hadn't Auntie just promised not to interfere? "You have it all figured out."

"And all you have to do is give it a try," Claire replied.

"Is that why you didn't tell him about me? It was better that we both get surprised?"

"Let's not argue, Sela, especially since we just professed forgiveness of the other only a few minutes ago."

Sela repinned her loose braid and grunted at her aunt's words.

"Also, I think it was best that you discover your similar link with Ben on your own."

"Auntie—" Sela tried to explain things from a different point of view. "He's nice enough, but there's more to consider here."

"Reverend Osborne tells me you two are getting along fine. You were both at the Wednesday supper."

"Yes . . ."

"But what?"

"His stay at the inn has started gossip." She filled in her aunt about Ben's run-in with various citizens. "The only people totally thrilled are Reverend Osborne and Fontella."

"I thought that might happen, but you can weather a few small minds."

"You know how I feel about the past—"

"Sela, there's no closing off your feelings. Use your instincts, listen to your heart, and the right one, your future, will come along."

She squeezed her eyes tight as she thought about it. "I'm not so sure anymore."

"Trust me—you do well by not living in the shadows. I would never allow anything that brings harm and ill will to enter our door. I promised Helena." Her voice dropped to an even tone. "I tried, and I couldn't protect her, but I swear that won't happen to you."

Sela bit her lip. She didn't like it when Aunt Claire spoke wistfully of their buried past. She swiftly changed the subject and, in the process, the mood.

"So, tell me where you are this week. From your postcards, I know it's somewhere in the Alaskan wilderness."

"First, I want to hear about those boys of Vanessa's."

Sela scrambled onto her knees in the middle of the bed. "You won't believe how much they've grown since you left."

They continued for a time with the light conversation about the goings-on in Fairlight. But they knew this process of familiarity was a shield to protect each other from all the things that go wrong when fate takes control. Lifting each other—it had always been their way.

Arranging the last-minute date with a delightful and eager Sherita had been easy for Ben; but, while she had only been too happy to accommodate him for dinner during the weekend, it hadn't been as easy as he'd thought to become the carefree suitor she expected.

Now that dinner was over at the restaurant she had chosen, and they had arrived back at her home, all he could think about was his return to the country town where he'd spent the last week and where he could strike up a hearty disagreement with Sela.

"I think your mind is miles away," Sherita said as he helped her from his car.

"At least a hundred," he answered honestly. It was clear the little red number she wore was meant to keep his thoughts on her rounded charms. "That's where my work project is located. I've got to return there soon."

"A girl could be insulted by that, Ben."

"You're right," he conceded as they walked up the steps to the front door. "You're a lovely woman, Sherita, and tonight you deserved a more attentive date."

When they stopped at the door, she reached up and stroked Ben's jaw. "I had a nice time, but you're the visitor and it was my job to show you a good time, too. I failed," she said simply.

He didn't want her to feel guilty, so he smiled. "No, I did. I have too much on my mind today." He took her hand, still against his face, and brought it down. "Why don't we do this again sometime? When I get another free weekend, can I call?"

As she inserted the key into the door of the apartment, she raised her eyes to Ben. "If you don't have to return tonight, that still leaves us the rest of the evening." The suggestion hung in the air like frothy cotton candy. "Why don't you come in for a nightcap?"

At that moment, Ben juggled the devil that was carefree Mont on one shoulder, and an angel in the guise of practical Sela on the other. While one egged him on, the other derided the very idea. And he, the man in the middle, could only satisfy one. He blinked to clear his thoughts beneath a cloud of spun sugar that had already begun its descent over him.

Sela was asleep when a series of knocks sounded at her bedroom door.

She sat straight up on the bed, not yet fully awake, and answered automatically. "Yes?"

"Sela, it's me, Ben."

Ben? He was back. "Just a moment." Leaping from the bed, she slipped her robe on and tied the belt, all in one motion, before she walked to the door and leaned against it. "Is something wrong?"

"Can I talk to you for a minute?"

She tucked a strand of hair behind her ear before

she flicked on the light. It was late, past midnight, so what could he want? She smoothed back her braid and slowly opened the door.

Ben leaned against the opposite wall. His dark suit hung open in a casual slant over a dress shirt with no tie. He held something in his hands.

"You want to go in the living room?" he asked.

"Sure," Sela answered and let him lead. "What's so important?" she asked when they got there.

When he turned to her, she saw that he held a white plastic box with a well-known bakery's logo on the top. Sela's arms were crossed and held defensively against her chest as she walked up to him. "Well?"

"I brought something back from Atlanta."

She took the box from his hand and peeked inside. A colorful slice of fruit torte sat nestled against a generous helping of cheesecake drizzled with dark chocolate.

"You woke me up for dessert?"

"Yep." He smiled as he produced two plastic forks.

"Ben." She looked from the dessert to him. "You've lost your mind. What time is it?"

"Almost two-thirty."

She strained her eyes at him. "In the morning?"

He nodded and indicated she should sit down. She set the box on the table before she curled her leg beneath her on the sofa. He joined her and set the forks and napkins next to the box in front of them. "We'd better eat it now. It's been traveling in the car for a couple of hours."

She looked at him curiously. "You're serious, aren't you? All right." She reached for one of the forks and scooped up a piece of the cheesecake. "So, why didn't you just stay in Atlanta tonight?"

The creamy concoction was still cool, and she let it savor for a moment in her warm mouth.

Ben looked at the expression on Sela's face and grinned. "I knew you'd like it."

She swallowed before she reached for more. "You didn't answer me."

"There was nothing in Atlanta to keep me, so I came back." He picked up the other fork and sliced from the torte. "And this is my way of apologizing for being rude before I left." He looked up at her before he continued. "When you get to know me, you'll find I'm pretty straightforward about most things. But, I did misread your signals."

While he chewed on the fruit, Sela almost choked on the cheesecake, her dark eyebrows slanted in suspicion. "What are you talking about?"

"That you were interested. In me, that is. I don't think there's any doubt that I'm interested in you. Even my brother recognized it. I admit it rubbed me the wrong way when you refused to go with me to Atlanta." He ate more of the torte, watching Sela all the while. "But, I'm over it."

Self-conscious from his stare, she busied herself and scooped up more of the cheesecake. "And your point is what?"

He smiled at her while he placed the fork on the table and turned to her, his arm now stretched across the back of the sofa, and within reach of her neck. "That I've declared myself. The next move, I believe, is up to you."

She was surprised at his open words, and had become giddily distracted by his romantic notions. She ate more of the cheesecake as she tried to reclaim her poise, though his proximity, along with his aftershave's tantalizing smell, didn't help matters.

"First of all, you got it all wrong about signals,"

she said. "There's no truth there because I would never allow myself to get involved with you."

"I see."

She thought she caught a glimpse of pleasure in his eyes, as though he enjoyed her struggle to explain things away. "No, you don't. I don't get involved. Ever."

"All right. That makes it clearer," he said. "Any reason?"

She was keen on his sarcasm and frowned. It had seemed a simple vow when she made it years ago; but without enlightening him on its meaning, her words would sound preposterous.

"Relationships don't work for me." She reached for more cheesecake and felt his stare follow her. "So, I've given up on them."

"Well, how will you know when the right one comes along?"

His almost identical quote of Aunt Claire's earlier warning rocked in her head. The piece of cheesecake teetering on the edge of the fork she held aloft slipped over the side and into the cleavage formed by her robe.

To stop the chocolate-tinged dessert's tumble, which had trailed to her left breast, Ben quickly grabbed up a napkin and pressed it to her skin.

Sela's breath caught in her lungs, and she grabbed his hand to halt its further movement. "I can handle it."

He stopped, but his gaze swept her face. "Am I reading you right this time, Sela? We can be friends, but leave it at that?"

She stared back at him, conscious of his fingers, cool and smooth, above her thumping heart. "I . . . I believe so," she said.

As Ben leaned into Sela, she still didn't suspect

his intent; then his mouth, feather light, touched hers in intimate persuasion. Her eyes closed as she succumbed to the heady sensation. She didn't think, but parted her lips and raised her face to meet him fully.

When Ben pulled back, Sela was slow to open her eyes, only to find his stare pinned to her, his brows narrowed. At the same time, his hand moved recklessly to her neck, his fingers warm as they began a rhythmic stroke there. Before she could focus, and clear her head, she fell back against the sofa, and he followed her. But this time his lips parted hers.

As her mouth softened under his seductive assault, she tried to hold on to her drifting sanity. Her hands, caught between their bodies, pressed into his hard chest.

What am I doing? While she asked herself the question, she met the rhythm of his lips on hers, and gave herself freely to the passionate kiss. Just this once.

And then, it was over. Too quickly. He sat back with a deep sigh as Sela's eyes fluttered open and she sank into the cushioned sofa. Her hand flew up to her mouth, still moist from his kiss. She could see that his was, too.

"I've wanted to do that for longer than you probably think," he said, and pushed farther away from her. "But now that we're past it and have gotten it out of our system, we can go on and become friends, like you said." He didn't wait for her response, but stood and grabbed up the box and forks.

"Good night, Sela." He gave her a brief nod before he walked briskly across the room, and out of her view.

It was all happening so fast. She could hardly lift

her voice above a whisper as, drained and left to puzzle over what she had done, she belatedly wished him the same.

Fourteen

After almost two weeks, the kiss remained an unresolved barrier between Ben and Sela. He had begun to suspect she preferred it that way. Even on the occasional breakfast when they had appeared at the same time, Sela had been polite, but always seemed to find a reason to leave.

And, so it went. The weekdays flew by as Ben threw himself into the analysis of the church's architecture. The small town weekends were a different matter. There wasn't much to do if you ruled out helping with the Fourth of July parade decorations—except to contemplate the enigma he'd become attracted to named Sela. Even though she made herself scarce, they did manage to arrive for Sunday church services together, to the delight of Reverend Osborne, the twins, and what seemed like most of the congregation. Never mind that they were crammed together when the twins chose to sit on either side of them on the already crowded pew. It was a fate Ben gamely accepted, though Sela would wear a pained look the entire time.

Ben had mulled over things time and again. He wasn't sure what he had expected in the aftermath of their intimacy, but he knew it wasn't her continued indifference, especially when her true attitude had slipped through that night—if only for a moment. In that significant moment, she had wanted him every bit as much as he'd wanted her. When he had glimpsed the passion that lined her eyes, and when her mouth opened under his, it had been easy enough to figure out. He wouldn't seduce her, though—not until she acknowledged that she wanted him equally. Until then, he was content to let her stew.

He shook off the steady stream of thoughts and stretched from his cramped position inside the church wall. To Ben's chagrin, it seemed his pointed suggestion to Sela that night—that they could now become friends—might actually happen. He smiled broadly. Friendship was hardly the first thing he wanted to explore on that woman.

Even before he read his watch by the light from the octagonal window set in the wall, he knew it was turning late. The sun had begun to settle in the western sky, and the church's Saturday evening activities had quieted down until all ancillary sounds were nonexistent.

The space behind the wall where Ben stood was less than two feet wide. He shifted his shoulders in the confined, dusty space and grabbed his set of blueprints. He then followed the long corridor that would lead him back to the church basement where he had started out from.

The large, spacious church was a mix of old and new construction with a maze of passages and dead ends that surrounded the main sanctuary. It sported a number of hidden walkways like this one, which ran along the outer wall, and which could be accessed from one of many doors camouflaged by the church's decor. The trick was in discerning their disguise.

Ben had learned that the best way to reveal an unmarked passage was to overlay successive blueprints. Unnamed spaces invariably turned out to be hidden rooms and halls. While some of the crawl spaces were results of expansion, where doorways and alcoves had been sealed over, others had been created and maintained to allow access to out-of-the-way locations in the church, like the steeple tower and the basement. Still others were the simple results of attempts at concealing poor plans. For a building with a history that spanned a hundred and fifty years, all of the reasons were valid.

As Ben navigated to the end of the wall, he heard a noise—sort of a muffled and repeated thump. It echoed from somewhere ahead of him. Surprised that anyone else was still around, he stepped onto the sharply angled steps that led to the lower-level basement door, his way out of the wall passage. He checked to make sure his flashlight was handy, and then moved on, confident in the knowledge that, based on the spiderwebs and dust levels in the passage, he was the only person who had walked these old walls for some time.

When he stepped off the bottom stair, he moved to the red oak door ahead and turned its worn, gray metal knob. It moved only slightly before Ben tried again. The door was stuck. Or locked.

Ben was sure he had left it unlocked when he entered through it earlier to explore the wall cavities. He pushed against the jamb now with his shoulder.

"Hello?" he called out, and hit the door. No answer. "Hello?"

The door wouldn't budge, and no one answered his call. He slammed his fist against it. This was one for the books, getting locked in a wall. Ben sighed as he leaned against the door and unrolled the floor plans. He trained the flashlight on the blueprints, one at a time, until he found one that contained this hallway. And, just as he suspected, there was no other opening marked for exit. The passage simply ended at the wall on the other end of the hall where he'd just left.

Ben let out a deep sigh and tuned the flashlight to the corners in the murky shadows. Luckily he wasn't claustrophobic. Otherwise, this could really be hell. For now, it was simply an inconvenience.

Thump.

Ben stiffened. That noise again, and this time he was sure it was coming from the other side of the door.

"Hello, is anybody in there?" he shouted as he hit the door. "Can you open this door? Hello?" No answer. Was someone in there or not? And, if so, was this their idea of some sort of silly game? He listened for more sounds, but heard none.

Ben decided to retrace his way back up the stairs to the main level where he might be able to find a hidden door in the wall. It was either that or sit here until church services tomorrow morning, then hope someone would hear him through the thick walls.

As he walked along the corridor, he flashed the light across the walls in the hope that a latch, an uneven board—something—would signal an exit. By the time he reached the small, decorative window again, he'd had no success, and he peered through its double glass.

He had a clear view of the sanctuary's side yard and the Life Center next to it. It was dusk, and this part of the building was on the edge of the floodlight's coverage. So, all he could discern was the outline of shrubbery settled in with the shadows to his right, and the parking lot's periphery to his left.

At first, he couldn't see much in the faint light, but gradually, his eyes grew accustomed to the dark. It was then that he made out a figure as it moved away from the church and across the wide expanse of lawn. The path taken was one used often by parishioners to cut to the parking lot from the basement and the rear of the sanctuary.

But, the figure didn't move to the left for the parking lot. Ben flicked the flashlight on and off at the window as a signal, but the fast-fading figure never looked back. It took on the movement of a dark tumbleweed that steadily drifted farther away, to the right, until it disappeared into the distant field.

Ben was puzzled. Frustrated by his efforts, he returned his attention to the walls ahead of him and, setting the flashlight on the floor, began to search in earnest for a way out. Almost immediately, his keen eye spied the uneven floor molding. He kicked it, and realized it was loose. He kneeled down and set to work.

Sela did prefer that the matter of the kiss remain unresolved—at least for now. That evening two weeks earlier had clearly tapped into emotions best left buried and the ensuing time had given her a chance to sort through them. She had not intended to fall under the spell of romance again and couldn't figure out what had come over her.

When Ben entered a room, a vaguely sensuous spark would pass between them. Granted, it had been a long time since she'd been kissed so thoroughly, and by someone who, admittedly, attracted her. The thought of it had the power to make her, literally, squirm.

Sela twisted uncomfortably on her bar stool pulled up to the kitchen counter in the inn.

"What's wrong with you?" Vanessa asked. Standing next to Sela, she looked up from the bowl of cookie dough she stirred and smiled. "I haven't seen you twitch like that since last summer in the park when you sat in those ants."

Sela snatched her head around, guilty about the drift of her thoughts. "I'm thinking about something, that's all." She grabbed a cookie from the plate and began to nibble.

"Let's see, now. Is it about six-three with a killer smile?"

"It's about what I'm getting myself into when he's around."

"I've already told you," she reminded Sela. "You won't get any answers until you commit yourself first."

"And what do you think our kissing each other meant?" she asked sarcastically.

"It only counts if it was a really good one." Vanessa glanced at her and grinned. "Well, was it?"

Sela remembered and the answer was reflected in her smile as she fidgeted in the chair again.

Vanessa laughed as she dropped the spoon and turned to Sela. "Listen, the man's interested, so why don't you find out if something's there? This avoiding him at every chance isn't you. I mean, maybe all you two have is a simple case of—"

"Lust?" Sela finished for her.

"It's not unheard of, you know. Of course, I don't think you'll jump into a one-night stand."

She snorted. "Maybe that's what I should have done before. Plain old sex was never my problem.

It's only when there's a relationship attached that I seem to get in trouble."

"Sela." Vanessa dropped her hands to her hips as her tone became serious. "I hate when you talk like that. If you give yourself a chance to start over, for heaven's sake, you'll see that what happened before was just a horrible fluke, a bad turn in fortune."

"Wrong. What happens to Ben if I'm right and we act on our feelings? The accidents, that's what. I'm cursed, my whole family seems to be, and you know it." She smoothed her hands down her face, muffling her next words. "Everybody knows it."

Vanessa heard her. "That's not true," she insisted, and returned to the cookie dough. "It's more like everybody's rooting for you to beat that rap and be happy for a change."

"They're waiting to witness another train wreck."

"Would you stop talking like that? And, Mrs. Thornton's not the entire town." She spooned batter onto the cookie sheet. "You know, Miss Claire called us the other night, and she asked about you and Ben." At Sela's frown, she added, "She's just worried, that's all. She wants you to spread your wings outside of Fairlight, and she knows Ben can help you do that."

Sela let out a deep sigh. "I hate to disappoint her, but the sooner Aunt Claire and you and everybody understand that I'm going to be here for a long time, just like Auntie and my mother, the better we'll all be."

"You know you re only hiding out here, and it doesn't have to be that way—"

The doorbell sounded, only to be followed by three more rings in quick succession. Almost at once, they heard the door open and twin voices chatter.

Sela straightened up. "Ron and the boys are back."

"Hey, where's everybody?" Ron called out as he trailed Brett and Brian into the kitchen. Walking up behind Vanessa, he swung his arms around her protruding middle and nuzzled her neck. "How's my favorite pregnant woman today?"

Brett and Brian made a beeline for the batch of cookies next to Sela just as Vanessa sounded her warning at them.

"They're for dessert, guys."

Even as she saw Vanessa's grimace, Sela held the dish out for them. They each grabbed a couple as their eyes stretched wide in delight.

The boys were Sela's personal godsend, and she enjoyed spoiling them. Ever since their birth, they had been her sanity amidst the craziness foisted on her by fate. She believed they acted as a grounding force in her life, since she would most likely never have children of her own. Vanessa seemed to understand the connection and allowed her as much time to coddle and spend with the boys as Sela could stand.

Tonight would be one of those nights. Sela had agreed to baby-sit the boys at her house while Vanessa and Ron spent a little time together over dinner.

"If you two are ready to leave, I can finish up the cookies, Vanessa." She looked away from the boys and saw that her friends were whispering. "Anything wrong?" she inquired.

Ron raised his head. "Where's Ben?"

Sela hunched her shoulders in disinterest. "I don't know. I guess he's still at the church doing his research. Reverend Osborne says he loves rummaging about in that big old place. Why?"

"Well, it's Saturday night, and no one's at the church, so I figured he'd want to do a little something with you, like maybe go out. Vanessa says you're baby-sitting for us, though."

Sela smiled and nodded to the boys, who were busy comparing cookie pieces. "I already have two dates, right, fellas?" She turned back to Ron and lifted her brow. "And, what makes you think he wants to go out with me? He's just as liable to go back to Atlanta and do his carousing."

He nuzzled Vanessa's neck again. "Why is she so touchy tonight, baby?" A devilish grin split his face as he said, "Oh, I know. You're still mad at him 'cause you didn't take him up on his last invitation, and then he left for Atlanta without telling you."

"I am not," Sela declared. "I don't care what he does. He's barely around here, anyway."

"And whose fault is that?" Ron asked.

Incredulous, Sela looked at her friends. "What are you talking about?"

"The man's been interested in you since the first day he showed up, but you keep sidestepping."

"So now it's my fault if I'm not interested in somebody?"

"You know I would have been the first one to tell him to back off if I believed that."

Taken aback by Ron's candid comment, she looked to Vanessa for support. "I . . . I don't even know him, so I'm definitely not interested in him." When neither said anything, she began to clean up the counter and dug in with her denial. "I'm not."

"She's not interested," Brett said to no one in particular.

Brian mumbled his agreement, too, as both twins

continued to show more interest in the chocolate chips embedded in their cookies.

"I told you, big ears," Vanessa whispered, and moved out of her husband's arms. "Come on, guys, let's get washed up." To Ron, she said, "We can leave in just a minute, okay?"

"Sure," he said. When Vanessa left, he leaned on the island next to Sela. "Why don't you admit the man's got you hummin'?"

The warmth of a blush filled Sela's face, but she still boldly faced down her friend. "He's done no such thing. You know me better than that. I mean, I can't remember the last time somebody really got me going that way."

"I do. It was Charles."

The smile slowly drained from Sela's face. "Ron, you're my friend. Why are you saying these things?"

"Because somebody needs to." He stood away from the island and motioned to her. "Come here, Sela."

They came together and hugged. Sela ultimately slumped against him, wanting the support. "For some reason, I'm a little sensitive this evening. I know you didn't mean anything by it."

"You're the closest thing I have to a sister," he said. "And I love you. But, I also know you and I'm gonna call things the way I see them. You deserve that." He set her away from him. "Now, I think you're unhappy and preoccupied by something. I don't think you've been happy for a while, and Vanessa's noticed it, too."

Sela turned her face away, not thrilled at his insight but he gently tilted it back to him.

"Maybe it's time to shake things up," Ron added. When she started to protest, he laid a finger to his lips. "Hey, I won't say anything else, but think about it."

She nodded. "All right. And I promise to work on getting happy real quick."

"In that case, you can start now. Come to the diner with us."

"But I promised to look after the boys."

"Not anymore," he said. "Fontella is our backup. Worst case, we'll take the kids with us. But, I don't think you should sit home tonight. We'll have fun . . . listen to some jukebox music, dance a little, pick up on the latest gossip, what do you say?"

"Hmm . . . maybe I will go with you." She smiled, then nodded at her decision. "Okay, but I have to run to my room and change first, and you can finish cleaning up our cookie mess." She started across the kitchen just as Vanessa returned.

"Take your time," Ron called out. "I want to use your phone before we go," he said.

She waved her okay from the door, and heard Vanessa's low spoken question to Ron.

"Did you manage to get her to come with us?"

Sela didn't break her stride, but continued on with a smile, the couple's earlier private whispers now clear. Warmed by their concern, she felt good and decided to change into something fun . . . and feminine. Yes, that's exactly what she'd do.

The diner was simply and aptly named The Diner, and was located in a two-block area loosely referred to as downtown. The owner, Wally Rutherford, was Fontella's brother. He offered three meals a day, six days a week, and a buffet on Sunday. In a small town like Fairlight, where family dinners were still a staple, a night out meant plans for The Diner.

Wally whipped out the white linen for the dinner and buffet meal, complete with the obligatory cloth flower and candle in the middle. Each meal could become as intimate or as exposed as the diner chose, with a jukebox nearby and space for dancing if the mood hit you. And Wally made it his business to encourage everyone to enjoy their visit. If the jukebox fell quiet, he would have it crooning again in no time, courtesy of the management.

Sela leaned on the table and rubbed her arms, bared by the sleeveless short dress she wore. They had only been seated for about ten minutes, having detoured to Fontella's to drop off the boys, and were now a part of the late wave of diners. Only a few other tables were taken so far—by teenagers, probably on a date, and a couple of families.

"Why does Wally hike up the air-conditioning?" Sela asked as she fiddled with the locket that hung from her neck.

"Some of us are hot-blooded in the summer," Ron laughed. He leaned over and nuzzled Vanessa. "You know what I mean?"

Sela rolled her eyes at the playful couple. "Yeah, and I see where it's gotten you. It must be a year-round thing since your babies seem to be born in the summer," she said, referring to Vanessa's belly. She loved to see them enjoy each other, and secretly yearned for the same herself. She sat back against the chair just as Vanessa's eyes trained on a point beyond Sela. Ron stood from his chair and stepped out, his attention taken, as well.

"Hey, man," Ron said. "Glad you could make it." He stretched his hand out in greeting as the man approached their table.

Somehow, Sela's heart knew who it was, and had already begun its thump, but she managed to follow

Ron's gaze, turning in her chair with her head strained up as the familiar, smooth baritone filled the air.

"Sela, I didn't know you'd be here."

She swallowed a hard lump before she met Ben's dark gaze straight on—a gaze that, before her eyes, softened into a caress. "Then we're both surprised."

Fifteen

"Come on and sit down with us," Ron offered as he shook hands with Ben, who then came around the table and pulled out the chair next to Sela.

Giving Vanessa a quick frown, Sela made room for Ben at the table as everyone settled down again. "When did you invite him here?"

"I got him on his cell," Ron explained pleasantly. "I think you were changing at the time." He took a sip from his water glass and eyed Sela from over the top, and dared her to complain. "We all promised we'd get together, so why not tonight?"

"Why not?" Sela echoed, sure that she had been blindsided. Despite her fears of what the evening had in store for her, she felt a hot and awful joy at his presence. He had come casually dressed in a light jacket and slacks, and looked every bit the forbidden fruit he represented.

Ben turned to her, interest bright in dark eyes that boldly raked over her. "I hope I didn't keep everyone waiting. I stopped by the house to change."

"No, we only arrived a while ago." Keenly aware that she was the object of his stare, she brushed her fingers across her gold locket nestled in the deep

V made by her collar. "We're also pretty casual around here. You were probably fine."

"After climbing through dusty church walls all evening, I needed to clean up a bit."

"Why were you doing that, for heaven's sake?" Vanessa asked.

"I told Ron what happened, but it's a long story that's not worth repeating, though I would like to know if there's anything in that field beyond the church."

"The cemetery," Sela said.

"Oh." Ben's brow rose in surprise. "Operated by the church?"

She nodded. "It's set way back on a little trail. The plots are mostly owned by family of the oldest members. You can get to it from the main street on the other side of the church."

"Or," Ron continued, "you can take the shortcut across the churchyard, like most of the members do."

While Ron and Vanessa discussed the menu, Sela turned to Ben. "If you'd like, I'll show it to you tomorrow."

He smiled at the offer. "I'd like."

Relaxing against his chair, Ben stretched his legs out, but they promptly collided with Sela's crossed ones.

"Oops," she muttered, and hastily drew her legs up.

"Sorry," he said.

Under his diligent eye, she uncrossed her legs and tugged at her short dress before she grasped her chair to slide over. However, Ben did the same thing. So, when their hands brushed with electric impact, it drew each other's attention. With only a moment's pause, they laughed with sincere amusement, the tension finally dissipated.

"Okay," Ron said, having watched them. "That ice y'all been storing up ought to be melted by now. Ben, let's get Wally to bring you something to drink before the two of you do any more damage to each other."

Sela looked across the table at Ron and, in spite of herself, smiled. "You're incorrigible. Ignore him, Ben. He just wants to be the center of attention, that's all."

Ben let his eyes roam her face. "That may be true, but for my money, I'd say you're beating him by a mile." He then gave her a devastating grin. "You look fantastic tonight."

"Thank you." Warmed by his steady gaze, Sela studiously unfolded her dinner napkin into her lap before she glanced up at her friends.

"When will you tell her about us?"

Claire selected two bottles of juice from the bar and returned to the bedroom where the heavy male voice with the clipped accent had come from.

"I don't know." She spoke from the door before she moved to the rumpled bed and looked warmly at Edward Powell as he sat casually against the overstuffed pillows.

Claire wore his gift, a long silk robe to cover her nakedness, and now caught its fullness up in her hand so she could perch on the edge of the bed.

"Are you angry because I continue to put it off?" she asked.

"Of course not." He accepted the juice she handed him. "That's a decision you have to make." Like Claire, Edward also wore only a robe.

"She won't admit it, but she's fragile, you know." She reached for his hand. "If she knew we wanted to get married, she would insist that she was just fine, and that I should get on with my life." When he squeezed her hand in understanding, she continued. "But, I can't accept your proposal to marry and move off to England with you and just leave her there."

"I know that," he said.

"I believe she'll find her way soon. But right now, she's been left too many times before."

He sighed. "I don't like the idea of you putting your life on hold, that's all."

"I know that I can't continue to presume you'll wait until my life rights itself."

"Claire, we've known each other now for five years, and we've planned our trips together for the last three. Are you having second thoughts about us?"

She shook her head. "I can't. You've become a part of my joy. But, so is my niece."

"I know. That's one of the reasons I love you. You have more compassion in your hand than some people have in their entire bodies." He set the juice on the nightstand before he raised her hand to his mouth. "This is a pretty powerful tool, you know." He kissed her palm.

She watched his dark, bowed head. "You don't think I'm a freak." It was a statement of fact.

He raised his head. "Never. And the fact that your abilities no longer work on me pleases me more than you know." His dark brown eyes crinkled with his smile. "It means we're emotionally bound."

She smiled, too. "I've always thought that little quirk was a good thing."

"Oh, I didn't tell you. I talked with Mr. Little from

his home in Texas. He asked me to tell you that, though their baby was premature, the little guy is doing fine."

A few weeks before, Claire had received a powerful vision through inadvertent physical contact with the junior officer, Mr. Little. It had concerned his pregnant wife, a fact of which Claire had no prior knowledge. Because of the serious nature of her premonition, she had cautiously shared it with him.

"I'm glad to hear that," she said. "Just don't mention my part to anyone, okay?"

"I don't see why you don't crow more about your abilities, Claire. In my home country, Senegal, you would be honored."

"When I'm quietly in the background, I'm in control"—her voice dropped—"and I can also interpret what I see without pressure of consequences. Otherwise"—her tone rose again—"I'd feel as if I were performing for a sideshow, like some crone attempting to get it all right for the audience's pennies."

"Hey, you're definitely no crone, and I should know." He rose up from the bed and came toward her. "In fact, I can confirm that you're one sultry handful."

Claire smiled. "Is that all I am to you?"

With that challenge, he playfully pulled her from the bed's edge, and into his embrace.

"Stop." She laughed as he drew her to him. "You're spilling my drink," she warned, but it had already splashed against her chest.

"Then I'll have to clean it up."

Her laughs and protests stopped when she found herself trapped underneath Edward.

"I love you." She managed to get the words out before his mouth covered hers.

"And I, you." He kissed her.

* * *

Dinner had been pleasant, with orders for Wally that ranged from the meat loaf special to grilled fish. All had gone well among the four of them, too, especially when Ben considered the simple fact that not once had Sela tried to disappear. As he watched her gracefully animated motions, he suspected she didn't realize she was stoking a gently growing fire that was laying to waste his "no seduction" plan.

Maybe it was because she had dropped the cautious and serious face she usually wore and allowed her more playful and inquisitive side to show. No way was she as staid as her severely pulled back hair would suggest. It was a carefully laid out guise she had perfected, but why? The more he learned, the more he wanted to know about this quietly private woman. Ron and Vanessa had turned out to be an unexpected source of information while they all waited for Wally's special dessert of the day, sweet potato pie garnished with whipped cream and pecans.

"I didn't know you've had your articles published in the *Atlanta Journal-Constitution.*" Ben gave Sela his full attention after Vanessa's revelation. "With their circulation, that's some accomplishment."

"The newspaper did a special series on education and youth in the rural counties. I was just a contributing writer for the piece, that's all."

"She's also had articles published in a few magazines," Vanessa continued.

"Have you ever considered exploring your journalism talent?"

"Ben, I'm blue in the face from telling her that. She's really good, but she won't follow it to its natural conclusion."

"Vanessa—" Sela's protest was interrupted.

"Oh, my God," Vanessa muttered to no one in particular, her attention snatched away. "Look at who just walked in."

As everyone's attention turned to the door, Ron spoke first.

"Luther and Rosalie. Now, that's a hoot. She's gonna drive your boy crazy with that mouth of hers before they get to order."

Vanessa punched him.

"I think they're kind of cute, and it's nice that they're out together," Sela said. "You think someone set them up?"

"Now, why would anyone in this town try to set somebody up?" Vanessa grinned.

"They do look comfortable together," Ben said as he joined in with an observation. "Maybe it's not arranged."

Luther's round face beamed as he escorted Rosalie to a table not too far from theirs. But, when he saw them, he and Rosalie turned in their direction.

Sela nudged Ben. "Are you enjoying your first gossip session?"

Ben thought back on their conversation and felt a rush of humility. "You're right, I'm guilty."

"Don't get all bent out of shape," she said. "I was just teasing. Anyway, we weren't being mean-spirited. Next time, don't be so judgmental about what you think only small town people do. You were just doing the same thing."

Ben started to grin. "I see my words are coming back to bite me. Okay, I promise to be more prudent with my words," he said, and turned as Luther came up to the table to shake hands.

"Ben, it's good seeing you again," he drawled.

"Same here," Ben replied.

"Glad to know you and Sela mended your fences."

He glanced over at Sela as she engaged in conversation with Vanessa and Rosalie before he responded. "We're getting there."

After everyone exchanged hellos, and the couple had returned to their own table, Vanessa spoke up.

"You know, Luther's so sweet. Charles was, too. In fact that whole family's charming."

"Who's Charles?" Ben asked the others at the table.

Ron coughed as he looked from Sela to Vanessa. "He was a young local around here, Luther's cousin."

"He was a boyfriend years ago," Sela offered.

"Oh." Ben looked between them. "I take it he's not around anymore?"

"No," she said.

When the table fell quiet, he knew he had come against another of Sela's private doors.

"Didn't Mrs. Thornton mention his name at the church the other night?" Ben asked.

Ron frowned. "She did?"

Vanessa began to rise from her chair. "Honey, why don't we get up and stretch our legs before we eat that dessert," she suggested.

"You want to dance now?" he asked.

"As long as you don't spin me around like you did last time."

"All right, then," Ron said, and stood from the table. "Come on, let's show everybody how to bust a move." He referred to the two teens who were dancing spiritedly near the jukebox. "Y'all should come on and join us, too," he said to Ben and Sela.

As her friends walked to the dance floor, Sela took a deep breath. She knew Ben well enough by now to know he had lots of questions, but it was still her call as to how much she'd reveal. When she turned back to him, his gaze was like a burn, and she flinched.

"What?" she asked.

"I got the distinct feeling they left to give us some privacy. I suspect it was so you could tell me about Charles."

"Why should I tell you about him, and what's it to you, anyway?"

Ben pushed his chair out from the table and turned so he could face her. He leaned forward and caught her hand in his.

"Because the other night you kissed me back; and no matter how much you try and avoid the subject, something happened between us." His head slowly inched toward her. "You can deny it, but I think if I were to kiss you right now, in here, you'd kiss me again."

Sela believe his threat, and looked around quickly. "Don't you dare do that," she whispered.

He smiled at her. "I think there's more to Charles's story and I'd like to learn more about you, so tell me, okay?"

Sela pulled her hand from his. "All right, what do you want to know?"

"Were you two, you know, serious?"

Sela smiled vacantly. "You could say that. We were almost engaged."

His brows drew together in a thoughtful frown. "How long ago did this happen?"

The memory of that afternoon in her room of saints swirled around her, and threatened to make her dizzy. "About three years ago."

"I remember you saying relationships didn't work for you. Is this why? You're not over your breakup?"

"Do we ever really get over losses, things like that?" It was a hypothetical question, but she rubbed her temple with her fingers, tiring of the subject. "What we do is work it into the pattern of our being and move on. It's still there, just lost in the detail of our life." She looked at him as he studied her. "Anyway, I'm just not ready to commit myself to anything. It's as simple as that."

"Maybe it's not simple at all, Sela. Maybe you haven't resolved that previous love affair and that has everything to do with how you're reacting to me."

"I thought we were having a nice time tonight with friends, Ben, so why do you have to mess it up by trying to make this into some kind of a twosome for us?" She sighed deeply and dropped her eyes to her hands. "Can't we just have a good time and not be—" She searched for a word. "Coupled off?"

He also let out a deep sigh of frustration at her words.

"So, why didn't you tell me you heard Mrs. Thornton that night?" Sela asked.

"If you remember, you were already upset, and I figured at the time you wouldn't want to know."

"How much did you hear?"

"Most of it."

Sela looked at him, some of her good humor returning. "You must really think we're all screwy around here, huh?"

They both looked up as another customer entered through the bell-rigged door. It was Deacon Freeman and his wife, Alice.

Ben watched as Sela's smile slipped a little.

"There's something about him that doesn't sit well with you," Ben said.

"It's nothing. I just don't like how he always puts down Aunt Claire."

"Come on, let's get rid of some of your pent-up anger on the dance floor."

"No, I don't want to," she said.

The song that played on the jukebox was about to come to an end, and Ben stood up. "I'll be right back."

She watched in silence as he approached the jukebox, inserted a coin, and quickly selected a song. Curious as to what he'd do next, she swallowed hard when she saw him return to the table like a man with a purpose.

He didn't speak, only picked up her hand and drew her from the chair. At first Sela offered a feeble protest, but deep inside, some part of her did want to dance with him, did want to have fun and experience some part of the intimacy they'd shared before. Under pressure from inside, she relented.

He pulled her along behind him out to the low-lit dance floor where Luther and Rosalie were now headed, as well.

As the strains of the classic Stevie Wonder ballad, "All Is Fair In Love," picked up steam, Ben turned her into the fold of his arm and clasped her hand in his. With his arm firmly fitted around her waist, he held her close as they began to move as one to the music.

Sela, not unaffected by his dancer's embrace, was extremely conscious of his virile appeal on her senses, and attempted to regain a smidgen of decorum as she took a step back.

With one tug of his arm, though, Ben reclaimed the gain.

She held her head back to look up at him. "Do you always contrive to have your way?"

"Whether or not I get it, that's always my goal." He whispered near her ear, "Do you always smell this good?"

His mouth was a feather's brush against that sensitive organ, but it was enough to shake Sela's foundation, and she held on to him now for dear life. As the music swelled, Sela squeezed her eyes tight with her head close to his chest, and let Ben guide her through the slow movements.

Finally, at least two beats beyond the music's end, they broke away from each other, and to the utter shock of Sela, the other diners and dancers began to clap.

Sela, mortified by the attention they received, looked at Ben. He grabbed her hand and squeezed it.

"Come on, let's get dessert over with. Maybe we can find some privacy later on." He looked at her, the double meaning in his gaze obvious.

Sela didn't protest and let him lead her back to the table. Whether it was true or not, the gossip mill would consider them a couple, and she needed to warn Ben about possible rumors. A dinner table with her best friends as monitors was not the place.

Sixteen

After dessert and good-byes to Ron and Vanessa, Ben and Sela left for home in his car.

"Why so quiet?" he asked after a few minutes of her studied silence. He glanced at her from across the shadowy car. "Are you okay?"

She nodded with a sigh. "Yes, I'm fine. Just thinking, that's all."

"I like your diner. I guess what I had expected was, well, a diner—not the cozy place Wally created."

Sela shifted in her seat to face Ben. "I should remind you that this is, after all, a small town, and after we made a spectacle of ourselves tonight, people may misunderstand. And, it doesn't help that we're occupying the same house."

"I'm not concerned about what people think if you aren't." He tried to read her face. "Are you?"

"No, but there might be fallout when you're paired with me."

"Mrs. Thornton thought so."

"Exactly what did you hear that night?"

"Something to the effect that your house has an unsavory past, and that I was bound to hear things about your boyfriends." He smiled at her before he continued. "Oh, and that your aunt travels around like a Gypsy."

Sela settled back in the seat and stared ahead. "I think I'm impressed by your patience," she said. "I thought you would have demanded to know what she was talking about on the spot."

He laughed. "I generally don't buy into rumor, and the truth has a way of making itself known. I figured she was talking about that 'black magic in the basement' stuff Mr. Freeman brought up at the house." He looked to her for agreement.

"Go on," she said.

"And, you've told me about Charles and that affair. Of course, Rosalie had already mentioned your short-lived relationship with college sweetheart Andrew." He glanced at her again, seemingly satisfied with his interpretation of events. "I think that about covers your former lovers."

She glanced at him at his use of words, then turned away.

"I'm sure there won't be some bogeyman who'll jump out at me just because I'm staying at Claire's Inn and I danced with her niece."

The wind whipped at her from the open window, and Sela caught up a wayward strand of hair from her face and slicked it back with the rest of her tightly wrapped braid. It was a dangerous game she had begun to play with fate. But did it operate by appearance alone, as in when she was coupled with Ben, for everyone to see? Or, was it the emotion made aware inside of her that really mattered, like when she took delight in secretly studying him, or the way her heart fluttered when he entered a room? Maybe it was some strange mix of the external and internal.

That was the predicament she now found herself

in. She didn't know quite how destiny was supposed to work. Isn't that why she had forsaken relationships these past years in order to be safe? She still had to take care, not so much for the rumors that might swirl around them, but for something far more ominous—the dangerous fortune that would somehow find her and, ultimately, Ben.

The car had come to a rolling stop before Sela realized they had made it home.

"That was fast," she said.

"I think your mind was somewhere else the entire time," Ben said, as he cut the engine and twisted in the seat to face her. Glossy black wisps of hair had managed to escape near her nape. He reached out and lightly fingered a loose tendril.

"Why do you wear your hair so severe? I don't think I've seen it loose once."

The comment caught her off guard, and she dipped her head away from his hand. "What are you looking for, anyway?"

Ben showed genuine confusion as he dropped his hand. "What are you talking about?"

"What do you think?" Tilting her head back, she peered at his face. "I'm not the cosmopolitan type you look for. My hair isn't permed, and I don't wear makeup. In fact, I'm very much small town, and don't fit the mold for the kind of company you're used to."

Ben's grin lit up the dark car. "First, you do yourself an injustice talking that way. Second, I think I like it better when you're silent." He leaned toward her and, lifting her chin, brushed a gentle kiss across her pliant mouth.

Sela's eyes slipped closed at the same time a soft and unexpected sigh left her throat. But, it was enough to remind her of where she was, and she quickly pulled away from him and reached for the door latch.

"I'm tired, and it's late. We should go on in."

As she managed to slide from the car with her modesty intact from the twisted dress, she heard Ben's remark as he exited, as well.

"I suppose you don't want the neighbors to see us."

She ignored the sarcasm and proceeded to the front door, leaving him behind. By the time he joined her, she had already unlocked the door and entered the foyer. As she stepped into the living room, Ben caught her hand to stop her progress.

"What's your rush?" he asked in a husky whisper.

When she recognized the dare in his eyes, she flushed, embarrassed that he thought she was a coward. Well, she would enjoy proving him wrong.

"Contrary to what you think, Ben Russell, I didn't kiss you in the car because, seeing as we're both grown adults, we don't have to grope around like raunchy teenagers in the backseat parked at Hunter's Pond."

"All right, you've made your point." He tugged on her hand and hauled her against him. "I want to kiss you good night. Properly," he added, and dropped his hand to where it lightly draped her shoulder. "Here and now works for me."

A pleasant shiver swept through Sela. What was it about him that made her react so? He was so damn self-confident, and good-looking, and . . .

Ben's mouth captured hers, the touch of his lips delicious in their mastery as his other hand pressed into her back and blocked her retreat. She held on to him for support and enjoyed the heady desire.

But, when Ben's hand lowered down her back on its journey to seek out her waist, pulling her intimately into him in the process, Sela's knees weakened.

She broke from the dangerous kiss. "I thought we were only saying good night?" she whispered thickly.

He lightly traced a path along her cheek. "I think we're ready to handle a little more than that."

Folding her within his arms, Ben kissed her deeply, her delicate mouth equally intoxicating as her breasts that crushed against him and the taper of her back under his hands. Sela's arms had found their way inside his jacket and now curved around his back. With his own senses afire, he hungrily parted her lips. His tongue traced their soft fullness before he explored the recesses of her mouth. Her quiet whimper told him she wanted this as much as he, and nothing she said later could ever change that.

His hand glided to her neck where he massaged and stroked the sensitive skin there in an ageless, rhythmic beat.

The locket's sudden contact with the hardwood floor was like a cymbal clash in the quiet space Sela and Ben had momentarily created. They came apart abruptly, and both looked around for the source of the interruption.

"It's probably my locket," Sela explained as she felt her neck for the offending item, then looked around the foyer floor for it. The search allowed her the necessary moments to collect her thoughts and demeanor.

"Here it is," Ben announced from somewhere behind her, and picked up the jewelry, which had taken a roll toward the living room. Near it was a folded slip of paper. "What's this?" he called out to her as he picked it up, too.

Sela began to speak, but he had already unfolded the paper and read her mother's words. She tried to forget the taste of him as reality settled within her. He turned and handed her the paper.

"Is this yours, too?" he asked.

She nodded and accepted the locket and paper that Ben placed in her palm. "Just something of my mother's. They both are. That's all." She turned away and replaced the paper in the locket's compartment, the earlier meaning of the intimacy with Ben fading.

"I've got to get this clasp fixed," she exclaimed in a light, almost shaky voice. "By the way, if you're going to church service tomorrow, let me know. I'd like to leave early."

"Sela." Ben came up behind her and placed a restraining hand on her arm.

She shook her head, and dissuaded him to continue. "It's been a long day." She slipped away from his hand and walked to the doorway. "I'll see you tomorrow."

Ben pushed his hands deep into his pockets and watched as Sela slowly walked away, her hip's soft sway beneath the short dress wreaking havoc on his body, until she disappeared from view. He could only marvel at her chameleon-like ability to mask her feelings in an instant. On the other hand, he was a smoldering volcano in need of a cold rain. He scratched his head in confusion before he went in the opposite direction to climb the stairway.

Surely his thoughts would eat him alive this dark night. Frisco quickly gave his head a hard shake, lest he scream from the invading visions and bring on undue attention. In times like these, it took all his strength to contain his anger, which he was more than aware could spill over at any moment. It had been a problem that had dogged him since he was fifteen—the very reason he had been sent away from home in the first place.

He could control it; he knew he could. But the idea that he had to withstand this open embarrassment by an outsider was something else altogether. Maybe the outsider would take heed of his warning and back off. Yeah, that would be for the best. For now, he had to fight the urge to solve the problem swiftly.

He needed to think, and he needed some time alone. It had become a craving of late, and to learn that his solitude in his private place had been violated was more than he could stand. But, he had shown that outsider, hadn't he?

Frisco massaged the throbbing tic near his eye and chuckled with no one in particular. He was beginning to feel better, though. Perhaps he could do with some solitude down by the pond right now. He was out of his seat before he knew it, but then stopped and looked around. He batted his eyes, and stared as if he had only just noticed, for the first time, the other people who surrounded him as they went about their lives. Uncertainly, he retook his seat, a quick trip to the pond no longer an option at the moment.

Ben squinted up at the late Sunday morning sun that already preyed down upon the worshipers. The service was over and he and Sela were descending the church steps.

"Would you still like to see the cemetery?" she asked.

He had not forgotten, and looked across the churchyard as some members prepared to leave, while others prepared for additional activities. "Sure. You lead the way."

When she proceeded in the same general direction he had witnessed the figure take the night before, he said, "Are we taking the shortcut?"

"Yes, it's around the back."

They skirted the wide green lawn and kept to the uphill sidewalk, greeting members as they passed. When they crested the incline, he could see the pastoral scene the cemetery presented laid out before him. Its perimeter was edged by a white picket fence, with a meadow of flowers separating the spot and the sidewalk where Ben and Sela now stood. They could see a few visitors already in what could easily be described as a garden setting. He stopped and admired the view.

"Reverend Osborne kept this area a secret. It's a paradise back here." Ben could see the beginnings of Hunter's Pond in the cemetery's distance and the long, two-lane road that ran parallel to both.

"Everyone takes pride in it, so we have committees to keep things neat and trimmed, flowers fresh, that sort of thing. You met Mr. Lewis. He heads one of them. There's even a slave burial site preserved in one section."

"You've got some kind of history stored away in this church." Ben glanced at his watch. "If you don't mind, I'd like to look around the area. I don't have anything to do for a while."

They left the sidewalk for the grass, and worked their way to the well-traveled trail that took them through the meadow filled with patches of pale wildflowers.

The cemetery was quite large and consisted of

neatly marked blocks of real estate, each identified by a headstone that ranged from conservative to opulent, simple to complex. As they drew closer, Ben could see paths that ran through each area in a crisscross manner, every two rows, and allowed full view of each burial plot without the visitor trampling over adjacent graves. The older section was farther out, near the road. It was juxtaposed to what appeared to be a newer one, which wasn't quite as filled. Stone benches sat like sentinels at the end of each aisle.

They both remained silent as they walked the aisles, commenting only when an interesting bit of information came up from a headstone. Ben noticed that Sela seemed to lead him in a particular direction, toward the family plots.

Soon, she came to a stop in front of a headstone pockmarked by time. Ben read the name and the dates, and realized it was her relative.

"This is my great-grandmother Rhoda's grave. She died before I was born, but I've been told she was one fierce woman, and a superb storyteller. You have to hear Aunt Claire tell about some of her stories."

"Was she psychic, too?"

"From all I've heard, very much so. Auntie said she didn't care that people thought she might be crazy, as long as they believed she could predict the future or put a curse on them, particularly the Klansmen and their kind, who freely roamed around Georgia in those days. If their fears saved the ones she loved from lynching and hassles, she used it."

Ben laughed heartily. "She was smart, too."

Sela laughed with him, liking the sound of his humor that rippled through the air. "She knew what she was doing. But, she was only taking a page from her own grandmother's book of surviving during slavery times in this area."

They continued down the aisle of graves. "Well, are you going to share the slavery story or not? Don't keep me in suspense," Ben teased her.

"All right. Granny Rhoda's grandmother's name was Selah, too, but spelled with an *h*. She was enslaved on a moderate-sized farm around here. I think Auntie said it owned less than twenty-five slaves. Anyway, Granny Selah saved the plantation owner's baby son from some sickness or other, and in return for that, she became highly respected for her healing powers, and there was a hands-off policy pertaining to her while she lived on the farm."

"She was a clairvoyant, right, and somehow used that knowledge?"

Sela nodded. "After that and until the end of the Civil War, she pretty much became the owner's confidante. But the most interesting part in all this is that, at Granny's insistence, he started to allow his slaves to worship in the white Methodist church building, which still remains the base structure of our existing church. Soon, Granny Selah had performed so many *miracles* that he gave the church building to the slaves. It was called Hope Methodist."

"So your—" His brows furrowed as he thought. "Let's see, your great-great-great-grandmother was partly responsible for the existing church."

"That's only half the story," she said. "Since he held Granny in such high esteem, she used that trust and his fear of her power to her advantage. She would hide the occasional runaway slave who came through our area in our church."

"The walls." Ben looked at her. "I'll bet that's how they were hidden, right?"

"How did you know?"

"I knew there was a reason why the building has so many false doors and walls built into the base structure, and now it makes sense."

"The farm owner never interfered with his slaves' church. So, whatever went on there occurred without his interference. It became a safe haven for a lot of people who had nowhere to go, except to the little colored church in the meadow by the pond." She laughed at the irony. "If only they knew what was going on during all that preaching. The former slaves even started one of the first colored schools in their church after the war."

"Amazing," was all Ben could say as she stopped again, this time in a newer section at a deceptively simple granite headstone engraved in gold. Roses were etched along its entire length. Next to it stood a live, staked rosebush, flowing with unopened buds that showed a little yellow and white at their tips.

"Ah, they're ready to bloom," Sela announced. Her arms were crossed as she looked up at Ben.

"Another relative?" He leaned from the aisle toward the headstone and read the name out loud. "Helena Claire Bennett, a mother, a daughter, a sister, 1953 to 1978." It was her mother's grave and, God, she had been so young. Ben turned to Sela. "Your mother. I didn't realize how young she was when she died."

Sela nodded. "We were all young at the time—me, Auntie, and my mother."

Ben didn't know what to say, but from her solemn demeanor, he could still observe her pain, even after more than twenty years had passed.

"Do you mind me asking, how did she die?"

Ben saw her shoulders shrug as she turned to him again, her arms still crossed. Gone was her earlier playful air. And while she kept her features composed, it was her large, dark eyes that drew his stare. They glistened in the bright sun.

"No, not at all. It's common enough knowledge around here," she said matter-of-factly. "She committed suicide."

Seventeen

Ben's eyes came up to study Sela's face, and she could tell that he was taken aback by the disclosure.

"I . . . I had no idea, Sela."

She tried to blunt his shock by corralling her own disquiet. "It lessens with time," she said, and stepped around the gray, rectangular slab in the ground to inspect a stem of buds. "She loved yellow roses, so Auntie helped me plant this the year she died. You know, I think this poor bush has had to survive about as much as we have." She released the stem and rejoined a subdued Ben in the aisle.

When he reached for her hand in silent commiseration, she didn't hold back. As soon as her fingers became enclosed in the warmth of his outstretched hand, she was caught off guard by the comfort and safety the simple connection produced. She looked at him for a long moment.

His eyes swept her face. "The message on the paper in your locket," he began, then faltered.

She nodded as he squeezed her hand in support. "I was told she left the note for me."

"To have gone through something like that as a child. A person wouldn't know it to look at you."

"Oh, I have my days, but it's just one of those things." She made a tremulous smile. "Now you see why Reverend Osborne is so lenient with my family. Altogether, we've probably broken every tenet of the church." This time, he joined in with her smile.

"But," she continued, "he also acknowledges what my grandmothers did a long time ago. And, just between us, he probably does believe there's something unexplained about this clairvoyance business, but it's not too smart for a Methodist minister to openly admit it's anything other than the devil's work."

Ben smiled, now more comfortable with her admission, and brought the back of her hand up to his mouth. "I'm beginning to better understand your symbiotic relationship with this town and its citizens," he said, and kissed the smooth skin across her knuckles.

"Sela."

The call came from Mr. Lewis. They turned as he hailed her again. In his dark church suit, he looked decidedly different from the snoopy postman who asked questions as he ate muffins. Their hands dropped as they started down the path to meet him.

"Mr. Lewis, how are you, sir?" Ben shook his hand after Sela gave him a light hug.

He greeted Ben with a jovial slap against his back before he turned to Sela. "I see you been showing off your family tree, huh?" he asked with a blustery laugh.

"She's got a lot to be proud of, too," Ben said. "I understand you're part of the reason this cemetery is so beautiful."

Jim Lewis beamed with pride. "I call it our Memorial Garden. Nice, isn't it?"

"I don't think nice covers it, but yes, it is," Ben agreed, looking around.

"So, you saw the roses at your mama's grave?"

The older man walked past them to the burial plot they had stopped at only a few steps away. "I told you they'd bloom this year, didn't I?"

"Yes," Sela said as she followed him. "And I guess you were right again."

When she and Ben joined Mr. Lewis, his head was bowed reverently in respect at the grave.

"God rest her soul," the postman said, and nodded before he looked up. "She was a wonderful woman, you know, and it's a shame she died so young and beautiful." He turned to Ben. "If you ever see pictures of Sela's mother, you'll be amazed at how much they looked alike at this age. The same size and coloring." He pinched Sela's cheek playfully.

"I don't know why you insist on treating me as if I were still ten years old," she protested.

"And with the same attitude," he added as he grinned at her embarrassment. "Well, I got to be going. I'll see you two later on, won't I?"

"What's going on?" Sela asked.

He looked from Ben to Sela. "We're supposed to pitch the tents this afternoon over at the pond for the July Fourth picnics. I thought Ron said Ben was helping."

Ben stepped up. "It's news to me, but I'll be glad to give a hand."

Sela's eyes stretched wide as she remembered. "Ben, I'm sorry. Ron asked me to tell you about it, and after we got home last night, well, I sort of forgot to mention it to you."

"What happened last night?" He turned to Ben. "You behavin' yourself, right?"

Before Ben could defend himself, Sela cut in. "Of course, he is. What kind of question is that? We went out with Ron and Vanessa, that's all."

"We all ate together at the diner," Ben clarified with a straight face.

"You know, I was over at Wally's, too; but, it was pretty late, so I missed you."

"Thank God," she mumbled under her breath to Ben. "Since we're scheduled to work this afternoon, are you ready to go now?"

He nodded. "Mr. Lewis, I guess we'll see you later on at the pond after all."

"I'll be there." After a round of good-byes, he turned and left them, already hailing someone else he recognized.

Ben took up Sela's hand again. And, with an understood glance that hovered between them, they retraced their path back to the churchyard.

"We're gonna break for a while," Ron said, and reached into a large ice chest. "Take one of these to cool off."

Ben took a healthy swig from the bottle of ice-cold Coke Ron had handed to him. After the satisfying swallow, he inhaled deeply and wiped his brow. It was hot as hell, and he couldn't figure out how he had so easily agreed to sweat with five other guys over interconnecting pipe and line to pitch picnic tents. He could have sworn he had vowed not to get too involved with the locals.

It had been two years since he had been stateside on a July Fourth holiday, but he still hadn't done anything like this since he had been a kid—attend parades, picnics, and watch fireworks. Wait until Mont got an earful of this, and Ben would enjoy the telling, too. He laughed to himself.

The sun was unrelenting as he and Ron leaned back on the spectator bench they shared on the edge of the empty field where a pickup ball game had started with some of the men and older kids. With two tents completed, their group had three more to erect, which meant at least two more hours of sweat.

He took another deep drink and looked around. Straight ahead, and separated by the tool house, he saw Sela. She was sitting on a blanket with Vanessa's twins. Clad in shorts and shirt, with that braid twisted to the back of her head, she was an interesting eyeful. That braid pulled loose had already been the subject of a few stimulating dreams. He smiled at the thought until he remembered the tragedy she had revealed today, and his brows drew together.

"You probably realize she's not your ordinary woman." Ron nodded toward Sela before he gulped down the remainder of the drink.

"She told me her mother's death was a suicide."

Ron glanced at him. "I guess it shocked you a bit, huh?"

"I swear, it came at me out of left field." He leaned forward and rested his elbows against his knees. "What do you say to something like that?"

"I see your point, and I figure you don't want to say the wrong thing and lose the ground you already gained."

"What do you mean?"

"Last night. You two hit it off pretty well."

"We're okay. At least we're talking to each other." Ben smiled. "That's more than we were doing last week."

"Like I told you when you first got here, Sela doesn't open up too easily, and you'll do better by letting her take her own time with letting things out."

"You grew up with her. Has she always been sort

of standoffish and secretive about herself? I'm sure it was rough on her with no mother, or father to speak of."

Ron scratched his chin. "Everything worked out pretty normal for her with Miss Claire. And, except for the occasional crap from some, and you expect that, everybody liked her and wanted the best for her. Believe it or not, back in high school, I even dated Sela for a while myself."

Ben's eyes raised in a surprised smile. "You did?"

"Yeah, but before you even go there, let me tell you there's no story to it." He laughed himself. "She was always this good-looking chick to the guys, but during that time, she used to get teased real good about Miss Claire's powers, and there were some pretty unpleasant names tagged to her. We ended up being good friends more than anything else."

"So, she didn't date a lot?"

He looked at Ben. "She dated, but . . ." He seemed to hedge with his answer. "Maybe she ought to explain those high school days."

Ben sought out Sela again. This time she was playing catch with the boys. "After high school, she went off to college where she met Andrew?"

"Uh-huh, that's about right. I left for college, too, and met Vanessa. So, it all worked out in the end."

Ben turned to face Ron. "Except Rosalie said things didn't go the way Sela had planned with Andrew. What hap—"

Ron stopped him. "Listen, I know you're trying to figure her out, but she's my friend, and my wife's best friend. I prefer to leave it to Sela to fill you in on the details about her life."

Ben took a deep sigh. "Fair enough," he said, and downed the rest of the drink.

"I will say this, though. Don't read too much into what happened before."

Ron stood and dusted his jeans, effectively ending the conversation. "Hey, you want to catch a few balls with the guys before I haul them back to work on the tents?"

"Sure," Ben answered, and he, too, stood from the bench. He fixed his stare once more to the area where Sela sat with Vanessa.

As he accompanied Ron to the softball field, his mind raced ahead with the subtle message he had just been offered. *Don't read too much into what happened before.* So, what had happened?

Sela looked down the bank toward Ben and Ron, and saw that they were no longer talking but now heading to the ball field. While half of her attention was taken up with helping Vanessa set out a snack for the twins, the other half continued to return to the men as they walked away.

"What do you think those two were talking about?" she asked Vanessa, and nodded in the departing men's direction.

Vanessa shielded her eyes from the sun as she followed Sela's stare. "Probably you." She nibbled at some of the finger foods they had set out on the blanket in front of Brian and Brett.

"I'm serious," she explained.

"Me, too. I doubt if I could have shoved a ruler between the two of you last night on the dance floor. And knowing a man's mind, you are still on his, honey." She chewed on a baby carrot, a devilish smile pasted to her face. "So, what kind of dancer was he?"

Sela grinned and took her friend's bait. "Capable.

And, for future reference, we can rule out that he's a eunuch."

Vanessa chuckled loudly. "That can only be good news."

"Mama," Brett started.

"What's a yoo-nit?" Brian finished.

Both women burst out in a hardy, infectious laugh that, in no time, had spread to the two boys. When her laughs became so hard, Vanessa clutched her side in pain.

"Are you okay?" Sela asked, immediately sober, and scrambled to her knees to get to Vanessa's side.

Her friend took in a couple of deep breaths. "Lately, I've been getting a pinch in my side. I guess my little fellow is anxious, that's all. But, I'm okay," she said, as she blew breaths out in rapid succession. "I still have about four good weeks to go."

"Well, as long as you're sure we don't need to get Ron," Sela said.

"Just between us, you're doing fine. He'll want me to go to the hospital." She smiled as she said, "Lord have mercy on all of us if I go into labor and he's the only one around."

Sela pressed Vanessa's brow, then helped her recline on the blanket. "If you promise to rest a while, I won't get him just yet."

"I love that man to death, Sela, but as black as he is, he still turns white as a sheet when he sees blood or me in pain."

As she settled another blanket under Vanessa's head, she wondered at the comfort it must bring to know that you and the baby you carry are loved and cherished and very much wanted. That's what she wanted when she had children. *If* she had children. Sela wasn't sure about the circumstances of her own conception and birth; she and Aunt Claire had closed the subject long ago with no answers about her father.

She sat back on her knees, surprised at the inexplicable train of thought. The visit to the grave site, Vanessa's pregnancy, and Ben's ubiquitous queries—they all seemed to lead her to wonder about her own past and privilege.

"Sela?" Vanessa pulled on Sela's hand. "What about you? Maybe I should ask if you're okay."

She pulled from her reverie and gave her friend a reassuring smile. "Yeah. I was just thinking . . . about my father."

Reverend Osborne didn't quite fit the picture of the staid minister he portrayed on the first day Ben came to town. To accommodate his hands-on policy, today he wore jeans and a T-shirt that proudly proclaimed in bold words that he was a man of faith.

Ben's group had just completed the tents when the minister arrived with a host of deacons, all attempting to sign up volunteers for jobs related to the July Fourth festivities. Ben left the group and hiked over to the tree where Sela was sitting on top of a stack of folded blankets.

"Tired?" She offered Ben a cool, wet hand towel.

"Ah, that looks nice," he said, and took the proffered towel. He immediately spread it over his upturned face.

"Where's Ron?" she asked.

"He's in that crowd back there somewhere, signing our talents away."

"Well, you are getting the hang of how small town folks do things. Congratulations."

He pulled the towel from his face. "Don't rub it in. I didn't say I liked it. I'm just doing my civic duty while I'm a town citizen. Now all I want is a hot shower and a chance to raid somebody's fridge for a giant bowl of ice cream." He rubbed the cloth over his forearms and hands.

"Before dinner? Vanessa cooked for us today and wants us to join them later. She's already left with the boys, so we'll have to drop Ron off."

"In that case, the ice cream can wait. I'll grab this stuff up and then find Ron."

Even though he had protested his good intent, Sela suspected he enjoyed the team effort with the other men, and said so.

"You know, I think our small town life is beginning to rub off on you. Go on, admit it."

She saw the gleam in Ben's eyes too late, and before she knew it, he had swooped his arms under her legs and back and proceeded to swing her around.

"Ben," she squealed and held on to him for dear life as he swung her again, impervious to the stares they were attracting from the few people nearby. "Put me down."

He slowed down just enough to speak for her ears only. "Uh-uh, not until you admit something to me."

"Okay, what?"

"Admit that you're beginning to like me just a bit."

"I am not."

"What, you don't like me or you won't admit it?"

"Both," she blurted out.

He spun her again and again, ignoring her squeals.

"Okay, okay," she said on the third turn. "It's true. I like you."

Ben stopped the spin and slacked his arms just enough so that she easily slid to the ground. When her feet touched the grass, she stumbled back a step, and eyed him with exasperation.

"I think you're the devil, Ben Russell. You don't play fair."

"I just play to win." He smiled innocently as he reached for the folded blankets. "And, I'm going to win you."

The underlying sensuality of his words captivated Sela; and, as she tugged her shorts back into some semblance of order, she eyed him thoughtfully from a safe distance.

"Come on," he said.

There was something potent about a man being so open with his intentions. She made a mental note to be careful, especially since she had grown acutely conscious of that arrogant man and had admitted she liked him. Sela drew in a confused sigh and followed Ben across the grassy bank.

Eighteen

Sela leaned back from the cardboard box on the table and wiped her brow. A promise was a promise, and she had made one to Reverend Osborne, even if it had been under duress. She had sorted her way through two of about ten boxes stacked against the wall in the little basement room, and it hadn't been a lot of fun.

The water-damaged files were a mishmash of church memorabilia and correspondence, and made up only a part of the great crush of disorder that permeated the room she had promised to sort through by the end of summer. There were a few racks of outer clothing, as well as a virtual lost and found of personal belongings boxed on the tables, all unclaimed property that had multiplied over the years.

Her only company in the downstairs office was a portable radio, and it sat next to the remnants of a sandwich she had nibbled on hours earlier.

The door, already ajar, was pushed wider before Irene Bruton, the church secretary, filled it with her formidable figure.

"Girl," she exclaimed as she rapidly perused the room, her braids fanning out, "you got your work cut out for you. Reverend Osborne knew not to ask me to come down here in this dust and mold, not with my asthma. The cleaning service people don't even come down here."

"Nobody in the congregation volunteered, either. That's why he blackmailed me into it." Sela put her hands on the hips of her jeans and joined the observation. "It's a mess, huh?"

"It's been like this ever since that water pipe broke last year."

"But, if I don't clean it out now, Reverend Osborne says we might not pass the insurance inspection for the renovation this fall. And only God knows what all is buried in this rubbish, so we can't just throw it all away." She dragged another box to one of the tables.

"Sela, bless your heart. You're the only one I've heard who cares about this old stuff. Well, I'm just about getting ready to get out of here and call it a day. You don't need me for anything else, do you?"

"No, I'm fine." Sela looked up. "Is Ben still around somewhere?"

"The last time I saw him, he was rattling around in the rafters like a squirrel," Irene said, and shook her head. "I'm scared of heights and there he is, just hanging over one beam after another." She saw the cleaned-up files Sela had already set in another sturdy box. "Why don't I take some of this stuff you've already cleaned out back upstairs with me? I can have Deacon Freeman bring the heavier boxes up tomorrow. He's already left for now. He'll be back later to make sure everything's locked up."

"Sure. I marked everything that was salvageable so you can refile it."

"Don't you be staying down here too long, now," Irene said as she gathered up the box. "The shadows can get pretty long in this drafty place and make it downright spooky."

"I'm not scared, Irene. I grew up running around here. But, maybe I'll find Ben. That way, I won't need your keys."

Irene smiled as she glanced toward the door. "It won't be much of a surprise. He's been watching you since you first got here this afternoon."

"She's right," Ben said from the door.

Sela turned, her surprise eclipsed by the pleasurable flow of energy that surged through her.

"I'll see y'all later," Irene said, and backed out of the door with the box.

As Ben strolled to Sela, she noticed that he, too, wore a simple shirt and jeans to work in the basement. She crossed her arms and smiled. "You were watching me?" At his nod, she added, "Where have you been? I haven't seen you once all afternoon."

"Checking out structural integrity inside the roof shelving, and going over some preliminary findings with Reverend Osborne and Mr. Freeman. You've been busy in here, so I didn't bother you. He planted his feet in front of her. "It's good seeing you."

The words pleased her. "It's not like we don't see each other every day."

"Ah, but it's the quality of the time that counts, don't you think?" He leaned forward, and with a feather touch, kissed her cheek.

She sidestepped around him. "You know, I used to run all over this place as a kid. Why don't you show me what you've been doing down here?" She glanced up. "Or, maybe up there?"

"I take that to mean you don't disapprove of . . ." He brushed her cheek with his mouth again.

The pleasure was palpable, yet she guarded her

reaction in case he read more into it than she was ready to reveal.

"Never mind," he teased, and drew her hand into his. "Don't answer. Anyway, Irene told me no one ever comes down here." They started for the door.

"Irene doesn't come down here." Amusement lifted her eyes. "I can probably show you hiding places even the reverend didn't know existed."

"All right," he said, rising to the challenge. "Let's see how much you really know about this place."

Sela stood with Ben in the church's spire tower and looked through a tall, mullioned window. From more than three stories up in the vaulted ceiling, the view—all the way across the floor of the sanctuary to the altar below the arched window at the eastern end of the church—was magnificent.

She moved around the scaffolding that was set up against the tower walls, her head now stretched over the high safety railing, but Ben was right there with her. It was as far as he would let her venture out while he held her tight at her waist—an additional safety measure.

"Ben, it's beautiful. So, this is what you do all day?" she asked. "Climb around up here and admire the view?"

"It's an old building, so I've been checking out the roof fascia. I have to recommend to your building committee what needs replacing, what can stay, that sort of thing. For churches like yours with historical significance, the trick is to preserve as much of the history as possible while still making sure it's safe and meets current building codes." He spoke at her ear as his hand tightened at her waist. "And, that's what I do best."

She could feel the pride swell in his chest. "And then you draw up a set of plans from your ideas?"

"Right. Now, come on away from the edge. Reverend Osborne would have my hide if he knew I let you come up in the tower. We were supposed to be checking out the basement, remember?" He gently pulled her away from the tower window.

"I still haven't shown you my favorite place at the church," she said as she turned to him. "Maybe you've seen it, the tiny oval chapel with the stained-glass saints circling the wall?"

"It's in the west transept, right?" He smiled. "Reverend Osborne told me." When he saw her outright blank look, he laughed. "This church, like many, is built using a cruciform plan, cross-shaped, and the transepts would be the arms."

She smiled in understanding. "I didn't know that, but it makes sense now."

"You've noticed how church windows tend to be large and elongated?"

"So, there's more to that than the fact that it looks good?"

"Of course. Somebody figured out, say about a thousand years ago, that taller windows lead the eye heavenward and allow more light to pour into the building."

"Amazing," Sela said, and started for a simple wooden ladder that disappeared through a square floor opening. "Let's take the ladder back down instead of the stairs."

Ben moved ahead of her and shook his head. "I don't know."

"Come on," she said and playfully tugged his arm. "I'm getting a kick out of all this. I haven't had this much fun exploring in a long time."

He saw the glow in her eyes and looked again

at the ladder that could take them down two floors of open space where they would then use the circular stairway in the corner wall to get to the main floor.

"I use it during the day because it's quicker, Sela. I don't know about you climbing on it."

"That's the point," she argued. "It's faster, and we can still look around downstairs."

He relented, but spoke firmly. "All right, but I'll go first and you follow close behind. Keep your head up, don't look down, and you'll move more surefooted, okay? No games."

Her smile broadened. "Yes, sir."

In close single file, they climbed down the wall ladder, with everything moving smoothly as they came to the next floor.

Then, the unexpected happened.

Ben felt the fissure in the step before his entire weight came down on it. He instinctively drew his foot back to drop to the next step and avoid catastrophe. Unfortunately, that step was also broken and when his foot came down, he lost his balance; his grip loosened from the rungs as he slipped down the rail. Knowing that within the moment, Sela would reach the same step, he called out.

"Sela, don't—" Too late, she stepped down on the first weakened step and it gave way, all in one motion.

"Ohh—" Her surprised exclamation came out in a whoosh as her foot sank through the cracked stair. With no means of support, she scrambled for a hold, then lurched backward. As she emitted another shriek, she tumbled down, against the ladder, and to the floor. Ben had preceded her fall to the floor, and now waited there in the guise of a soft pallet to break her fall.

* * *

His eyes were tired and bloodshot. Frisco squinted at his visage in the bathroom mirror, not sure he wanted to see what stared back at him any clearer than he already had. He hadn't forgotten his shame. In his haste to punish the outsider, Frisco had hurt her.

He stepped back from the sink and pulled open the medicine cabinet. His eyes darted about in no clear pattern as they searched for the small brown bottle he had tried to ignore, but knew he'd have to come to terms with again.

When he located the prescription-labeled bottle on the top shelf, the discovery triggered another wave of nausea that had become a constant of late. He picked it up and read the label. Trazodone. And what about her? Would she desert his dreams if he dosed himself again?

Something in his pocket bumped against the counter, and he remembered. His hand burrowed deep, and he pulled a small leather-bound book from his pocket. Though the leather was aged, it was daintily worked and embossed with a golden rose. He'd have to return it to its safe place real soon. He set it on the counter before he pried open the bottle of pills.

As he shook a tablet out of the bottle and into his palm, his familiar waking vision tried to take root.

Frisco threw his head back and tossed the pill into his mouth. He then bent his head to the sink and drank tap water from his cupped palm. After he'd taken his fill, he straightened up and wiped the moisture from his mouth with the back of his hand.

His eyes settled on the leather book again. He

hadn't meant to hurt Helena tonight. It had been a terrible mistake, and one he couldn't repeat.

"Are you sure you're okay?" Ben's concern was evident in his voice as he spoke to Sela through her bathroom door, his voice rising above the level of the water that splashed into the tub.

"After I soak in this hot water for a while, my bruises will be fine. Why don't you do the same?" she called out. "I know you must be sore, too."

Ben smiled to himself as he crossed his arms and leaned against the wall. "Do you want to make room for me in there?"

He heard something bounce off the door from the other side, and knew it meant she had nixed the idea. "Okay, so this is how you treat me after I save you from disaster tonight. My plan worked, didn't it?"

"That was a plan?" Sela's sass came through the door loud and clear.

"And it played out just right. I dropped to the floor so I could catch you and break your fall."

"Only you weren't off the floor yet, and I landed on your side."

"I'm a big boy. I can take a little bumping." He heard her come to the door, and he straightened from the wall.

She opened the door a few inches, enough that they could talk. "Seriously, Ben. You think it was just that the ladder rungs were rotten, and that's all?"

He could see that she wore a robe and a fragrant oil had already begun to permeate the steamed air. Ben also noticed how her loose hair softened her already beautiful features. He swallowed hard at the familiar tightening in his loins. She affected him much more than he realized.

"Hey, stop worrying yourself over that. Of course it was probably just rotten wood." He tried to fathom a reason for her now serious expression. "I promise you I'll check it out tomorrow; then I'll recommend a replacement."

"All right, as long as you're sure that's all it was." Her smile returned. "I'm going to sit in this tub of hot water, alone, and I'll be fine. I guess your plan worked after all."

She closed the door and Ben pressed his hands deep into his pockets as he walked back to the living room. He couldn't let her see how troubled he was by the evening's turn of events. He had been up and down that ladder all week, and easily at twice the speed they had carefully taken tonight; and, not once had there been an indicator that the ladder was unstable.

He rubbed his neck in thought. So, why tonight? And what was worse, had she not been on the ladder with him and caused him to be extra careful, he might not have discovered the rotted sections until tomorrow, when he was working. Tonight's discovery was the difference between a few bruises and a broken neck. It was an unsettling thought, but he couldn't share it with Sela. Not right now. She was too rattled over the accident. Still, he believed he owed her his life.

At that moment, the phone rang.

Ben looked back down the hall and called out to Sela. "I'll get it and tell them to call back." He reached around one of the numerous figurines and picked up the phone. He then uttered a brusque, though clear greeting to the caller.

"Ben Russell?"

His surprise was immediate as he recognized Claire Bennett's distinctive inflections. "Yes. It's been a while since we last spoke, Miss Bennett."

"More importantly, are you getting any worth from the trip I encouraged you to take?"

He laughed at her choice of words. "So, are you admitting you finagled me into your town?"

"I admit no such thing. You are not a man to be persuaded unless you choose it. Am I right?"

He smiled again. "You are. And the trip was worth your persuasion. The church is a great study, and Reverend Osborne seems to like my ideas. So, everything is working out for us."

"What about my niece? Are she and Fontella keeping up the Claire's Inn tradition of pampering our guests?"

"I think I lost my guest status for Sela the first day I arrived. Fontella, on the other hand, is in full operational mode."

"Ah . . . Sela hasn't come around yet?"

"Oh, no, she's done very well by me, considering our introduction and my intrusion on her summer. She's fair-minded and helpful and, well, she's been great."

This time, Claire's smile could be heard in her words. "Then, everything is going well. Where is Sela?"

Ben looked around the corner. "She's, uh, in the tub." When Claire didn't respond, he explained. "Soaking from a few bruises."

"Oh?"

He tried to get it right this time. "You see, we were at the church and there was an accident—"

"What kind of accident?"

"Nothing serious, just a rotten ladder rung that gave way, and we both took a tumble. We're fine, she's fine, and the ladder will be replaced tomorrow."

"I'd like to speak with her, Ben. Get her for me."

Surprised at her directness, he looked down the hall again before he answered. "Sure, just a moment."

True to his word it only took him a moment to change to a portable phone, knock on the bathroom door, and inform Sela that her aunt wished to speak with her.

Ben heard the water splash as she left the tub and shortly thereafter cracked open the door. He handed the phone to her towel-clad body through the opening, before he whispered his concern.

"I sort of told her about the ladder, and now she seems a little anxious about it."

Sela nodded and closed the door.

"Auntie," Sela said brightly, and dropped to sit on the edge of the footed tub.

"Ben told me about the fall you took. He's well, but what about you?"

"I'm fine. But, you said you wouldn't be calling before the holiday. Is everything okay?"

Claire's voice was a soft breeze of humor. "Now that I know you're all right, I am, too. He explained what happened, and I trust his judgment. Should I continue to?"

"It really was no one's fault, just a silly incident, which I probably created being stubborn."

"I know it well. But, he's up to the challenge, isn't he?"

Sela sighed. "Well, I have no argument with your judgment of character. He really has been patient with my attitude. He's even been a good friend. And, Auntie, as much as he pretends to hate country life, he helped the men pitch tents for the holiday picnic."

"You seem to have picked up on his finer qualities, and he has noticed a few of yours, as well. Now, what am I to make of this?"

She blushed at her aunt's insight. "First, don't read so much into it, Auntie. We're friends. I'm sure you'd rather have us civil than at each other's throats in the same house."

"You're right, and I'm properly chastised."

Sela reached over the edge of the tub and ran her fingers through the sudsy water as she gathered her thoughts to broach a closed subject.

"Auntie, I've been thinking about something. What if the reason I don't relate so well to men is that, maybe, I don't have any knowledge of my own father?" The pregnant pause from the phone told Sela she had managed to unnerve her composed aunt.

"You have been giving the subject thought, but your conclusion is flawed. You've had father figures. Your minister, your grandfather for years, and—"

"I know you don't like to talk about my father, and we haven't had this conversation in over ten years; but lately, it's been uppermost in my mind, and you're my only source for information. Please."

"We'll talk more when I see you."

"Okay, but I won't drop the subject. I will ask again." Her voice broke slightly. "I love you."

"I love you. Take care of yourself."

Claire hung up, shaken by her niece's insistence on answers she, herself, wasn't sure should be unearthed. She looked at the tarot cards piled atop each other on the table, the result of her reading for Ben, and realized she never did tell Sela her reason for calling so soon. With Ben confirming that everything was okay, it was just as well.

One card was separate from the others. Claire picked it up now. It was the inverted Three of Cups, and she had divined it accurately. There had been danger afoot, and she wasn't quite convinced it was over with, yet.

Nineteen

"Yep, it looks like the steps broke clean through," Deacon Freeman said, echoing Reverend Osborne's earlier words.

"We'll get it replaced right away." Reverend Osborne walked around the ladder the men had hauled down from the hooks and placed in the middle of the tower floor. "Ben, you will check out the other ladders, won't you? We don't want any more accidents in God's house."

Ben had knelt near the ladder and studied it closely. "I did that before you got here, sir, and they're fine." He looked up at the men. "Only the middle rungs on this one seem to be weakened from . . . well, I'm not sure, but it doesn't look like rot."

"Maybe it's just a case of a simple splinter in the wood itself," the deacon suggested. "After heavy use, that would weaken it more, and before you know it, it cracks from the weight."

"Probably," Ben replied absently. The others standing around also agreed with the deacon's conclusion.

As the men filed out to take the wall stairway back down, Ben stayed behind, still intrigued by the wood. When he looked up, he was surprised to see

Reverend Osborne there. The older man was regarding him from beneath furrowed brows.

"I imagine that was some experience last night," he said to Ben. "And Sela, she's all right today?"

Ben rose from the floor and slapped his hands against his pants. He nodded, relieved that he could share his thoughts with someone. "I was more concerned for Sela than anything else. She was a little bruised, but that was the extent of it, thank God."

"Claire called me last night, after she talked with Sela. And, we're both assured that Sela will be okay. That's mainly due to you."

"Well, thanks for the confidence, sir, but I didn't do any more than anyone else would have done."

"You've helped where it counts." He tapped the side of his head. "Mentally. Your presence helps Sela, and that's appreciated." He looked toward the stairway and saw that the men had left, before he turned to Ben.

"Do you have any other explanations for what happened? I've seen you go up and down those ladders for the last three weeks, yet you say you never noticed a weak rung."

Ben rubbed his chin. "I don't know if I'm satisfied with the deacon's analysis, but since I don't have any other theory to float, wood stress is plausible."

"Okay, enough of this." He lightly slapped Ben's back as they both headed for the stairs. "Are you looking forward to our Fourth celebration? With the parade, picnics, and fireworks, it'll be an all-day busy affair."

"I've been hearing about it," Ben admitted, "but, I'm not much for parades and fireworks. The picnic, now, I can work with that."

"We're famous for the food. But if you find a pretty lady to wave to in the parade, and later on sit at your table, maybe you can both share a blanket under the sky while you watch the fireworks explode."

Ben stopped and laughed. "Reverend, are you setting me up?"

The minister smiled. "All I'm saying is Sela loves a parade, picnics, and fireworks."

"The entire package. I know." As he held the stair door open for the minister to precede him, Ben began to think out loud. "Maybe I'll take her to dinner tonight. After last night, she might need it."

"Now you're talking," Reverend Osborne agreed, as they both took to the stairs.

Ezra Harris was the town's only internist, who also doubled as the medical examiner when the need arose. He had been practicing in the county for over thirty years, and had earned the moniker of Doc Harris, which he touted with pride, from the legion he served.

One of his patients, whose file was now spread across the desk, had called earlier and needed a prescription refilled. In a day that had run the gamut of problems, from a migraine headache to a broken limb, the doctor's time was a guarded prize. He attempted a quick perusal through the file when his door was thrust open.

"Doc, are you ready for Mrs. Gandy?"

He waved off the nurse. "Let me take care of this first, okay? Give me a few minutes; then I'm sure you'll remind me." He glanced at her over the rim of his glasses. "Again."

With a humorless grunt, she closed the door.

Doc shook his head and quietly resumed reading the previous diagnosis of the patient. "Patient has a schizoid personality with intermittent periods of extreme anxiety. See extended diagnosis on consultation sheet with Doctor Victor Holliday."

He switched over to the consult sheet from the clinical psychologist, and upon reading a few lines, remembered that the patient had been in some form of treatment for mental instability since he was fifteen years old. The suggested method of treatment had been followed, but the patient admitted to "falling off the wagon" due to the medication's side effects.

Somehow, the patient would detect his limitations during extreme bouts with his illness, and would request to be remedicated. Apparently, this was one of those times. Trazadone, a low-dose, psychotropic drug, had worked fine in the past. He tapped his pen on the desk, and decided he would continue with the treatment.

He wrote instructions for the prescription in his notes, and prepared to hand the file over to the nurse. But, he stopped. It had been more than three years since the patient had last been seen. Was there a trigger that caused his schizoid attacks? Maybe another consult with the psychologist was warranted.

He decided he would see the patient, and wrote additional instructions for the nurse to schedule an appointment. As soon as possible, he added.

It was late afternoon when Ben arrived at the house, and the first thing he noticed were the two—no, three, he counted—extra cars parked around the house. The inn would remain closed until the fall, so why all the cars? he wondered.

He parked and scooped up the bouquet of flowers from the back seat. Smiling, he figured Sela would have to agree to go out with him tonight. None of her excuses would fly in the face of flowers from her hero of the moment. She had become less rigid and had begun to warm to his advances. He'd take her back to Wally's diner, and as long as they could dance in the back with the lights low, he'd be just fine. His smile broadened as he opened the front door.

At first, the door wouldn't budge more than a few inches, before it finally gave way with a second push, wherein a pair of kid's eyes peered from around it.

"Aunt Sela, it's Ben." Brian's little voice made the announcement loud and clear as four other little faces stopped their play in the foyer and riveted their gazes on Ben.

Ben suffered a mild shock. The normally quiet house was thunderous with noise. Laughing adult voices floated in from the den area. The children—they all appeared to be preschoolers—had lost interest in him and now resumed their chatter while they played on the foyer floor, which was filled with toys of every size and shape. The toys became a never-ending trail from the foyer clear through to the living room. Ben stepped forward and felt a metal form of some sort beneath his sole.

"Hey, you're stepping on my sailboat."

Ben looked down at his accuser, a boy he didn't recognize. "Sorry." He moved his foot dangerously close to a stuffed animal.

"Ben." Sela came from around the corner and stopped at the foyer entrance. She wore a giant pink gift bow that dangled from her neck. "I didn't expect you'd be home so early. Some of us got together to give Vanessa a baby shower."

"I figured something was going on, what with all this." His hands swept out at the room. So much for his plans to orchestrate a romantic evening. And Sela, looking as cool as a cucumber on the hot summer day with her midriff exposed, did nothing to dampen his enthusiasm for a night alone with her. He looked around, his senses still not yet digesting all of the commotion.

"Have you met the kids?"

"More or less," he muttered, and tried to make his way to her through the swell of kids and toys.

"Things are a mess, I know, but I told the parents it was okay to bring the kiddies, too." When Ben reached her and sort of pushed the bouquet at her, her eyes lit up. "Flowers. Ben, thank you." She took a step closer and accepted them. "What's the occasion?" she asked as she sniffed at the blossoms.

He shrugged. "Nothing special, just something for you."

She hooked her arm in his. "Come on and let me introduce you to the ladies—"

"No, no." He unlinked his arm. "I'll just go downstairs and do some work. That way, the noise in here won't bother me down there."

"Okay, but there'll be lots of food left, so don't worry about going out to eat. I can bring down a plate later."

He had already walked off, but raised his hand in acknowledgement, avoiding most of the toys as he worked his way to the staircase.

Sela walked back to the door of the den and watched him disappear, noting how he seemed distracted and almost unhappy this evening. She started to go after him, but one of the children had sidled up to her and she placed an arm around his shoulders.

"Is everything okay, Sela?" It was Fontella in the den.

Sela turned to the door and looked in where a dozen women sat around Vanessa amid stacks of gaily decorated gifts.

"Yes. It was Ben." She brought the bouquet to her face and inhaled. "He brought flowers . . . uh, for the house," she improvised. "But, I think the kids scared him away."

"He stepped on my boat," the youngster under Sela's arm exclaimed to everyone. "He's got big feet."

"Hmm, that's not a bad thing," Juanita, the hairdresser, teased, "if you know what to do with them."

"We know who got the flowers, so I'm figuring he won't mind showing her," Fontella chimed in.

While the other women laughed at the wicked joke, Sela shared an uneasy smile with Vanessa.

It had been more than two hours since he had arrived home in the middle of a baby shower, and the noise that had emanated from upstairs in a steady rhythm had dropped considerably in the last half hour. And, while he had completed some of his site work in the form of preliminary sketches in the downstairs office, it was obvious that his mind was otherwise occupied. In fact, it was upstairs, and performing a slow dance with Sela, to be exact.

He tossed the pencil across the desk and took to the stairs, two at a time.

When he reached the top stair, he heard Sela's voice as she implored the twins to stop their play for a while and help pick up the toys. He sighed. Company was still afoot in the form of little people.

As he left the hallway and walked into the living room, Sela was busy collecting toys that lay strewn through the house. The kids in question were totally oblivious to her pleas as they built a tower from blue and red blocks.

He stopped and, crossing his arms, called out, "Fellas, didn't Sela ask you to pick up your toys?"

When the boys paused with their construction to look up at him, he cocked his brow and said, "Well, get to work. Now."

They glanced at each other, and silently scrambled from the floor and started to stuff toys into the giant toy bag Sela dragged to them.

"When we finish, will you read us a story?"

Ben wasn't sure which twin had spoken, but he played it by ear. "Let's get the room picked up, first; then we'll decide what to do next."

"Okay," the other twin said, though he seemed to eye Ben in a new light.

Sela joined Ben and they both walked to the kitchen.

"You don't think I was too hard on them, do you?" He looked back over his shoulder. "I don't want to damage them for life."

She laughed. "Oh, no. They ignore me every now and then because I'm more a play partner than the disciplinarian in their life. They can tell who can be faked out a mile away. Now, Ron has the same effect as you. He walks in and gives an order only once. Poor Vanessa doesn't even try these days."

"Where are the ladies, anyway?"

"They've left, but Vanessa wasn't feeling well, so I'm watching the boys until Ron picks them up later on."

She had changed into shorts and a shirt and looked delectable. Ben tried to keep his eyes raised to her face.

Sela looked at him oddly. "Did you come upstairs because I forgot to bring a plate down?"

"Yeah." He smiled. "I'm hungry."

"I never got around to it. I'm sorry." She walked toward the counter where trays of food were covered with aluminum foil. "Come over here and fix yourself something."

He followed her, enjoying the sway of her hips. Distracted as he was, when she abruptly stopped, he almost crashed into her. She indicated the plates and he picked one up. "Where are your flowers?"

She leaned against the counter and watched him ladle food onto the plate. "I put them in my room. They really are beautiful. But you know, I don't believe for a minute that you just happened to bring them home for no particular reason."

He stopped a moment to look at her. "You're right. They were an offering to get you to agree to dine out with me."

Surprised by his admittance, she glanced at her hands before she looked back at him. "Oh. I guess that's why you looked sort of lost for a while? You arrive here and the place is filled with kids, toys, and wild women, some even pregnant."

He smiled. "Maybe." He set the plate away from him and moved around the counter next to her. "I'd like to spend some time with you, that's all. On neutral ground, where we can get to know each other better."

"I know even less about you."

"All the more reason we should try, don't you think?" He bent to kiss her mouth. At the last moment, she slanted her head and the kiss fell innocently against her cheek.

"I'm not used to doing this so easily," she breathed.

This time, his hand took her face and held it gently. His lips brushed against hers as he spoke. "But, it is easy. Just follow my lead."

His lips took the lead well, and she returned the kiss with a hunger that coursed through her body.

"We're finished."

"Now can you read us a story?"

The twins' high-pitched voices sent a shudder of reality through Sela. They would be in the kitchen any second now.

She pulled away from Ben, and wiping her bruised mouth in the process, stepped to the other side of the counter.

"Saved by the kids." He grinned a devilish smile as he crossed his arms and studied her. "I can wait because I play to win."

"You're mine, no one else's. Why can't you see that?"

Frisco whispered his plea to no one in particular, least of all his love, Helena. He sat in the grass on the near side of the woodshed, less than fifty feet from his obsession, and pondered the moonlight that filtered the shadows across the gazebo.

He was more distraught than angry and, if he would admit it, confused. He had been sorry to cause her pain only the day before, and now . . . well, it had started again. Why did he continue to go to her, and allow her open affair to tear him apart this way? She was no longer responsible, he knew that. It was he, the outsider. Everything was fine until he showed up. Frisco kicked at the damp earth.

He had seen them again. Together. It had been hard to watch, but tonight they openly carried on in the kitchen for anyone to see. They wouldn't learn except through pain. She and her daughter were his, and it wasn't right that another man could lay claim to something so sacred. He wasn't to be trifled with, and soon, he would have to show them again.

It was well past midnight and Sela's twists of protest in her bed were to no avail as her subconscious slipped into the dark corridors where she dared not go during the waking day. . . .

It had been warm, painfully warm that spring day, and Sela had already stripped her sweater from her back where it now dragged from her school backpack. As she skipped from the bus, she said good-bye to the preschool bus driver. By the time she reached the front door of the house, she had already collected three interesting rocks, a wildflower, and a colorful piece of glass.

She would show her prizes to Mama while they had milk and cookies.

Putting her weight into it, she turned the big knob on the front door.

"Mama," she called, and dropped her bags in the middle of the foyer floor. "Look at what I found." She marched into the kitchen, expecting to see her mother at the table waiting with cookies. She wasn't there.

"Mama," Sela called. She dropped her prizes on the table, and went to find her.

After checking the backyard and the den, she took her search upstairs to the bedrooms. She bounced up the stairs, finding a game in every part of the day, as only a five-year-old could. Today, each stair step was an invisible dragon, and she had to step carefully to avoid their fire-

breathing mouths. Happily, she bounded across each step until she safely arrived at the top floor. . . .

Sela groaned on her bed, a subconscious warning to her dream-self, but like all the other times, it went unheeded in this perpetual replay of destiny. . . .

"Mama, where are you?" Little Sela stepped onto the top-floor landing and skipped along the hardwood floor to the room at the end, which belonged to her mother.

When she reached the door, she turned the knob to enter, but it wouldn't open easily. Never having had so much difficulty in finding her mother, Sela grew tired of the chase. She used both hands to make the knob turn; and finally, it did. But, as soon as the latch unlocked, the knob flew from her small hands and the door jerked partly open.

"Mama?" Sela entered the doorway, and her eyes were drawn upward and to the horror that swung from the ceiling.

"Mama!" She stumbled backward, against the wall, as her scream repeated itself over and over. . . .

"Mama!" Sela screamed from her bed as she tried to extricate herself from the dream's clutches, but to no avail.

"Mama!"

Twenty

Ben was in the kitchen, and when he heard the cry that emanated from the hall, he dashed for Sela's room.

He reached her door and pounded it. "Sela, are you all right?"

Another whimper, almost childlike, floated from the room.

He twisted the knob, but it was locked. "Sela, it's Ben." He hit the door with his fist. "Open the door." When no response came, he called out, "I'll break it down if you don't answer in two seconds."

"I'm coming." It was Sela's voice, strained but clear.

Ben ran his hand over his face, not sure what was going on or what to expect. He felt an eternity pass as he waited for her to open the door.

When she did, his eyes roamed over her in a quick study. She stood wrapped in a long robe, her eyes damp from where she had wiped away tears. Her hair was loose and thick as it brushed her shoulders.

Something was wrong. He grasped her arms. "What's going on? I heard you from the kitchen."

"It was a dream, that's all." She hugged her arms to her chest. "Nothing more serious than that."

"No, it sounded more like a nightmare." He held her from him. "Does this happen often?"

"If you're asking has it happened before, the answer is yes."

"Sometimes it helps to talk about it. Do you want to do that?"

"No, I've already kept you from—" Her eyes dropped to the T-shirt and short sweats he wore.

"I was working late downstairs, that's all." He looked past her and into the unlit bedroom. "There's no point in you trying to go back to sleep just yet. Why don't I get you something to drink? Say, hot tea, maybe?" Though he worried over her being terrified by a dream, he forced himself to smile in encouragement. "How about it?"

She inhaled a deep breath and nodded. "Tea would be nice. Thanks."

"I'll be right back." Ben squeezed her arms before he released her, and headed back down the hall to the kitchen.

As he disappeared around the corner, Sela leaned back on the door and closed her eyes, still a bit shaken by the dream that had come back to haunt her. It had been years since she'd awakened with cold sweats, calling out for her mama. Ben was right. Returning to bed now would only cause her mind to revisit the tortured scene.

She treaded wearily back into her dark bedroom, the hall light her guide, until she found herself standing at the jewelry box where she stored her locket. She removed the keepsake before she returned to her bed and switched on the bedside lamp. With the gold locket suspended from her fingers, she dropped to the edge of the bed and sat with her foot tucked beneath her.

Sela looked up as Ben returned with a tray. She

closed her hand over the jewelry and slipped it into her robe pocket.

"That was quick," she said.

"The teapot was already heated from when I used it a while ago." He set the tray between them before he made a seat opposite her on the bed. "The tea should be nice and hot."

Sela watched him as he turned and looked around the large bedroom that came complete with a sitting area. When his eyes lit on the flowers he'd bought for her, now displayed in a cut-glass vase atop her antique dresser, she saw him smile. He continued to look around the room until he saw the huge chifforobe that commanded an entire far corner.

"I can tell that you and your aunt are alike in some ways. You both share a love for old pieces." He nodded toward the chifforobe. "From this distance, that wardrobe chest could be a good reproduction, but it looks early 1900s. Is it?"

She nodded. "Auntie found it years ago in some place she was poking around, and had it sent here."

"I'm surprised you don't travel more, like she does."

Sela remained silent, not sure what to say, but equally sure that he would rebut any explanation she managed.

"If you ever decide you want to take off somewhere, I'm game to go just about anywhere."

"You're not afraid of much, are you?"

"I don't think travel is a brave venture, but you do have to be open to change, and that can be a hard thing for some." He cocked his head at Sela. "Maybe that's what keeps you here."

A tenuous smile formed on her lips. "What makes you leave your home?"

A wry expression crossed his face. "I don't know. Maybe it's partly that I'm restless, but I spend a good deal of time chasing and digging into the past." He gave Sela his undivided attention. "And, now I'd like to hear about your dream."

While their tea steeped, Ben's inquisitive gaze was a living thing as it enfolded her. She pushed strands of hair from her face and returned his stare with darts of her own. He had strong eyes that she believed sprang from his equally strong sense of self. If she were his prey, she suspected, those eyes would never waver as he came in for the kill.

"Why do you do that?" she asked.

"What?" He spoke in an innocent enough tone.

"That look of yours—it goes right through me." Her tired voice belied the beginnings of her smile. She removed the teabag from her cup. "Do you really want to hear about a bad dream?"

"Only if you want to talk about it."

Sela realized she did want to tell him. She took a sip of the hot tea, and it began to melt the cold knot in her stomach. "I dreamed of my mother and the day she died."

"You said her death was by suicide."

She nodded. "I was the one who found her."

This time, she saw through Ben's barrier and read the horror in his frowning eyes as his teacup stopped halfway to his mouth. She wondered if she had been wrong. Maybe he wasn't ready to hear all of it.

"What happened?" In quick afterthought, he added, "This is probably difficult for you, Sela. You don't have to—"

"I do, and I want to." She curved her hands around her cup and let the recollected images flow forward. "The dream starts off innocently enough. I've just come home on the kindergarten bus."

Ben's frown grew deeper. "Take your time, you don't have to rush, and I'm not going anywhere."

"Thanks." She set the cup on the tray and quietly relayed the recurring dream to him. When she faltered a moment at the end, her hand clenched into a fist in her lap.

"And, that's where I find her," she finished, and raised her eyes to Ben. She saw that his eyes also searched her face, as though he tried to reach into her thoughts. It was then that she realized he had caught her hand between his. "She's . . ." Sela swallowed. "She's swinging by her neck from the ceiling beam."

"My God." Ben reached out and drew her into his arms. "It's no wonder you still have nightmares."

She relaxed against his shoulder. "Even now, I can remember how much she resembled a fragile rag doll."

They pulled away from each other, and Ben asked, "It happened in this house?" He brushed her hair back from her face.

She nodded. "Upstairs."

"The room I wanted to stay in at the end of the hall," he surmised. "That's why you acted peculiar when I wanted to use it."

"Aunt Claire has always been here when we use it for guests. So now you know another town secret." She sat back as she regarded him.

"You do a good job of keeping it together." He reclaimed her hand.

"I'm no different from anybody who has problems to overcome. It's stored deep inside. But sometimes, it makes me feel frozen and empty, like there's nothing there."

"That's not good, Sela, but I think it's called grief."

"But, it's been twenty-two years now, and I should have found peace with it. Most of the time I think I have, except when the dream comes back."

"What happened to you would've been a shock for an adult, and you were a five-year-old child."

"When I was in elementary school, I was very angry for a time because I decided Mama must not have liked me, after all. You see, she did hang herself so I could find her."

"But, you learned that wasn't true, right?"

"Let's see, after about three child therapists, I'm sure I've come to terms with that part of it."

"Did she leave a note to explain why she took her own life?"

"I think that would have helped me, to know why she did it. The unanswered questions bother me most. Auntie, like the rest of us, was completely taken by surprise, and the autopsy didn't show any hidden disease. She did leave one thing for me, though." She pulled her hand from his, then reached into her pocket and withdrew the locket. "I keep it inside here." She released the clasp and the folded paper popped out.

"The note on the floor the other night." He looked at Sela before he read the words again on the slip of paper. "She wrote good-bye and that she loves you."

"It was found with her." Sela shifted so she could peer at the paper with Ben. "It seems kind of cryptic, don't you think? For years, after Auntie told me about it, I decided it was some sort of secret message, and it was left up to me to decode what it meant. I would sit for long stretches and just stare at her handwriting and analyze her words."

He ran his fingers along the torn edge of the paper. "Did she leave other notes?"

"No, that was it. I keep this one because it was her last good-bye to me."

He carefully folded the note again. "It doesn't look like she planned things too far in advance. It was a spur-of-the-moment decision."

"When a person is desperate, nothing makes sense." She made an uncomfortable smile. "So far, the only thing I know about that day is that she left me."

Ben dropped to his elbow and stretched out across the bed. "But your aunt stepped in. She didn't leave you."

"You're right. I don't know where I'd be without Aunt Claire. I can't help but wonder at what would make a person leave their child without even a father left to care for her."

Sela untucked her foot and now extended it out as she mimicked Ben and propped herself on an elbow to face him. Her long robe draped each sinuous move, all under Ben's watchful eye.

"So, are you feeling better?" he asked.

She covered a growing yawn with her hand as she nodded. "I am. Maybe talking does do a body good."

"Sleep does that, too," he teased. "Maybe I should go and let you rest." He rose and picked up the tray between them, but her hand on his arm stopped him.

"No, we've talked about me this entire time. "I'd like to know more about you."

Ben smiled as he seriously contemplated the statement. He set the tray he held on the floor, then resumed his propped position across from her.

"Fair enough, but earlier, you said you *had to* tell

me about your mother's death." Ben's face became serious. "Why did you put it like that?"

She studied her hand. "We're traveling an interesting path, and I guess I want you to know a little of what you're getting yourself into when it comes to me." She looked at him. "I'm really complicated, Ben Russell. To the point of not being worth the effort."

He laughed at her words, as if he were sincerely amused. "The way my parents figure it, I'm about five years past my prime for marriage and family. I don't have roots in any particular place, so I'm the one not worthy of your time."

Sela looked into his face as she tried to gauge whether he meant what he'd said. "I'm serious."

"So am I." He raised his hand in a casual salute. "I'm the middle son, the complicated birth order number that usually begets a rebellious personality, not to mention a tendency toward unconventional thinking."

"You sound more like an entry in a psychiatry book." Sela laughed. "No wonder you impressed Auntie. So, if your family's not too happy about it, and I know how you feel about small southern towns, why did you take up Auntie's offer and come here?"

He laughed with her. "I'll tell you why but you have to promise not to say anything to anyone else."

She crossed her heart. "Promise."

"I needed a quiet, unassuming place where I could think through an important decision that affects my future."

"It already looks pretty bright to me. What more could you want?"

He raised his brows. "It's something I don't want. I don't want to partner into my father's business."

"Why? Isn't that what sons are supposed to do? You'll have it made."

"Well, I'm odd like that, I guess. I don't want to have it made. I'd rather blaze my own trail, and I'm doing pretty good specializing right now. Who knows, I might even do some consulting under my own name. Anyway, my brothers can aptly fill my shoes at the corporate office."

Sela was proud of the stance he'd taken, and thought he should be, too. She had a decision to make, too, but hers was more about finding courage to carry it through.

"Do they know how torn you are?"

He nodded. "I think it was obvious after I cut ties with a lot of things connected with my planned future. And so, I've been traveling for my father's firm the last few years, and picking up a new language here and there. Through it all, I've managed to teach as well as collect material for my own project."

"That would be your case study volume on religious structures?"

He nodded. "I've become pretty knowledgeable on the subject, and on occasion I get to teach what I know to eager students abroad. Meanwhile, my father is right there, dangling the business at me, like a carrot, every chance he gets."

"Didn't Auntie tell me the whole lot of you are professional something or other? Sounds like there was a lot of overachieving going on."

"Yeah. At my house, it was a given."

"So, have you made up your mind?"

Ben reached out and gently drew a finger along her jawline. "It seems my mind has been occupied lately with more pleasurable thoughts."

She flushed at his touch and the suggestive words. "I told you I can only complicate things for you."

"I love a puzzle." He touched her hair and drew his fingers through its length. "Soft." His baritone voice had dropped to almost a whisper. "I think I could get a kick out of taking you apart and putting you together again. At our leisure."

She held her breath as, once again, his words released an erotic wave within that unnerved her to her very core. She dared a glance at him and exhaled.

"Auntie goes on and on about the depth of your character. I wonder what she'd think about you saying these things."

"I'm in bed with a beautiful woman and I'm actually watching my manners. Nothing says character better than that." He raised himself and molded his hand to her robed waist. "And all the time I'm asking myself, how many different languages can I whisper in her ear to say she is one damn beautiful woman?"

Sela looked at Ben's face as it neared hers, and felt she would drown in the masculine power he exuded. It was pointless to deny her attraction for him.

She didn't. "Why not give it a try?"

His large hand at her waist pressed her back onto the bed. He lifted his body half atop hers, and captured her hands on the bed at either side of her before he lowered his mouth to her neck.

"Vous êtes une belle femme," he whispered against her skin before he kissed, then nibbled at the bottom of her tender lobe.

Sela strained against his mouth and released a heady sigh while she further exposed the delicate lines of her neck to his mouth.

He kissed her cheek, her nose, and then moved down to her mouth where his lips brushed hers as he spoke. *"Lei sono una bella donna."* His thick whisper was quickly buried within her mouth as his tongue traced the soft fullness of her lips.

Sela thought she would pass out from the exquisite euphoria he summoned. She wanted to touch him, and revel in their contact, but he held her hands, and intensified the sensations even more.

His lips left hers as they traveled across her chin to kiss the pulsing hollow at the base of her throat. *"Usted es una mujer hermosa."*

Sela's groan pleaded for release, but he wouldn't have it. Instead, he moved to cover her hips with his hard body, until they fit like hand in glove. Their closeness was a drug that lulled her to a silky pleasure.

"Ben, what have you done to me?" She made a desperate whisper through her roused passion.

"Everything you're sensing, I'm feeling it in spades. *Ebu nwanyi mara-ma."* His mouth created a path from her neck to her chest. As he nudged the robe away from her breast, he released one of her hands. *"Lei sara la mia donna."*

Sela brought her hand up to caress his neck while he pulled loose the looped belt on her robe. He slipped his hand inside and let it glide down her taut stomach to the swell of her shapely hip where he began to stroke those soft lines.

Sela gasped in torment as he explored her sensitive, naked skin. Naked skin.

Both the knowledge and the cool air doused her ardor as her eyes flew open. Ben had already raised up on his knees. When she saw the hunger and lust in his gaze that remained frozen below her face, she realized why. She quickly sat up on the bed and pulled her robe across her nakedness.

"Sela. You . . . you don't have anything on."

"I forgot," she said, and looped the belt close.

"You forgot what?" he asked. He sat back on his legs, his ragged breaths finally returning to normal.

"That I didn't have anything on beneath my robe."

Ben tilted his head in confusion.

She stumbled over her explanation. "I don't sleep in much, and when you came to the door earlier, I just threw on a robe, and then, one thing led to another."

"I see." Ben rubbed his hand down his face. "You know, a man can get carried away with a surprise like that." He moved off the bed, and away from her. "Not that I'm complaining, but from what I've figured, you're not ready to go there just yet."

"I know." Sela's body still vibrated with hunger. "I didn't mean to let things go so far."

"Unless it's what we both want." When the silence lingered between them, Ben broke it. "It's almost morning, and your parade is tomorrow." He picked up the tray from the floor and started for the door. "You have a lot to do later on today, so you should try and get back to sleep. This time."

"Ben," Sela called to him when he reached the door. "What were you saying to me, you know, in the different languages?"

"Only that you're a beautiful woman. And in time, I wager you'll be my beautiful woman." He smiled at her. "Go on, get some sleep." As he left, he closed the door behind him.

Sela pulled her knees up to her chest and contemplated his words. Would she ever become his woman? How could she when she was a danger to him? Of course, no one close to her had ever held that belief, but it was how she had decided to live her life. But, the thought of the pleasure she might experience with him made her dizzy with expectation. She dropped back and hugged the pillow to her chest. How could she win against a stacked deck dealt by fate? She had to tell Ben all of it, every ugly part of it, and soon. It was only fair.

Frisco opened the shed door at the pond and stepped out into the dark, humid morning. It had been a simple enough matter to weaken the electrical wire casings so he could expose them at a moment's notice to create his own fireworks show tomorrow.

He had learned a lot from helping his uncle, New Hope church's janitor and all-around handyman for thirty-two years before he died. It would all be quick and final. A touch and that would be it. But most important, things could return to normal.

He looked around the deserted banks as the mist rose from the pond after the light rain had cooled everything off. He liked how the white fog made everything clear. Frisco smiled, nowhere near tired this early morning. His best ideas came to him when he had the edge of restlessness about him.

He sighed as he shook his head clear, the nervous tic at his temple brazen with its incessant hammering. It would be all over soon, and he'd have them again. Helena and Sela. He began the long hike to his car on the other side of the ball field.

Twenty-one

"I want to get picked up, too, Mr. Russell."

Ben looked down at Brian, and scooped him up. "Can you see now?"

He settled down on the safe perch of Ben's wide shoulders. His answer was the clap of his hands in time to the band music with his brother, Brett, who also sat tall on their father's shoulders.

The two men stood in the back of a deep throng of onlookers in the thickest part of the countywide parade route that would end just beyond the few blocks of downtown. They had rocked with the bands, laughed with the clowns, been awed by the fire trucks, and endured the politicians in open-top cars, as all of it paraded in front of them. But, they still searched for sight of Sela. Now, another local county high school marching band had begun to high-step for the crowd in their loudest percussion glory.

"Ben, thanks for helping out with the boys," Ron yelled above the din. "I forgot I'd need two sets of shoulders to view the crowd at one time."

Ben adjusted his sunglasses with one hand as he laughed and waited to answer until the band had passed. "I wasn't doing anything else today, anyway;

and, Sela told me I'd never hear the end of it if I didn't show up."

"She should be coming along the route any minute now."

"Is Vanessa feeling any better?" Ben asked.

Ron grunted in concern. "She says yes, but I don't know. I think she ought to check into the hospital, just to be safe, but she says it's normal to have false contractions in the last weeks. So, she stayed home to pack the picnic basket for the afternoon. Right, guys?"

"Right, Daddy," they answered in unison.

"Look." Brett pointed down the street. "I can see Aunt Sela."

"And, she's got Petey in the parade," Brian added.

Ben looked down the parade route and smiled. He recognized her and the little fluff of a mutt that marched proudly in front of her. Their banner proclaimed their group as the Fairlight Humane Society and Animal Shelter. She, along with at least thirty other pet handlers, paraded the leashed animals of various breeds, sizes, and colors down the street.

As expected, the animals were a hit along the route. Squeals broke out from the old and young, along with the ones that came from Brett and Brian.

"Last year," Ron said, "they dressed the animals up, and it was not a pretty thing to watch." They both laughed.

"Daddy, when can we get our dog from the shelter?"

Ron looked at Ben. "Vanessa told me that would be when hell freezes over." To the boys, he replied, "We'll talk with your mama about it later, okay?"

Ben smiled, oddly at peace in this motley crowd of strangers. The warm sun felt good on his arms, a happy kid sat on his shoulders, and a parade of dogs were being led down the middle of the street by an incredible woman. An indelible sense of stability, like a long-delayed epiphany, washed over him. He sighed, as all seemed right with the world. This must be what it was like for his married brother every day, what Ron took for granted, and what his parents had raised him to look forward to. Maybe this settling down thing didn't have to be a contrary experience. But, then again, maybe the difference in his thinking was Sela. As she passed in front of them, like the twins, he waved wildly at her to attract her attention.

Sela stood at the counter in Vanessa's kitchen, deep in thought as she wrapped another sandwich in cellophane before she passed it on to her friend to be packed with the other food.

The parade was over, and now it was time to meet the men and boys at the pond for the picnic. Sponsored as a group effort by the local churches and county government, the Fourth of July celebration was an event that had gained popularity each year. That was caused, in part, by a fireworks display, which had also grown as the years passed.

"I was sure I had it all figured out, Vanessa. I really did. And now, I just don't know."

"Well, I think it can only be a good thing if you get rid of the notion that you're responsible for what happened to Andrew and Charles. Let it go."

"No matter what you say, I'll never accept that they were just coincidences."

Vanessa left the picnic basket and grabbed Sela's hand. "Just stop one minute, and listen to yourself."

Sela's expression turned mulish; it was her way

when she didn't want to listen, ready to argue her point at a moment's notice.

"That's guilt talking because you couldn't prevent what happened," Vanessa argued. "Not you, and not even a clairvoyant like Miss Claire. Now, Ron and I, we've let you walk around in this fog of your own making because nobody's come along that you've even raised an eye to. But then Ben steps in. He's a wonderful guy, and I swear it's like he was made to order for you, girl. And you're going to walk away from him because you have a feeling he'll die a horrible death if you form a relationship?"

"But, what if—"

Vanessa stopped her with a look.

Sela let out a deep sigh. "I care about him." This time, when Vanessa arched her brow, Sela smiled. "Okay, I admit it, but I don't want anything to happen to him. I'd sacrifice myself first before I let him get hurt."

"Sela, you two have been getting close for a while, and nothing odd has happened. That's a good sign, don't you think?"

"You're right," she agreed, and her smile widened as she hugged her arms around Vanessa. "You always help me see the other side of things."

"I admit, I've become a good substitute for Miss Claire when she's not around."

"Who knows?" Sela said, her eyes bright. "He might even decide to stay and oversee the church renovations this fall."

"Everything will be all right. How can it not be? You've got too many people cheering you on not to win." Vanessa squeezed Sela's arm. "I think fortune has dealt you the right hand this time."

* * *

It had turned dusk, and the picnic area was dotted with townspeople who milled between the game field and the tents where food still remained. Others relaxed on the grass and chose their favorite spots for the fireworks that would soon begin.

Ben and Sela had picked a grassy spot located under a copse of trees. The blanket was spread so they could enjoy an unobstructed view of the sky above the water. It was also located just down from Vanessa and Ron's picnic table.

After their afternoon full of food and games, Sela now settled on the blanket. Weary, though quite happy, she closed her eyes and leaned back on her arms.

Ben dropped down beside her. "This has been some kind of day. I don't think I'll remember half of the names of the people I met, let alone all the kids."

"What's important is the kids will remember they met a well-known African-American architect. That'll mean a lot when they come to realize that they can be anything they want."

He turned to face her. "You really love this town, don't you?" Smiling, he said, "I already know the answer to that."

Sela shifted uncomfortably. "I've invested a lot here—my friends and family are here."

"I figured I spoke prematurely about the town when I first got here." He looked around. "It has a lot going for it after all."

She smiled with obvious enjoyment. "I'm going to take that as an apology, and I accept it." She reached out and touched his cheek. "I'm glad the day has turned out this way."

He caught her hand and fitted his fingers with hers. "We should do this more often."

Sela felt a warm glow flow through her as she observed the promise in his eyes.

"Did she ever tell you about how we used to skinny-dip out here?" Ron had walked over to their blanket.

Sela tossed her head at her friend and grimaced at the reminder. "No, I didn't and I'll thank you not to, either."

Ben gave her an incredulous look before he laughed. "You skinny-dipped out here?" He drew her hand to his lips and, with good humor, said, "There's a side of you I don't know yet." He then whispered for her ears only, "Maybe that explains that penchant of yours for sleeping with no clothes on."

"Seeing as they were both ten years old at the time, neither one of them had much to hide," Vanessa added good-naturedly from her seat at the table.

"All of the kids used to do it," Sela admitted. "And, that's probably the extent of my wild and crazy life."

Vanessa stood and stretched her back. "Ron, don't you have to make sure the equipment is collected before the fireworks start?"

"You're right," he agreed. "I'll go and do it now."

"The boys and I'll walk over with you."

He looked at her with concern. "Are you sure that's not too much walking for you?"

"Positive." She walked over and slapped him on his back. "Let's collect the boys from Luther and go." To Sela and Ben, she said, "We should be back before the fireworks start."

"Okay," Sela said, and watched them walk off.

"I like that woman," Ben said as he bent his head

and offered Sela a smile as intimate as the kiss he was about to give her.

Sela closed her eyes and received his kiss, though she was uncomfortable by this display of affection in public. However, she knew the arrogant Ben Russell thought nothing of throwing caution to the wind.

He moved his mouth over hers, and devoured the softness. The surprisingly gentle kiss seemed more a caress, and escalated her own passion. When she parted her lips, he spoke against her mouth.

"Let's not start anything out here." He pressed his lips to hers again before he raised his head. "Do you know how many times today I've wanted some privacy with you? I even considered inviting you into that toolshed with me."

She smiled at the exaggeration, though it flattered her. The sound of chuckling came from nearby. They turned and saw two young girls walk by, and after having thrown a glance Sela and Ben's way, giggled again behind their hands.

Sela groaned. "That's why I can't do this in public."

Ben smiled. "A couple of your students?"

She nodded. "I run the media center. They're all my students."

"What was it I said about small towns and gossip?" He made her laugh as he hugged her against him.

"Ben." The deep hail was unmistakably Luther Matthews's voice.

As Ben and Sela separated, they saw Luther as he came their way. Dressed in casual picnic clothes, the young deputy was obviously off duty.

"Luther, how's it going?" Ben stayed on the ground, but stretched his arm out for a handshake.

"Not bad," he drawled before he greeted Sela in

turn. "Just doing a little patrolling of the grounds, that's all, for the picnic committee." He looked up at the sky. "I guess we'll get the fireworks in for another year, and without the rain."

"It's been nice all day," Ben agreed. "I was telling Sela that your town really knows how to put on a holiday party."

"Everybody looks forward to it every year," she said.

"They even assigned you a job, huh?" Luther asked.

Ben laughed. "From what Ron said, I don't think anybody gets out of one. Mr. Freeman asked me to handle the lighting, and so far, so good. In fact, when I power the lights back up on the ball field after the fireworks show, that'll be it for me."

"Well, he wanted to remind you to bring up the entire bank of lights after the show, not just the ball field. I think you can only do that from the disconnect box in the toolshed."

"No problem," Ben said. "I'll take care of it."

Luther turned to leave, but he stopped. "Oh, and one more thing," he advised. "Don't turn the lights on too soon. Make sure you wait until the last firework charges are spent. It's more excitement for the crowd if it stays dark until the very end."

Ben and Sela smiled at Luther's thoroughness. "I'll remember," Ben said.

The fireworks were loud, plentiful, and spectacular, and had been set off to a rousing, looped score of "America." Ben smiled to himself as he bent to hug Sela while she sat squeezed between his knees. How much more apple pie could this town get?

He whispered at her ear, "The show is just about

over. I'm going to jog on over to the shed so the lights will be on when this is done."

"I guess Vanessa and Ron got stuck somewhere else when the fireworks started," Sela said. Her head remained upturned as she watched the sparkle of multicolored lights explode across the sky over the pond.

He glanced around, then brushed a kiss at her cheek. "I still don't see them, so you're probably right. When I finish with the lights, I'll meet you back here." In one swift motion, he was on his feet. He squeezed her hand again before he let it go.

For at least two minutes, Ben made his way through the scores of people who lined the bank before he saw the toolshed in the distance. When loud applause erupted all around him, he knew that signaled the fireworks were coming to an end. As he drew nearer the building, he waved when he saw Ron and his family together watching the fireworks, just as he and Sela had thought.

He passed Jim Lewis. He was being his usual gregarious self as he held court at a table with others from the church, including Mrs. Thornton, the Freemans, and a few others whose faces were familiar, but whose names now eluded him. Ben threw his hand up to greet them, but continued on to the toolshed.

When he reached the building, Ben opened the door. The large, one-room reinforced shed had no windows and it was now pitch-black. He stepped in and immediately stubbed his toe against a hard object.

"Damn." The sharp expletive was spoken aloud. What happened to the light, and where the hell was the switch? He took another tenuous step into the black room. As he touched the walls in search of the switch, the door swung shut. It didn't matter; there wasn't much light coming from outside, anyway. He tried to wait until his eyes adjusted to the dark. So, where was the disconnect box?

A long, wooden worktable lined most of one wall, and using it as a guide, he moved across the floor. When his next few steps didn't reveal the wire box, he stopped, deciding this was ridiculous. Then, he remembered the automatic lighter he had used for the grill. To keep it away from the twins, he had stuffed it in his pocket. He pulled the short-barreled plastic lighter from his pocket, and squeezed the trigger a couple of times. A small flame, albeit steady, flickered from the barrel's end.

"Voilà," Ben said with a smile, and held the flame high. A naked lightbulb hung from the center of the ceiling, but the string pull was missing from the ceramic apron.

Ben's eyes flowed to the other side of the room where he saw the faint shape of the rectangular disconnect box. He had walked past it.

"Finally," he murmured, and moved toward it with the flame; but, in the same breath, he let out a long expletive and stopped in his tracks.

Trained to understand basic wiring, he immediately noticed the live power-supply wire that had come loose and now dangled in contact with the outer metal casing of the circuit box. Instinctively, Ben took a step back. He knew a touch to the metal box would have electrocuted him in short order.

The adrenaline rush honed his senses to a fine edge. He swallowed hard as he judged the situation and decided on what to do. He looked around the room. This was a toolshed, after all, so he began to pull open the drawers in search of something he could use. Then, he spied just what he needed: a pair of insulated needle-nosed pliers.

"Hey, Ben, what's taking so long?" He heard the faint male voice from somewhere outside the shed as a succession of others agreed with him. They were curious about the continued darkness, and here he was about to get fried.

He grabbed up a short length of two-by-four wood that rested on the table. Holding it in the hand with the lighter, he brandished the pliers in his other as he moved toward the power-supply wire. Ben held his breath as he caught the wire and bent it away from contact with the metal box. Finally he exhaled, his eyes now following the wires to the floor and latching upon the green insulated one, in particular.

The door flew open, and the lighter flame flickered as Ben turned to it.

"Ben, do you know what you're—" It was Ron, followed by Mr. Freeman and Luther. They all stopped just inside the door as Ben's hand shot up in caution.

"There's a live wire exposed over here at the disconnect box," he said in hushed tones. Then, he motioned to the thin green wire that ran separate from the others down the wall. "And our ground wire has, somehow, disconnected." He handed the wood block to Ron.

Luther came from around Ron, his eyes wide with concern. "Oh, my God."

Ben looked at his discovery before he stooped to reconnect the ground wire. "That was my feeling exactly. Only, I think I put it a bit differently."

Sela looked up from her seat on the blanket, and laughed when the twins raced to jump in her arms.

"Where has everyone been?" she asked the boys as she hugged them.

"Mama's coming."

"Daddy and Mr. Russell are coming, too."

No sooner had they informed her of the circumstances than the three adults appeared. Sela thought they seemed a little preoccupied, especially Vanessa, and her smile dissolved.

"Are you all right, Vanessa?" Sela stood up from the blanket as she corralled the boys with her hands.

Vanessa pressed her hand to her back. "Maybe that walk did me in."

"When it took so long for the lights to come up, Ben, I began to wonder if you ran out on us." Sela saw his grin stretch across his face, and she smiled, too.

"Never." He looked at Ron as he said, "We had a slight glitch; but see, the lights are back on and everything's fine."

"Yeah, Vanessa and I are going to get on home with the boys," Ron said.

"Then I'll get the baskets together," Sela said. "And you, Vanessa, sit down."

When she led Vanessa to the picnic table to sit, Ben turned to Ron and spoke in a low voice.

"Maybe you shouldn't say anything to Sela about the wires in the shed." He looked across the grass at her. "She's having a good day, and she deserves a lot more of them." He turned back to Ron. "And, there's no point in having her worry about what could have happened. Look at how upset it made Vanessa."

Ron buried his hands deep in his pockets as his brows furrowed in thought. "You're right. Sela will be upset, too."

Ben smiled. "I'm learning more and more about her."

"Yeah, you are." Ron also trained his gaze on the two women. "And since we're her friends, we have to do our best to save her from herself."

Twenty-two

Sela had been at the chore of working through the old boxes of church paraphernalia all afternoon. The windowless little room in the unused section of the basement didn't offer much excitement, and she longed to get back outside, though it was doubtful she would see the sun. The rain had kept up all day. She also craved a glimpse of Ben.

The thought brought a smile to her face. She couldn't help it, but when he was around, it was as though the air she breathed turned electric. She hoped it was the same for him. Based on the goodnight kiss they had shared each of the past nights, she thought so. True to his word, he had not pressed for more. And for that, she was grateful. He seemed to understand that she needed time to come to terms with the path their relationship would take.

She readjusted the latex gloves she wore on her hands and dug deeper into the box. Besides the mold and mildew she could see, it was anybody's guess at what else she might come across in the forgotten room.

The intimate talk with Vanessa had helped Sela see things from her past in a different cast. She yearned for more of that helpful bolster from Vanessa. However, since the picnic two days ago, each time she had tried to draw Vanessa into conversation about Ben, she no longer had an opinion, and changed the subject. When Sela mentioned Vanessa's odd behavior to Ron, he quickly surmised that his wife's skittish moods stemmed from the baby they expected to arrive soon.

As Sela continued to unpack the box, she decided that she agreed with Ron. Vanessa was having as hard a time with this pregnancy as she'd experienced with the twins. But, she suspected Vanessa thought the discomfort was worth the pleasure of motherhood.

She looked down at her own belly, still flat inside her jeans, and wondered at the possible fortunes that might lie ahead for herself, something she had dared not think about not too long ago.

As she allowed the pleasant thoughts to invade her soul, she lifted folded blueprints from the bottom of the box. They were spotted and weathered with age. She held them away from her, not sure what creatures might be attached to the pages, and placed the prints on the table.

When she returned to the box, she saw two other pieces of paper; one was twisted and lay on top of another, and both resembled writing paper. Familiar writing paper.

She reached into the junk box and picked them up, not quite sure why, but intrigued by the color and their quality weight. It was a heavyweight paper almost bleached white from what was probably already a pale color. The two sheets were obvious matches as she unfurled the twisted sheet first, disappointed that nothing was written on it. Its ends were charred, as though a match had been set to it, and the outer edge was stylishly ragged. The other sheet was also blank, and it had the same ragged outer edge; and, both sheets were notepaper size. Even though the paper had been in a box of clutter for who knows how long, Sela thought they were well preserved. It was probably acid-free paper, an expensive blend. Then again, maybe it had been recently tossed in the box.

Sela frowned and, in a spurred thought, held up, first, the twisted sheet she had flattened, then the other, to the light hanging from the ceiling. And she saw it both times. It was a watermark, and it matched one she had seen on some of her aunt's writing stock.

She brought the paper down and folded both pieces. As she tucked them in her jeans pocket, her mind blazed its way through one explanation after another, discounting a coincidence. No way would Aunt Claire have thrown away her stationery, and it wouldn't have been disposed of this way if she had. So, how did it get down here?

Ben followed the narrow hallway he'd come upon in the lower basement until it led to a pine door set into the concrete block wall. He took a couple of photographs before he rattled the door, surprised to find that it opened easily. He led with his flashlight as he peered through. It was a regular size room, and with the exception of a few hanging cobwebs, nothing else greeted him but the dirt floor.

The ceiling line of the room slanted away to his right and into the distance for at least the twelve feet he could see, until it rose no more than a few feet off the dirt floor. He suspected this room lay beneath a set of stairs, and wondered what he would find beyond the arc of his flashlight.

Not sure when the church last had a good survey, he thought this discovery simply hammered home the fact that there was a lot of new territory in this old place not marked on the available blueprints. Reverend Osborne had agreed with Ben's conclusion, and had recommended that he take the opportunity to survey as much of the place as he could.

Ben stepped through the door and, by the time he'd made it halfway, resorted to a stoop as he moved farther into the space. The flashlight played with the shadows on the inclined ceiling until it reached the end and . . . nothing. When he could no longer move forward in a stoop, Ben jutted his shoulder against the concrete slab wall for support. He tried to aim his flashlight as far into the linear opening as he could. It ended in a hole, a black opening that probably dropped into yet another space.

He shook his head and relaxed against the wall. He wasn't sure how far down it dropped, and right now, he wasn't willing to climb in there until he had, at the very least, made a record of this find.

Ben aimed the flashlight around the space again when something caught his eye. He returned to the spot and beamed the light over the area until it lit on several balled-up pieces of paper. Next to those was something partially buried in the dirt. A candle? Had someone else been down here? Surely that couldn't be. Who in their right mind would purposely spend time down here?

"Ben, where are you?"

He cocked his head toward the faint call from outside the room in the basement. It sounded like Sela. He edged his way back to the doorway before he called out.

"I'm down here." The place was a maze of catacombs on this level, and he didn't want her to get lost in them. He dusted himself off as he left the room and began to retrace his steps, and literally ran into her as he turned the corner.

"Oh, there you are," she said, smiling. "Irene told me you were still down here when I thought you'd be gone by now. Working hard, I see."

"Yeah." He dusted his jeans once again before he held his flashlight high. "You shouldn't be down here. The light is poor and this area should be officially closed off you know."

"I know, but it should be okay if you're down here."

He smiled at her. "Since you're here, let me show you something I uncovered. He took her arm and led her back down the hall she had just traveled and stopped at the corner, where a small plaque had been set in the projecting angle of the wall near the floor.

"It signifies your original church," Ben said. He curved the light over the engraved stone. NEW HOPE AFRICAN METHODIST EPISCOPAL CHURCH, 1878.

"You found a cornerstone."

He nodded. "One of the foundation stones of the church with its new name. Everything up to now has been built on and around it."

She knelt down, and as she traced it with her fingers, read it again. "The church added 'new' to the name when they joined the A.M.E. denomination after the Civil War," she said. "Did you show this to Reverend Osborne?"

He nodded. "Yesterday. We'd like to clean up around it so that the renovations will preserve this stake and the members can see it in the future."

"You know, when I was little, we used to sneak down here and play hide and seek. But, it never looked this dark . . . and uncomfortable." She stood up and rubbed her arms while she looked around. "I guess we never saw the danger."

He smiled. "We both need to get out of here and get some sunshine before this lack of light drives us nuts."

"It'll have to be the liquid variety, I think."

"Maybe it'll get better by the weekend."

"Ah, yes." She laughed. "The weekend in Fairlight. Now that the Fourth is over, what can I introduce you to? How about the fine art of gardening?"

"I have a better idea." He turned her around to face him. "Why not let me treat you to an evening out in Atlanta?" When he saw her brows draw together, he added, "Let me finish. Dinner and a movie, or maybe a stage play at the Alliance Theatre, if that's what you prefer."

Through the dim light, Ben could see that her large eyes were charged with uncertainty. "And, no pressure to stay overnight," he added. "Unless you want to."

Her eyes darted away from his hold for just a moment as she nibbled at her lip. Then, the indecision seemed to pass. She looked up at him and smiled. "Okay, it sounds like fun."

"It's a real date, then, tomorrow afternoon, and no reneging."

"A date," she agreed.

They both left, arm in arm, for the stairs that would return them to the sanctuary above them.

The Saturday theater in Atlanta had been entertaining, and they decided to end the evening at a supper club where their digestion was aided by the soft sounds made by a local jazz ensemble. Ben and Sela had completed their meal and relaxed in their chairs at the linen-covered table as the waiter cleared away their plates.

"We missed the chance to hear Jill Scott at the Tabernacle," Ben said. "She was there last night."

Sela smiled as she nodded. "I like her. Maybe next time."

He liked how she said that. He lifted his water glass and gazed at Sela over the edge as the longing stretched inside him.

"Good. Next time." He watched her draw up the lacy spaghetti strap that had managed to slip down her arm again. Besieged by a vision of what he'd expose if he could pull the strap farther down, he gulped a swallow of water.

"Have I told you how beautiful you look tonight?"

She laughed brightly. "I sort of got the idea when you walked into the wall when you first saw me at the house. But I'm not complaining. I don't get enough chances to dress up."

"And let your hair down." He grinned. "You look comfortable, Sela, and the city was made for you; so, for the life of me, I don't know why you won't pursue opportunities around here. It's close by your hometown, and it could open up another world for your teaching and writing."

Sela shifted in her chair, as though she wasn't sure how she'd respond. "I have considered it." Her eyes turned up to meet Ben's. "I've even received an offer. It's for an editing position."

The surprise was written on Ben's face. "That's great. You are going to take it, right?"

She laughed. "Hold on. I'm seriously considering it, and for me, that's a big step."

He joined her in a laugh. "Don't I know it. I'm just glad you're taking the chance."

"To be honest, I think you've made me want to

see more. I sure seem to be seeing things a lot differently than before, just like Auntie said I would."

He reached across the table for her hand and stroked it lightly. "How often is Auntie right?"

"Well, her record's pretty good. Why?"

"When I met her in Italy, she told me my destiny would lie here."

"And, it makes you uncomfortable that she might be right?"

"No," he said honestly. "It did make me curious as hell, though." He grinned. "Who would throw away a chance like that?"

"That's the kind of thing you'd do, Ben." Her face turned solemn. "You take aim at fate, then fight to get what you want."

"Take a chance with me, Sela." Ben's face now became serious. "Play with fate and stay with me tonight in town."

She pulled her hand from his and turned it so that she grasped his, instead. "I'm getting there, Ben, I really am. Just give me a little more time."

He smiled and, for her sake, masked his disappointment. "All right, I will."

Frisco took a careful pace up the stairs to the second floor of the inn. The only other sound in the house was the rain against the windowpanes that managed to drown out his own staccato breathing.

He had entered the house with the extra keys that lay hidden in the gazebo. Fontella wouldn't need them again until the morning, and by then he would have let himself out again.

When he reached the landing, he made deliberate steps to the room at the end of the hall. He turned the knob and was disappointed that it was locked. He raised his hand above the door and took the key he knew would be wedged along the jamb. When he entered the room no more than a step, he felt her presence. Helena.

It was a preternatural stillness that rose from the room where his Helena enjoyed her last sleep. A rare reality entered his head as he, in this clear and thoughtful moment, relived the private truth that he couldn't confront. She didn't want him and didn't want him here. She had damned him to hell.

Frisco covered his ears to protect them from her words. He looked up at the ceiling beams and felt his rage begin to build. Her words screamed to him from the walls; and after all this time, her words still hurt. He had to get out of here, before she divined his plans for the outsider. He dropped the room key in his haste to leave. The door slammed behind him as he made his way down the stairs, and out the back door to the gazebo.

The rain poured down on the two-lane blacktop and showed no signs of relenting. Ben peered through the windshield as he made the turn off the main highway to Fairlight.

"We should be home shortly."

Sela had slipped her shoes off and sat with her feet tucked under her with her wrap pulled snugly about her shoulders. "Good. There's nothing like sleep in the middle of a storm."

Ben glanced at her. "There are others things just as good. I'll have to remember to tell you about them."

"I'm sure you won't forget," she said, and snuggled deeper into her wrap.

They drove on for a while in companionable silence, the CD player and the dancing rain the only sounds.

Sela must have drifted to sleep momentarily, because when Ben put on the brakes, she was jarred to reality.

"What's wrong?" She blinked her eyes as she sat up. "Why are you stopping at this intersection? This isn't our turn."

"Look." He pointed. "Across the street on the sidewalk."

Sela followed his hand and saw the sorry, soggy animal that stood there as though in a daze. "Oh my goodness, Ben. It's Petey." She reached for her door handle.

"No," Ben said. "I'll get him." He opened the door, and darted into the rain.

Sela watched as he grabbed the little dog in his arms, and rushed back to the car. She scrambled to her knees on the front seat and reached to open the rear door so Ben could put the dripping dog there.

"Poor Petey," she cooed. The dog whimpered as Ben set him on the seat, then slammed the door. "You look so sad." She pulled her wrap from around her neck and began to mop the rain from the dog's coat.

Ben had already regained his seat in the front, and wiped the rain from his face. "What's he doing this far from home?"

"He probably sneaked out the same way he did the night we saw him. I'll bet Mildred is worried to death." The dog's whimpers became louder. "He's scared, Ben. Let's take him home."

While Sela calmed Petey, Ben turned the car in the direction of home.

Sela leaned over and kissed Ben's cheek.

"What's that for?" he asked.

"You forgave Petey by rescuing him tonight. You could have driven on past, you know."

"No, I couldn't." He glanced at her. "No matter what I think of the mutt, you care about him."

She laughed, and returned to looking after the dog. "You can't fool me, Ben Russell. I think Petey is growing on you, too."

They arrived at Mildred's house shortly thereafter, and found her standing on the porch. It was obvious she had been looking for Petey. When she saw Ben come up the walk with the wrapped dog in his arms, she ran to meet him along the walk.

He returned to the car and saw that Sela's eyes were also damp.

"Don't tell me you're crying, too," he said as he started the car.

Sela thought she was happier than she'd been in a long time, and told Ben so. He sat there a moment before he leaned across the space that separated them in the car and kissed her hard on the mouth.

"I think you deserve all the happiness you can get," he said. He turned back to the steering wheel and pulled out onto the street.

"Don't forget to stop at Vanessa's. We have to see how she's doing before we go home."

Frisco sat slumped in his car parked down the street from the inn. He should have left an hour ago, before anyone returned. But he had stayed, and planned. The electrocution didn't work out, but he had overcome problems in the past. He knew that if you bided your time, a new opportunity always presented itself.

He pulled out and began to drive through the

pelting rain when he met them. They drove past the inn, to another house. He continued to watch them in his rearview mirror. They were pulling over now, farther down. An opportunity. He doused his lights and drove a block to the end of the street, then turned around.

The rain was still coming down when Ben came to the pastel-colored house. He waited for the slow-moving car coming toward them to drive past before he brought his car to a stop along the street edge.

"Do you want to wait until the rain eases up?" he asked Sela.

"No," she said, and turned in the seat to get the umbrella from the floor. "I'm making a run for it," she teased.

She opened the door and released the umbrella. And with a little squeal, she leaped from the car and ran up the drive to the front porch, hopping over puddles as she went.

She rang the front doorbell and began to shake out the umbrella. As she did this, she turned back to the street. Ben had turned the car off, and she now waited for him to take his turn in the rain and meet her.

And then, she saw a blaze of bright lights. Ben had left the car, and stepped into the road to come around the front, when the high-beamed lights lit on him. As his hands came up to ward off the blinding light, a car appeared from nowhere to screech across the wet asphalt directly at him.

Sela's eyes stretched in horror as she screamed. "Ben!"

Twenty-three

The umbrella dropped from Sela's nerveless fingers. Oblivious to the rain, she raced across the porch and into the night toward Ben.

In a moment that was like a flash in her eyes, Ben dove for the edge of the road as the blurred car reached him.

Sela reached the edge of the dark yard and screamed his name again. Vaguely aware of Ron's voice from somewhere behind her, her attention remaining focused on reaching Ben in the street. She slipped through the gate and gained a flood of relief when he picked himself up from the hard gravel. Then, he stepped back into the street and looked in the direction the runaway car had taken.

"Ben," she cried, and threw herself into his arms before she buried her face against his chest. "I thought you were hit."

"Hey—" He dropped his arms around her, and held her in their tight circle. "I'm all right, but I sure would like to know what that driver was thinking."

"Ben, what the hell happened?" Ron yelled as he jogged up to them. "We heard Sela and the car as it sped off."

"That was about it, but I'm still in one piece," he

said, and glanced at the adjacent houses that had begun to light up. "You may have to explain this to a few neighbors tomorrow, but right now, let's get out of this rain."

Sela and Ben, arm in arm, turned and trotted back to the house as Ron followed them.

Vanessa met them at the door with towels. And, as they dried off, Ben and Ron talked quietly in the living room about what had happened.

Sela, finally satisfied that he was all right, now battled the familiar tugs of guilt that had begun to stir, and quietly separated from the others to walk to the guest bath.

"Our street is pretty settled," Ron said. "Maybe the driver was lost."

"The lights came up out of nowhere through the rain, as if the driver had them off before he saw me," Ben explained. "So, maybe I was just as much a shock to him as he was to me."

Sela stood in the bathroom and looked into the frozen mask that was her face from over the sink. Ben's deep voice floated in to her, and with each inflection of his explanation, the chill around her heart grew colder, tighter. What if?— She blinked at the incomplete thought as Vanessa joined her.

"I brought you some hairpins and bands." She placed the items on the counter, but didn't leave the bathroom.

"Thanks." Sela began to brush her damp, unruly thick hair back into its familiar braid.

"Did you enjoy Atlanta with Ben?" She reached out and touched the delicate, soaked lace on Sela's dress. "Even wet, this dress is still beautiful. It was a good choice."

She knew what Vanessa tried to do, so she attempted a smile as she busied herself with the braid.

But, she couldn't forget what had almost happened to Ben. "That car came close to hitting—"

"I know what you're thinking, but don't," she said, and leaned against the counter next to Sela. "Ben is fine."

"But what about the next time?" She whispered her fear as she secured the braid with a pin.

Vanessa's tone turned sharp. "You can't go back to thinking like that."

Two deep lines of worry appeared between Sela's eyes as she turned and faced her friend. "Ten minutes ago he was almost killed."

"No, he wasn't. He moved out of the way of a car," Vanessa clarified. "Accidents are a given in life, so we accept them." Her soft, brown eyes now settled on Sela. "And you might as well know, Ben avoided one at the picnic, too."

Sela frowned. "What are you talking about?"

"I wanted to tell you before now, but Ron and Ben thought you'd misunderstand what—"

Sela fled the bathroom and returned to where Ben and Ron sat and talked in the living room. They both looked up when she suddenly appeared, but her agitation was what drew the frown to Ben's gaze.

"What happened at the picnic that you didn't tell me about?" she blurted, scarcely aware of her own voice, though fearful of what his would reveal.

He glanced at Ron before he deftly answered, "Nothing to be concerned about. A few electric wires got crossed in the toolshed. Someone was careless, that's all."

The only evidence of Sela's shock lay deep within her, the ability bolstered by years of masked emotions. Vanessa came up behind her, and now squeezed her hand.

As Ben rose to his feet, he smiled in amusement.

"I was telling Ron that if I were superstitious, I'd swear I was jinxed since arriving in town."

"Why would you say that?" She managed to stutter the words through stiff lips.

"Well, let's see." Ben began an absurd enumeration with his fingers. "I was locked inside a wall at the church, fell from a ladder, was almost electrocuted at the picnic, and I just missed being hit by a car." His smile broadened. "If I'm not careful, I think my luck could soon run out."

Vanessa sucked in her breath, shocked by his casual announcement. "That's four accidents since you've been here?"

Sela's panic heightened as she involuntarily clutched at Vanessa's hand.

"Oh, God, it's started again." Her emotions had surfaced to her face. She knew what this meant and looked to her friends as a thread of hysteria entered her voice. "It's happening to Ben."

The humor in Ben's face drained away when he saw Sela's fear. "What's wrong?"

Ron tried to allay their qualms. "Nothing to get upset over, nothing at all."

"Yes, it is," Sela argued, and backed away from them all. "He's had four accidents. Four, and he's barely been here a month. That's no coincidence."

Ben watched as Sela's demeanor turned from concern to alarm before his eyes and he reached out for her, but she sidled away.

"Sela . . ." Vanessa begged with a whisper. "Don't do this."

Ben inched toward Sela. "I don't know what it is, but you're acting pretty strange because of a few accidents. Somebody want to explain?"

"I've got to get out of here," Sela muttered as she backed into the door. "I have to think." She reached behind her and turned the knob as she spoke. "I'm sorry, Ben, but the only way to save you is to let you go."

When she slipped through the door with those words, Ben leaped forward, but the door slammed shut, and Vanessa stopped him before he could run after her.

"She's only going home, and I'm the one to go after her. She won't listen to anyone else right now," Vanessa said.

"What did she mean about saving me?" Ben looked from Vanessa to Ron for an answer.

Vanessa exchanged an understanding glance with her husband before she grabbed an umbrella from the coat tree. "I'll be back as quickly as I can." In a matter of seconds, she had left by the same door as Sela.

When the door slammed again, Ben turned to Ron, the events of the last half an hour now an even greater puzzle.

"All right, you want to tell me what the hell just went on?"

"Ben . . ." Ron dug his hands deep into his pockets. "I don't know if I should—"

"The hell with that. How about the truth?" Ben's concern for Sela battled his anger over the fact that the ones who protected her still considered him in her outer circle. Ron's hesitation confirmed it.

Ben paced across the room and darted a glance to Ron time and again. "I'm beginning to feel like I'm the straight man for the whole town's joke. Everybody knows what's going on, and I'm the poor schmuck who gets the surprise pie in his face."

He finally came to a stop in front of Ron. "Listen, I . . . I care about Sela. Maybe it's even more than that. Hell, it's a lot more than that, so I deserve to, at least, know why she just told me to kiss off."

"You're right," Ron said, and looked up. "You're the only man she's let into her life in a long time, and I know she cares about you, too. You should be told the truth, once and for all."

Ben sucked in his breath, not sure what to expect. "And, what is that truth?"

"Sela won't let you get close to her again."

Ben said nothing as his frown deepened.

Ron sighed. "Not as long as she believes that she caused all those accidents to happen to you."

Ben frowned. "I don't understand."

"She doesn't believe the accidents are that at all. She thinks they're predestined. Fate. You see, the two men Sela was last involved with seemed to always have these . . . accidents."

"You're serious?" Ben asked, incredulous of Ron's words.

He nodded. "And they both died as a result of an accident."

Ben digested the words for a full minute, his mind whizzing through this implausible idea that, in this little town, suddenly seemed not so far-fetched. He smoothed his hand across his head.

"Start at the beginning, Ron."

And while Ron told the story behind Sela's vow to avoid emotional entanglements, Ben pieced together the tortured existence Sela must have lived most of her life. She'd survived more than her share of tragedies, and at the same time she had to live with a foot in both the normal and paranormal worlds.

"It seems most everyone she loves gets taken away," Ben said as Ron finished with the explanations.

"Or leaves her, as she sometimes sees it," Ron added. "And she's decided it's all her fault."

"Damn." Ben spit out the expletive in frustration before he headed for the door.

"Where are you going?"

"I've got to see her and tell her I don't believe this crap."

"It won't be simple, Ben."

"Haven't you heard that anything worth having seldom is?" He cleared the door and, without a pause, jogged through the rain to his car.

When Ben arrived at the inn, he met Vanessa in the foyer. She started to speak, but he held up his hand to stop her.

"You don't have to try and cover what's going on with Sela. Ron told me everything."

Vanessa took an audible breath. "That's good. You should know." She reached for her umbrella, before she turned back to him.

"Where is she now?" Ben asked.

"She won't see you.

As Ben looked past Vanessa, and into the living room, she touched his arm and looked him hard in the eye. "Listen, she's in her room, and she's really fragile, loaded with guilt. Now, I don't pretend to understand why you've had so many accidents—"

"If it makes you feel any better, that's all I think they are."

"Then, if you care about her, you'll go in there and make her understand that you won't leave her, too."

He nodded. "Ron and the boys are on their way for you in the car."

"I'll check back with Sela tomorrow." She walked

past Ben through the doorway, and without looking back, pulled the door closed.

Ben locked the door behind her, and then strode through the foyer toward the hall that would lead him to Sela's bedroom, determination in each step.

Twenty-four

Sela was curled around a pillow on the bed, her shirt and shorts rumpled from the experience, when she heard his knock. Before she could raise her head and tell him to go away, he had already come in.

She could have sworn she'd asked Vanessa to lock her door on her way out, but in view of the fact that her friend had tried to dissuade her from the course she wanted to take, Ben's easy entrance was no great surprise.

The coverlet Vanessa had thrown over her felt good against the humidity and air-conditioning, but she threw it back now, and sat up quickly. As she watched him at the door, she rubbed her arms against the sudden chill. He wore his confidence like a crown, certain that he could wear her down. She spoke to him from the bed.

"Ben, I'm sorry about the scene I caused at Vanessa's."

"You don't have to apologize. Are you all right now?" He stepped into the room.

"I'm calmer, yes. But, we can't continue to see each other, and I don't want to talk about it, either. I just want you to go." Sela watched as his dark, observant eyes searched her face.

"I don't know if you heard me with Vanessa before she left a minute ago, but Ron explained everything, or at least all that he knew."

Ben's words scraped at her dignity and Sela dropped her chin to her chest, not sure if what she felt was relief that he finally knew or humiliation from his pity.

He came farther into the room. "You've had a lot of difficulties, I know, so your confusion about things can be expected."

"Difficulties"—she punctuated the word he'd used—"don't have to be all bad." She moved to sit cross-legged and drew the coverlet over her shoulders as she looked up at him. "We can take something away from the most impossible of events."

"And, you took on guilt."

"The threat is real, and has nothing to do with guilt." She shook her head. "Ben, how do I make you take this seriously? And, I'm not confused. At least not anymore. I don't know . . . some things can't be explained. You just go on faith."

He stopped when he neared the bed. "This is what's been tearing you up about us since the first day we met?"

"I was scared, yes, that this might happen if we became too close." She looked at him. "I told you I didn't want to get involved."

"These last days we've been very close. Why didn't you tell me what you feared?"

Her resolve gained strength as he reached the edge of her bed.

"I wanted to tell you, but I didn't know how to explain it without sounding as if I were crazy. Don't you see, Ben? I don't want you injured, or worse. And, the only way to keep you safe is for us to stay away from each other."

He started to reach for her, but stopped, and pushed his hands deep into his pockets. "You've got a lot going for you, but you don't have that much power."

Sela was ashamed of her past. She didn't want the man she loved to pity her, or even laugh at the dilemma she found herself in. Love . . . the unbidden word interrupted her thoughts. She swallowed hard and bit back the tears that threatened to flow.

"I can't explain it, but I do have that power. Things happen to people who return my affection. And, I don't want you to be a victim."

In a flash, he was sitting with her on the bed as he tried to use reason. "Sela, why don't you trust me? I won't let anything happen."

"You can't stop it." She looked at him as she pleaded, and the tears that had threatened all evening came forward. "Don't you think Andrew and Charles wanted to live? They couldn't stop it from happening."

"And neither could you."

"Ben," she sobbed. "I might as well have killed them."

He grabbed her shoulders and shook her. "But, you didn't." He shouted the words. "And stop saying it."

"I did, and I'll be responsible for your death, too, if you stay around me." She searched his eyes. "I couldn't live with myself if something happened to you."

"Sela, nothing will happen."

"When it does, I'll blame myself."

He hated that she was so hard on herself. He looked in her eyes, wet from tears, and pulled her into his arms. He tried to hug the fear from her, fear nurtured since she was a child, and take it over as his own.

Her voice from his shoulder was flat and quiet. "You can't stay in the same house with me. You have to leave, you know that?"

The unspoken threat that this could be the end no longer hung in the air for them. Ben felt as if he were fighting every prejudice and superstition that had lingered about in Sela's family. But, it wasn't this battle that he feared. It was the war he would ultimately lose. It couldn't be won without her consent, and she wasn't ready to give it. At least not tonight when everything was so fresh in her mind. He'd abide by her wishes for now.

He squeezed her hard in his arms, then set her from him. "I know. I'll do it tonight." He got up from the bed and left for the door. "Before I change my mind."

When he cleared the door, he held a hope that she would call him back, tell him that he was right all along, and that it was nonsense that she was the fault for the accidents. But, it didn't happen. She never called to him, and he continued on to his bedroom upstairs.

Ben zipped the small carryall bag that sat on the bed. In a little over fifteen minutes, he had managed to change clothes and grab a few things to tide him over for a day or so until he could arrange for other long-term accommodations. Lightning flickered through the window just as a peal of thunder vibrated through the house. Ben walked to the window and peered outside.

The rain had not subsided in the least. If possible, it was coming down harder. It was, indeed, a rainy night in Georgia—a night that started out as a promising one for lovemaking; instead, he was being sent away from his love. He made a wry smile at the thought. His love.

Another flash of lightning lit up the sky for a brief moment, and illuminated his car parked at the gate. He dropped the curtain back in place and picked up his bag from the bed on his way out.

As he closed the door behind him, his glance fell to the end of the hall, and the room that had belonged to Sela's mother. He walked up to the door, and only now did he remember it had been locked the last time he had tried to enter. This time, to his surprise, the knob turned under his hand.

Ben set his bag on the hall floor, before he slowly pushed the door open and entered, his interest more pointed on this, his second visit. He flicked the light switch and looked up into the open ceiling and saw that the beam her mother had most likely hung from had since been camouflaged with ceiling fans and track lights.

As he moved in farther, he was drawn to the dresser where a framed picture was propped near the mirror. He picked it up. It was a young woman, Sela's mother. Their resemblance was nothing short of remarkable. He set it back down next to the writing box.

It was a gilded metal box with three compartments. The two outer sections carried notepaper and envelopes, and there was a rest for a pen. The middle section was empty. He picked up a sheet of the paper and observed that the heavyweight paper seemed to be the same as that that Sela kept folded in her locket. Ben replaced the sheet and turned to leave.

When he reached the door, he almost stepped on

the small, shiny object before he saw it. A key. Its silver, boxed shape resembled the one he'd been given for his room. He stooped to pick it up. With only a passing curiosity as to why it was on the floor, he placed it on the dresser before he left the room.

He quickly strode to the stairs and descended to the first floor. When he walked through the foyer and reached the front door, he heard something behind him and turned. It was Sela.

He drew in a sharp breath that seemed to pain his heart. She stood at the foyer entry, her feet bare and her hand on the wall, as though for support. She looked as fragile as Vanessa had suggested. Her face was drawn and her large eyes were two bright spots as he captured them with his own. He dropped the bag and began the hard steps that took him back to her.

"I'll get a room tonight at one of the motels we passed on the main highway. You're upset and I don't want to give you more pain tonight."

"Ben, I'm sorry to do this to you." Her resigned voice shook with emotion. "But, it's for the best."

He stopped in front of her as his eyes continued to cling to hers. "We will work this out, Sela. I don't want to lose you."

When she dropped her eyes before his steady gaze, Ben swooped his head down and claimed her mouth in a quick ravishment. As his arms wrapped her waist and she swayed backward, his mouth slanted across hers again and again in reckless abandon. While the thunder and lightning raged outside, their own elemental passion exploded inside. Ben meant to leave his mark on her, and he did. Sela's knees buckled and she sagged against him in defeat, his last words almost smothered on her lips.

"I won't lose you simply because I love you."

No longer compliant, Sela fought against him now, and pulled away. She stumbled backward as their eyes met and understood.

With a last glance, Ben picked up his bag and left through the front door, and as the latch sounded to announce the finality of it all, Sela ran up and turned the lock. She slumped against the door as her tears poured down.

Her arms were wrapped around her waist as she slid to the cold, damp floor. It was going to happen again, she could feel it; her heart, almost numbed now, cried out against this thing she couldn't understand. He loved her, but it no longer mattered. She had to sacrifice their love to try and save him.

The phone's incessant ring finally woke Sela. She had cried herself to sleep, and didn't want to wake up. But, the caller was more insistent. Reaching from the bed, she answered the phone.

"Sela, this is Luther," he drawled.

The announcement fully awakened her, and she sat up on the bed and rubbed her eyes. "Why are you calling at this time of night? It's way past midnight."

"I know, but this storm is pretty bad, and I promised Vanessa earlier that I'd get over there and talk with Ben about that accident he had tonight in front of her place."

"She told you about it?"

"Yeah. I know it upset you, too, but I'm calling 'cause I can't get over there tonight, seeing as the state patrol's helping us out with so many accidents in this weather." The phone line broke up as a boom of thunder sounded.

"Luther, are you there?"

He laughed. "Yeah, I better get off this phone. I'm headed out to a pretty bad one right now. Somebody got their car wrapped around a telephone pole out on the main highway near our turnoff."

Sela jerked upright. Ben. Was he all right? She threw the covers aside and reached for her robe as Luther continued to talk.

"—Tell Ben I'll see him tomorrow."

"I will, Luther. Thanks for calling." She hung up the phone and dialed Vanessa. Her friend answered on the second ring.

"Sela, is everything all right?"

"Ben left the house tonight to find a motel. And . . . and Luther just called to cancel seeing him tonight because there's a bad accident on the main road." Sela sniffed back a tear. "I just wanted you to know I'm driving out there to see if Ben was in that accident."

"No, Sela. I'll get Ron up and he can go."

"Vanessa, please. I have to do this myself." She took a deep breath. "I'm okay, I promise. I'll call you back and let you know something."

"But—"

"If I don't call, then you can tell Ron."

When she received Vanessa's agreement, she hung up. Within a few minutes, she had dressed and left through the rain to find Ben.

Twenty-five

Sela leaned forward and peered between the bobbing windshield wipers as she drove down the main highway. She frantically racked her brain to remember the direction in which the new motels were located; with it being late and stormy, Ben likely pulled into the first one he came to.

She strained to make out the images on one side of the street, then the other, as the tears behind her eyes burned for release. What if she had asked Ben to stay until morning, what if she had agreed to stay with him in Atlanta, what if . . . She shook her head to clear it of the useless game.

She had offered up prayers repeatedly. *Please don't let the accident that Luther investigated involve Ben.* She had steadfastly denied to herself that he could be hurt, so there was no way she would go to the accident site. Instead, she decided to search him out at the motels, and she would find him at one. Safe. As her tears started to emerge, she saw a sign up ahead, a bright yellow and red one. With her heart hammering against her chest, the car came upon the two-story rectangular structure with room doors that faced the outside. She slowed down and turned into the parking lot.

* * *

Claire pushed back from the hotel room desk and dialed the phone at the house a second time. After an anxious minute, there was still no answer, only the voice-mail pickup. She replaced the phone in the cradle and, in an impatient gesture, drummed her fingers on the table. By now, Claire was desperate to contact her niece, so she picked up the phone again, and decided to check with Vanessa.

When Vanessa answered her phone after only a few rings, Claire breathed a relieved sigh. She would know Sela's whereabouts.

"Vanessa, dear, this is Claire. I realize it's late, but I'm trying to locate Sela, and she doesn't answer the phone at the house."

"Miss Claire." Vanessa's voice was cautious, though respectful to the older woman. "I'm glad that you called. I wasn't sleeping, anyway."

The strain in the young woman's voice made it clear that something had happened, so Claire spoke without preamble. "I'm concerned for Sela, and I need to speak with her. Do you know where she is?"

"You're right to be concerned. She's upset because Ben was almost hit by a car tonight."

"He wasn't hurt, was he?"

"No, but Sela panicked at his accident." Vanessa went on to explain the events that had occurred that day, the news of Ben's multiple accidents, and where Sela might be now. "She said she had to find out for herself that he was safe, and she'd call me back when she learned something."

The incident with Ben was more a confirmation than news to Claire, but Sela's reaction to it provided her with an additional worry.

"Sela won't let go of her guilt easily, Vanessa. No matter how often we tell her that she's not to blame, she has to believe it herself. Ben will help her."

"I just pray that he's okay. With you not around, I worry about Sela if something does go wrong."

"Take my number down and call me if you hear anything new from her tonight. I'll call again in the morning." She gave Vanessa her number; but, before they said good-bye, a tangential notion flitted through Claire's mind. It was an event that occurred quite often with Claire, and she did something she didn't often do. She shared it.

"The baby is coming soon, so prepare for the event."

"Yes, but we still have almost a full month to go."

"No," Claire said, and frowned thoughtfully. "There's not much time at all, and you should be ready when the rain stops." Before she was asked for an explanation that she couldn't give, she exchanged good-byes and hung up the phone.

The news Vanessa had shared from home became an additional worry for Claire. It was imperative that Ben went about his business in town unfettered and free of presumptions; it was the only way he could affect her niece's surefooted fate.

Claire picked up the man's silver bracelet that was entangled in the silk scarf on the table, and held it between her hands. When she rose from her chair, she became light-headed, startled by the images that flashed through her mind.

Regaining her balance, Claire walked to the sliding glass doors, pushed them open, and stepped out onto the balcony. As she stared into the distance, her decision became as lucid as the clear Vancouver skyline. She would contact Edward on the ship and tell him, too. It was time for her to go home.

* * *

Sela's heart beat in triple time inside her chest, but she shook off the fearful images that had built up in her mind. She would find Ben, and he would be okay. He had to be.

The nondescript row of cars parked in front of the equally nondescript row of motel doors suffered her scrutiny as she drove past them in the parking lot. Within a minute, she spotted a dark car toward the end of the row. Though it resembled Ben's, she couldn't be sure through the rain.

Sela swung her car into a parking space across from the motel rooms, and jumped from it. She sloshed through the standing water as she crossed the driving lane to get to the black car parked in front of the motel doors.

Oblivious to the rain that pelted her, she squinted through the car's window. She couldn't see anything familiar, but wasted no time with a guess. She ran onto the sidewalk in front of the car and knocked hard at the motel door.

"Hello," she yelled above the rain and sporadic thunder. "I'm trying to find Ben Russell's room." She beat at the door a second time. "Hello, does this room belong to Ben—"

A lock rattled before the door made an abrupt swing inward for maybe six inches, and an elderly man peeked out from behind the looped chain.

Her heart sank. "Oh, I'm sorry. I didn't mean—"

"Sela?"

She yanked her head around to the next room and followed the deep voice that had called her name. The room door opened.

"Ben." She said his name as she turned and headed for the figure that was about to step from behind the door.

When Ben appeared, a cry of relief broke from

her lips, and she ran into his arms, an emotional wreck. "I was afraid you were in the accident down the street," she said, her voice choked from her sobs. "Thank God, you're okay."

"What are you talking about?" he asked, puzzled. "Of course, I'm okay."

Sela gulped hard as she drew back to look up at his face, and witness the stony expression that she had helped create. Assailed by a tumble of confused thoughts and feelings, she broke her tenuous control and yielded to her tears again. "I'm so sorry. I've messed everything up."

"Come inside. You're soaking wet."

The hot tears streamed down her face as Ben led her into the room and closed the door. There was much she managed to observe about him while she bit back her tears. For one, he had hastily donned his jeans—they rode low on his hips and were only zipped, while the snap hung open. His undershirt stretched across his broad chest and left his muscular arms bare.

She watched his long, quick stride to the other side of the small room where he disappeared into the bathroom, only to reappear just as fast with a towel. Rather than hand it to her, he proceeded to mop the water from her hair, then blot her tears, his touch surprisingly gentle.

Sela looked up and tried to read his handsome face, but it remained somber and reserved. And as her sniffs settled down to no more than a few, he took her hand and drew her to the bed, where he settled her on the edge.

"Give me your foot," Ben ordered, and dropped to one knee.

As she stuck out her foot and watched him untie the lace to her sneaker, she studied his big square hands. Her eyes darted to the powerful set of his shoulders as the muscles flexed in movement, and the top of his beautifully shaped head.

God, she loved him. He was everything she'd ever desired, and in the short time they'd known each other, she thought he understood her more than she did herself. In any event, she'd shared more with him than any man she'd ever been close to.

But, even so . . . Sela couldn't form the words for the hapless thought. She wouldn't think about the bad things. At least not for the rest of the night.

"Ben," she started.

He peeled off the wet cotton anklet and tossed it with the shoe, then started with her other foot, before he glanced at her and spoke.

"You said you didn't want me in your life anymore, Sela, and that our relationship wouldn't work." His words were sharp as he pulled off the wet shoe.

Sela nodded in agreement, and watched the frown form across his brow. "I know."

"Then, why did you come to me tonight?" He slipped off the other sock, then released her foot to the floor.

She dropped her head to study her hands, and wondered if he'd believe her.

He raised himself up and spread his hands to either side of her on the bed. "What is it that you want?"

She looked up at his rigid expression. "You."

He closed his eyes a moment as he seemed to enjoy a deep breath. Then, opening his eyes, he captured Sela's. Her dark eyes were as beautiful as black satin. "Show me," he whispered.

Sela leaned toward him and, taking the initiative, cupped his face and led his mouth to her lips. She allowed the kiss to develop as a slow, thoughtful caress. And though she wanted him crushed against her, he didn't move, and she was affected even more for it. A tiny moan slipped from her throat as she dropped her hands and stroked his chest.

Ben deepened the kiss; his persuasive tongue explored her mouth with a lusty vigor, which she savored. When he began to unbutton her shirt, he realized she wore nothing underneath. He pushed the material aside and gently outlined the circles of her bare breasts as they surged at the intimacy.

He raised his mouth from hers, unsure if she wanted to continue on this path. But, when he gazed into Sela's eyes, he received his answer.

"That's what I wanted to see," he said, his stony facade finally broken. He slid the damp shirt off her shoulders and down her arms, before he tossed it aside. They quickly rose to their feet, with Ben already drawing his shirt over his head.

Silent anticipation made them both vibrate with fire. Ben smiled and reached down to unclasp her waistband.

"We don't have protection," Sela whispered as she stroked his busy hands.

"Yes we do." He motioned to the nightstand. "In case you forgot, I had earlier hopes that we would be together tonight."

"You're beautiful." He gazed at her breasts, mesmerized by their perfection and the sensitive, swollen tips. "Of course, I saw that the first day we met," he said, his voice thick with passion. He pulled her hard against him and took her mouth in another deep kiss.

Sela felt safe, protected in his arms, and wanted this happiness to last her forever. It was a sensation—an emotion—that awakened her senses, and she wanted to experience more. She reached for his waistband and slowly worked his zipper down. He caught her hand midway and broke the kiss so they could discard the rest of their clothes. And in the moment they stood naked beneath each other's gaze, there was no denying their desire for each other.

Ben drew Sela to the bed, where his kisses to her neck and shoulder nudged her backward. He captured her hands under his and began the discovery he had been denied only a few nights before.

He kissed his way along her shapely body, his ardor contained as his hands and mouth searched out and teased her special pleasure points. At Sela's moans of encouragement, he took her hands and engaged them in their own exploration, and she rose to the challenge.

She exalted his strength and relished his possession of her senses. Like honey on a warm day, love flowed through her.

As the rain continued outside, so did their turbulent passion become an exquisite pain. And when Sela finally pleaded for release, Ben complied. Amid their whispered words of love for each other, she welcomed him into her body in a shared tempo that bound them together, shattering the hard shell she had so carefully built. In a final pounding wave, they yielded to the little death that confirmed their souls as alive.

When their world had righted itself once again, and the fire within had been reduced to a manageable flame, Ben raised himself from Sela and kissed her brow before he turned on his side and drew her back against him.

She squeezed his hand that was wrapped around

her middle. "I think I said I love you," she breathed, sated and satisfied in his arms. "More than once."

"I heard. I love you, too." He kissed her ear and settled in the bed with her, their legs, their hearts, finally intertwined.

Sela sat on the edge of the bed, demurely wrapped in a corner of the top sheet. That was because Ben lay partially twisted in the rest of it. She hung up the phone at the bedside and glanced at him over her shoulder. He was napping due to the little, if any, sleep they'd taken during the last six hours.

Suddenly self-conscious of how she would look in the morning's light instead of through Ben's sheen of passion, she brushed her loose hair back with her hand. At some point during a wilder moment last night, Ben had freed her hair from the band. He had said he didn't care that it was thick and unruly. He liked it that way. She smiled at the memory, one of many she'd treasure from the last hours.

"For a woman who sleeps without a stitch on, why are you all wrapped up in that thing?"

Sela jerked from her reverie and turned as Ben tugged the sheet away from her. She caught the end of it and laughed as she joined him under the sheet. When she became comfortable, spoon fashion, in his arms, she told him about the phone conversation she'd just finished with Vanessa.

"Aunt Claire called last night. Vanessa told her everything, and that I'd gone looking for you."

"Will your aunt approve when she learns you stayed with me last night?"

"Auntie never liked the idea of me putting brakes on my life after Charles's accident." Still not quite comfortable with the subject, she squirmed in Ben's arms. "She doesn't share my fear about the accidents."

He quietly stroked her stomach. "Can we talk about that for a minute?"

"I do feel less threatened right now, but that has more to do with the fact that we're in each other's arms. It's when I feel safest, and when I know you're okay."

"That's the key, Sela. We should work together with this fear of yours. You don't have to carry it all on your own. Tell me what's going on in your head."

"Did Ron tell you that even the few boyfriends I had in high school seemed prone to accidents?"

"He mentioned it, but that doesn't prove anything. Teenagers are clumsy."

"For me, it was the beginning of proof that I was like my mama. I not only looked exactly like her, but everyone in town was determined to cast me in her image."

"I saw her picture on the dresser upstairs."

"So, I was bad luck to boyfriends, and it became a joke that started in high school. Aunt Claire, herself, even predicted a dangerous fortune for me when I was only five years old."

"That was around the time your mother died."

She nodded her head against the pillow. "Auntie told me she was haunted by these particular visions. She and my mother even argued over them; and when my mom wouldn't do anything about it, Aunt Claire resorted to something she's never admitted to anyone else. And, don't you dare tell her I told you, either." Sela smiled as she remembered. "She tried a spell on me."

"She must have really been worried," Ben said as he squeezed her. "I thought you said your mother had more defined powers than your aunt. Why didn't your mother see these bad visions?"

"With a clairvoyant, it's a matter of interpretation, especially if it has anything to do with someone close to you. My mother read the signs differently, and they disagreed."

"Maybe your mother was right." He squeezed her in a hug. "If it's a matter of interpretation, what your aunt saw may not have had anything to do with you. It could have had something to do with your mother."

"Ben, I've never tried to explain my aunt's powers. In fact, I've belittled more than embraced them, but I can't deny that they're there. I've seen the results too often."

He shifted her around so that they faced each other. "Humor me for a moment, okay?" When she nodded, he continued.

"I won't deny your mother's and aunt's powers or your observations. But, I'm not that big on the paranormal and I don't believe your theory that you're bad luck." When she started to speak, he quieted her. "That's because I believe most things can be explained if we investigate them hard enough. And these accidents that have put the fear of living in you can be explained."

"What's to investigate, Ben? They've been happening since I was sixteen years old."

"If you let it, your mind can take you places you'd never want to venture. You're thinking in a box. I'm not, and I'm going to figure this one out."

She smiled at his self-satisfied theory. "How about this? Vanessa said Auntie knew something was wrong yesterday. That's why she was trying to find me in the middle of the night."

"You two are close; but, how does she, you know, connect with you here?"

"She keeps a personal item of mine with her, a silk scarf, when she's away like this. It's a link we can share."

He grunted. "Something personal, huh?"

Sela grinned. "Uh-huh. What did she manage to separate from you?"

"She's something all right." He smiled as he remembered. "I have a sterling silver ID band I've worn almost every day since I went off to college. She won it as a joke in a friendly game of poker, and promised to return it when I came to Fairlight."

They both laughed as Ben drew her close to him.

"Now you see what I've had to put up with for so many years," Sela declared. "I love her dearly, but she always gets her way, you know." Suddenly, she pulled back from him. "Didn't you say you saw my mother's picture upstairs? How? I've kept that door locked since you moved in."

He began to nuzzle her neck, and spoke between his gentle bites. "It was unlocked when I left last night. You must have gone in there, because you dropped the key on the floor."

Sela had difficulty keeping her thoughts clear as he lowered his mouth to her breasts, giving each deserved attention.

"I don't think so," she murmured through a fog. "It was probably Fontella."

She grasped his head in delight as they began another journey to fulfillment.

Twenty-six

"And you say this car came from out of nowhere?" Luther refolded his arms as he leaned against the wall in Ron's office.

"One minute I was about to cross the street, and the next, these headlights just blinded me." Ben stared out the window and into the early morning sunshine as he spoke. "It was the craziest thing."

He sat forward on the sofa and clasped his hands as he continued. "You know, I don't think the car just appeared. I think it was there on the street, but with no headlights on. In all that rain, who would have noticed?"

"So you think the driver tried to hit you on purpose?" Ron asked from behind his desk. "How did they know you'd be there at that very moment?"

"Nobody from around here would try a thing like that," Luther said, taking exception to Ben's theory. "Things like that go on in Atlanta all the time, but not here in Fairlight."

Ben looked at the two men. "I didn't say they intended to hurt me, but it's strange how the lights came up only when the car was almost on me." He frowned as he mentally sorted through information. "And, why didn't he stop?"

"So it was a he?" Luther asked, and shifted his

position on the wall. "Maybe he was scared. Did you see a man behind the wheel?"

"No, Luther." He sighed and looked at Ron. "But, just suppose for a moment that I was the target."

"Who would want to hurt you?" Luther asked.

"And why someone from around here?" Ron chimed in.

Luther stepped away from the wall. "Maybe they're not from here. You weren't in any trouble before you came here, were you, Ben?"

Ben smiled. "I like the way you think, Luther. And no, I didn't have any trouble before I came here." He turned to Ron again. "Remember how I told you I thought I heard someone in the church the night I got locked in that wall?"

"When did that happen?" Luther shifted again as he looked from one man to the other.

Ben quickly brought him up to date about the locked door incident. "Suppose we take the question, *how did I* get trapped in the wall, change it around, and ask, *why would someone* trap me there, or booby-trap my ladder, or electrocute me, or even hit me with a car?"

"The only thing you're doing around here is working on the church—" Ron started to say.

"—And paying special attention to Sela," Ben finished.

"So, maybe the accidents do have something to do with Sela?" Ron asked, picking up Ben's drift.

Ben felt as if a lightbulb had just been turned on as a kernel of an idea began to grow. "Yeah, they have everything to do with Sela, and nothing to do with bad luck. Think about it. Friends of Sela's don't have these accidents, and boyfriends who turn into friends don't have them anymore. Isn't that what happened to you, Ron?"

"I get it," Luther joined in. "You think somebody's trying to separate Sela from her boyfriends. So we need to find out who would want that."

"That's it." He stood and slapped a beaming Luther's shoulder while he glanced over at Ron. "I told you. Luther would help figure this thing out."

"But, that would mean this person has been around here for a long time—at least since we were back in high school," Ron said.

"Exactly," Ben said. When he saw Ron's frown, he warned both men. "You can't mention this to Sela right now. I'm still having to convince her that she's not anyone's bad luck. But, I still don't know what it is we're trying to find, so I need both of your help."

"Sure," they said almost in unison.

"First," Ben said, "the same question we asked earlier, we now ask it about Andrew's and Charles' accidents. Why would someone want to hurt them?"

Luther smiled again. "Because they were paying special attention to Sela, too?"

Ben nodded. "That has to be it. A person is behind the accidents."

"Man, do you know what you're saying?" Ron sat up in his chair and shook his head. "You're thinking crazy."

"Maybe," he agreed. "But, it's no crazier than everybody believing that Sela has the ability to kill the men she's attracted to. And, until we consider my theory as a possibility, we won't know if it's crazy." He looked at the faces of the two doubting men. "So, why don't you tell me all you know about her boyfriends?"

* * *

Sela was worried as she stepped onto the front porch and looked down the street for a sign of Ron. Vanessa was not well, so Sela had left a message on his voice mail to get home soon. She glanced at her watch again.

It was late morning, and Fontella had already left the inn for the day. And though Ben had mentioned he'd planned to do research at the house, she couldn't reach him on the phone. Of course, that could mean he was simply using the line. Maybe she should send the twins for him, just in case.

"Sela, what you doing over here?"

It was Mr. Lewis delivering the mail. Instead of stuffing it in the Stewarts' mailbox, he slipped through the gate and walked up the path to greet her.

"Vanessa's not well," Sela answered. "And I think the baby might come early. The other night, Aunt Claire said it would be here after all the rain cleared out."

"Well, it's been sunny all morning so far." He handed her Vanessa's mail. "We need it after that stormy weekend."

"Mr. Lewis, can you do me a favor? When you get to the inn, would you ask Ben to come over here? Ron will be on his way home soon, but if Vanessa gets in trouble, well, I'd feel better with Ben here."

"Sure," he agreed with a nod. "I saw you and Ben at the picnic. Anything going on you want to tell me about?"

She smiled as she playfully feigned offense. "Will you stop asking questions? Just get him over here, that's all."

"Sela, you can't be too careful these days." His eyes became pensive. "You know I've always looked after your welfare, as if you were my own daughter."

He was right, and it was why she had accepted his interference, along with that of others from the community, so easily. But, she had promised Ben she would stay strong and not let the past be an omen for her future.

"I do know," she said. "But stop worrying over me. Ben is helping me work through some things. I wish you'd get to know him because you'll find he's a good man. Even Aunt Claire likes him."

"Sela . . ."

She darted her head toward Vanessa's weak call from inside the house, then faced the mailman again.

"Mr. Lewis, I've got to go." She backed away to the door. "Don't forget to tell Ben to get over here."

She ran into the house and met the twins at the bottom of the stairs. They had sensed something was wrong with their mother and had begun to cry. She ran up the steps past them to Vanessa's bedroom.

When she reached the door, she saw that Vanessa was still in bed, but had turned onto her side. She was propped up on one elbow and grunted with pain. "Something feels wrong," she panted. "And, my water just broke."

"Oh, Lord," Sela cried, and reached for the phone to dial 911.

Internet access from his laptop computer was an easy enough process for Ben, but it was also a slow one via a dial-up line. Attempts to get into the *Journal-Constitution*'s on-line files were moving at a snail's pace; so, he considered it a victory when he finally gained access to a small article on Sela's mother.

Ben knew that to examine any problem, its root

had to be unearthed. Sela's fears had started with her mother's death, and that's where he would start.

Under the heading of NEWS AROUND THE STATE, the death was given a two-inch space in one column of the paper. Even that small entry, though, was geared more to the sensational fact that Helena Bennett's hanging body had been discovered by her young daughter, rather than the sobering knowledge that a young mother had chosen to take her own life. Still, it gave him a new sense of the horror Sela had already related to him.

He supposed the town's weekly paper at the time, the *Fairlight News*, had a more detailed article. The best place to check on their story would be in the library archives.

The door chime rang. Ben frowned at the interruption, and wondered who had stopped by in Sela's absence. He closed the laptop, then bounded up the stairs to the front door. When he opened it, Mr. Lewis stood there and greeted him.

"Good morning." Ben returned his greeting with a handshake and pushed the door wide. "If you're looking for Sela, she's visiting Vanessa up the street."

"I already saw her over there. Is Fontella still around?" He peered around Ben's shoulders and into the house. "I thought we could all have a cup of coffee."

"No, you missed her and her muffins by about an hour. Aren't you making rounds a little late today?"

"Well, it's a slow start when my load is a lot heavier because of the Fourth holiday. Then, I have to deal with these migraines." He rubbed his temple. "You know, even though these migraines get to me every now and then, I still make it to church." He dropped his hand and squinted at Ben. "I didn't see you and Sela at Sunday service. Any problems?"

Crossing his arms, Ben frowned at the older man's audacious inquiry. "No," he answered. And, as the two men exchanged frowns, Ben spoke bluntly. "I care about Sela, and I know—"

"You don't know nothing."

Ben was taken aback by the vitriolic remark. "What?"

"You don't know what she's been through . . . the pain, the problems she's had dealing with men and love, and then losing both. You don't know any of it. And it hurts all of us who care about her, that you're gonna end up leaving her, too."

"Where is all this coming from?" Ben took a step forward, his anger awakened at the man's presumption that his intentions were less than honorable toward Sela. "If you cared about her, you'd want her to get on with her life, and not hide behind the town so everybody here can tell her what to do."

A siren blared in the distance and stole their attention. As both men looked out to the street, it quickly became obvious that the sound was in their close vicinity.

"I wonder if that ambulance is going to Vanessa's," the mailman mused out loud.

"Why would they be heading there?" Ben stepped out onto the porch with him and looked up the street as the red glow from the ambulance's light could be seen flashing in the air. "Vanessa is all right, isn't she?"

"Sela said to tell you to get up there, just in case." He gave Ben a glazed look. "She can't find Ron."

"Why didn't you say it?" Ben pulled the door closed and jogged to the gate, with the mailman somewhere behind him. When he reached the sidewalk, he saw Sela trot toward him with the twins in tow. Brian's and Brett's cries had become an effusive choir.

He ran another fifty feet before he met up with them. "What happened?"

Sela was out of breath as she tried to shush the twins. "I need you to take care of the boys while I ride with Vanessa to the hospital. Her water broke, and she's in a lot of pain." She pressed the unwilling Brett and Brian toward Ben. "They're scared, that's all, and they'll stop crying; but, I have to go with her."

"What do I do? Where's Ron?" Ben looked at the bawling, teary-faced children and felt a panic in his chest as he'd never experienced.

"Ron called me and he's meeting us at the hospital. I'll call and let you know what's going on as soon as I can." Her eyes were pleading.

He bent and gave her a fleeting kiss on the cheek. "You go on, and take care of her." He swallowed hard. "And don't either of you worry. I'll . . . I'll take care of the kids."

She touched his arm in a silent gesture of thanks, then turned and ran back up the street to the ambulance.

The boys had not let up on their wails as they turned and watched Sela disappear. Ben dropped to one knee and tried to calm their fears.

"Fellas, listen. Your mom's going to be okay. She's got Sela and your dad with her, and they're all going to get the new baby ready to come home."

The twins looked at each other and slowly the wails began to subside to simple cries.

"By tonight, you could have a new baby brother or sister." He grabbed their hands in his. "Come on, let's go."

As they trudged back to the house, Ben met up with Jim Lewis again. He had waited at the mailbox.

"Mr. Lewis, we'll have to take our differences up some other time. I've got my hands full right now with the kids, and I want to get them in the house."

"What about Vanessa?" he asked Ben, his eyes still trained to the street up ahead.

"From what I can figure, the baby's coming, and they're on the way to the hospital." Ben looked back in thc direction of the Stewart house. He could tell that the ambulance had pulled away.

When he turned back, the mailman had already started to walk away, presumably to the next house to deliver the mail. Ben shook his head at the odd-acting man, and walked through the gate with the crying boys alongside him.

"Mom," Ben said hesitantly into the phone, surprised to hear his mother on the other end. "What made you call in the middle of the day? Is everything okay?"

As he held the phone, he looked up from his computer and turned toward the stomping noise that came from the stairs. The twins seemed to have made a game out of just coming down the stairs. As they appeared in the doorway, he saw that each had a muffin clutched in his hand, mindless of the crumbs that trailed below. Ben shook his head, and decided he'd have to clean up the mess later. Belatedly, he realized his mother was talking.

"Mom, I'm sorry. What was it you said?"

She let out a loud sigh. "What are you doing? And what is all that commotion?"

Barbara Russell was not used to being ignored by

clients or family, and Ben knew he was testing her patience. "I'm baby-sitting a set of twins."

"Is that Aunt Sela?" Brett asked.

"I want to talk," Brian chimed in. The twins had joined Ben at the desk, and as he pried their sticky fingers from the computer keys, he also attempted to carry on a conversation with his increasingly impatient mother.

"I'm sorry, Mom, but things are a little busy around here right now."

"Twins? You, baby-sitting? My goodness, Ben. Whose children are these? Not the young woman who runs the inn?"

"No, no." Ben laughed at her questions. "They belong to a family friend who went to the hospital to have another one. It's a long story."

"Oh. Well, I called because I happened to overhear your brothers talking about you and the young woman there, Sela. I'll admit it unnerved me a bit. What's this about the people you're staying with being some kind of fortune-telling cult?"

Ben talked as he directed the twins to play with the toys spread out on the floor. "Knowing Mont, he was teasing you. It is true that Sela's aunt is a clairvoyant, though."

"What?"

"Everybody around here knows it."

"You haven't gotten yourself into anything, you know, weird in that little southern town, have you? I mean, there's no telling what they believe and practice in those backwoods."

This time, Ben laughed. "Mom, they're nice, friendly people, and not as backwoods as you might think. And, listen, I want you to meet Sela. She's, well, she's pretty special to me."

"You sound like you're involved with the young woman."

"You know, I guess I am. Of course, some odd stuff is going on right now."

"Odd? How?"

"I don't know, but it looks like somebody's trying to cause trouble for the people she gets close to. I'm trying to find out who would do something like that."

"You're not serious, are you? This all sounds dangerous."

A crash sounded in the corner of the room and Ben turned to see that the twins stood near the up-ended room divider.

His mother was quick to comment. "Ben, what in the world is going on there?"

"Don't worry about it," he said, and held the phone in place under his neck as he righted the divider. "Listen, the twins are a handful. You can't take your eyes off them. I've got to go now, but I do want to bring Sela to meet you and Dad."

"Of . . . of course, son, but what about this danger—"

"Don't worry. I'll get back with you soon. Right now, I've got to go." The twins ran past him to the other end of the room, and he wondered what they would crash into next. He bade his mother a quick good-bye and ended the call.

The phone immediately rang again. Ben held his fingers up to the boys and motioned them over to his desk while he answered the phone, sure that it was Sela with news from the hospital. It wasn't. It was Luther.

"Ben, I got a copy of the reports you wanted to look at."

"Great," he said. "Right now, I'm stuck at the

house with Vanessa's boys. Sela is with her at the hospital."

"I heard. You want me to drop these off at the house?"

"I really need to get to the library for a while," Ben said. "Why don't you meet me over there, say, in about an hour?"

Luther agreed. When they hung up, Ben looked down at the twins' matching grubby faces and hands. If he didn't get them out of the house, they were going to destroy it.

"All right, you two, you're always looking for a good story to be read, right?"

"Right." The boys cheered.

"Okay, first, you're going to pick up your toys and the rest of this mess; then we're going to the library where you can spend a little quality time—with a storyteller."

Twenty-seven

It had only taken Ben a few short hours to acquire a healthy respect for anyone who had to raise children. That appreciation had been extended to Ophelia Glover, the librarian who had swooped the kids away to a reading room shortly after their noisy arrival at the Fairlight Public Library.

When he explained to her that he wanted to find some old news stories that may have been reported in the *Fairlight News,* Ophelia directed him to a section next to the front desk. The area was gated for restricted entrance, and carried a sign that announced it as a research area, and no materials beyond the gate could be checked out.

Ben passed through the gates and set himself up at a table that boasted a row of dated microfiche machines into which he'd feed the thin microfilm that the news stories had been stored on.

He first sought the facts on Andrew Grant, the first of Sela's boyfriends to succumb to an accident. The news story was much the same as the account Ron and Luther had given him that morning. Andrew had been a newcomer to the town seven years ago, and had drowned when his car plummeted into Hunter's Pond in the late night to early morning hours. It was suspected he had lost control of the car in the heavy fog, unfamiliar to him, which was known to linger in the area. Unable to swim, he was trapped in the car, where he was later found by authorities.

Ben frowned as he read on. A citizen had come upon the car as it bobbed in the lake and had tried to extricate the man from it, but to no avail. The article did not identify the Good Samaritan.

He then read the story about Charles Matthews, Sela's most recently deceased boyfriend. He had died of a self-inflicted wound to the chest, accidentally caused with a shotgun. It was an item Charles had gained some familiarity with, since he had been an avid sportsman for some time, and it wasn't unusual that he would have access to one at his home. The prevailing theory had been that he was cleaning the instrument for an upcoming sporting event and, somehow, it had gone off, and Charles had been the victim.

Ben shook his head at the inconceivable accident, and could only wonder at Sela's pain upon learning that a tragedy had visited a second boyfriend. No wonder she had been frantic about his safety. He adjusted the microfiche under the machine lamp so he could read the remainder of the article. There, he read that Charles's body had been discovered by a neighbor who had heard the shot earlier in their quiet, rural neighborhood, and had gone to investigate.

Were these two accidents just horrible coincidences? Or, was there a connection somewhere? True, their accidental nature was shared, and both accidents seemed to have occurred with no witnesses. But, there seemed to be no other connection. All of the information he had learned swirled through Ben's head, and he rubbed his chin in thought as he prepared the next piece of microfilm for viewing. He wanted to see what the local paper had said about Helena Bennett's suicide.

He had been reading the various articles for a good part of an hour when he looked up and saw that Ophelia had returned.

"Ben, do you need any help?" she asked.

"It's coming along okay," he replied.

She saw the microfilm highlighted on the screen and recognized the article from the *Fairlight News*. "Oh, you're reading about Sela's mother." She grunted. "That was really bad."

"Do you remember her?"

"We were in high school together. She was very pretty, but quiet, an introvert, probably because she thought of herself and Claire as different."

"Because they were clairvoyant?"

Ophelia nodded as she crossed her arms, warming to the subject. "Claire was a few years younger than Helena, and her opposite, socially. Whatever people dished out to Claire, she returned it in spades." She chuckled. "She was never anybody's victim. Helena was a different story; but, I never thought she'd end her own life that way."

Ben slid the film from the tray. "Were there any more stories, maybe follow-up pieces, after she died?"

"Let's see," Ophelia said and leaned against the table to think back. "The *News* was weekly back then, and this story didn't go away immediately. I'm sure another story came out a week or two later when the cause of death was confirmed by the medical examiner. What with all the rumors that were flying around, they probably had to."

"What rumors?" Ben asked, and searched

through the film box for the next edition of the paper.

"Well, at the time, I don't guess Claire wanted to believe that her sister had killed herself and left her body to be found by little Sela when she came home. Helena loved her little girl, and it's hard to believe she'd let that happen."

"So, what else could Miss Bennett do? The only other explanation was that her sister had been murdered, and that was unlikely."

"I know, and Claire finally accepted the suicide, but not before she brought up all the reasons her sister wouldn't have committed such a thing."

"What kind of reasons?"

"Well, the suicide note was odd. It didn't make a lot of sense, and it was left for Sela, not Claire. I mean, Sela was only five years old. Why would she leave a suicide note for her five-year-old who probably couldn't read?"

"Yeah, I thought the same thing, too."

"The other thing Claire argued was that the suicide note came from some kind of diary she had given to her sister; but nobody ever found the doggone thing in the house. The police said that since it may have contained personal things, maybe she destroyed it before she took her life."

Ben located the follow-up article as Ophelia talked. "Here it is," he announced, and manipulated the machine's lever a few times before the story fit onto the screen.

"That's the one," Ophelia said, and peered at the screen. "The medical examiner ruled out everything else before he declared the obvious."

"Is that medical examiner still around?"

"Sure. He still has a private practice, too. Everybody goes to him," she said. "His name is Ezra Harris, Doc Harris to the folks in town."

"It says here that he concluded that her death was by hanging. The police agreed it was a self-strangulation. Suicide." Ben read on until he reached the end of the piece. "It also says that while the family is puzzled over her suicide, they've accepted that their daughter and sister was deeply depressed over recent personal events."

Once again, Ben turned to Ophelia. "What were these recent personal events? Do you know?"

"The only personal thing I know of that was ongoing with Helena had to do with Sela's father. And frankly, I don't know why her family would think that it suddenly depressed her so much that she'd kill herself." She grunted in disdain. "The time to kill herself would have been when she first came back to town, pregnant and without a husband. That's when she was depressed."

Ben knew that the subject of her father, or the lack of one, was a sticky issue with Sela. This piece of gossip made it clear as to why.

Ophelia chuckled a moment when she saw Ben's face. "So you didn't know all that, huh? Helena left town to get married. But, then she came back, not married and with no explanation. Soon after, it was obvious she was pregnant."

"Maybe the family was still reeling over her death. Maybe they were just holding on to any *possibility* to explain away the *impossible.*" Ben gave her a meaningful glance. "It's no different from people in town thinking that something must be wrong with Sela because her boyfriends have accidents. It was a way for the town to explain the impossible."

Ophelia properly blushed at the accusation hurled at the town. "You know, those of us close to the family have never embraced that idea, but everybody knows about the accidents, and sort of came to expect them. I know it's a ghoulish thought, but a lot of the older folks around here actually think she's cursed by her own mother's failure with her father."

Ben frowned. "Can you think of anyone who would want Sela to fail like her mother?"

"Of course not." Her brows furrowed in thought as she slowly shook her head. "Why would you ask that? There aren't that many unattached young bucks around here that are her age, anyway."

"I'm talking about somebody older, say you and her aunt's generation?"

She looked at Ben, confused. "Nobody."

At that moment, the gate opened and Luther was heading for their table.

"Hi, Luther," Ophelia said gaily, then turned to Ben. "I'd better get back to the front desk. I only came over here to tell you that the twins are having a great time in the storytelling room."

Ben thanked her for her time and information, and as she left him, Luther pulled up a chair and joined him.

"I brought those reports for you," Luther said, and set an envelope on the table.

Ben spilled the contents of the envelope out on the table and saw copies of the medical examiner's report, along with the accident reports filed by the police, as well as the one for Helena Bennett's suicide.

"This is great, Luther," Ben said as he poured over the reports. When he saw the accident report for Andrew's drowning, he read it quickly for details of the scene, and when he saw a particular item, he looked at the deputy.

"Why didn't you tell me it was Mr. Freeman who found Andrew's car in Hunter's Pond?"

"I don't know." The young man hunched his shoulders. "I didn't think it was important. Is it important?"

Ben shrugged as he returned his attention to the reports. "I don't know. Sometimes little things like that make you see things differently, that's all. The newspaper article didn't have his name."

"That's because Deacon Freeman didn't hang around afterwards for the press. He didn't want nothing to do with that story, and the police didn't give out his name."

"The paper called him a Good Samaritan."

"Yeah, Deacon was pretty shook-up over seeing Andrew's car in the water. When he was out on the road by the church, he saw the car, jumped in the water, and tried to save Andrew, but it was too late." Luther sighed. "He tried being a hero."

Ben stacked the reports and replaced them in the envelope. "I'll keep these for a while, if you don't mind."

"Sure," Luther said and stood up. "Did you find out anything new on that theory of yours?"

"No, I'm still sorting through the facts behind the accidents. I mean, you just filled me in on something I didn't know."

Luther chuckled. "I guess I did, huh?"

Ben smiled as he nodded. "I'm going to the church in a few minutes. Maybe I can catch Mr. Freeman over there. He might be able to tell me something else, so I'll let you know what I learn later."

When Luther left, Ben waved for Ophelia's help once again. She left the desk and came over.

"Ophelia, you wouldn't happen to keep the high

school's annual yearbooks around here, would you?"

She smiled. "Hey, it's your lucky day. Look." She pointed to a locked, glass-front bookcase against the wall in the gated area. "You can browse to your heart's content."

"Thanks." He joined her as she walked to the case, his hands pushed deep in his pockets. "Maybe you can hang around and make a few quick IDs for me?"

"Sure," she said, and unlocked the glass doors.

He stooped in front of the bookcase, and selected the yearbook for Helena Bennett's senior year. "Okay, let's see how many of your old friends stuck around town."

Twenty-eight

True to his word, Ben soon left the library with the boys in tow. When they arrived at the church, they went to the secretary's office, where she promptly asked if there was any news yet from the hospital.

Ben shook his head, amused that everyone in town knew Vanessa was at the hospital. "Nothing to report yet."

He then asked if Mr. Freeman was around.

"I haven't seen him, though he's usually around here by the afternoon." Irene looked at her watch. "But, if you don't see him, give him an hour or so, and he'll show up. He always does."

"I need to go down to the basement," Ben said. "I left my clipboard and some sketches from last week down there."

Noise from the hallway drew their attention. When they went out into the area, they saw that the twins were playing with a colorful ball they had found in one of the rooms along the hall.

Smiling, Irene leaned over and chucked the boys under the chin. "And, hello, guys. I hear you're gonna have a new baby at the house soon."

The kids, suddenly shy, dropped the ball and stepped behind Ben's legs.

"I see they've taken to you," Irene observed as she straightened back up. "Are you taking them downstairs with you?"

He let out a deep sigh. "I don't know," he said, and contemplated whether it was a good idea or not.

"We want to go with you," Brian piped up.

"Please," Brett wheedled.

"Aw, let 'em tag along," Irene said. "They rip and run around here during the weekends, anyway. In fact, the kids at the church probably know the place better than their elders."

"Well, okay, but on one condition," he said to the boys. "You have to do as I say."

They readily agreed and scooped up their ball as they took off in a run for the stairs.

Ben quickly caught up with them and grabbed a hand in each of his. "First rule," he said. "You don't run off without me."

The boys thought Ben was funny and began to giggle as he led them down the stairs and into the basement. When they reached the cement floor, he released their hands and first sought the work items in the room Sela had been working in. He took a quick look around the room and realized that the clipboard was not there. Then he remembered. The cornerstone. Maybe he had set them on the floor when he had explored the area. He left the room and saw the boys bounce the ball off the wall farther down the dimly lit corridor, and started for them.

"Fellas, let's go to the other side of the basement." Ben saw their ball scoot away from them and roll farther into the muted light. Then, to his surprise, they both took off in a race after the errant ball.

"Let's play hide and seek." The childish voice echoed through the basement.

"Hey, kids, come back here." Ben's stride picked up speed as he hurried toward the running twins.

"You're it," they screamed back to Ben in unison, enjoying their impromptu game.

"No, I'm not. Come back here." All he could hear was their childish laughter as they turned into a corridor ahead and were no longer in his sight.

"Well, I'll be—" He whispered the expletive under his breath. He finally reached the bend in the corridor and almost tripped over the forgotten ball they had abandoned for the opportunity to play hide and seek. He picked it up and slowly started to walk down the hall. The place was a maze and the kids could be hiding along any of the halls.

"Okay, Brett, Brian, the game is over." He pulled a small flashlight from his pocket and moved along the corridor.

"I'll find you both," he yelled. "So, come on out."

Frisco had pressed himself against the wall of his private hovel and watched the two chuckling children hug each other as they stooped near the door. Their laughs meant they hadn't seen him. Yet. The candle he used burned a bright single flame at the back of the room. It had been set in the soil, and they would see it soon. Suddenly, his place, his own space, was suffering from daily violations. It was all the outsider's fault. Frisco's ears perked at the sounds beyond the door. He could hear him now, calling to the children.

As the voice outside the door grew closer, he watched the two children back up on their heels, and move farther into his space. It was too late for

Frisco to retreat undetected to the back of the room and escape. No. He'd have to take his chances on the kids leaving before he was seen. He tightened his grip around the metal tube at his side.

As the kids backed up even more, one of them turned and saw the candle and its flickering flame. Like a moth, he was drawn.

"Look," he whispered to his brother, and pointed.

The other child turned his head and saw it, too. Fascinated by the discovery, they sidled along the dirt floor toward the flame. The one who had spoken stopped for an instant as his head jerked away to something in the dirt. Just as quickly, though, his attention returned as he joined his brother and looked up at the tall shadow against the wall. They crouched frozen in place as the shadow moved toward them.

The outsider's voice floated into the room. "Kids, if you come out from hiding, we'll go and get some ice cream."

Frisco took another step and knelt down to the twins' level, giving them his angry stare. How many times were they told not to play down here? The outsider again. He'd brought them.

"You know not to be down here, don't you?" His voice was gruff and spewed venom.

The twins nodded in unison, their eyes wide with caution, their mouths unsmiling.

"Then get out of here. If you tell anybody you saw me down here, I'll make sure you pay for being bad." He leaned toward them. "Go on," he growled, and hefted the metal tube. "Get out of here."

The twins never took their stare off him as they

scurried backward to the door, and scrambled through the opening.

Ben flashed his light from down the hall as the boys tumbled through the opening of the crawl space.

He stopped in his tracks a moment. "This is why I don't trust you little people. You told me you'd do like I said, and then you don't. Get your butts over here."

The twins ran to Ben and stopped in front of him. He looked at their wide eyes in somber faces and guessed what was wrong.

"You two look like you've been scared out of your wits," he said, his voice now softer. "So, you don't like it when the rooms are really dark, do you?" He played the flashlight along the door behind them.

"There's nothing in there to hurt you," he said. "Come on, I can show you." He started for the door, but the twins pulled him back.

"No, no, we want to go."

"And you promised us ice cream if we came out. I want some ice cream."

"I guess I did, huh?" He smiled down at them. "Okay, let's get out of here, soon as I get my clipboard."

The kids clung to Ben as they walked around to the next corridor and retrieved the work he had left. But, as they climbed the stairs back to the main floor, Brett dropped something he had in his hand, and it clattered on the stairs. He pulled from Ben's hand and scurried down the steps to retrieve it.

"Hey, what's that you have?" Ben asked the child.

"I found it in the hide-and-seek room." He climbed back up the stairs and showed it off.

"Let me take a look." Ben saw that it was a tiny rectangular metal box, about the size of a regulation domino, and about as thick. Old and beaten, the gold was just shiny enough to attract a child's favor. Ben saw the clasp and pulled it open. To his surprise, he discovered it was a pillbox, complete with a collection of pills. So, what in the world was a pillbox doing in the crawl space? He turned it over and could see no monograms or other identification.

"You found this a while ago, when you played hide and seek?"

The youngsters nodded.

"We saw a candle—" One child started to speak, but abruptly stopped when he looked at his brother.

Ben frowned, his curiosity raised. He had wanted to go back and check out that space ever since he'd discovered it a week ago. But, that was out of the question right now. He couldn't go back in there with the twins.

"Can I have it back now?" Brett asked.

"Listen, why don't I just take these pills out of here and then you can keep the case, okay?" He shook the pills into his palm and dropped them into his pocket before he handed the case back to Brett.

"Now can we go for the ice cream?" Brian pleaded.

Ben smiled. "Now we'll go for the ice cream." He held the door as the kids ran through it at top speed.

It was late in the night, and Sela was exhausted as she unlocked the door to her house. Ron's loopy grin was still pasted to his face. He had become the father of another healthy boy earlier that evening, and he would probably look stupidly proud for at least another few days, Sela surmised.

"Do you want to leave the boys with me tonight and just get them in the morning?" she whispered.

"No, I promised the twins I'd pick them up when we talked on the phone from the hospital. More importantly, I promised Ben I'd pick them up. I figure if I take them home tonight, we can get to the hospital early in the morning and have breakfast with Vanessa."

When they entered the foyer, they could hear the TV as a Disney character talked. Although a few toys were visible, it was not as cluttered as Sela had been expecting.

"I wonder where they are," Sela said, and headed for the den.

She got her answer when she entered the room. Ben was on the sofa with Brian nestled under one of his arms, and Brett under the other. The boys had changed and each now wore what looked like one of Ben's white T-shirts. All three were asleep as the VCR tape of a Disney adventure droned on and on. The coffee table in front of them was filled with leftover popcorn, ice cream wrappers, and an assortment of other junk food; all a parent's nightmare, but food nevertheless.

Sela sighed, overcome by an emotion she knew to be love. He was wonderful. Who'd have thought just a little over a month ago that he'd ever allow himself to be put in this position?

"I think you've got yourself a winner, Sela." Ron had come up alongside her. "Ben's all right."

"Yeah," she replied, and continued to watch the trio sleep. "Don't I know it."

* * *

Later, as Sela curled around a pillow in sleep, she heard a faint knock against her door. She raised a tired eyelid and saw a sliver of light enter the room and then just as quickly disappear. Alerted, she remained still when she recognized the form that moved across her dark room. A tingle of expectation shot through her.

When she heard the rustle of clothing being removed, her heart pounded an erratic rhythm. Soon after, the covers were pulled back as a warm, hard body joined her naked one in the bed.

"What took you so long?" she inquired of Ben. Her arms joined around his neck as his slipped down her naked back and caressed its curves. "I missed you."

"I thought you'd be tired from all that happened today. But then, I remembered what I'd been through baby-sitting, and I figured you couldn't possibly be more tired than I was keeping up with those four-year-old dynamos."

Sela let out a tired laugh. "I'm just thankful you're not reporting a new accident of yours to me." Before he could chastise her for worrying, she added, "I know, I promised to put it out of my mind and trust our love. Well, I still had Luther check on you for good measure."

"That explains why he was so easy to locate every time I needed him."

"Exactly." Sela shared a kiss with him, then asked, "So, what did you do today? We know you fed the kids enough sugar to keep them hyper for the rest of the week." She let his hand, now pressed against her backside, insinuate her soft curves against his rock-hard body.

"You mean besides dream about this—" He

planted a kiss in the hollow of her neck, then worked his way around to her mouth again.

Sela giggled against his lips. "You did not. I talked with Luther on the phone this afternoon. You've been doing some investigating."

He stopped his lusty perusal of her body for a moment. "You aren't angry, are you?"

"No. Actually, I feel better that you know all the bad stuff."

"Oh, I meant to tell you that I spoke with Fontella this morning."

"About what?"

"The key on the room floor upstairs," he reminded her. "Remember?"

"Yes. So, did she know about the key and the door being unlocked?"

"No. She said she hasn't been in the room since I arrived."

Sela raised up from the bed so that she could look into Ben's face. "That has to be a mistake. She must have gone in there to clean it, or something, and just forgot. Are you sure you discovered the door unlocked and the key on the floor?"

"Positive."

"That's weird," she said with a frown.

"No more weird than everything else that's been going on around here."

"What do you mean?"

"I don't know," he said, "but, there's this nagging in the back of my head that says all of these inexplicable incidents, my accidents, even your boyfriends' accidents, all of it's connected."

"But how? I don't understand."

He pulled her back down to him on the bed, then rolled with her so that he was on top, his knees tucked between hers. "If I knew the answers, I'd be clairvoyant like your aunt."

"If Auntie were home, maybe she could help you figure this out."

"If Auntie were home," he said, drolly mocking her as he lowered his head, "we wouldn't be doing this."

Ben's lips teased her breast while his hands explored the soft lines of her waist and hips. And as Sela's gasps urged him on, the events of the day took a temporary backseat to the current, sweet agony that gripped them.

Sela twisted away from the noise and light that had awakened her, and knew instinctively that it was morning. After a few attempts, she raised her weighty eyelids and saw that light streamed obscenely through the open blinds in her room. That would be Fontella's doing. She closed her eyes again and stretched her arm out to the space behind her, and then she remembered that Ben had slipped from her side sometime in the early morning hours.

Relieved that he had left before now, she turned in the twisted sheets toward the noise in the hallway. She opened her eyes just as her door was flung wide, and Fontella appeared.

"Sela, get on up, girl." Her voice bubbled with attitude.

"Fontella," she grunted. "It's still early. What is it this time?"

"It's Claire."

"What about her?" Sela replied sleepily as she pulled the pillow to her chest and closed her eyes for a few more minutes.

"I'm home."

The unmistakable voice that belonged to Claire Bennett wasn't lost on Sela. She was too surprised to do more than sit straight up with her sheet clutched around her, and grin from ear to ear as she exclaimed her shock.

"Auntie."

Twenty-nine

Sela sat at the table in the kitchen with the others, her pride immense as her gaze flowed from Ben to her aunt. The two carried on an animated discussion of Claire's recent travels, and compared the places they had seen.

It had been months since she'd sat with her aunt like this, and it bolstered Sela's resolve to move out of the past and get on with her life. She thought her aunt Claire looked great—her thick, dark hair, fashionably streaked with a shot of gray, was worn stylishly short, and her intelligent eyes looked out from a lineless face. The flowing caftan she wore had probably been bartered from some Mediterranean street vendor she'd met along her journey. Still, Sela suspected a disconnection, as though part of her aunt's thoughts were occupied elsewhere.

"By the size of that trunk you had them drag in here, you brought back half of what you saw," Fontella declared as she delivered another basket of hot muffins to the table.

Claire laughed as she reached for the bread. "That's not everything," she called out at Fontella's back. Her resonant voice was meticulous. "The rest will be delivered later." She turned to Ben. "I even brought something back for you."

He smiled. "It wouldn't be that ID bracelet you won off me, would it?"

A shadow flitted across her eyes, but it was quickly gone as she smiled. "No, but I did promise to return it, and I will." She tilted her head slightly. "You don't look the worse for wear without it, and I trust you're enjoying your stay?" Her eyes seemed to make the shrewd assessment from across the table.

"Very much," he answered. "Though I figure you knew I would from the beginning."

"And does my niece have anything to do with that?"

Ben glanced at Sela next to him, then leaned back in his chair. "Actually, most of it has to do with Sela," he answered.

"We, um, haven't had a chance to bring you up to date on much of anything." She kicked him under the table when she thought he was about to laugh. "So much has happened since you've been gone and Ben arrived."

"It all worked out, I see." She looked at them both, and smiled. "For both of you."

A blissful peace swelled up in Sela. "Ben wasn't sure how you'd react to us seeing each other," she explained as he covered her hand with his.

Claire's smile was serene as she looked at Ben. "Don't you know I would never have sent you here to meet my beauty if I held reservations about you?" she asked smoothly.

"I realize that now, and I'll make sure you never regret your trust." He cleared his throat. "I was surprised to find you back this morning, though. What happened to make you cut your trip short?"

Sela had yet to ask the same thing, and saw that her aunt's face revealed nothing.

"Auntie—" She shifted in her chair. "Did you

come home because I was upset the other night about the accidents?"

Claire didn't answer, but raised her eyes to Ben. "You've been digging at old wounds, and asking questions around town, haven't you?"

Unsure of her mood, Ben frowned as he nodded. "Just a few."

"Then, speak up. Tell me what you've learned."

Sela sat up and jerked her head toward her aunt. "You saw something, didn't you? That's why you came back early."

"You had some sort of vision, Miss Bennett?" Ben asked.

Claire nodded. "I came home to its source. I need to get a better feel for this change in the air I've detected ever since I first met you in Italy."

"Can you describe it?" His voice urged her on.

"That doesn't always help. You see, I'm the only one who can interpret what I see. And, while I've taken measures to keep the two of you close to me, I'm afraid I'm no better than average at predicting what will happen when it affects the ones I love and care about."

Sela reached across the table for her aunt's hand. "This change. It's not a bad one, is it?"

Claire's look to Ben was a deft assessment. "I do know that Ben is the catalyst."

"Me?" he asked.

The older woman nodded. "You've already started the changes with these questions you've begun to raise."

Sela turned to Ben. "What kind of questions?"

The lines of concentration on his brow deepened. "I think I'm on to something. I just don't know what it is."

Sela shook her head. "I don't understand."

"I didn't want to say anything to you prematurely," Ben explained. "I ran some of my thoughts and ideas past Ron and Luther, and they both agreed to help me."

"Go on," she encouraged him.

He gave her a hard look for a moment. "I'm going to get to the bottom of these accidents. The ones that involved me, the ones that killed your boyfriends, all of them."

Sela couldn't believe what he was saying. He was purposely dredging up an ugly past.

"You don't think they were simple accidents." Claire spoke the statement matter-of-factly.

"I can't explain them away, but a lot of things don't make sense where they should."

When Sela clamped her jaw tight and stared at them, Ben darted a glance at Claire before he faced the stubborn set of Sela's shoulders.

"I'm not ignoring the fact that the accidents happened," he said.

"But, you just said they're not accidents. I thought you wanted me to accept them for what they were—coincidences that had nothing to do with my so-called bad luck."

"That's right." He reached out and took hold of her stiff shoulders. "But, suppose it has nothing to do with coincidence either? Suppose there's a person behind the accidents?"

Sela paused a moment, her brain in a whirl. "Why? For what reason?"

"Yeah, that sounds just crazy," Fontella added as she joined them from the sink. "Nobody's gonna buy that story around here," she said, and propped her hands on her hips.

"Ron and Luther said the same thing. At first."

Ben explained why he believed someone had

caused the accidents, though he admitted he was still working on the who and why. He felt confident he would find some thread of commonality that had been previously overlooked.

Fontella shook her head and threw her hands up. "Now I've heard everything, Ben."

Sela also looked skeptical. "I don't know what to say." She saw her aunt's calm expression, and twitched her brows. "Don't tell me you think there's something to his speculation?"

"I don't know. I've never considered it before, Sela." She looked at Ben. "But, your points are intriguing."

He looked at Sela's unconvinced face. "Even if you just consider the strange things that have happened since I've come to town, that alone should make you think something isn't right."

"What strange things?" Claire asked.

He enumerated the four near accidents he'd experienced. "And, I'm not clumsy," he added with a laugh.

"I have to admit you may be right about the strange events," Sela said. "Remember the odd stuff with the upstairs door key?"

"What about the key?" Claire asked Sela.

"We still don't know why the corner room was unlocked and the key was on the floor."

Fontella explained the mystery to Claire. "Something like this happening is downright spooky. And, I don't like the idea that someone could've been right here in the house with us, going right on up the stairs, and then walking around in the rooms."

Ben looked at Fontella. "When you made breakfast for me that first morning I was here, didn't you tell me you let yourself in with a key that's kept in the gazebo?"

"That's right," Sela answered, and she, too, looked to Fontella. "Is it out there? Do you still use it?"

Fontella frowned as she nodded. "Yeah, I do."

Claire spoke their thoughts out loud. "Then, it's possible that someone else might know about it, and could have helped themselves to it while no one was home."

An arctic chill surged through Sela, and she hugged her arms. "It never bothered me that a key was out there until now."

"But that explains how someone could get in the house and enter the room without any of us knowing," Ben said.

"Oh," Sela blurted, and jumped from her chair. "I just thought of something else that's odd. I'll be right back."

When Sela left the room, Fontella stood up and promised that while she did the chores, she would check around the house to see if anything was missing. She also vowed she wouldn't put the extra house key in the gazebo anymore. She left the table, mumbling to herself about the craziness in the world.

Claire's deep voice dropped an octave as she spoke her thoughts. "Maybe this is the impending danger I detected."

Ben could see that. Claire's inability to explain her visions bothered her.

"I wouldn't worry about it, Miss Bennett," he assured her. "I'm not going to let anything happen while I'm at the house."

"I'd think your hands would be full avoiding accidents." When they both broke out in grins, it eased the strain of the serious subject.

"Sela will believe the danger I see is centered on you because of her fear of these . . . accidents,"

Claire said. "But, the danger is spread out. Maybe it affects the whole town."

Ben now leaned forward and lowered his voice, too. "For something as bad as that about to happen, you sure seem to be taking it in stride."

"It's a practiced outer calm," she snapped at him good-naturedly. "And, I've had years to perfect it, so let's not get off the subject. Sela will return shortly."

Ben smiled at the testy, though utterly likable woman. "All right, what level of danger are we talking about here? Tornado, flood, serial killer, what?"

"Usually, this kind of vision could be any of those things, but it could also simply mean that our way of thinking is turned upside down, our personal lives and those of others around us could be changed forever. Things will happen, and you, somehow, are involved, along with a number of other people whom I can't seem to identify. She arched a brow of caution at him. "Don't ask, because I've tried, but I can't separate the other bodies."

She reached across the table and pulled Ben's hands into hers. "Do you know that, for me, your aura turns azure, a beautiful combination of pale purples and blues?"

"And, on the psychic scale, is that a good or bad aura?"

"Neither, you nonbeliever. It's simply you. Everyone I come into contact with exudes some manner of colorful aura.

Claire looked him straight in the eye while she squeezed his hand. "And, even though I detect excellent strength in your character, there is a bit of hubris there that could use some work." She smiled as she slowly freed him. "So, promise me that you'll be careful when you pick apart these accidents and search for a truth even you may not recognize."

Ben saw a pain in her eyes—a minor crack in her outer calm—as though she were trying to eke out the clarity she'd seen through the touch of his hand. Suppose she did have this power?

"I promise." He spoke the words soberly, respectfully.

"Good." Claire released his hand just as Sela rejoined them at the table.

When Ben pulled out a chair for her, he saw that she had something in her hand, and inquired about it.

"We were talking about strange things. Well, you know how I'm cleaning out those old boxes in the basement for Reverend Osborne, since Irene won't do it? Well, I came across these near the bottom of one."

She laid two pieces of paper on the table; Claire picked up the smooth sheet, while Ben lifted the crumpled one.

He sniffed at the sheet's black edge. "This has been scorched. Looks like nice writing paper, though. And you found these in the basement?"

She nodded. "They were mixed in a box with a lot of other stuff. The only reason I picked them up is that they looked a lot like your pale blue notepaper, Aunt Claire, and I couldn't figure out why your paper would be down there."

"True," she said. "I don't usually write personal notes at church, let alone in the deserted basement." Claire's brows furrowed as she studied the paper closely. "But, if I had to hazard a guess, I'd say it's my paper, down to the watermark."

"So, what's it doing in the basement?" Sela mused out loud.

"You know, I saw some balled-up paper in a crawl space area down in the basement, too." Ben turned the paper over. "I'll have to check that out."

"Actually," Claire said, "this color more resembles the stock I keep replenished for the guests. I originally gave this paper design to your mother years ago, Sela."

"That's where I've seen this before—in my room," Ben said. "These old pieces look like it, down to the faded block design."

"I imagine they could have been pale yellow once upon a time," Claire observed. "In which case they would perfectly match Helena's writing set, complete with the yellow rose journal I gave her."

Ben's head shot up. "The journal?"

Both women looked at him. "What about it?" Sela asked.

"It's just that I learned yesterday about how your mother's journal disappeared after her death."

Sela and Claire exchanged a quiet glance before Claire answered Ben.

"You have been busy with your questions," Claire said. "It didn't disappear from her writing set so much as it became lost."

"If it's the same set in her room upstairs, I saw it. The middle section is empty. That's where the journal would fit."

"Unfortunately for us, my sister's journal must have been lost before she died. That's why we couldn't find it later."

"That's what makes this paper all the more interesting," Ben said. "Maybe she lost her journal at the church years ago."

"I never considered that," Claire said, "but, she wouldn't have been writing in the basement."

Sela reached inside the neck of her shirt and

pulled out her gold locket. "I just thought of something."

She opened the locket and carefully unfurled the paper before she placed it next to the sheet of paper Claire had set on the table.

"Look at that," she said.

"My goodness." Claire spoke with surprise. "They match."

"How can you be sure?" Ben asked.

"The edges." Claire's voice dropped. "The paper from the basement has a ragged edge, just like one of the short edges of Sela's note." She looked up at Ben. "That edge isn't on the notepaper. The ragged edges were on the journal's pages."

Sela simply stared at her discovery. More coincidences? She turned and looked at Ben. "I don't understand this."

"One thing is certain," he said. "It all falls in the strange category."

As Sela sat at the kitchen table next to her aunt, her mood had turned to brooding. Ben had left to return to the church after he talked with some others who might have answers. It seemed she now had more cause than ever to worry over Ben's safety, though he was convinced that the answers they sought were in the church basement. Her only comfort now was his assurance that they'd get to the bottom of things, one way or the other.

"Stop frowning," Claire said to her. "When Ben is around, there's a shine to you." She reached over and touched Sela's hair. "I even like your hair loose and on the shoulders. Ben again?"

She nodded. "I have to admit, he's made a difference in how I see things, lately. I know, you've told me a lot of the same things in your own way. Ben, though, let me find out for myself that I should move on."

"That was wise of him, considering your personality." She smiled. "Your mother also preferred to learn through experience."

"Auntie, when we talk about my mother, I marvel at the fact that I don't know her at all." She raised her eyes to meet her aunt's. "I've decided that no matter how much your intention was to protect me, you've done me a disservice by not telling me all that you knew about her."

"But, you do know everything, Sela." Claire gave her an earnest smile. "She loved you.

"Then why did she take her own life? Why don't I have a father that I know?"

Claire reached over and took Sela's hands in hers. "You're moody and prickly . . . just like your mother," she said with a smile. "I believe Ben will have his hands full with you."

A reluctant smile crept to Sela's face. "Tell me some more about her, please; and, tell me about my father."

Claire lifted the locket around Sela's neck into her hand. "This was a gift to your mother from your father."

Sela's hands flew to the necklace. "I didn't know."

"It was his gesture of love, I imagine. Your father sent it to Helena before she left to meet him in New Orleans to get married."

"They were going to be married?"

Claire gently released the locket, then sat back in her chair. "Helena met Geoffrey Smith when he was a medical student at Tulane, and she was in her last year at Southern University. Your mother became pregnant with you soon after she graduated. When she finally told Geoffrey, he asked her to come back to New Orleans so they could be married. The locket arrived with the letter."

"Where were you at the time?"

"I was in college, but she promised that, when the arrangements were made, she would send for me and our parents.

"Within a week, though, she had returned to Fairlight with no husband and very little explanation for those outside of the family. Soon, you began to show, and she never spoke of Geoffrey again."

"I guess people talked and made up their own explanation."

"She was irritated by it, so she devised a story to protect her privacy. She simply told anyone who had the gall to ask that your father was in a fatal accident just before the marriage. While some probably didn't believe her story, they kept their doubts to themselves around her."

"That's how the rumor got started that I was like my mother."

"One that gets perpetuated every now and then by Mabel Thornton."

"What was the true story, then? Why did she come back?"

Claire sighed and rubbed her fingers across her temple, as though the truth were a painful process. "I didn't learn the real reasons myself until after you were born, Sela." She took her niece's hands into hers. "You see, Geoffrey only had Helena travel to New Orleans for an abortion."

Sela's hopeful face dropped and her eyes darted away at the knowledge.

"Of course," Claire continued, "Helena refused. He said he loved her, and wanted to marry her some day, but he didn't want a child—not right away. He told her if she had you, he wouldn't support her decision."

"Auntie, why didn't you ever tell me this?"

Claire's expression was pained. "Because Helena made me promise to never divulge how he had spurned the two of you. She felt the greater hurt would be if you tried to find love in a man who wanted nothing to do with you. And when I couldn't save Helena from suicide years later, I felt the least I could do was keep my promise to her."

Sela experienced an acute sense of hopelessness and felt her tears push forward. When she replied, her voice was low and tormented, but hopeful. "People can change, can't they? Do you think he ever regretted the decision he made about me?"

"I don't know. It's possible. I almost tried to find him after Helena died. But, you had just lost your mother, and I had no idea who Geoffrey had become or if he would reject a five-year-old child and foist another painful loss on her. So, I vowed I'd raise you as mine."

Claire's eyes had become cloudy with tears. "I break my promise to my sister now because I realize that you and I, we're the living, and we have to find the best way to make our place here on earth, and then move on."

"Is that why she took her own life? Because she never got over my father's rejection?"

Claire shook her head. "We were as close as sisters could be, but to this day I don't know why she chose that route. I do know it wasn't because she was depressed, Sela. She had you, and you gave her all the joy she'd ever wanted, and all the reasons to live."

Sela gave in to her tears and reached out for her aunt, her arms wide. "I love you," she whispered. "Thank you."

Claire pulled her niece close to her and returned the hug. "I love you, too, my beauty."

The doorbell only rang once, and Claire was already there. She had seen Jim Lewis from the window as he entered the gate. She didn't have much time to chat foolishness, not if she was to join Sela and the Stewart family at the hospital any time soon. When she opened the door, she relished the surprise on his face.

"What are you doing home?" he asked without preamble, and pushed his hands into his pockets.

"And why do you need to know?" Claire responded, her arms stretched akimbo.

"Yep, you're back, all right, haughty as ever with that mouth of yours." He grinned wide. "Welcome back."

"So I've heard," she commented and turned to go back into the house, leaving him at the door as her caftan swirled in her wake. "And thank you, I'm glad to be home."

Jim pulled off his cap and followed her through the foyer. "I knew you'd get on back once you heard Sela was carrying on with this man you sent to town."

"Carrying on? Please, Jim." She walked through the house to the kitchen. "Even Reverend Osborne doesn't sound that bad."

"You mean you're not gonna do anything about her seeing this new fella?"

"His name is Ben in case you forgot, and what do you suggest I do? Send her to her room?"

"No, but it's for her own good if you remind her of who she is and what her place is. She'll listen to you."

Incensed, she turned and began to advance on him, her finger pointed. "You sound like a crazy old bear. I want you to know that I like Ben Russell, and she likes him, too. They're good for each other, so I don't want to hear of you or anyone else standing in the way of their happiness with stories of what's already been."

She had reached him now and her finger dug at his chest. "And, if you can't live with her seeing him, then don't come around. Is that clear?"

Jim stumbled back and away from her advancing figure before he brought his hand up and clutched hers tightly to push her back.

Claire looked at him as a swirl of color surrounded her head, and an acrid odor bit into her nostrils. She turned her hands so that she now grasped his tightly. Jim's brow pulled into an affronted frown as he snatched his hand away.

"You can't keep me from seeing her, all right? While you go flittin' around the globe every year, I'm the one who's here making sure she's okay, and I say she needs to leave this man alone for her own good."

Claire studied Jim with a curious eye as he retreated to the front door. "Why did you do that?"

"Do what?"

"Snatch your hand away from me, as though it burned. Come to think of it, you seem to always avoid my touch, even though you're not afraid of me like some others." She stepped nearer to him. "So, why is that?"

"Why don't you just take care of Sela like her mama wanted you to, and things will be fine."

He backed away some more before he turned and headed for the foyer. Before Claire could reach him, he had already cleared the front door. As she turned, there, near the foyer wall, she spied his work cap on the floor. He must have dropped it, she thought, and picked it up.

As she grasped the cap in her hand, she was struck by a vision so intense that the room seemed to, suddenly, tumble as she lost her balance and teetered against the wall.

"Oh . . ." she whimpered as the pure, vivid reds and yellows in the image threatened to burn her closed lids. But, this particular vision wasn't new. She had seen it before. With Ben.

She heard the front door open. Claire opened her eyes and saw Jim rush in. Without a word, he came up to her and snatched the cap from her hand. Then, just as quickly, he pivoted and left. The door slammed behind him.

Drained, Claire leaned against the wall and covered her face with her hands. She was no closer to understanding what she'd just seen; but, she'd have to tell Ben about it as soon as possible.

Thirty

Ben's long strides through the hospital corridor took him closer to the pediatric nursery floor at the Talbot County Hospital. He didn't have to search long for Ron. He was standing in the hall and peered expectantly through the window at the sleeping babies.

He stretched his hand out to greet Ron. "Congratulations on the new baby. Vanessa told me I'd find you up here. I wanted to give you something for the little one." He presented Ron with an envelope. "Seeing as the cost of kids keep going up, I figured I'd help out with your college funds."

Ron grinned as he opened the envelope. When he saw the U.S. Savings Bonds, one for each of the boys, he laughed out loud.

"Ben, this is great; Vanessa will like it, too. Thanks."

He then pointed out little Brandon to Ben and they spent the next couple of minutes admiring the sleeping child.

As they walked away from the window, Ben asked Ron, "Have you seen Mr. Freeman lately?"

"No, not today. You still haven't caught up with him, huh?"

Ben sighed. "Not yet. Maybe I can catch him at

the church later." He stopped a moment. "Maybe you can answer a question about the accidents, Ron."

"Sure, what do you want to know?"

"The papers said a neighbor found Charles and then called the police."

Ron rubbed his chin in thought. "Oh, that was old man Garfield who lived out near Charles's family's house. He died sometime last year. That whole area where they lived was pretty isolated back then."

"Did you know anything about him, and how he happened to find Charles's body?"

"I know he told Sela he felt pretty bad about not acting sooner when he heard the first gunshot. If he had, maybe Charles wouldn't have bled to death."

"So, why didn't he act quicker?"

"He said he didn't think it was anything, at first. Then, when Mr. Lewis came through with the mail delivery, he mentioned the sound he'd heard, and Lewis urged him to check it out."

"Interesting," Ben mused. "Maybe I'll learn something from this Doctor Harris that will decipher some of the stories I'm hearing. I'm headed there in a few minutes for an appointment Luther set up for me."

"Listen, man, if you need me, I'll be here."

"Sure, Ron. In the meantime, you take care of your beautiful family." Ben bade him good-bye, and headed for the elevator. It would be interesting to hear what the doctor could toss into this muddled salad of information.

When Ben arrived at the doctor's office, the parking lot was close to full. For a small-town practice, it appeared to be a thriving one.

As he parked, and then prepared to lock the car, Ben looked up and saw Mr. Lewis leave the doctor's office through the front door, his thoughts clearly on whatever it was he held in his hands.

Ben supposed he was delivering the mail, and started to greet the older man; but, then decided against it. The man didn't like him and, even though Ben wanted to ask him about the accidents, maybe now was not the right time.

He locked the car, and by the time he started for the door, he saw that Mr. Lewis had already moved through the parking lot.

Within ten minutes of his arrival at the reception counter in the busy waiting room, Ben was shown to the doctor's private office by a rather sullen nurse who kept referring to the doctor as Doc Harris. And, as he sat for yet another five minutes in the small office, he studied the crowded walls. They were lined with awards and trophies, all unrelated to medicine, as well as an assortment of mounted fish and animals, an obvious sign that the doctor had taken an active interest in his personal life.

"Mr. Russell."

Ben turned to the opening door and saw the doctor enter. He was tall and ascetic with longish, graying hair, and a neatly trimmed mustache to match. He wore a white lab coat over his street clothes as he peered at Ben over the top of his wire-rimmed glasses.

"I'm sorry it's taken so long to get in here," he said absently as he came across the room. "One day I've got to take the time to find a partner."

Ben smiled as he stood and greeted the doctor with a handshake. "How do you do, sir? And, please, call me Ben. I appreciate you giving me a few minutes of your time."

"Not at all, Ben. You've got a good reputation. Actually, I'd already heard about you coming to town to look over the renovation work at New Hope church. You know, it's one of the biggest churches in all the adjacent counties." He took a seat behind his desk and placed the folder he held to the side.

"Luther Matthews, the local deputy around here, suggested I talk with you." Ben reclaimed his seat, as well.

"You know, not only is Luther a patient, but he's an okay fellow in my book. Glad I could grant him a favor. He told me you had a few questions about the ME reports I filed a while back on three deaths in town."

Ben nodded. "That's right."

"I had a chance to review all three before you arrived. What did you want to know?"

"Is there a possibility that any of the deaths could have been other than what they appeared?"

"You mean, like, foul play?"

"Something like that."

"Well, that distinction is something a criminal investigation team would determine, and to the best of my knowledge, that was never the official police finding in these three cases. Of course, as the medical examiner, I determine the cause of death, and these deaths were a basic, by-the-book drowning, gunshot wound, and hanging."

"Let's consider Helena Bennett's hanging, in particular. Could she have been dead before she hung from that makeshift noose?"

He shook his head. "I remember the family wanted to believe that. It was a rough time for them and the child. But, the autopsy would have revealed badges of foul play." He frowned a moment. "There was one odd thing about the Bennett hanging."

Ben's head jerked up. "Oh?"

"She had a soft-tissue bruise across her right jaw. It wasn't the cause of death, of course, and the police decided it could have occurred in an earlier suicide attempt or fall as she set up her death. In either event, it didn't change the facts."

"And those facts would be?" Ben asked.

"Well, in these three instances you point to, the facts of each case coincided with the cause of death. There was just no competent authority to point to a foul play suspicion."

Ben clenched his jaw in frustration. He could think of nothing to further the conversation on the deaths. They had been straightforward investigations, and surely he couldn't change all that because he had a gut feeling something wasn't right.

"Can I help you with anything else?"

"Well, there is one more thing." Ben stood and reached into his pocket. "While working in the church basement, I came across an antique pillbox. I thought that maybe identifying the medication might point to the owner."

"Sure," he said. "I can take a look."

Ben dropped the pills into the doctor's palm. "I can tell some are over-the-counter drugs."

"Let's see . . ." The doctor examined the pills. "You've got extra-strength Tylenol as well as a pretty potent-strength dosage of prescription Motrin. This person must walk around with a hell of a headache," he joked.

"Now this one I can't identify right off," he continued. "And, it doesn't look familiar." Doc Harris held the pill up to the light. "Good, the inscription is still intact. It's a simple matter of looking up the numbers, but I'll have to get back to you," he said.

"That's fine," Ben said. "I'll leave you my cell number."

Soon after they exchanged a few more pleasantries, he left the office. When he got to his car, he dialed Sela on his phone.

"Hi," she answered. "Where are you?"

"I'm on my way to the church to recheck that basement and see if I can find Mr. Freeman. I want to ask him some questions, but I can't seem to catch up with him. You think he's avoiding me?"

"Stop seeing intrigue everywhere," she teased. "This is Fairlight. Now, what did you want to know?"

"Since Freeman was the one who found Andrew at the pond, I thought he could tell me what Andrew had been doing that night. Would you know?"

"Well, he did have a church meeting."

"He was leaving the church the night of his accident?"

"Yes. He was a youth leader and had planned a trip that needed approval by the youth board. So, he met with them earlier that evening."

"You wouldn't remember who all attended the meeting with him, did you?"

"Sure. Let's see, Reverend Osborne, of course, and a couple of other young people. Um, Mr. Freeman and Mr. Lewis attended that night, too. I guess that's everyone. Does that help you?"

"To be honest, I'm not sure. The paper said there was heavy fog that night. Is it always bad over on that road?"

"It can be bad, but there was controversy about whether it was foggy or not on that particular night. I remember it had been presumed that fog was a contributing factor, but the weather reports didn't indicate any for that evening."

Ben's thoughts raced through this information.

And, for the life of him, while he suspected something important may have been relayed in all he'd heard, he didn't quite recognize it yet.

"Ben, promise me you'll call me at home if anything new comes up. I'll be leaving the hospital soon to help Fontella at the house. We're planning a welcome home drop-in for Aunt Claire, and we invited a lot of neighbors. I want you to attend."

"I wouldn't miss it, and I promise to call you the minute I find something interesting."

"Please be careful," she warned him.

Ben smiled. "I will." He shut off the cell phone and, finally, turned his car in the direction of the church. It was time to do a bit of digging.

Frisco had pulled alongside the road and waited for the bout of nausea to pass. Taking his medication in his recent, haphazard way had only added to the depression and elation that hit him in hard, vertigo-like waves. He was torn between his craving for this medication that stopped the dark urges, and the freedom of mind and spirit he enjoyed when he wasn't bound by the drugs.

He had dangerously stretched out his use of the last pills, and now his brown bottle was empty, and he couldn't find his pillbox. Damn. He squeezed his eyes tight. Doc Harris wouldn't give him a new supply until he met with that feeble minded Doctor Holliday in Macon.

He gripped the steering wheel and tried to figure out when things had gotten this bad. Had Claire's return done it? Maybe. But, he had begun to suffer the heavy depression days ago, ever since he'd visited Helena's room. That was it. He shouldn't have gone back to the house. He shouldn't have followed her upstairs. As he shook his head clear, his eyes opened and fell to his hand. As he stretched his fingers, he willed energy through the veins.

This didn't have to happen. It was all because of the outsider. He continued to flaunt his affair in everyone's face, and now it was becoming common knowledge. Again.

Frisco closed his fingers into a fist and punched the steering wheel with all his might, and the pain felt good. Right now, he recognized that he was at the end of his rope, and somebody would pay.

Ben turned the car into the church parking lot. As he reached for his cell phone to place in his pocket, it rang, as if on cue. When he answered, it was Doc Harris.

"Ben, glad I caught you. I knew I'd stay busy for the rest of the afternoon, so I thought I'd call you now and give you the information on the pills you left."

"Great." Ben reached for a pad to take notes.

"What you've got here are low-potency doses of a psychotropic drug called Trazodone."

"All right. Now say it in plain English," Ben joked.

"Sure. It's a medication for someone who is mildly depressed, possibly delusional. I suspect the Motrin is taken in tandem because of the side effects, which include severe headaches, nausea, the whole nine yards of just feeling bad."

"So why does someone take something that makes them feel that bad?"

"It's sort of a 'damned if you do, damned if you don't' situation. You have to take the medication to curb the delusions and depression. The side effects just come with the territory."

"Could a person taking this drug hurt someone?"

"Well, that's a relative question. We're all capable of inflicting pain, even death, but it depends on the situation. But, if they haven't hurt anyone yet, the chances are slim that their delusions are dangerous to others." Doc Harris chuckled. "I suspect whoever this belonged to was probably in a bad mood a lot of the time."

"That could be the case," Ben agreed as he thought over the doctor's words. He thanked the doctor for the quick results and clicked off the line.

Ben dropped his head back against his seat. He now had a profile of his basement dweller. He was most probably a male who suffered from headaches and delusions; depression, even. So, who around town hadn't met that description at one time or the other? Ben sighed as he got out of the car, and headed for the church office.

Thirty-one

Ben moved the flashlight in a wide arc as he made his way through the narrow, faintly lit basement corridor. He both relied on and trusted his instincts that some of the answers he sought would be found down here.

He shrugged off the creepy feeling of being watched and moved on.

The church had already been emptied of the summer school students for the day, and Irene had closed down the office at three sharp, so he was pretty much on his own down here until Freeman came by later to check on things.

Ben had worked his way deep into the basement of the huge church. When he reached the door of the crawl space, he threw the latch and wrenched it open. Leading with the flashlight, he peered into the yawning black halo.

He followed the slanted ceiling line with the flashlight until the ceiling met the dirt floor far in the back of the unfinished room; and then he played it back again. That's when he saw the light dance off the paper he had seen the other day. The balled-up sheets were near the middle of the far wall, and next to a wax candle.

The humidity was not comfortable, and Ben

wiped his forehead. He pointed the flashlight across the back of the room and saw how it ended in a black chasm, an opening that might easily become a dungeon and trap him there.

Regardless of the danger, he had to see what might be hidden in there. If, indeed, there were a delusional individual living in the church's basement, it had to be revealed. He set the flashlight down and unbuttoned his shirt. At least when he came out, he'd have a clean shirt to put on, he thought wryly.

Once his shirt was off, he wiped his hands across his dark jeans and went into the room at, first, a walk, then, a stoop, and, finally, a crawl. As Ben played the flashlight ahead of him, he could see that the black hole was an opening that dropped down into the floor at the back wall.

When he reached the edge of the drop-off, he carefully manipulated the light toward the space that descended a few feet. It was reinforced with wood on the three sides, and the bottom was dirt. Ben could see nothing on the far side he'd shone the light on; but, when he stuck his hand down there and felt around the near wall and corner, he struck a plastic bag. Ben strained to reach deeper until he finally eased the bag between his fingers. He clutched the bag tight and pulled his arm out of the hole.

Cramped and dirty, he crawled backward out of the humid room with his prize, and into the relative coolness of the hallway. He thought he would go back and check around one more time; but, after a few deep breaths, he allowed himself to savor this first success and to open the plastic bag. He quickly peeled back the plastic from the sturdy object.

When he saw the single gilded rose etched against

the aged leather book, he knew what he had found: Helena Bennett's lost journal.

Ben dusted the flecks of dirt from the cover and reverently opened the soiled book. He did not take the time to even consider the how and why. He just wanted to see if the woman's words were still intact after more than twenty years.

And so, first, he simply inspected the book, and deduced that the blank sheets they had found around the basement had been torn from the unused back pages. Whoever had kept the book had been careful to preserve the pages on which Helena Bennett had written.

As Ben's hunger quickly grew for answers to why she had killed herself, it became awkward to even consider reading the woman's words. Somehow, it seemed only fair that Sela should be the one to receive the book and gain personal knowledge of her mother's deepest, maybe her last, private feelings.

As the pages fluttered open past his gaze, he noticed that one of the written pages had been torn. He opened the book to it and recognized Helena Bennett's precise, cursive handwriting on the short journal entry. But, the bottom fourth of the page had been ripped away. Still struggling with the dilemma to read or not, he did. Her words were simple.

I can't imagine being without Sela for a few days, let alone a few months. She has brought all of us a joy we never imagined. So, how do I explain to my little girl that when she goes to her big school next year, her mama will also be going away for a few months to a big school, too? Claire keeps telling me not to worry about her, and that everything will be fine. For me, though, the hardest thing in the world would be to say

The page abruptly ended. The remaining words had been ripped away. Slowly it dawned on Ben what he was likely looking at. "Whoa," he blurted out loud as the realization fully hit him. The suicide note in Sela's locket. The first word on Sela's note, *good-bye,* easily made sense fitted on the end of the passage.

Ben's thoughts churned at an extraordinary speed. What if Helena Bennett didn't commit suicide after all? What if someone set it up to look like one? The possibility caused Ben's heart to thump in a triple beat.

As he read the passage again, fitting as much as he could mentally recall of Sela's note to the end, his initial excitement began to ebb. The journal alone was not going to be enough to change a suicide to homicide. Unless the journal offered a clue as to why she was murdered.

Ben glanced up the shadowy corridor before he browsed the pages dated around Helena's death. And, as he turned through a few pages, he saw that Helena Bennett's words were seldom depressing, though they were fiercely protective of her little girl. They were not the words of a woman who planned to kill herself. He read a passage.

Frisco is so possessive, and of all people, it's over my Sela. I'm at the point where it worries me. He actually tells me how I should dress her for nursery school. I wonder now if he goes by the school and watches her, too? I don't like it, and I told him so. I don't think he believes I'm serious. Well, we'll see. I feel he's a man of good intentions, but he has problems he has purposely hidden.

Frisco. Although the name was vaguely familiar, Ben couldn't recall where he'd heard it before. He turned to another page where the same name jumped out at him:

Frisco asked me to marry him. Again. I'm beginning to wonder where he gets the idea I'm interested in him that way. It has to be in his head. He truly believes I've been greatly wronged by Sela's father. But like most things you see from the outside, there's a greater depth to be pursued. If only he knew the whole story.

Ben frowned as he turned to Helena's final entry and realized it was dated the day she died.

Now that I have made peace with my decision to tell Sela's father about her, I feel a great burden lifted. When Claire returns tomorrow, I'll discuss this with her, and she'll help me locate Geoffrey again. I can only hope Sela will one day forgive me, too. While he may have much to atone for, he has the right to know our child, and I had no right to return his letters out of anger, even if my anger was righteous. I worry over how Sela will take this news that's sure to come out. Everyone has always believed that her father was dead and

The passage abruptly ended in midsentence. She had planned to find Sela's father, and let him back into their lives, Ben mused. He went back to the name on the other pages and spoke it aloud in measured tones.

"Frisco, Frisco. Where have I heard it before?" He snapped his fingers as the startling answer came at him in a rush. It was at the library, where he'd read the articles on the microfiche. Ophelia had waded through the pictures in Helena Bennett's high school senior yearbook. She had pointed out their classmates, and at Ben's request, had named the ones who stayed in town. And, she had rattled off their nicknames, too.

"Frisco." Ben said the name again, amazed, and sat back on his heels. "He was the crazy kid who transferred in from San Francisco."

Ben punched in Sela's number on his cell phone at the same time as he worked his arms back into his shirt. The line was heavy with static interference as she picked up.

"Sela, can you hear me? I'm down in the church basement."

"Ben? Did you learn anything new?"

He let out an elated laugh. "You're not going to believe it, but it's all beginning to make sense. I found your mother's journal." Static followed his words.

"What?"

"I know who's behind all this." A movement to his left drew Ben's attention away. He raised his eyes and, as he began to turn, he took the full force of the blunt object that came down on his head.

The phone popped from his fingers, but Ben fought to stay upright as he fell backward to the cement corridor floor; and, too soon, all had faded to black. . . .

Ben's inert body lay sprawled in the corridor. Frisco surveyed his handiwork as he leaned the lead pipe near the crawl-space door. A moment of silence confirmed that no one else was around. He took only a brief moment to press his hand against his pulsing temple before he got to the chore at hand. Frisco was a big man, but so was the outsider, and he had to store the body until he decided how he would plan his accident.

He hefted Ben up by the armpits, and with the first of numerous grunts of pain, dragged him through the crawl-space doorway.

"Hello, hello?" Sela transferred the phone from one ear to the other before a quick and disturbing thought came to her. The phone on the other end had gone dead. And Ben would have called back. If he could.

Sheer black fright swept through her. Something was wrong, and she had to get to the church with Ben. The knife she had held clattered to the chopping board and she hurried across the kitchen, untying the apron from around her rust-colored pantsuit as she moved. Sela had planned to surprise Aunt Claire by wearing the gift she had brought back from her trip to the drop-in this evening, and now she didn't have time to change so it would stay fresh.

Fontella had not returned from the market, either, and there was no time to leave her a note. Sela decided she'd worry about it all later. What was important now was getting to Ben. Grabbing her keys and purse in the foyer, she rushed out the door.

The drive to the church was a nerve-wracking experience compared only to the one she'd made through the storm. When she arrived, she quickly left her car to run to the office door. It was locked.

Sela looked around and saw no one to help. She ran around to the back of the church for the basement door, and beat on it.

"Ben, are you in there?" When there was no answer, she tramped across the grass and tried to peer through a glass block window.

"Sela, what are you doing?"

She turned at the voice. Deacon Freeman was coming her way from across the grass.

"Oh, I'm so glad to see you. You've got the church keys. I need you to let me in the church."

"Hey, slow down."

Sela took a deep breath before she sped through her explanation. "It's Ben. He called me about twenty minutes ago from the basement, and something happened to our connection. He found something downstairs, and I think he may be in danger."

Deacon Freeman looked at her as though she'd grown another head. "What are you talking about? What kind of danger?" He walked past her and moved toward the parking lot. "Ophelia told me he was at the library playing these dangerous games, talking about accidents, and bringing up old mess—"

When Sela pulled with all her might on the deacon's arm, it spun him around, and he grabbed hold of his glasses before they could sail from his face.

"Now you listen," she screamed. "This is not a game. He's in that basement and you're going to open those doors right now and let me in, or I'll take the keys from you and let myself in." She took a threatening step toward him. "Right now."

"All right," he agreed, and stomped off to the basement door.

"Hurry," Sela pressed as she stood at his elbow.

He worked the key. "Okay, okay." When he threw

the door open, Sela ran ahead of him and called out, "Ben, are you down here?" She headed for the stairwell that led to the lower level where Ben had located the crawl space he'd mentioned.

"What are you doing now?" the deacon asked.

"I'm going downstairs. That's where he probably is."

She was surprised to hear the deacon follow her through the doorway and traipse down the stairs. When they reached the bottom, she opened the stair door and stepped into the cool, dim corridor as she called out to Ben again. There was no answer. And, as she looked around, she realized they had another problem.

"You wouldn't happen to have a flashlight on you, would you?" She continued down the hallway, cautiously looking from left to right as she maneuvered in the dim corridor, entering deeper into the basement.

"Not with me. Where did you say he was supposed to be?"

"Somewhere near the cornerstone he found last week." She saw a turn up ahead and swallowed her growing fear. "I think we should go this way. Ben?" Her voice was high-pitched and nervous. "Are you down here? Ben?"

As she cleared the corner, she heard a bump, then a loud grunt, both coming from behind her.

"Deacon Freeman?"

She looked over her shoulder, then turned just in time to see Deacon Freeman stagger a few steps into her, his hands extended.

"What's wrong with you?" she screeched. She stumbled backward, and into the wall as the older man fell against her, before he dropped like deadweight to the cement floor.

Sela screamed, but only part of the scream came out. The other part died in her throat as she realized he'd been hit from behind with something. She stooped to the floor and tried to find a pulse on the deacon when she heard the footsteps. She looked up as someone came at her.

Claire was worried and could no longer contain her agitation.

"Miss Claire, what's wrong with you?" Vanessa asked from the hospital bed.

"Vanessa, I have to go." She sighed and closed her eyes a moment. "I haven't heard from Sela, and I left a message at home that she was to call me as soon as possible. I've called the church, and there's no answer there, either."

The phone in the hospital room clanged loudly, and jarred Claire's senses. It was Fontella. She bowed her head silently and waited.

Someone in the room had picked up the phone and now called out, "Miss Claire, Fontella wants you on the phone."

It was passed to Claire and she answered from her chair.

"This is Claire."

"I heard your message," Fontella said, "but I thought Sela was back at the hospital with you."

"Explain," Claire said simply.

"Well, when I returned from the grocer's, she was gone. Course, she left the knife in the middle of the chopped celery, but her purse and car aren't here, so I figured she was at the hospital."

"And Ben?"

"Not around. He's gone in his car, too."

Claire bit her lip, mildly frustrated. "Fontella, stay

near a phone, please, and let us know if you hear from Sela at all."

"All right, but you sound worried. Is anything wrong?"

"Let's just say something isn't right."

"You're still coming home a little later this evening?"

"Yes," she said absently. "I'll be there later."

As she replaced the phone on the hook, the twins, rambunctious as ever, rushed over to her chair. Brett's golden trinket dropped from his chubby hands into her lap. Claire picked it up, and her breath was taken away. She attempted to stand for air, but she still couldn't overcome the strong rush of electric energy that filled her space. Colors, reds and yellows bursting in the air like a raging fire, danced before her eyes. She blinked as she looked at the trinket she held in her hand.

"Miss Claire, are you all right?" She could hear Vanessa's question. "Somebody, get her some water."

Sela and Ben were together and they were in danger. But, where? Ben had promised he'd take care of Sela. And she was supposed to look out for him. Claire now turned to Vanessa.

"Is Ron still at the hospital?"

Vanessa nodded. "Yes."

"Send for him. I need to talk with him now."

When Fontella hung up the phone, worried over Claire's concern about Sela, the front door chime rang. She sucked in her breath. If it wasn't one thing, it was another. She looked around the kitchen at the food that still needed preparation, and felt like pulling her hair out. She'd have to call Rosalie and get her over here, then hope Sela would show up before Claire and their friends came by tonight.

The doorbell sounded again.

"I'm coming, I'm coming," Fontella yelled at the offending bell and now stepped lively to the front door. She threw it open and looked at the two people who stood there, a handsome couple that was a young man and an older woman not from around here.

"Well, hello there," she greeted the two, and crossed her arms. "Can I help you?"

"Yes," the woman spoke up. "Are you Claire Bennett, the owner of this bed and breakfast?"

The woman was shorter than Fontella, but she hid the fact in the high heels and dark suit she wore on this warm July evening.

"No," Fontella answered, stretching out the monosyllable. "I'm the housekeeper. Sorry, but the B and B isn't open for business until Labor Day weekend this year."

As she stepped back from the door to close it on the would-be lodgers, she watched as the young man began to grin—one that quickly spread to his eyes. Fontella squinted at him. Doggone if he didn't look like a younger, more playful version of Ben Russell.

He stuck out his hand to Fontella. "My name is Montreal Russell. This is my mother, Barbara Russell." As they shook hands, he added, "We're looking for my brother, Ben. He's an architect visiting town."

Fontella now grinned with him, and pushed the door wide. "Then you're at the right place," she said. "Come on in." As they stepped into the foyer, Fontella counted herself as lucky. She had two more hands to help with the food preparation.

* * *

Ron was with Claire outside the hospital room, and had stooped to the twins' level.

"Listen, fellas, you're not in trouble, but we need to know where you got this pillbox."

"In the basement," Brian answered, and looked at his brother.

"We're not supposed to say where in the basement, though." Brett's attention had not moved from his toy that Claire still held.

Ron sighed. "And why is that?"

The twins exchanged a glance before Brian said, "Mr. Russell told us not to play down there, but we did."

"And we got in trouble when we went in the hide-and-seek room."

"Ben was angry with you for disobeying him?" Ron asked.

"No, Brett whined, tiring of the explanations. "It was—"

Brian nudged his brother, and Brett fell quiet again.

Claire stooped to the boys. "So, you found this in your hide-and-seek room. Tell me, who was angry with you in there?"

"He said we were in his hiding place," Brett said, and began to twist uncomfortably.

"And we better not tell anybody about it or we were gonna be in trouble," Brian continued as he twisted his hands.

"Ben told you this?" Ron asked the boys gently.

"No, he didn't," Claire said and smiled at the boys. "But, I think I know who did. Do you want to tell us now?"

"It was Mr. Lewis." They spoke together.

As Claire and Ron stood, she said, "I gave this pillbox to Jim years ago, and connecting with it is like standing in the center of a fire. I'm seeing the same vision for Ben."

"Then, we have to find out where Ben and Mr. Lewis are."

"I can't find Sela anywhere, either," Claire said. "I believe all three are together."

"Ben was going to the church today." He looked at. Claire. "Let's find Luther and get over there to this hide-and-seek room."

Thirty-two

Sela stumbled as Jim Lewis pushed her ahead of him and into a dark room that was briefly lit by the dim hall light—enough to outline another body crumpled on the floor inside—before everything was once again blanketed in darkness. It was a man's body. Shocked by the possibility of that horror, Sela became numbed to everything else. When the door slammed shut, she spun around, and knew she was locked in.

Her attention quickly returned to the body she knew instinctively was Ben's, and blindly made her way to him. Sela used every bit of willpower she could harness to make him all right. With gentle touches under his unbuttoned shirt, she tried to locate a pulse, and was quickly rewarded with a deep groan. He was alive.

"Oh, Ben. Thank God." With her limbs quaking, she tried to nudge him awake in the dark. "Come on, wake up. You'll be okay."

He groaned louder this time; but, with her help and a painful wince as he raised his head, he was finally able to roll from his back to his side.

He let out a heavy sigh. "Sela? What are you doing down here?" He straightened up until he sat next to her.

She smothered a tearful sob. "When your phone line went dead, I came to find you. And Mr. Lewis, he's totally out of his mind. I mean, he just came at Deacon Freeman and knocked him out; then, without saying anything, he dragged me in here with you. What happened to you?"

"He blindsided me while I was talking with you on the phone."

When his arms reached for her in the dark, Sela allowed him to gather her to him. She buried her face against his chest.

"I didn't know what to think when I realized it was you in here," she sobbed. "I thought our worst nightmare had come true after all, Ben."

"It has nothing to do with fate or bad luck. Mr. Lewis wanted to stop me from warning you that he's the one behind these so-called accidents going on in town; all of them. He's a murderer, Sela."

"What?"

"He's sick. I found out from Doc Harris that he's taking medication for delusions and schizophrenia. And, from what everyone has told me about the accidents, he seems to always be in the background when they happen," he whispered in her hair.

"How . . . why?" She was unable to form a question, unsure what to ask first.

"Only he can give us the details, though I suspect the murders have something to do with his longstanding fixation on you and your mother." He pulled back from her. "I think some of our answers are in her journal I found in here."

Sela's mind was reeling as she peered through the dark at Ben's face. "You have her journal?"

"I did. There's a drop in the floor at the back wall where it was hidden. But, Lewis probably got it back after he knocked me out." His hands captured the sides of her face, and followed a stream of tears. "He didn't hurt you, did he?"

She shook her head between sniffs as she took all this in. "He hurt Mr. Freeman, and I don't know how bad; but, I tried to stop him." She raised her fingers to his face and gently stroked it. "I know you're hurt. I've heard you groan more than once."

He dropped his hands. "I'm still a little woozy, and I'll probably have a hellish headache tomorrow. Right now, we need to figure a way to get the hell out of here before he gets back."

"Let me help you stand up."

With Sela's help, Ben tried to stand, his groans increasing as he stood taller.

Sela pulled him back down to sit on the floor. "You need to rest a minute, Ben. You've probably suffered a concussion."

The door let off a creak, and a light flashed from where it was opening.

Blinded by the sudden brilliance that penetrated the blackness, Ben and Sela shielded their eyes, suspecting that it was Jim Lewis behind the bright halo of light.

"So, you finally woke up?" It was Jim's voice.

Sela helped Ben rise to his feet again. He whispered to keep silent, but she ignored the caution, unwilling to accept that the man she'd known all her life had become a monster.

"Mr. Lewis, what's wrong with you? Why are you doing this?"

"Helena? Get over here with me."

Puzzled, she turned to Ben.

"This is Sela," Ben said to Mr. Lewis. "Helena is dead."

"Get over here," he demanded again. "And

you"—he motioned to Ben with his free arm—"shut up."

"Go ahead," Ben whispered to Sela. "Do as he says. Play along."

She slowly stepped toward the door. "Mr. Lewis, for heaven's sake, what's going on? You have to stop this before it goes any further. Let us go."

When Sela was within his reach, he grabbed her wrist and snatched her to him.

"You're hurting her, Frisco. Stop it," Ben's voice boomed.

The words penetrated Frisco's brain like a lightning bolt. *Stop it, Frisco.* She'd said the same thing that day. He released her wrist as though it were a hot poker, and watched as she rejoined her lover at the wall, his arms open to receive her.

Frisco blinked. Sela? No, Helena. The outsider was with her—living proof that she still hadn't learned. He blinked hard again as he rubbed the pulsating tic near his temple.

The love and hate that had tried to reside mutually in his heart for all these years now swelled for a showdown. He leaned back against the door and, brandishing the outsider's flashlight in one hand, reached into his pocket and withdrew a small-caliber gun with the other.

He heard her gasp and knew the power he possessed. It was like all of the other times.

"Why are you doing this?"

Frisco looked up as she made her plea. "Because you don't know what's good for you. You never did."

"What are you talking about?" she asked.

"I don't think it's you that he sees anymore," Ben said, his eyes leveled at the man.

"What do I have to do, huh? Keep teaching you a lesson until you learn?" Frisco asked. "And I'll do it over and over again until you realize what's best for you."

"And what's best for them is you. Right, Frisco? You're best for Helena and Sela?"

"Yes." He hated the outsider's smug voice. "I won't hurt her or leave her with a child to raise. I wanted Sela for my little girl." He motioned with the light. "She should've been mine from the start."

"But, you did hurt Helena, Frisco. You hurt her and Sela real bad, didn't you?"

His heart pumped feverishly at the outsider's words. He aimed the light at him. "What are you talking about?"

"I'm talking about what you did to a woman who had a little girl she loved and who wanted to live so she could take care of her." The voice turned heavy with accusation. "You killed her."

"Ben, no." She turned to Frisco. "You hurt my mama?"

"No . . . no, it wasn't like that at all." Frisco's hand tightened on the gun as he remembered that day and the secret. He had to set them straight about what really happened. "It was an accident."

"Tell her how you killed Helena Bennett, Frisco."

"I swear." Frisco looked at them. "It was all an accident. I can explain."

"Frisco, it's you." Helena Bennett unlatched the screen door to the porch. It was midmorning and she was attired in a dressing gown and carried her journal in her hand. "Do I have to sign for mail or something?"

"No," he answered, enjoying the way she always called him by the nickname that had stuck since he'd showed up in town as a cocky kid from the San Francisco Bay area. It meant she wasn't angry with him anymore.

"Well, I'm busy right now and I don't need any company."

"I'm still a friend, right?" he argued. "Whether you want to marry me or not?"

She looked properly chastised for being cool toward him and smiled. "Sure," she relented, and stepped aside as she held the screen door open to him. "Do you want a cup of coffee? There's still some on." She turned and walked back inside.

"Yeah, that'd be nice," he said, and followed her.

As Helena passed through the dining room, she stopped long enough to lay the journal, faceup with a pen holding her spot, on the linen tablecloth before she continued on to the kitchen.

Frisco came through a few paces behind her, and he slowed as he neared the open journal. When he saw that she had cleared the door and entered the kitchen, he stopped to read her journal page. The words she used were disturbing to the emotions he had always kept under control—anger, resentment, and helplessness.

She wrote that she would tell Sela's father he had a child. The outsider who had turned his back on them was being invited to take Helena and Sela away from him. Even though Helena wouldn't tell him who Sela's father was, Frisco was willing to accept Sela as his own once Helena married him. And, he knew it would only be a matter of time before she said yes. He loved that little girl. She could so easily be his . . . she should've been his.

He now picked the book up with both hands and read the words again, his anger a palpable thing. Helena had broken off their earlier relationship in high school, only to go off to college and get pregnant, then mope over a man she wouldn't even name, who didn't want their child.

"What are you doing?"

He twisted around in time to see the hot coffee slosh over Helena's fingers as she swept into the room. Frisco didn't back away from her fuming face, though; instead, he lifted the journal up so she could see it, and held open the page with his searching finger.

"What is this . . . some kind of confession for your soul? You're letting a stranger come here to take you and Sela away?"

"It's none of your business what I do." She set the cup down before she snatched the journal from his hand. "How dare you come into my house and invade my privacy this way." She pushed at his unyielding chest to force him out of the room. "Leave now."

"All you have to do is accept my offer to be your husband. I'll be good for you and Sela," he said as he backed away.

"Where did you get the idea, Frisco Lewis, that I would marry you? You're possessive to a fault. Even so, I thought we were, at least, friends." She pushed him again. "I want you out of my house."

Frisco grabbed her hand in his, and the familiar spark of clarity, as though she could see clean through a thing, came into her eyes. Frisco knew what it meant.

"So, what do you see, huh? That sight of yours and Claire's is pure evil." When she narrowed her eyes at his words, he frowned. "Yeah, I've been looking in on the two of you every now and then." He squeezed her hand tighter. "I even saw Claire through the window working a spell on my Sela in that basement."

"Now you're spying on us? You are sick, Frisco."

"That sight you two have is the devil's work, and I thank God Sela's not tainted by it."

"You stay away from Sela."

"All I ever wanted to do was make a good and honest woman out of you again. But, no. You want to go crawling back to some outsider who caused you nothing but pain and trouble."

Helena turned her hand in his. "You're wrong about

most everything you think. You're the evil one with your thoughts." She now thrust him away from her. "Get away from us. I don't ever want you around Sela again or I'll call the sheriff."

He looked at the set of her face. "You don't mean that."

She had turned away and was headed to the front door. "I do. And now I'm sure it'll be for the best if her father takes her away from you and all the other small-minded people around here."

Now it was Frisco's turn to fume at his possible loss. "You can't do that." He caught up with her in the living room. "I've practically lived my life for you and Sela. I won't let you."

"You won't let me?" she sneered. "Just watch. Now, get out, and don't come back, ever."

"Why, you ungrateful—" He backhanded her with his flat hand, and she whirled away in a free fall, the journal bouncing to the floor, until she landed on the sofa.

Helena screamed. It was a bloodcurdling howl that would alarm the neighbors. Frisco fell upon her.

"Shut up," he growled. "I didn't mean it. I'm sorry." But, she would have none of the apology.

As she let out a steady stream of vitriol that she hated him and would see him arrested, Frisco had to stop the words. He grabbed up the pillow cushion and thrust it into her face.

Helena fought against the pillow, but he held it tighter, only wanting the screams and the hate words to stop. Then, finally, they did. When he removed the pillow from her face, she was quiet and still. He sighed as he studied his beautiful Helena. And, as he sat there with her unmoving body, it dawned on him. He had stopped her words, but at what price?

What would he do now? Claire would manage to blame him for this. He had to stay clear of her and away from her touch. He picked up the journal and stuffed it in his pocket. He then gathered the limp, compliant Helena in his arms and climbed the stairs to her bedroom. Once he was there, a hellish plan began to form.

It didn't take him long to fashion a noose from electrical cords, and tie the other end to the doorknob. Then, he used the main ceiling beam as a fulcrum from which he suspended the cord that would hoist the noose around her neck.

As Frisco methodically planned the suicide, he tore a passage from her journal for a suicide note. He lifted her in his arms again, and climbed the chair to the noose. When it was snug around her neck, he couldn't contain his own grief any longer at what he was about to do. He slowly released her to gravity, then jumped from the chair, knocking it over.

A groan rose up behind him and became a choked scream that echoed in his head. He turned and looked up, only to stare into his beloved's own shocked eyes as she twisted wildly above him. She hadn't been dead after all. . . .

"Oh, my God, Ben, he hanged her alive." Sela choked back her sobs before she turned on Mr. Lewis. "She was alive," she yelled, "and you killed her."

Before she could launch herself at the man, Ben held her back, and wrapped her in his arms again. She clung to him as she broke down in tears, sickened by the mind-reeling confession they had just heard.

"You killed her," she cried out at the man she no longer knew. "And you let us think she took her own life all these years."

Mr. Lewis stared ahead, seemingly unaffected by her grief, as he continued to explain. "It was an accident, a stupid misunderstanding. I didn't know she was still alive." The gun hung at his side as he sagged against the door. "I . . . I just didn't know."

"But you kept on killing, didn't you?" Ben held Sela to his chest. "You killed two more in accidents."

The older man looked up and wiped his face with his arm. "When I saw them with Helena, it just wasn't right. All they were gonna do is make a fool of her again. I wouldn't have done that."

"So you got rid of them, is that it?"

"Shut up," he shouted back. "It wasn't like that."

"Sure it was," Ben replied. "Somehow, you drowned—"

"I got a ride with him when he left the church in his car," Mr. Lewis interrupted, "and, it was so easy to hit him over the head when he got on the straightaway. After that, he lost control and drove into the pond."

"What about the other one with the gunshot wound?"

He studied the gun in his hand and spoke in a toneless voice. "I was delivering mail out his way, and went inside his house where he had all those guns he collected."

"Oh, God, no," Sela gasped in disbelief, and buried her painful moans against Ben's chest.

Ben quietly comforted her. "And, your plans for me?"

"You were slippery and got away a few times." He shook his head as he moved to the door. "I couldn't even hit you with the car. So, I had a dose of nightshade all ready for you yesterday, when you were home by yourself. Then, you went running out the door and down the street. Nothing worked out until tonight."

"But, Sela showed up."

He rubbed his temple. "Would you shut up? You're trying to confuse me."

"What are you going to do about it, Mr. Lewis? Or, should I keep calling you Frisco right now?" Ben dropped his arms from Sela and stepped away from her, his brows arching sharply in a frown.

"My Helena called me that; now, I told you to shut up." He waved the gun.

But Ben ignored him as he sniffed the air. "Smoke."

"I smell it, too," Sela said as she looked around. "Is that what you meant by nothing working out until tonight?" Ben asked. "You're burning down the church with us in it?"

Mr. Lewis slowly nodded. "I'm tired. I have to put an end to all this."

"For God's sake, let her out of here, then." Ben edged closer to the man. "If you loved Helena like you say, let her daughter go."

Jim Lewis backed up to the door. "I know what I have to do." When he turned to open the door, Ben saw his chance and pounced on him.

With loud grunts, they crashed into the door, then the wall as the flashlight, followed by the gun, popped from Mr. Lewis's grasp and bounced soundlessly to the dirt. The two men grappled to the floor and rolled in a heap toward the door, both in a frenzy to retrieve the weapon somewhere on the shadowy floor.

Sela grabbed the flashlight to help locate the gun.

"Get out of here and run," Ben yelled as he swung his fist.

"Be careful," she screamed amid the commotion, ignoring his orders. That's when she saw the gun near the door, but watched in dismay as the men fell onto it. In a deadly dance, they now rose from the floor, grunting as they struggled against each other. Her heart lurched as she saw both of them try to gain control of the weapon.

"Ben, the gun—"

The gun released a terrible blast in the small room. Sela screamed as Ben backed away from the gun that was now leveled at him. Mr. Lewis retreated toward the door, his arm held close to his body. He had been shot.

"Okay, you got your blood," he said to Ben. "Now, it's my turn to get mine one more time."

When he backed out of the room, Sela followed Ben as he ran to the door, but it had already been latched again. Just as quickly, they heard a loud whoosh go up outside the door. Sela turned the flashlight's beam on the door. Smoke had already begun to filter up from under the door.

"He started another fire," she said with a cough.

Ben shook the knob. "With the number of timbers down here in the old construction, it won't be long before this smoke explodes into flames."

At that moment, a faint, high-pitched whine sounded in the distance.

"The fire alarms," Ben said, and looked around. "We've got to get out of here."

He turned to the back of the room. "Let's see if there's another way out."

Sela didn't like the idea. "Do we have to go out that way?"

"Come on," he said, and took her hand. "It'll be all right."

With the flashlight as a guide, Ben helped Sela slide under the stair incline and drop into the opening at the back of the room. He then climbed in behind her and began to kick at the reinforced wood sides.

"What are you doing?" she asked, and stifled a cough as the acrid air reached her nostrils.

"Kick. It's the quickest way to discover a secret door."

She joined in, but their resolve revealed no escape route.

"Ben, look." Sela's upturned face was fixed on the slanted ceiling line that almost covered the opening they stood in.

"Well, I'll be damned," Ben said, and reached to finger the wood. "Our secret door turns out to be a ceiling." He took the flashlight and poked at the slit in the wood above their heads. The panel easily dislodged.

"I'll bet this is how Mr. Lewis made his way in and out of here without being noticed," he added.

With the panel moved aside, they could see that the opening led into the stairwell through the bottom step. Ben swung up and lifted himself through first, then he reached down and pulled Sela into the area with him.

As they sat in the small corridor a moment to catch their breaths, Sela's eyes began to burn. "Ben—"

"I know, the smoke's stronger." He scrambled up, then helped her do the same. "We need to go back up these stairs to the next level and try to get out there."

He followed her up the wooden staircase that had brought them down to the second level of the basement. When they tried the red oak door, it wouldn't budge.

"Damn, it's been locked. Mr. Lewis was thorough; he's made sure we wouldn't get out." Exasperated, Ben hit the door. "What does he have, his own set of keys to the place?"

"That's possible," Sela said. "His uncle was the custodian for years before he died a while ago, and Mr. Lewis used to help him out." She looked at Ben. "What do we do now?"

A spark of hope shone in Ben's eyes and a smile began to split his face. "We're going to get out through the wall."

"Huh?"

He took her hand again. "I'll explain on the way. Let's go."

Thirty-three

Claire, Ron, and Luther could see the smoke and flames from the police cruiser's windows as they turned onto the road that led to the church.

Claire's eyes were fixated on the bright reds and yellows that lit the sky as they danced along the tented rooftops of two of the church's outbuildings. She thought it resembled a surreal pastoral landscape.

"It's just like you said, Miss Claire." Ron turned to her in the backseat. "Fire and smoke, even the colors."

Claire sat very still, her worst fears realized. Once again, she had been unable to decipher her own vision and another loved one was in danger. She held Sela's crushed scarf tightly in her hand. It was wrapped around Ben's silver band.

"Luther, try to go faster," she urged. "When we get there, you must go directly to the sanctuary. Break in if you have to."

Luther picked up speed. "Yes, ma'am."

Ben led Sela out of the stairwell and back up a short set of wooden steps. Soon, they were in a tight corridor no more than a couple of feet wide that snaked along the wall. He didn't stop, though, and continued on until they could see the corridor's end ahead of them.

"Ben," Sela said, coughing. "I can smell the smoke, even see it, but there's no fire."

When they reached an octagonal-shaped window set in the wall, Ben stopped and looked out.

"Sela," he called out to her. "Come take a look." He pointed at the window.

Sela strained to look through the window and saw that the neighboring church building was already engulfed in heavy flames.

"Oh, my God," she exclaimed.

"He must have set that building on fire first. I'm not sure if the sanctuary and basement are engaged that heavily; but, from the way the smolder is seeping in, there's a fire ready to ignite."

She looked around for Ben and saw that he was kneeling on the floor as he faced the wall at the end of the corridor.

"Ben, what about Deacon Freeman?" Sela's voice had become hoarse and her throat hurt. "We can't leave him down there."

"Where did you see him last?" He stripped away a piece of wall molding and tossed it aside.

"In the hall, around the corner from the room we were in."

He straightened up from the floor and began to take off his shirt. "Okay, listen. I want you to get out of this building through the sanctuary. Take the easiest way out—that'll be through the front doors, and then head for Reverend Osborne's house."

"They're away and won't be back until tomorrow. But, how do I get to the sanctuary from here?"

"Through here." He moved and Sela saw that he had uncovered what looked like a swinging trapdoor straight ahead. "It leads into the sanctuary. All you have to do is hop over the railing and get out the door. I'll take the stairs back down and bring the deacon out this way." He handed her his shirt. "Stay down low, but use this to wrap around your face if the smoke gets bad, okay?"

She nodded her head as her fear threatened to take over. "Oh, Ben, I love you so much." She threw her arms around his neck. "Please be careful."

"Hey." He spoke gently and soothed her with strokes to her back. "You and I are just getting started. I love you, and I don't plan on going anywhere any time soon."

Ben gave her a hard kiss before they separated and he helped her through the trapdoor. When she exited it, she found she was on the landing behind the pulpit. The large, open-air sanctuary was already filling with smoke from flames that licked the far wall.

Sela gasped as much from the loss of her church as from fear; but when she looked back to the trapdoor, Ben was gone. She knew the fire would reach the front of the church soon, so she climbed over the railing for the short drop to the choir stand; but, she landed badly on her foot.

After a quick test of her ankle, she hobbled between the chairs, down the two steps, and to the sanctuary floor, where she could now feel the heat from the nearby flames that had started to eat at the walls. She pressed Ben's shirt to her face and headed for the middle aisle and the front door.

As she moved, Sela stared in awe at the wall of flames. Mesmerized by the elongated yellow and red licks, she tripped on the runner beneath her feet and tumbled to the floor under the pain of her ankle.

"Here, let me help you."

Sela looked up, and it was Mr. Lewis. The gun hung down in the hand of his arm wrapped at the forearm with a bloodstained cloth. She shrank away from his other outstretched hand.

"What do you want? Haven't you done enough already?"

"What are you talking about, Sela?" He grinned oddly as he talked. "I have to get you out of here before the walls come down. Don't I always take care of you?"

Sela scooted farther away from him, fearful of yet another change to his personality. Ben was right. The Jim Lewis she had known and trusted most of her life was gone and had been replaced by a sick, desperate man.

"What about everything else you've done? You tried to kill Ben."

"Everything's fine. He's gone now."

Sela looked behind her, toward the trapdoor, then turned back to Mr. Lewis, her eyes wide. "What did you do to him?" she railed. "Tell me, what did you do?"

She saw his eyes drop to her neck where she wore her mother's locket.

"You're still wearing that damn locket from the man," he growled at her. "You're not gonna learn, are you?"

Indistinct voices came from the other side of the sanctuary doors, and they both turned. Then, the doors shuddered as a breach attempt failed.

"Help," Sela called out and, raising to her knees, tried to stand.

Mr. Lewis grabbed her arm, though, and pulled her up with him. "Come on."

"No," she protested as he dragged her with him

back toward the choir stand. "Where is Ben? What did you do?"

"Turn her loose, Lewis. It's me you want."

Ben. Sela's heart leaped as she looked up and saw that Ben was already climbing over the railing trying to get to her.

At that same moment, the sanctuary's double doors burst open from the outside, and Luther rushed through with Ron only a step behind.

"He has a gun," Ben yelled from the choir stand. "Watch out."

Jim Lewis let go of Sela's arm and took aim at Ben with the gun.

"Police," Luther called out. "Drop the gun now or I shoot."

Mr. Lewis calmly turned from Ben to face the deputy. With a final bow of his head to Sela, who continued to sidle away toward Ben, and without a word uttered, he curved his arm and pulled the trigger against his temple.

The deafening blast tore through the sanctuary.

Sela screamed.

Luther shouted, "No," and ran to the fallen man.

Ben reached Sela and pulled her into his arms just as Ron and Claire came running down the center aisle.

"Sela," Claire called out as Ben moved aside and allowed her to embrace her niece.

Fire engines could now be heard as they piled into the church's drive.

"Everybody, get out of here now," Luther ordered as Ben and Ron joined him near Jim Lewis's body. "The fire's spreading, and there's nothing we can do for him. He's shot himself dead."

"I brought Deacon Freeman as far as the landing. He's alive, but he's lost blood," Ben said.

"We'll get him," Ron said. "You get Sela and Claire clear of the building."

"I need to check his pockets, first." Ben slipped his hand in the man's back pocket, and immediately found what he searched for.

"What are you doing?" Luther asked.

"It belongs to Sela," Ben said. "It's her mother's journal."

While Ron and Luther ran to retrieve Deacon Freeman from the landing, Ben handed the book to Claire. "You might want to hold on to this," he said to her. Then, he scooped Sela up in his arms. "Let's get out of here."

They met the firemen coming in as they moved down the aisle and out the door.

"Aunt Claire?" Sela called from Ben's arm.

"I'm right here," Claire answered.

"There's so much to tell you, so much that can be explained now."

Claire clutched her extended hand and brought it to her lips. "I know, and I'll be here to listen. I'm going to help you get through all this."

"We'll both help," Ben added solemnly, and led them both away from the escalating fire to the safety of the nearby pasture.

Thirty-four

Ben's arms were still tight around Sela's shaking shoulders when they all arrived back at the house hours later. As she leaned against him, she saw the cars parked along the street, and the full bank of lights on the main floor of the house. That's when she remembered the planned celebration that night. It all seemed so long ago now. In the span of a few hours, the world had been turned on its axis more than a few times.

"Auntie." Sela turned in Ben's arms and looked for her aunt, who was being helped through the gate by Ron. "I forgot to tell you that we planned—"

"I know all about it."

"And, Ben." Sela turned back to him. "I'd planned on surprising you tonight by wearing this new outfit Auntie got for me on her trip. Now it's ruined."

"I was surprised and I think you look beautiful in it," he teased.

They all grinned tiredly and climbed the steps to the porch just as Fontella threw the front doors wide.

"Lord, bless me," she cried and threw her arms around Sela and Ben together. "You're okay. Lord, have mercy, you're okay. Luther just called to say

Deacon Freeman regained consciousness on the way to the hospital. He should be okay."

"Thank God," Sela whispered. The others joined in with her relief.

Fontella pulled them into the foyer where she made a loud announcement. "They're here, everybody."

Ben released his arm around Sela until she was standing on her own next to him as the others all crowded around them in the foyer, everyone asking questions at once.

"Let me get some ice for that ankle, Sela," Fontella said, and turned to Claire, who had made her way to Sela's side.

Before Fontella could ask, Claire smiled and said, "I'm fine, Fontella. You're doing great handling all these guests. Just go get the ice for Sela."

"You don't know how great," Fontella said wearily. "Mabel Thornton is here, and she's driving me and everybody else crazy."

"Just get some ice for Sela." Claire's eyes brightened. "I'll handle Mabel."

"Ben?"

The woman who spoke was unknown to Sela, but she stood with another man among the many neighbors in the foyer. Sela looked at Ben, who had stopped in his tracks, shock written on his face.

"Mom? Mont? What are you doing here?"

Sela's eyes grew wide as Ben took a long step toward his mother before she raced to him, her eyes brimmed with tears. She was followed closely by the tall young man who resembled Ben. All three engaged in a bear hug.

"I meant to tell you," Fontella said. "They showed up at the door tonight and helped me and Rosalie prepare the celebration."

When they came apart, his mother said, "I was worried about you when we had that last phone conversation, and when I couldn't reach you again, I managed to get Mont to come with me to see what was really going on." She started to cry.

"Mom, I'm okay."

"And then," she continued, "we were helping the housekeeper here out in the kitchen when someone called and said you and Sela were in a burning church." Her tears spilled over again.

"I know how you are when it comes to getting things done, man." Mont grinned at his brother. "So I knew you had it all under control. Still, it's good to see you made it through just the same." He turned to Sela. "So this is who you're always talking about."

"I want you both to meet Sela Bennett," Ben said proudly and pulled her into his arms. "And, this is her aunt, the lady who brought me here, Claire Bennett."

As they exchanged greetings, Sela thought if she had ever felt inadequate, it was now. With her dirty face and bedraggled appearance, this was as poor a first impression as she could ever make. But, her answer was a decidedly quick and warm hug from Mrs. Russell, followed by Mont's great one, which encompassed them both.

"I suggest we all retire to a room with chairs," Claire announced to the large group in the foyer. "Because I, for one, am tired and I think we have a lot to explain and talk about this evening."

"Not to mention all the food we have to get rid of," Fontella added.

As Claire led the gathering into the next room, Ben swung Sela up into his arms and whispered in her ear.

"She likes you. A lot."

Sela smiled. "Your mom? How do you know?"

He gave her a quick kiss. "Because she hugged you without a thought to how dirty you are." He grinned. "And because she knows I love you." When he saw her tears, he frowned. "Hey, you're crying?"

She nodded. "Despite all the horror that's happened tonight, I think I'm happier than I can ever remember, Ben Russell. And, it's all because of you."

He hugged her to his chest, his own thoughts mirroring hers, as he followed the crowd.

When Sela heard the faint knock at her door, she was ready this time, and she sat straight up in the bed as it was slowly pushed open and Ben quietly entered.

As she scooted over in the bed and made room for him, she asked, "What took you so long?"

He smiled as he knelt on the floor beside the bed. "I had to wait until everyone settled in for the night. But, I think my baby brother knew what I wanted to do. Anyway, he took extreme pleasure in keeping me busy with his asinine questions about everything."

"I think he's funny."

"Unfortunately, he thinks you're too gorgeous to waste your time on me, seeing as he thinks of himself as a ladies' man."

She giggled. "You know, since Rosalie is seeing Luther now, we could always introduce him to Juanita at the beauty parlor."

"Yeah," Ben agreed. "That'll keep him busy while he's here." He looked at her. "Are you okay after tonight?"

Sela nodded. "There's a lot to digest, but Auntie says we'll take it in a little at a time, that's all." She sat up. "Ben, why do you suppose he burned the church?"

"Well, besides the obvious plan to burn me up in it, I think he knew the end was near. He'd been burrowing himself down there for a long time, and probably knew every crawl space. Maybe it was his way of keeping his secret places untouched. I don't know. Maybe we'll never know what went on in his mind."

"You're right. I think all I want to do right now is have some quiet time to mull over everything that's happened." She held the covers back for him. "So, you don't want to join your bruised and broken girlfriend?"

"Just a minute," he said. "First, I need to tell you something" He reached for her hand and held it between his. "I love you. I know it's only been a while—hell, less than two months—and I'm the first one who'd ask, what can you learn in that short a time about a person you want to be with for a lifetime? But, that would've been two months ago. Now I'd say you can learn a lot. About yourself, about people, about life."

Sela thought her heart would burst with love for him at that moment. "Ben—"

"Let me finish. I've been thinking all evening, and wondering, what's next? And, you know what I say? I say let's just stamp this story of ours with . . . and they lived happily ever after."

Sela shook her head, not sure where he was leading. "What are you trying to say?"

"Will you marry me, Sela Bennett?" He opened his hand and revealed an exquisite, though simple, sterling-silver ring. "Until we properly shop for the one you want, and if you'll have me, I want to seal our future with this one."

"Oh, Ben." Sela was completely taken by surprise. "I want nothing more in the world than to be married to you."

"Then you accept me?"

"Yes, yes," she said and threw her arms around his neck, following it with a sweet kiss.

When they parted, she stared at the ring again, marveling at the simple detail. "Where did you get this particular ring?"

"I borrowed it from my mother." He took her hand in his and slipped the ring onto her finger. "She wears it on her bracelet, but it once belonged to her grandmother. Tonight, when she caught me looking at it, she said there's never a time like right now." He laughed. "And after all that happened at the church tonight, we know tomorrow is never promised."

"Should we wake everyone and tell them?" She held the ring up to the lamplight and admired the tiny treasure.

Ben climbed into the bed with her now. "Uh-uh." He nuzzled her neck as she fell back into the pillow. "Tomorrow is soon enough for their celebration."

"In other words," Sela said, laughing, "there's no time like right now for us."

Ben's lips touched hers like a whisper. "To celebrate," he clarified.

His words wrapped around Sela like a warm blanket. She raised her head, and the heady sensations of their delicious kiss sealed their betrothal.

Epilogue

Four months later

"Comfortable?"

"Quite," Sela answered Ben, and snuggled more comfortably against his chest.

It was a crisp fall night, though still too warm for November, and multihued leaves were scattered everywhere. They had slipped away from the noise and commotion in the house to relax on the big wooden swing in the gazebo. Sela looked idly toward the brightly lit bay window where she could follow the movements of Aunt Claire, Mrs. Russell, Fontella, and Vanessa.

The women were at the kitchen table, busy planning a wedding for next month. Sela smiled at the thought that she and Ben, the subjects of the plan, weren't even missed.

Ben squeezed her waist as they swung lazily. "You don't want to go back in there and look out for your best interests? It is your wedding, after all."

"And deprive them of their fun? No way."

Ben followed her gaze to the window, and chuckled at the women. "I see what you mean."

"Just look at your mom," Sela said. "With her eye for design, she's having the time of her life with

Aunt Claire's sense of adventure. Vanessa will keep them grounded in our generation, and Fontella will let them know if what they want is even possible in a month's time. And me—" She lifted her face to Ben's and received his kiss. "I just want to be here with you."

"In that case"—he spoke against her lips—"why don't we slip back over to our little motel on the highway? We can squeeze in some quality time."

Sela broke from the kiss and smiled. "We'll just have to keep being inventive until after this wedding. So, be patient."

"At least we had some time alone when you took off with me to travel last month. After all that happened at the church this summer, I think the time away did you a world of good. No regrets?"

She rubbed the pear-shaped diamond engagement ring she had worn for the last six weeks and smiled. "None at all, except, maybe, for that camel ride Mont tricked me into taking when he joined us in Egypt. My butt's still sore."

Ben laughed. "He'll probably still be apologizing for that when he arrives for the wedding."

"I did miss Auntie and Vanessa while we were gone. And, I'm going to miss my schoolkids at the media center, too; but, I'm looking forward to starting the next part of my life in Atlanta, what with the new job on the paper and . . . you." They kissed again.

"We can come down here pretty regularly, since I'm advising the contractors on the church renovations."

"One thing is for sure." Sela chuckled. "You'll have three lifelong friends here in Petey, Mrs. Vasser, and Deacon Freeman. You can do no wrong in their eyes."

"We'll both have plenty of opportunities to see everybody—the old and new friends." He smiled as he stroked her belly through her soft cashmere sweater.

"Maybe not for long." She sat up and turned to Ben. "I believe Auntie's going to accept the captain's marriage proposal when he comes for the wedding." She returned to her spot against Ben. "They'll probably live at his home in England, but she's decided we won't sell the inn. I'm glad of that."

"Are you happy for her and Captain Powell?"

"Very. They're in love, and have been for years. I didn't even know. And now that I've found my happiness, it's her turn."

"What about your father? When will you see him again?"

Sela sighed deeply and turned to Ben. "No matter how much I wanted to dislike him when we first met, he's really a nice man, after all. He admits he was young and stupid when he gave my mother that horrible ultimatum. Then, when he realized his error, and tried to make amends, she wanted nothing to do with him. We all lost."

"Has he decided to come to the wedding?"

"He wants to come, but doesn't want his appearance to take away from my day, so we'll talk about it some more."

"That's good," Ben said, and stroked her arm. "You're both talking."

"I don't really think of him as my father, just this nice man; but he wants to keep seeing me, and it's what my mother wanted for us in the end. He's insisted that I let him petition to have his name placed on my birth certificate."

"And what does Miss Bennett think of all this?"

"The truth about my mother's death along with the writings in her journal have considerably reduced both of their guilt. Auntie believes that it was my mother's murder she felt, which scared her that long time ago. But at the time, she couldn't separate the premonition from me and so she tried to protect me. She's still hard on herself about the mistake, but I think it's made all of us less anxious about embracing some real happiness."

"I think your mother would have wanted it that way, Sela."

She smiled. "I'll miss Auntie if she leaves. And Vanessa's little Brandon—I've barely gotten to know him."

"We'll have one of our own." Ben buried his face in her hair—soft, fragrant, and free, the way he liked it. "Soon."

"Do you think we should go ahead and tell everybody?"

"About the baby?" he asked. "Doc Harris said you're only a few weeks pregnant."

"No. Tell them that Reverend Osborne married us before we left for our trip out of the country."

Ben looked at the women through the window. "You said it earlier. I think we'd spoil their fun. Though, something tells me your aunt already knows everything."

Sela laughed. "I wouldn't doubt it."

"But, I'm glad we went ahead with a ceremony in your room of saints at the church. Even Reverend Osborne thought it was appropriate to bury the ghosts that might still haunt you. Once and for all, the whisperings about your dangerous fortune can be put to rest." He caressed her arm. "Your fate is right where it should be—intertwined with mine, Mrs. Russell."

"Mmm . . . I like the sound of that, husband." Sela shifted so she could lie more fully against Ben while he caressed her flat belly. "We can just tell them about our private ceremony when we return from our honeymoon."

"Our second honeymoon."

"It'll make an interesting story we can tell our little boy one day."

It was Ben's turn to smile. "Or, little girl."

Sela turned in his arms, her eyes bright. "You know, that motel out on the highway is looking pretty good right now."

They kissed again, deeply and gently, pleased with every discovery they found in each other. And, while Ben and Sela knew life wouldn't stay in this perfect moment, they were sure that whatever their fortunes, be it secure or dangerous, they would work through it together.

ABOUT THE AUTHOR

Shirley Harrison has been an avid reader and writer all of her life. She is employed in the tax accounting field and lives in the metro Atlanta area with her family. She is an accomplished artist, gardener, and Peachtree Road Racer. You can write to her at: P.O. Box 373411, Decatur, GA 30037-3411 (please include S.A.S.E.) or e-mail her at: sdh108@aol.com.